THE RIVERTON
PROJECT

THE RIVERTON PROJECT

PAUL ELLIOTT

MALEVOLENT BOOKS
Santa Monica, California

Malevolent Books may be purchased for educational, business or sales promotional use. For information, please write: Special Markets Department, Malevolent Books, a division of Quattro Media, 171 Pier Avenue, Ste 328, Santa Monica, CA 90405 USA.

Cover design by Roy Migabon
Typeset in Garamond

FIRST EDITION

Library of Congress Cataloging-in-Publication-Data is available on file.

ISBN: 978-1-936573-10-3

Malevolent Books, in association with Global ReLeaf, will plant two trees for each tree used in the manufacturing of this book. Global ReLeaf is an international campaign by American Forests, the nation's oldest nonprofit conservation organization and a world leader in planting trees for environmental restoration.

10 9 8 7 6 5 4 3 2 1

ACKNOWLEDGEMENTS

The author would like to thank some of the many individuals whose honesty, encouragement and talent have helped bring the town of Riverton to life.

First, a bit belatedly, my eternal thanks to my parents and my high school English teacher, Mrs. Lillian Paul Long, and my typing teacher, Ms. Roberta Hugley, whose combined efforts and determination led a sixteen year old class clown, kicking and screaming into a life-long career as a writer.

Next, I'd like to thank all my friends and family for all their support, especially...

Ellen Snortland and my fellow writers at the Writers Workout in Los Angeles,

The writers, actors and directors of Fierce Backbone in Hollywood

The Alliance of Los Angeles Playwrights (ALAP)

Kaaren Andrews

Diana Zimmerman

Sal Barilla

Jeff Wylie

Paul Messenger

and my immediate family, Ed, Keats, Kiersten, Johnnia and my brothers, Philip Richard and David.

Publication never happens without a lot of paperwork and legal maneuvering so I want to thank my entertainment attorney, Jay Cooper of Greenberg Traurig, and my publisher, Jim Strader of Quattro Media, for working so closely together to get this novel into your hands.

Most importantly, I want to thank Alan Brown of MeSolutions in New York for taking me on as a client and mentor and in bringing this novel to life. His talent, excitement, understanding and respect for the writer's voice, kept me wanting to dig deeper, ask more questions and be the best I could be. Everyone should be so lucky to have a man like Alan as a mentor and friend.

And to all of you who are now embarking on the journey that is The Riverton Project, I thank you.

Enjoy.

THE RIVERTON PROJECT

PROLOGUE

Dying never entered Shari Benton's mind as she expertly adjusted the speed of her car to keep it from sliding on the slick D.C. street. Easy on the brakes, she thought, remembering her father's admonitions when she was sixteen in Colorado and still a nobody. "You learn to drive in Colorado, Hon, with its ice and snow and you can drive anywhere," he liked to predict. He'd been right, and though she seldom had to drive anymore, she had to admit there was something strangely erotic about all that car's power and energy beneath her.

That had been twenty years and a completely different life ago, but Shari still smiled at the memory and wondered what her father was doing at that moment. Probably sleeping or watching late night T.V., or rather sleeping in front of the late night T.V. which had become his pattern since the death of Shari's mother.

The brake lights of the car in front of her flashed red and her focus snapped back to the road ahead. It was late and raining, and while the snow predicted for the DC area hadn't yet arrived, the roads were beginning to ice over with the drop in temperature. Shooting a film in Washington was always difficult, but during the winter it could be almost impossible.

Still, the rehearsal had gone better than expected. Working with Jeff Everett had been a risky choice on her part, but he was young and good looking and that was what she wanted. He was also a bit more erratic in his choices than she preferred but all in all, it had been a calculated gamble. And she'd won.

The press had been ecstatic about the choice and knowing that audiences could still accept her in romantic leads opposite someone as young and hot as Jeff Everett made Shari Benton flash that trademark smile into the darkness, the reflected image hanging like a ghost over the on-and-off crimson brake lights of the cars moving ahead of her trying to get home. Only in Shari's case, that home for the duration of the shoot was a suite at the W hotel.

This was one time, thought Shari, that she should have opted for a driver, but doing that would have been against type. While Shari no longer really liked to drive, she hated being waited on, always preferring, no matter what, to do it herself. It was that determination, dedication and low-maintenance reputation, plus a massive amount of innate talent and that dazzling trademark smile with just a flash of teeth, that had taken her from struggling young actress to an Academy Award winner, and according to the trade papers, Hollywood's number-one female box office star.

It hadn't happened overnight, and Shari never took it for granted. She still worked as hard as she ever had but now, producers and projects came looking for her, not the other way around. Shari Benton didn't have to go begging. She may have lost a little of her innocence along the way as well as a husband who proved that acting faithful was harder than it looked, but that was Hollywood. In spite of Nick's philandering, they remained friends and she had everything else anyone could ask for: money, fame and best of all, three and a half year old Leah with her soft Asian features and radiant black hair, now nestled in her car seat, sound asleep. Leah's adoption at eighteen months and Shari's divorce from Nick Harmon, both unfortunately happening at the same time, had kept the paparazzi on overdrive for months. It was not really the kind of publicity Shari wanted in her life. One was too personal, the other, she hated even now to admit, too painful. Still, as her agent liked to joke, "any publicity is good publicity as long as it's not an obituary or a Depends commercial."

Outside, the rain began to come down harder, pelting the roof of the SUV with ice now in a renewed attempt to dominate the night and frustrate travelers.

Shari glanced in the rear view mirror to see that Leah was still asleep, then checked to see if the rental car wipers had a higher speed. They didn't so she began looking for a place to pull off the road.

It was almost ten o'clock and the traffic on Queens Chapel Road had disintegrated into a veritable bumper to bumper parking lot. At the rate it was moving, or in this case, not moving, she'd be at least another hour before she made it back to Georgetown, if she could make it at all. There had to be an easier way. Spying a turn-off lane just ahead on her right, Shari made what was to be the worst decision of her life.

The lights from Big Ernie's Gas and Convenience store were the first thing she noticed after she turned. While she didn't need gas, she thought that maybe Big Ernie could give her some directions. The locals always knew the best ways around traffic jams; besides, she needed some more milk for Leah's breakfast tomorrow. Leah, at almost four, had become a *Fruit Loops* and *Apple Jacks* addict. Both had to be in the same bowl at the same time, every morning. While Shari knew it was probably the worst way for any child to start the day, any attempts at substitution, or dissuasion, had been met with her sweet little Leah turning into what Shari and Nick had sometimes referred to as "the demon child" – kicking, screaming, falling on the floor and other overly melodramatic displays of the injustices of the world. Leah's au pair, who came from a large Swedish family and was taking a well-deserved night off had assured Shari that this was just a normal part of every three-year-old's developmental behavior, and there were worst things than a sugar-rush first thing in the morning. In other words, she hadn't been any more successful than Shari in forcing a more nutritious start to little Leah's day. Somehow that knowledge secretly made Shari feel better. If the au pair, at eighteen, had been able to do what Shari couldn't, namely tame her child, then Shari's insecurities about motherhood might have come racing back to haunt her. But she couldn't, and so, Shari's didn't.

Pulling past the gas pumps at Big Ernie's, Shari parked as close to the front of the market's lighted glass doors as she could to avoid getting soaked by the icy rain, sheeting like a car wash in heat. Cutting off the engine, she reached for the scarf she always kept in her purse to cover her auburn hair and afford some sort of anonymity. She decided against the sunglasses, figuring anyone walking into a convenience store at 11:25 at night with dark sunglasses was just asking for more attention, not less. She sometimes felt foolish taking these precautions, but she'd learned in some not-so-pleasant ways that as her fame grew, she somehow became almost everybody's property.

"Where are you going?" came a sleepy voice from the back of the car.

Reaching back to reassure the child of her presence, Shari whispered, "Just inside to get some milk and directions, Honey. I'll be right back."

"Me too." Leah was already unbuckling her seat belts. The kid had fingers as agile as a safe cracker. It took Shari a good two minutes to get the child secured in her state-of-the-art car seat, and Leah's little fingers could fly through the releases in less than five seconds.

"No. Go back to sleep. You'll just get wet."

"But I want a root beer and cookies. I'm hungry."

"It's too late and you know it. I'm just getting milk for morning."

"Okay, no root beer, and just one cookie." Leah was never too sleepy to bargain. It must have been her Asian heritage, Shari thought, trying to hold back the smile. That hesitation was all Leah needed to recognize victory was just one step away. She was already crawling over and into the front seat, before putting the final cap on the argument, a winsome almond-eyed plea with dark lashes batting a thousand, "And I've been good?"

Shari could only shake her head and admit defeat. And the truth was she really didn't believe in leaving a child in the car alone, even for a second. Too many bad things could happen.

Scooping the child into her arms, she said, "Okay, hang onto my neck and we'll make a run for it. Just don't complain to me when you get all wet."

The mad dash for the door was as rain-soaked as Shari had expected, but somehow she had managed to shield Leah from most of the downpour. Inside the brightness of the store and the warmth was almost as overpowering as it was comforting. The same couldn't be said for the smell of the shriveling hot dogs that had obviously been cooking all day. The little old man in the mottled gray sweater and glasses behind the counter looked up as they entered, but then went back to scanning his *Recycler*. Obviously not Big Ernie, Shari thought, but there was enough disdain in that one look he'd given her that she knew he had to be a local. So he was probably good for the directions. But first the milk, then she'd go into the "helplessly lost" scene she was already playing in her head.

"Just a little cookie. I'll pick a little one," exclaimed Leah, already heading down an aisle looking.

"Honey, wait. I said, no cookie."

"For tomorrow. I need a cookie for tomorrow."

Again with the bargaining. "Okay, for tomorrow. One. Just one. A little one."

"Itsy, bitsy, I promise," came the giggling voice from the child Shari knew was already searching for the biggest cookies she could find.

"Yeah, sure," she shrugged as she headed for the giant cooler at the back of the store.

Quickly scanning the chilled dairy and cola products through the glass doors, Shari reached in for not the carton of milk she really wanted but one that would make due in a pinch and it was as she was closing the door that she saw the reflections of the two men entering the front door of the store. It really didn't register to her that something could be wrong until a blast shattered the stillness and in the reflective flash, she wheeled to see both men were armed. One, his gun smoking, was cautiously approaching the counter where the old man had previously been sitting.

Seeing there was no one still alive behind the counter, he reached over and opened the cash drawer. His partner, shifting nervously back and forth on his feet as though he was about to start a race, stood guard facing the front door, his modified shotgun ready to assure their getaway.

Quietly sinking down below the aisle shelves, Shari tried to remember where Leah was in the store. She had to get to Leah. She had to keep her quiet. She had to keep her safe. The men didn't know they were there. The men would go away. They just had to keep quiet.

Leah's frightened cry of "Mommy?" shattered the fantasy.

Both men wheeled at the sound. Shari behind a row of shelves could still see their images in the frosted glass of the cooler doors.

While the first gunman quickly returned to clean out the cash drawer, the other cautiously began moving towards the scared whimpering sound, the barrel of his shotgun leading the way.

With more terror and rage than she had ever felt, Shari leaped up and hurled the only thing she had at the man with the gun, her carton of milk.

"Leave her alone," she screamed reaching for anything else on the shelf she could throw. "Don't you dare..."

The first blast literally slammed Hollywood's number one female box office star back through the dairy case glass doors as another blast ripped through the cartons of milk...

Her child, Leah, screamed and screamed again but Shari was past hearing it.

The man with the shotgun reloaded and moved slowly towards the sound.

Leah was crouched in terror. The whimpering child whose adoption the world had cheered and championed was trying to cover her ears, the packet of cookies clutched so tightly in her hands crumbled into a thousand pieces.

A security camera captured the man as he advanced down the aisle, stopped, stood over the child, then aimed. Two blasts lit up the aisles. Not one, but two before the men raced for the door.

If the paparazzi and the country had gone wild at Shari Benton's adoption of little Leah, those two blasts were going to be the shots heard around the world.

CHAPTER I

Ishmael wasn't statistically labeled a hurricane by the time it reached the nation's capital, but it had proven to be a master of destruction anyway on its long march northward. Filled with what his southern victims referred to as biblical wrath, he had swept in unchallenged from tropical waters in the Bahamas as a category five, then capriciously skimmed along the outer surface of the east coast like a two hundred mile-wide skipping stone, digging irregular trenches of destruction as he touched down from Miami to Corral Gables, Charleston to Folly Beach, then flooding the Outer Banks, before heading straight for Washington and beyond. Constantly tracked by weather satellites and somewhat downgraded as he went, he still maintained enough force in his coming that most of the citadel streets had been emptied by the time the first wind-fueled waves of rain surged across the Potomac and into the corridors of justice, spinning stoplights and litter with equal abandon.

Power was out around most of the city, but inside 1600 Pennsylvania Avenue, the lights barely flickered as power was shifted from one backup generator to another. Though evacuation was discussed for the White House staff, it wasn't taken seriously. It would take more than the force of Ishmael to stop the machinations of this presidency if he ever hoped to be elected again.

In one of the more comfortably appointed, though deceptively insulated and isolated, executive conference rooms, behind six-inch-thick, mahogany-sheathed, titanium doors, the executive head of the country sat in darkness at the bow of the conference table, his outstretched manicured hands resting lightly on the coolness of its polished surface. He knew, were the lights on, he'd find himself faced with a large, inlaid emblem of his office; he also knew that were he to run his hands over that surface, he'd never be able to detect the artistry that had placed the design there. Like many things in the White House, the artistry was buried under layers of seeming transparency while in actuality, providing an impenetrable shield of protection to discourage close examination.

"Okay, here it comes," came a voice out of the darkness.

The President found himself leaning forward slightly, his eyes attempting to pierce the darkness, his ears catching the movement of somebody's body shifting in a chair on the opposite side of the room. Then he heard a hissing sound of a video monitor sliding out of its recess in the paneled walls. As soon as it stopped, the screen flickered once, drawing his focus, but then, it disappeared again into the shadows as dark as the room itself or the stormy streets outside. Softly and subtly, the room's state-of-the-art surround-sound system began filling the silence with the lush strains of "America the Beautiful" – deceptively peaceful, deceptively soothing in the now semi-darkness. Wait a minute, was that last dark flicker the image of child, the President questioned in his mind. The darkness and the question made him uneasy and he was growing impatient. "Well?"

"Just wait, it's…," came the reply from the man sitting next to him.

The wait was over before he was even able to finish the sentence. Suddenly, the serenity of the room was jarringly shattered by another tribute to the greatest nation in the world, but this time, in acid rock with images that ripped open the darkness of the screen in painfully bright shards of visuals. The President leaned forward as though trying to connect more closely with the images, then leaned back as though trying to distance himself.

The screen raged with a fast-cut montage of all the violence and crime riddling the nation's cities, expertly cut and layered to the music with effective, visceral results. Every aspect of America's failed legal system bombarded the senses as images of drive-by shooting victims, white-collar arrests, gang deaths, police brutality, gay bashings, lootings, car-jackings, elder abuses, serial rapists, celebrity mayhem, the carnage of employees' rage, a hostage situation that went terribly wrong, the anguish of a parent whose child has just been found sexually assaulted, pep rallies and protest-marches that had turned into riots. It seemed no major city had been spared and the President knew, without anyone saying it, that all of the images had been drawn from the headlines of just the past three months; each violent instance amplifying and making a mockery of the music that underscored it. But that was nothing compared to what it had done to the country.

Overnight, angry mobs and flash rioters raged through the streets of every major city in America, fire-bombing federal buildings, pulling government employees out of their cars and beating them, attacking police stations, even in one horrific case, allowing themselves to be arrested just so they could murder every detainee in the city's holding cells before committing suicide. All of it vigilante attempts at correcting the wrong that had become America.

The President had fought these images every night in his sleep and didn't need a compilation to remind him.

"Okay, okay, Bob, I get the picture," he shouted in a voice both worn and irritated. "It's not like I haven't seen these pictures already."

"Well, tomorrow, it's going to be you and the rest of the world, Mr. President," responded Robert Ryder, at forty-five, one of the President's oldest and closest advisors.

"The news media is going to have a field day. This video is going to be showing every hour, on the hour, on every channel, on every network, and every cable station, starting tomorrow. Probably going to win an Academy Award for best documentary though that's not why he was doing it. The 'he' being Nick Harmon, the ex-husband of Shari Benton, the actress murdered last month while filming right here in this city. This is his every hour, on the hour, eulogy to his ex-wife and their daughter, Leah. He's calling it 'Leah's America,' and everyone knows what he's saying. She was adopted, rescued from her own war-torn country, only to be slaughtered here in what was once the safest country in the world."

"Mr. Harmon is outraged and rightly so. And he's not the only one. This video is going to start a maelstrom and if you thought you've seen protest marches before, it's nothing compared to what this is going to trigger. Everyone is just looking for an excuse to keep rioting. They don't give a shit why, but all that shit is going to land right on our doorstep. Trust me, your opponents are already prepped and lining up to use this as another chance to blast even more holes in your administration and policies."

The lights were already coming up in the room, though scabrous images still continued to swirl on the screen. Joel Acresti, Ryder's young assistant, quickly and efficiently cut off the music and video mid-blast from his control-console and lowered the screen cover. A bright, twenty-five year old, law student, Joel had been working with Ryder for over two years; his loyalty and discretion were evidenced by the fact that in this meeting with the President, he was one of only three people in the room. It also spoke to the youth of the Presidency and his earnest, though quickly proven misguided, attempts at a new, more liberal, youthful, forward-thinking form of governing.

Neither man at the table spoke for a long moment, and then, the President, feebly flashing the smile that had won him the election, said, "I'm assuming there is more to this closed-door agenda than this because, unfortunately, I could have just stayed in bed and watched things about as bad on the evening news. At least there, I'd have had Dessa to keep me warm."

Ryder, because of his close friendship to the President and unquestionable loyalty, knew that what he was about to say, or rather to propose, needed to be firmly grounded in those two attributes; and whether the President listened and heard what he had to say would depend largely on that trust and friendship.

They had been classmates at Santa Cruz and Sanford in their home state of California, before heading to Northwestern University, and roommates from the moment they met in line at registration in their sophomore year until both had graduated with their doctorates, challenging both the universities and each other, never once questioning, in their idealism, that they were destined for great things, nor the friendship they shared. Ryder had been best man at the President's wedding, godfather to his two children, and closest advisor through campaigns that had taken him from governor to senator to President. They knew each other better than anyone else in the world knew either of them, and for those who criticized this presidency and its failed policies, and their numbers were growing, the question had often been, "Who actually was running the country?" Both men knew the answer to that. They were a team. The President was the President. He had always been the front runner, the one with the charisma, the one with the dreams, but Ryder had been the support, the sounding board, and then, the architect. Their bond had been strong, and they had been politically invincible, until everything went wrong. Not with their friendship. Not with their ambitions. With the country. What no terrorist had been able to do, the country did to itself.

After 9/11, the focus of America had been on retaliation and Homeland Security, and then on continually trying to justify to the world the steps former administrations had taken, as a nation, to meet those goals. No one realized, or at least no one listened to anyone who did, that the real threat to our democracy was not from those outside, but from those disenfranchised within. Not from foreign saboteurs, but from the reality of democracy and its inherent weaknesses. America was founded on the principle that all men were created equal, all having the opportunity to prosper, to better themselves. But that same principle was predicated on the assumption that for all that prosperity, for all that betterment, all men must put effort into making it happen.

That assumption was doomed by the millions of hand-out programs, perpetuated year after year, in what started as part of a partisan vote-gathering scheme, and ended up morphing into an unrealistic but very real sense of entitlement that every American now considered their birthright. Over half of this nation was supporting the other half that did not work, could not work, or would not work.

How could any administration, or President, solve a problem that was a ruling principle of our democratic process?

The President had idealistically been determined to make a difference when he took his oath of office, but it didn't take more than a month before the realities of Washington washed over him. Yet, still he fought to make changes, and in little ways, with Ryder's guidance, they'd both been successful. But not successful enough to make a real difference, or leave a legacy, or even, they both knew, get elected for a second term.

Ryder knew exactly what it would take to save America, but convincing a standing President to commit treason was not going to be easy. Fortunately, or unfortunately, dependent upon how this gambit played out, Robert Ryder was very good at convincing.

Joel sat quietly for his cue at the other end of the table, the room, to give them more space. He respected both of these men, but in the last year, his respect for the President's advisor had grown into a love that even he couldn't yet admit. Besides, he knew it would never be reciprocated. It would always be Joel and Mr. Ryder, never Robert, much less Bob. But that didn't stop Joel from wanting to do everything within his power to make Ryder's life run smoothly. Besides, that was his job, his position. No one else had to know it had also turned into his own personal raison d'être.

"You know as well as I do, somebody is always protesting something," he heard the President interject. "If it's not global warming, it's fast foods. If it's not fast food, it's crime in the streets. It's not like we haven't heard it all before."

"Maybe they don't think we're listening," suggested Ryder, turning to face his old roommate.

"I've got a god-damned war I'm still trying to get us out of," the President flashed angrily.

"I know, but this is not about the war. As bad as that is, the war is over there."

"Right! And...?"

"Over! That's the operative word. It's all 'over' there. This is here!" Ryder shot back, referring to the now blank screen. Not wanting to lose momentum, he pushed harder.

"That's here! That is now! I mean, it's bad enough over there, but 'over there' has a measure of distance to it. It's not the same as having it happen on your own street. This time, it's our innocent citizens who are being killed. Not just killed, slaughtered! And for tomorrow's big surprise, cutting straight to the chase, all those murders, those rapes, all those senseless killings we just saw on that video; all of them were committed by repeat offenders."

Pulling a sheet of paper from his briefcase, he slid it across the table for the President to look at. "Compliments of a friend at the Daily News. Tomorrow's headline. Video Documents Repeat Offenders."

"You're looking at a journalist who has decided to go for his Pulitzer and is doing a whiz-bang job of it. If this doesn't kick us over the edge and off the map, nothing will."

"I don't understand," the President said, as his eyes ran down the sheet.

"It's simple, Jack, most of the world don't have the luxury of working in the same house they live in like you. They have to drive to work in the morning, and drive home in the evening, and they don't like doing it in an armored tank. I'm telling you, according to this report, everyone in those video cuts had a prior history of arrests. Even multiple arrests. But no convictions."

"Jesus," the President whispered under his breath.

"Documented visual proof that our legal system isn't working."

"But that's the system we have," protested the President. "It just needs..."

"Jack, Mr. President, it needs to be thrown out."

"Oh come on, Bob, get serious," the President said, dismissively.

"I am serious," Ryder shot back a little more forcefully than he intended. Then, remembering who he was talking to, he took a deep breath and continued in a calmer voice. "Jack, remember when we were in college and we made that list, you know, the one that listed the most useless professions. What was number one?"

"How do you expect me to remember that? It was twenty years ago. I don't remember. We were just..."

"Yes, you do," Ryder cut him off. "It was judges. Why? Because they have no power. Because lawyers were turning courtrooms into circuses. Everyone knows the jury is the weakest link in our legal system. My God, look who's in the jury pool nowadays. They're like lemmings, they're so easily manipulated."

Moving his chair closer to his old friend, Ryder reached out a hand and rested it on the President's arm.

"Jack, you're President of what's supposed to be the greatest country in the world, and this country's scared. We all know it's not safe in the streets, but now it's not even safe at home. Do you know what the highest growth industry in our country was last year? Home security. Locks, dead bolts, barricades. And do you want to know the lowest? Tourism? It's down by half. Half! Do you know the impact that has on our economy? Our latest polls show..."

The President cut him off by pushing away from the table and standing up.

"Oh, come on, don't quote me polls, Bob. I know all about polls. And I also know about popularity ratings. I'm damned if I do, and damned if I don't. And what in the hell do they expect from me, anyway?" He was pacing now, agitated, and pounding on the table in frustration. "I didn't create this problem, my party didn't create this problem, and we're sure as hell not going to solve it. Because it can't be solved."

"But what if it can?"

There, it had been said, but the President didn't stop.

"It can't! What nobody is willing to admit is that," he jerked his hand to the screen, "that, that mayhem is built into our system, into our Constitutional Rights, our laws. Unless something changed in the last five minutes, in this country you still have the legal right to be a shit, to murder, to rape, to do God-damn whatever you want and nobody can do a thing until you're proven guilty. And we've turned 'presumed innocent' into a lifetime occupation, a career goal."

Ryder wasn't being put off. He reached out to the pacing head of the country and grabbed his arm. "But what if we could?" he said in desperation.

"Aren't you listening?" came the rebuttal, as the President pushed his hand away. "We can't. The fact is that in our court systems, we've bent so far over backwards, we ended up raping ourselves."

"But we can," Ryder pressed, not letting the President turn away. "Just hear me out. I'm not talking politics here, but I am talking re-election. And let's face it, unless we do something drastic, something besides shooting hot air and good-guy platitudes up their asses, you can kiss your sweet chances of holding onto your box seats at the Ford Theater goodbye because you're going to be shot out of office so fast by Serle Harland next term, you're barely going to have a chance to grab your jockies before you hit the gulf. Are you listening to me?"

A deathly silence followed this emotional outburst.

The President slowly returned to the head of the table and sank back into his chair. Ryder straightened up and unconsciously gripped the back of his neck, trying to rub the tension out.

The President looked up at his old friend, and indicating the seat beside him, said, "Well, go on, don't hold back on my account. I've known you long enough to realize you didn't shoot me down without some plan for setting me back up."

Ryder nodded, acknowledging the compliment, and sank into his own chair, but this time, faced the President square on.

"Okay Jack, here it is. The truth is with each party of this great two-party system of ours trying to stick it to the other, everyone's managed to lose what we were fighting over-our country. Well, I've got a suggestion. Why don't you be the President who gets it back?"

Quelling the objections he was already voicing in his mind, the President nevertheless kept them to himself. He'd learned with his old roommate to, at least, listen.

"Okay, I'm listening. Just don't tell me to push for more jails. We can't afford them even if we could find a place to put them."

"No, Mr. President," came Ryder's quiet, but pointed response. "I'm not proposing we build more jails."

It was what he said next that was going to keep both men in this private conference room for the rest of the night, and many nights to come. It was also going to open the door to a new country.

"I'm not proposing we build more jails," Ryder suggested. "I propose we eliminate them."

Before the President could even begin to respond, his attention was drawn to Ryder's assistant, Joel, who, as if on cue, was unlocking a secured briefcase and pulling out a set of sealed, white, legal envelopes.

Ryder took the first one and placed it on the table in front of the President, and then placed the second one before himself.

Nobody moved in the room, until the President, hesitantly, pulled his packet towards him to better read the words slashed across its white surface, *TOP SECURITY* and *FOR EXECUTIVE EYES ONLY*.

Looking up into Ryder's eyes, the President's own held a thousand questions and curiously something close to excitement, or maybe fear. Ryder's head nodded slightly towards the envelope, as though to say, "It's all in there. The answer to everything. Just like we planned all those years ago. But you have to take the next step."

Slipping his fingernail under the waxed seal on the packet, the President felt the waxy substance break away, and wondered if this was the beginning or the end of everything.

Slowly withdrawing the printed documents, he ran his fingers over the embossed words on the cover of the proposal, *The Riverton Project*.

He suddenly knew what he was going to find inside the document, maybe not the specifics, but enough to terrify him. It had been the topic of heated, often drunken, late-night debates all through their undergraduate years, a germ of an idea that by their post-graduate work had become a fully developed hypothesis that both knew would, or rather could, never realistically be put to the test. And yet here it was. The President felt his heart beginning to pound in his chest.

A sudden chill ran through his body as a sinking feeling settled in the pit of his stomach. *This must be what Pandora felt when she unleashed the evils of her mythical box*, he thought. She didn't know that that was what she was doing either, until it was too late. I don't have to do this, he said in his head. I can still walk away. But his fingers still toyed with the wax of the seal, and he found himself glancing at the digital display built into the desk, wanting to remember the exact time, this time, 11:52 p.m.

As the lashing rains of Hurricane Ishmael cleared the debris off the streets of Washington, he knew he was about to clear the debris off of over two hundred and fifty years of American political history.

CHAPTER II

Though there were no clouds directly over the commencement field, they, nevertheless, hovered in the background, towering pillars of slowly churning white that threatened to turn back to black at any moment. But, for the time being, the sun held forth as though it hadn't spent the better part of the past three weeks buried in the grayness of overcast skies. Even though spring was usually the rainy season in California, that year had been particularly wet. El Ninos and La Pinas seemed to fight with each other from December through May, bringing storm after storm to the Pacific Coast. This first reappearance of the sun, even if momentary, was a welcomed relief. If you ignored the threatening skies in the distance, and Angelenos had become adept at ignoring almost anything, it was just another beautiful day in Southern California; the kind long-time residents and transplants liked to point out as the reason they chose Los Angeles, chose to endure the bumper-to-bumper congestion and the cookie-cutter 1940's tract housing or stucco apartment buildings packed so closely, side by side, that any green, as in nature, was relegated to a ten-by-twenty-foot jungle of ferns and threatening, colorless prehistoric-sized Birds of Paradise, strangling out the requisite minuscule water feature that flanked either left or right of every security-locked front gate in the city.

For the graduates of the Los Angeles Police Academy, more than the sun was being celebrated as the caps of almost two hundred newly-graduated cadets sailed through the air in triumph.

It was a glorious celebration, and the sun's arrival only added to the cadets' excitement as they hugged each other, giving high fives all around, forgetting, for the time being, that they were now police officers and hugging in uniform was not exactly the image of dignity they wanted to display. Within moments, they were deluged with parents and family, racing from the bleachers into the center of the field, waving congratulations banners and brandishing mini-recorders and iPhones, capturing the glow of their proud graduates.

While police helicopters hovered overhead, on the dais, the Governor and the Chief of Police were posing for pictures that would appear on the front page of tomorrow's Los Angeles Times, as well as the Daily News and LA Weekly, announcing LAPD's largest cadet graduating class in recorded history. One hundred and seventy-five much needed officers for the city's safety-starved streets.

Seth Slavin, with his dark eyes and rugged, good Semitic looks, found himself surrounded by enough cameras to make a movie star jealous, except that all of his were being maneuvered by family.

They were capturing not only his momentous occasion, but a photo memory of his wife, Rachel, glowing roundly in her ninth month of pregnancy. Radiant and smiling as usual, she eased her oversized body into the familiar curve of his body and kissed him lightly on the cheek. To anyone watching, it was obvious Rachel was the most beautiful woman in the world in Seth's eyes, and it had always been that way since the first day they met reluctantly on a website called J-date, specifically for Jewish men and women to connect. Both were fending off almost constant harassment from their mothers, two remarkably similar women, who proclaimed, nonstop, that they just wanted what was best for their bubeleh, and both were set on the surety that what was best was a nice Jewish wedding.

He, in his last year of internship at Harvard Medical School and in a twenty-four-hour rotation, barely had time for dating, much less sex of any kind. It was not that he had never dated, or didn't like sex, but Seth had always been a boy, and now a man, who set priorities, and his priority at that moment in time was becoming a doctor. It was what his father had wanted, and it was what Seth had wanted, or at least thought he wanted, at the time.

Rachel, as a Social Science major working on her Ph.D. at USC, wasn't in the least bit interested in being a wife, or mother, or anything else that kept her from making a difference. She wasn't quite certain what that difference would be, but the one thing she knew was that she didn't need a man to achieve it.

Politically active in women's rights and the rights of children, Rachel was an advocate by nature, as strong and determined as she was beautiful.

Going on a date that Seth's mother had arranged with Rachel's in front of the meat counter at Jerry's Deli was the last thing either she or Seth wanted. And both had refused. Neither mother took rejection well, and to escape the nagging of their mothers, they each respectively put on a pretense of giving J-Date a try.

Scanning the bios and pictures, both had somehow ended up narrowing the search to the other. A phone call ensued, and both were quite up-front about why they would be meeting, if they decided to meet. Neither, of course, knew that the other was the blind date their mothers had arranged, and whom they had rejected.

Since both had the same goal, to get on with their lives without being badgered, they reluctantly agreed to meet for a non-committal cup of coffee that ended up lasting six years, through the completion of her Ph.D. Program, his being licensed to practice in the State of California, their union under the chupah, his joining the staff of the Bob Hope Medical Clinic in Los Angeles, the loss of her mother after a long bout with cancer, the publication of her first book on women's rights, and Seth's realization the previous summer that he really didn't want to be a doctor. It had been his father's dream, not his. He wanted a career in law enforcement and thought he could make a bigger difference.

That decision had not made Seth's mother, the formidable Mrs Slavin, happy, but Rachel understood how and why he had come to his decision, and supported and loved Seth all the more for it.

Seth meant it when he said he thanked God every morning for the woman pressed against his body on that graduation field. They were lovers, and they were best friends, an unbeatable combination.

Seth's arms instinctively encircled Rachel protectively, but it did not keep them safe from all the photo-seeking relatives, led by Seth's mother, who'd already moved in on the pretense of rearranging the young couple for another picture, when she really wanted to turn Rachel sideways so the picture would capture how gloriously pregnant her daughter-in-law was.

"Seth, another for Mama. Like this...for memories."

Rachel resisted in embarrassment, trying to turn herself to a more flattering position. "Mama Slavin, I know what you're trying to do and I look like a barn that way."

"You show me a barn that looks so pretty. Besides, my grandson will want to see how he was there when his father was head of his class."

Seth laughed, "Mama, I wasn't head of the class. Second. I was second."

"So, who else was Jewish?" scoffed his mother. "Like I said, first in your class."

Before either could say another word, she'd rearranged the couple once more to her liking, stepped back and clicked the picture, capturing Rachel in all her pregnant glory. Seth leaned in to kiss his wife gently as though to say, it won't last much longer, and then realized it may take longer than he thought as a dozen other camera-clicking relatives moved in for their turn.

Other cadets that afternoon also found themselves surrounded by their children, hugging proud Mommy or Daddy, who'd just become a police officer.

One such cadet was a strikingly good-looking young man with a surfer's body and the requisite blond hair. Jay Acresti was obviously adored by his three-year-old daughter, Kaaren, who rushed into his arms to be swept high in the air. It was also equally obvious that Jay was not so warmly received by his ex-wife, Erika.

Swinging little Kaaren around in a circle, he said, "That's my big girl."

"Are you a policeman now, Daddy?" she asked as soon as he set her down.

"Signed, sealed, and delivered," he beamed.

"Mommy, Daddy's a policeman now. A real policeman."

"I know, honey," she said without much enthusiasm, as she held out her hand to Jay. "Congratulations, Jay. So I guess this makes it official."

"Looks that way. The badge ceremony was last week and graduation is just the last step."

Erika just shook her head slowly, "I guess it just goes to prove, they'll take anybody these days."

Jay lowered his daughter and reached out to take Erika's hand, and said softly, "Erika, please. I'm sorry. I really am."

Erika did not reply, nor did she look away.

Jay held her gaze for a moment, and then looked down at their beautiful daughter, who was racing around his legs now with all the pent-up energy only a three-year-old can contain. "Thanks for bringing her."

"Well, she's still your daughter," she replied, coldly, "as long as you keep making the payments."

Fifty feet away, closer to the towering trees that surrounded the field, the situation was much less tense. Former cadet, now Officer, Angel Castillo was wrapped in the tattooed arms of her boyfriend, Enrique. No family bothered these two, and no cameras flashed, but they didn't seem to mind. They had other things to concentrate on, and it appeared to be each other's body.

"Whoa, I never kissed a cop before, Angie," laughed Enrique as he flicked a tongue over her neck. "Tastes good."

The red-headed Angel, Angie to her friends, with the morning sun glinting off the wisps of hair peeking from beneath her hat, pushed her lover away playfully and smiled seductively into his dark Hispanic eyes. "Well, if you're really good tonight, and I mean 'really good,' I might even let you wear my badge."

Enrique considered this for a moment and then gave her an even more knowing smile. "Oooooo, I like that. I get the badge and you get my gun."

Just then, Seth and Rachel pushed through the crowd to interrupt the couple's foreplay, stepping right in between them.

Of course, Seth was still being followed by his whole camera-toting family. "Hey, hey, air time. Break it up, you guys. Isn't that against the law?"

Enrique just smiled. "Not yet, but I was getting there." Then, everyone was laughing again and cameras flashed as Enrique shook Seth's hand in congratulations and Rachel hugged Angie.

Rachel and Angie had been friends ever since they met six months earlier, and it had been right on this field on the first day of Seth's training. Rachel has come to the academy that morning on the excuse of having lunch, but in reality, to make sure Seth was fitting in with the other cadets. It was not that he wasn't physically capable of doing anything; it was simply that he was at least ten years older than most cadets, having already established a successful medical career before making the switch.

The Police Academy could very well have been a hidden resort in the Canyon. Built in the 1920's and having lost none of its rustic charm, it came complete with restaurants, gift shops and a swimming pool. Were it not for the sounds from the firing range shattering the silence, the illusion could have been complete. The guard, an elderly Middle-Eastern gentleman, at the front gate passed her through and directed her to the cafe overlooking the pool. She later learned that his name was Mr. T because most of the students had trouble pronouncing his real name, which seemed to have more consonants than vowels. But that day, Rachel felt as if she was betraying Seth's trust, following him like some teenager on his first day at a new school. And she knew he would be embarrassed and upset, if he knew. But she couldn't help herself. She had never loved anyone as much as this man. In fact, she doubted she had ever loved anything as much in her life. It sometimes frightened her that she had become so vested in every aspect of his being. She wasn't worried about infidelity. That had never entered her mind. She worried about his safety. She was just a child when she saw her father gunned down while making a deposit at a Wells Fargo bank. People in your life could disappear in just an instant, and she didn't want that to happen to Seth. This was the first day of a big change in both their lives: His as a police officer. Hers, as the wife who had to secretly worry every single day that he might not come home safely.

Of course, she would never let him know that, and she promised, that morning, she'd never repeat this type of surveillance, if that was what it was, and she'd keep that promise. She'd even gotten up from the table, and started to make her way back to the parking lot but the temptation to see the training field was too great. It was just across from the restaurant, practically on the way back to the car, so she decided to take a detour up a couple dozen steps carved into the hillside. She climbed, trying to keep her head down, trying to pretend she belonged, trying to catch just a glimpse of the man she had made love to that morning.

And there he was, in a field of other cadets, a head taller than most, and for her easy to pick out even when dressed in the mandatory LAPD Academy gray tee-shirt, which, in his case, was already soaked in sweat. There he was, squaring off with a statuesque redhead, similarly attired and equally soaked, her hair chiseled into almost a buzz, and Seth was trying, unsuccessfully, to throw this woman to the ground.

That was the first glimpse Rachel had of Angie, and it was the one she could bring up the easiest in her mind, and it always made her smile. Angie was Hispanic fire captured in female form; and she wasn't giving an inch that morning. Evidently she had more than held her own throughout the entire training, competing, and eventually, beating out Seth for top honors by less than a point. Rachel liked that there was no bullshit about Angie, no using her femininity to court favors, and surprisingly, no jealousy. Though vastly different in background and education, she and Rachel had become great friends from the first moment they met several weeks later, instant rapport, like the sisters both had always needed in their lives.

"Congratulations, Angie," Rachel beamed at her friend, then added, because she knew how much it meant to all of them, "Officer Casillia."

Angie almost laughed at the sound of it, though she was secretly pleased. This was her family, The Slavins. They had taken her into their hearts and homes when her own family had rejected her. In more ways than one, they had saved her life, and she would not hesitate to lay down her life for any one of them. For the time being though, she just patted Rachel's tummy and said, "Congratulations to you, too."

"Congratulate me next month," shot back Rachel with a grin, "if I last that long. Why do they say nine months, when it's actually ten? If I get any bigger, they're going to be rolling me to the hospital."

"Picture time," chimed Mama Slavin, pushing forward to hug Angie, her camera already clicking at god-knows-what. Not really a great picture-taker, Mama Slavin was at least a prolific picture-taker, and Angie was family as much as Rachel. "All together now," she directed, "and I promise not to cut anyone's head off this time."

Seth moved in closer to Rachel, Angie and Enrique, and then suddenly got a better idea. "I want the whole gang."

Everyone took to this idea with enthusiasm.

"Where's Miles and Jay?" said Seth, already trying to peer above the crowd on the field.

Everyone scoured the crowd until Angie yelled, "I see Miles at two o'clock," as she broke ranks, and headed into the crowd at an angle.

Miles Hadley was a tall, ruggedly good-looking young man with the dark eyes and almost blue-black skin of his undiluted African ancestry. Of course, he was also surrounded by his own very large and boisterous camera-toting family and friends.

"Picture time," Angie squealed as she raced into the group and gave Miles a big hug. "The whole gang."

Rachel, Seth, Enrique and the rest merged moments later with Miles' family, easily exchanging hugs of congratulations and the requisite family boasting about their own personal graduate.

In Miles' family however, the major-domo of picture-taking was his mother, the small but indomitable, Harriett Anderson Wilson Hadley, and she was, as she liked saying, always in charge and would be until the time they shoved her, still fighting, into some coffin. And "even then, they better sit on it. Cause I don't give up easy, or ever." Her six sons and three husbands had never doubted, for one moment, that Harriett was not to be questioned. Or if they did, it was only once. Iron hands had a tendency to be listened to, especially when they were wielded with love. And nobody doubted Harriet loved her family, and no one in that family ever thought of disappointing her. So when she said, "Line up everybody for a big shot," waving her arms to expand the entire group, everybody did as she said.

Rachel moved in with Seth, sliding slightly behind him, but Harriet, like Mama Slavin, was having none of that either, and pulled the expectant mother out from behind her husband.

"Not on your life, Missy, and not in one of my pictures," she exclaimed, and then nodded to Mama Slavin, as only mothers on the same wavelength can do.

Of course, Miles took center with his arms around Seth and Angie, and all were beaming.

"The four Muske...," cheered Seth to mutual cheering, then remembered, "hey, where's Jay?"

That stopped everyone, and started another search of the crowd.

"There he is," shouted Angie, as she pushed off into the crowd without another word.

Everyone watched Angie disappear again into the crowd like a hunting dog on a good rabbit day. Then, Miles laughed, and pointing his outstretched hand like a park ranger, said, "Follow that Policewoman."

Laughing, everyone did, parting the crowd like a multinational red sea, causing ripples of laughter to erupt in their passing.

They arrived just as Jay was saying goodbye to his daughter. Angie who, of course, was leading the pack, arrived first, and instantly gave Jay a huge affectionate hug.

"Thought you'd hide from us, did you?" she enthused. "Congrats...," was barely out of her mouth before she saw Erika, leaving the "...ulations," to get lost in the arrival of the others. The excitement of the group suddenly became extremely subdued and awkward, as though seeing Erika had drained the energy out of not only the immediate group, but the entire graduating class as well.

Seth, as always, was the first to rebound. Quickly giving Erika an awkward hug, he barreled through, "Hi Erika. Good to see you. You're sure looking great." Then, not even waiting for a response, or afraid of what the response might be, he quickly turned his attention to little Kaaren and picked her up in one fluid flying movement. "And you too, big girl. How about giving your Uncle Seth a big hug?" Kaaren did, enthusiastically.

Miles quickly jumped in and gave his own hug to Kaaren. "Come on Honey, it's picture-taking time and we got more cameras than God has grass." And it was true. Between Seth and Miles' families, the Canon stock had leapt two points.

Little Kaaren was all for pictures, but Jay still looked to Erika for permission. Erika hesitated for just a moment before nodding and letting her go.

Racing to find her place, Kaaren realized her mother wasn't following, and turned back excitedly, "Come on, Mommy, the picture. Come on."

This was, of course, followed by a chorus of hurried agreement from everyone else trying to sound like it was their own idea.

Jay stepped forward and reached for his wife. Though she wouldn't take his hand, and in fact, seemed to avoid it, she did reluctantly move over to stand next to Rachel. Rachel put her arm around Erika, wanting to include her in the group.

Mama Slavin and Mama Hadley were already in position. "Now, on the count of three, everybody say 'Cheese!' One, Two, Three, they both chorused, as one and the field rang with laughter as each of the subjects responded with their own personal favorite. "Gouda." "Provolone." "Cheddar." "Mozzarella." Cameras flashed and pictures were captured. It was a wonderful, wonderful day and the only ones with forced smiles were Jay and Erika.

No one knew in that moment of rightness, of togetherness, of unified oneness that in Washington an order was being signed that would change their lives for ever.

CHAPTER III

A worried President looked up at Ryder as he slid the freshly, signed documents across the darkly, polished surface of his desk. "And you really think we can keep this quiet?"

Avoiding his eyes for a moment, Ryder retrieved the papers, and slipped them into the envelope Joel had prepared with an auto-destruct lining, should its seal be breached by anyone outside a chosen few. "Not necessarily quiet, but on a very strict 'need-to-know' basis—you, me, Jarrod at DARPA—a very few others," he said, as he sealed the envelope and wrote across its front in bold letters.

"Sorta gives new meaning to *Executive Eyes Only*, doesn't it?" the President mused, as he looked at what was being scribbled.

"By the time we're finished, we may find the concept of Executive itself obsolete."

Placing the envelope inside his attaché case, Ryder clicked it shut and thumbed the locks, including the one that linked the case to his wrist. "Okay, no more inner-office memos. Nothing electronic either way. My updates will be on your private line. I've got it secured, and Joel will sweep your office and that line daily, immediately before I call. If you see Joel, you'll know it's time. Joel will remain in the room, monitoring for interference from the moment you pick up the phone until you hang up. At that point, he will erase all traces of the call, its origin, and that it was ever made."

"I know all of this is necessary, but it makes me feel like I'm in a fucking spy movie," swore the President, trying to break the tension he was feeling.

"That's not a bad analogy to keep in mind," replied Ryder, picking up the locked case. "Until this project is fully activated, we're talking treason here."

The President exhaled slowly and nodded his head in agreement as Ryder leaned across to shake his hand.

For just a fraction of a second, the President thought about not taking his friend's hand. Maybe if he didn't, this experiment would go away, maybe they could come up with some other solution, maybe they could just go some place and hide, his feverish mind raced. But, he knew it was too late. He knew it was too late even before he signed the document. Once the idea had been spoken that first night in the storm, the thoughts explored, the possibilities envisioned, it was already too late. It was already in motion. The groundwork had been laid and an idea once released could never be recalled, like an avalanche of ice that breaks off from a mountain's peak, it's beyond recall. It's already roaring down the slope. "I guess this is it, then," he said as he shook Ryder's hand, and realized both their hands were as cold as that glacial ice.

"Yeah, this is it," was Ryder's only reply as he shook his friend's hand, then turned and left the Oval Office, its heavy door swinging silently closed behind him.

The President watched him go and realized that, in spite of the cold hands, he was actually beginning to sweat and could feel the perspiration trickling down his back. "No turning back," he heard himself whisper and then quickly scanned the expanse of the room around him to make sure he had not spoken loud enough to be heard. He was alone and, for the first time in his life, he actually understood the meaning of the word.

Less than a mile away, another man who understood the word, alone, only too well, sat in his darkened townhouse, sipping his second Chivas Regal in as many hours. Marshall Foster, at thirty-eight, had everything anyone could ever ask for in this life: money, power, prestige, and almost any woman he wanted in his wide circle of acquaintances; but the role of playboy had never been his style, and with his current work schedule, there just didn't seem to be any time for anyone else. It was almost two in the morning. The studio driver hadn't gotten him to his door until after midnight, and he had an appointment at nine in front of the Lincoln Monument, which meant he had to be ready by eight-thirty, which meant he had... Damn, he thought to himself, *no wonder I've got no fucking life.*

Then he smiled, realizing he actually enjoyed the life he had. Taking another sip of the Chivas and rolling it around his tongue, Marshall enjoyed the feel of the smooth liquid slipping down his throat. Hell, he knew his strengths and he knew his weaknesses, and while he had no trouble talking to the world, a one-on-one conversation with a woman was beyond him. It wasn't that he didn't know the right questions, or understand the female mystique and anatomy, it was just... He didn't know what it was. Maybe it was fear that if he let anyone get that close on a permanent basis, she might discover that the man behind the facade he presented daily was nothing like the image he projected. And image was everything in his line of work.

Marshall Foster, with his cultivated ruggedness, tousled blond hair, and gym-toned body was lead anchor at WJLA in D.C., and his ten o'clock broadcast was transmitted nightly in whole, or in part, to every ABC affiliate in the country and overseas. His face was the face America watched; his views, both the initiator and barometer of public opinion. Though broadcast journalists were supposed to be impartial observers, this thirty eight-year-old newsman, and that was what he considered himself, a newsman, not a journalist, a newsman...with old-school, bull-dog tenacity, unquestionable integrity, and fortunately, a real concern for what was happening in this country. His was a no holds-barred approach to television news coverage. His personal news team was the secret eyes and ears of the political scene. Marshall didn't care who you were screwing, just as long as it wasn't the American people. It was taken as a given that if anyone tried to pass a pork-barrel anything through D.C., Marshall Foster would be on your ass like a striking leopard, dragging you and your limp-dick, lame-duck project into the public eye, and personally attacking you on air. And when he spoke, people listened. And when he focused his attention on a political issue, he was an undeniable force to be reckoned with. Marshall Foster was both loved and feared in the nation's capital. Just where one fell on that scale depended solely on one's own moral compass on any given political issue.

As editor of his Glendale High School paper, Marshall's writing skills had earned him a full scholarship at Medill Northwestern. Of course, he was the first to admit the scholarship was based more on the fact that he was from California and would provide diversity to the campus than his actual writing skills. But those nascent skills, as well as his amazingly keen eye for the real story, were honed by Medill professionals to such a degree that he was quietly recruited even before graduation by CNN. Continuing his education in Atlanta at CNN headquarters, Marshall's reputation among the staffers grew until he was given assignments that usually were open only for more seasoned reporters. It was because of his age, and because there were just so many nights he could go back to his empty Atlanta apartment without people questioning why he wasn't dating, that he requested and was given the assignment that would take him into national headlines.

Marshall was twenty-five at the time and realized that most of the young men and women fighting the on-going wars in Afghanistan and the Middle East were his age and younger. He wanted to cover the war from their perspective. And that's what he did; his daily reports reaching a whole new market of young people who had never before watched much more than You-Tube videos. It was also during that assignment, and because of it, he learned first-hand how America and its touted democracy were perceived outside its insular borders.

Although he had always liked to consider himself a protester, when faced with the actualities, however, it was a time of real disillusionment. That was enhanced, when he also discovered how incredibly exposed our American service men and women were. Stationed in those barren lands, they were charged with protecting America's rights and freedom, but saddled with equipment that, at best, was merely inadequate, if not downright non-functioning.

With the entire country coming up on two decades of economic inflation, with budgetary cut-backs following cut-backs, with military supplies and equipment held up from within, Marshall began to dig deeper. In the process, he uncovered and exposed an incredibly corrupt military accounting and fulfillment system, with more than half of its massive budget being derailed and funneled into the pockets of political supporters, military advisors, criminal interests, and even oil companies.

That Pulitzer Prize winning story catapulted him out of the field and straight to the nation's capital where his continuing reports of corruption won him both the admiration and the disdain of the political elite.

After two and a half years of reporting for CNN, and moving back and forth between the futuristic Atlanta headquarters and the depressingly insular single green-screen studio in D.C., Marshall accepted an offer to move to D.C.'s Channel 7 where he was promised his own studio, his own news room, and his own news team who answered only to him. Most importantly though, and the real reason he accepted the position, was that he was promised less censorship and fuller freedom of expression.

While Marshall had loved working with CNN and the professionalism of its news-gathering team, and recognized that CNN's drive to get to the core of a story had allowed him to capture the public's eye, he had never found their news-reporting style personal enough for his own taste. Marshall was just not a man capable of distancing himself from his stories. The bloodshed and violence flowing through his country and cities, with drug-cartel viciousness, ripped at his soul. He was determined to convey that rawness to the rest of the country until that country decided to finally stand up and fight back.

But tonight, he needed sleep, and throwing back the rest of his drink, he moved through the darkness to his bedroom where he fell asleep with his clothes on like almost every other night.

CHAPTER IV

Tucked in among the trees on the upper crest of the Verdugo Hills, the tiered terraces of the Castaway Restaurant offered soft music, good food and drinks that were actually worth the price. Above all of this, the Castaway offered the most spectacular night-time view imaginable of the San Fernando Valley and the Los Angeles Basin.

Sitting at their table, overlooking the glimmering lights of the city below, Seth reached out to gently touch his Rachel's hand. The candle, flickering in the center of the table, gave her face a soft glowing warmth.

"You are so beautiful," he whispered, and meant it.

Rachel smiled at the love she always found in his eyes. "Thank you," she blushed as she looked down and smoothed the fabric over her pregnancy. "This table is very flattering. It covers everything from the waist down. I'd lean over and kiss you, but my body doesn't bend that way any more."

"Mine does," her husband grinned as he leaned over to brush his warm lips on hers. "Thanks for being there."

"Where?"

"Beside me. Through all this. I know it's not exactly what you bargained for. You marry a doctor and end up with a cop."

Rachel took his hand gently in her own and, unconsciously, traced the lifeline in his palm, "Seth Slavin, you listen to me. I got everything I bargained for and so much more. All of it perfect. There are more ways to save the world than being a doctor, or like me, a social worker, and a good honest police officer is one of them."

"The money won't be nearly as good."

"So, we'll manage. I come from a long line of managers and trust me, I'm not my mom's daughter for nothing. You are exactly where you're supposed to be and you care. That's what's going to make the difference. Today, I was so proud of you...all of those accommodations and awards."

"Don't tell anyone but I bribed the committee," he joked, then became more serious. "I just get worried sometimes, hearing all those horror stories about what being a policeman does to your family. I just don't want that to ever happen to us. If anything bothers you, tell me. You're more important to me than anything else in this world, and I mean it."

Rachel reached across the table to gently touch his face, "Honey, when have I ever kept my mouth shut if I felt something was wrong. I come from strong stock and I'm not going anywhere. I'll always be here. Always. And that's a promise."

"Whoa," she exclaimed with a wince as her hand dropped to her protruding stomach, "and pretty soon, someone else is going to be here."

The look on Seth's face was a cross between panic and excitement. "Now? You mean, now?" He was already standing up.

Rachel had to laugh. "No, no, no! Relax, daddy. He's just testing his legs. I've still got a while. Your mom warned me not to count by months, cause when you reach the ninth, you've still got four more weeks to go."

Rubbing her hand over the rounded lump that had suddenly bulged out in her maternity blouse, she looked like she was gently trying to push an alien back into a capsule where it belonged.

"Are you sure you never played soccer?" she teased. "Cause if this kid is any indication, you better start learning."

Seth had to laugh. Then he picked up his glass to toast her. She quickly joined him in that toast before reminiscing, "You know the one thing I really miss the most?"

Seth clinked her glass and teased, "Sex? Please tell me it's sex."

Rachel laughed, "No, my little stud muffin. Oh, I miss that, but there's something else I miss even more than that."

Seth protested, "What could you miss more than that?"

From the look on her face, whatever it was, she was already imagining it. "A tall, cool, bourbon and coke," she stated. "Do you have any idea how old this flavored water gets after nine months?"

Seth playfully pulled his glass out of her reach. "Okay, here's a promise. The minute you drop the package, I'll let you go on a bender. Large economy size."

On the steps of the patio, two dark-suited men kept their eyes on the laughing couple, as they had since following them from the graduation to their lunch celebration with Angie and the Slavin clan in Chinatown, then back to their apartment, where they watched from an alley across the street, and now here. They were not supposed to make their move until they got their call. Neither man knew why this couple was of such interest, but both knew what they were required to do when the signal came.

At the table, a waiter was assisting Seth and Rachel in their dining options when that signal came: an insistent, three-pulse vibration from the small device the first man held in his hand. He quickly punched in his own three-pulse response that signified he had received the go-ahead and was progressing as ordered. Pocketing the instrument, the first man nodded to his partner, and they quickly cut through the tables.

Seth looked up and knew, even before they identified themselves, that they were government agents, probably FBI. Neither man offered his hand, though both were reaching into their coat pockets.

"Seth Slavin?" one of them inquired, though it was obvious he knew the answer.

"Yes," Rachel heard Seth respond with a tenseness in his voice that suddenly warned her this was something he had not prepared for.

Withdrawing his credentials, the first man held them out for Seth to peruse.

"Samuel Harding, FBI. And this is Agent Winston," he supplied, indicating the other man. "Sorry to interrupt your evening, but I've an executive order here requesting that you accompany me to some place where we can speak... privately."

"Executive?" Rachel questioned, looking at Seth. "What executive?"

Seth was beginning to rise, and Rachel found herself pushing back from the table as well.

"What is this? Some kind of joke?" Seth protested. "Some kind of haze, just because I..." His voice suddenly trailed off as he realized, from their eyes, that something more than a joke was going on. His throat suddenly felt very dry. Looking from one agent's face to the other, Seth's mind raced for a reason or a meaning, as he lowered himself back into his chair. "You're serious, aren't you?" It was more a statement than a question.

"What's all of this about?" Rachel asked. "And how did you know we were here?"

The answer from the second agent, Winston, was simple and direct. "We followed you here."

Rachel slowly reached for Seth's hand, suddenly aware that all of this was happening in a crowded restaurant, and yet, nobody had turned to look in their direction. A chill ran down her spine, and even the baby stopped moving inside her.

"That ID? I think we better look at that again," she thought without realizing she had actually said it out loud.

Both agents complied, pulling out their identification cards again, and this time both Seth and Rachel looked at them closely, and then at each other.

What do they want? Rachel's eyes questioned. Seth could only shrug.

Turning back to the agents, Seth challenged, "Okay, I repeat, what is this all about?"

Agent Harding suggested, and they both knew it no merely a suggestion, that Seth and Rachel follow him and Agent Winston outside. Without a word, both slowly complied. Seth momentarily wondered who was going to take care of the bill, and Harding, as if reading his mind, snapped a finger in the direction of the waiter, causing Agent Winston to move quickly in that direction.

The other guests at the other tables continued to dine, oblivious to the young couple being escorted from the premises.

At the same time Seth and Rachel were being led from the restaurant, and into a waiting van, Miles and his family were celebrating his graduation, East L.A. style. Every friend and relative Miles knew, or had ever known, were packed into Mama Hadley's tiny backyard on Vineyard Ave. where charred chicken, burgers, and hot dogs were disappearing almost as fast as the smoking oil drum grills could be filled.

Large tubs of iced beers and sodas formed veritable obstacle courses for dozens of per-school children who played tag around their adult's legs.

Miles was obviously the center of attention, getting hugs, kisses and congratulations from everybody. His girlfriend, Rhondene, was also there, looking as enticing as ever. With her golden-brown skin and flashing eyes, Miles' girl could turn eyes where ever she went. And tonight, in the fuchsia knit blouse that clung tightly to her body and which had been picked especially for the occasion, Rhondene was right where she wanted to be, by Miles' side, her arm wrapped possessively around his waist. With all those so-called "sisters" coming out of the woodwork, she wanted to make sure everybody there knew where she had staked her claim. If nothing else, her eyes flashed, "Hands off my man."

Many of the guests looked like former or current gang members, and they were. Others were dressed in business suits and their Sunday finest. Nowhere was the dichotomy of East Los Angeles more evident than on Vineyard. There were those who worked, and those who took advantage of those who worked. Within reason, everybody had been welcomed to this celebration. That was one of the unspoken rules in this neighborhood. You never wanted to be accused of sending anyone away. It was not a ghetto party, but it might as well have been. Ghettos came in all shapes and sizes; and Vineyard, with its blend of struggling family homes and drug houses, was just another example. The music was blasting, but nobody was going to complain. On Vineyard Ave., complaining could lead to a lot of hurt.

Miles had been raised in this neighborhood; and the only thing that saved him and his brothers was the no-nonsense, forceful hand of his mother and her focus on education, and getting her sons out of the mind-set of Vineyard. Even her husbands, and she'd had several, had been carefully selected from outside of Vineyard to further the boys' chances of survival. One had been a carpenter, and worked with the boys on remodeling their mother's house. Another had been an artist whose creativity and sense of texture and beauty captured the imagination of their growing minds. Some of the boys' earliest paintings and collages still lined the walls of the living room. None of the husbands had lasted for more than a year or two, but their leaving was sort of understood from the day of their arrival; and all were loved, and all held a part of their sons' souls, and all were available where ever and when ever the boys needed them.

Miles sometimes wondered why his mother hadn't just taken her sons out of the neighborhood. She certainly could have. Any one of the men in her life would have gladly moved the entire family, but she had always been adamant. A home is made from the inside out, and this was their home. This was their community. You couldn't help a community by moving away. And she'd been right in some respects. Their community had improved. Though some of the houses still catered to drugs and prostitution, almost all, following Mama Hadley's lead, were freshly painted with mowed lawns and flowers. In fact, Miles smiled when he realized some of the former, or maybe current, gang members in the neighborhood were now mowing lawns for money, or just to help out when a neighbor was in a tight fix. Mama Hadley was a force to be reckoned with.

Miles smiled, as he looked out over his neighbors, and thought of his own private celebration he planned to have with Rhondene, if and when the party broke up. Without warning, something caught his eye and the smile left his face. Mama Hadley was coming down the back-steps from the house, a worried expression on her face. And he knew, without a doubt, she was looking for him, and that something was wrong, something she didn't feel she could handle. If Mama Hadley couldn't handle it, it was bad.

Miles slipped Rhondene's arm from around his waist and whispered into her ear, "Something's up. Stay here."

Rhondene stepped back, her eyes questioning and tinged with wariness. This was East L.A. Being wary was what kept you alive. She watched as Miles quickly set down his plate and made his way through the crowd to his mother. Rhondene couldn't hear what was being said over the music, but Miles' mother indicated something inside the house.

"Who?" she saw him question, his shoulders tensing. Mama Hadley just shook her head, and even from this distance, Rhondene could feel the worry in the exchange.

Rhondene instinctively found herself moving through the crowd towards Miles' mother. Miles had already entered the house. Slipping her arm around Mama Hadley's waist, both women waited in the yard.

Crossing the living room, Miles quietly opened the closet door, retrieved his service revolver from the top shelf, loaded it, and then moved cautiously to the front door. Standing with his back pressed against the wall, his free hand reached for the knob. Not knowing what to expect, but considering the neighborhood, he slowly eased open the door enough to hear, "Miles Hadley?"

"Who's asking?" Miles called back, still flattened against the wall.

Whipping around the doorjamb, before the stranger had a chance to answer, gun aimed and ready, Miles found himself facing a man in a dark suit, his credentials already out. The man didn't even flinch. He just said, "FBI."

In her darkened bedroom, Angie and Enrique were having a celebration of their own: a very, very, private, intimate one. Two beautiful glistening bodies slid over each other in the moonlight. Fingers, lips and teeth escalated sensuality to a fever pitch. Angie's body arched as Enrique's head slides down between her legs, even as his fingers reached up to tease her quivering lips. Her breathing was just about to crescendo when the doorbell rang. She almost cried out in pain.

Enrique groaned and tried to ignore the interruption, but Angie's concentration had been broken.

"Shit!!!" she hissed, trying to re-catch her breath.

"Don't answer it," pleaded Enrique, still buried between her legs. His body, he knew, was just strokes away from explosion. "They'll go away."

But Angie pushed him away and threw her legs over the side of the bed. Reaching in the darkness for her blouse, she said, "It could be my folks."

"They wouldn't dare," groaned Enrique in anger as he reached for her arm and tried to pull her back onto her back. "If they couldn't make the fucking graduation, they sure as hell are not welcome at the party afterwards."

The doorbell rang again, and Angie was torn between getting up, on the chance that it might really be her parents, or saying "fuck you" to them as they had so obviously done to her.

Again, the doorbell rang. Enrique rolled onto his back; the moonlight caught the glistening sweat on his chest and the still urgent need of his body. He knew when he first met Angie, he was dating damaged goods. She had not kept it a secret. Disowned by her fundamentalist mother and old-school Mexican father at thirteen for getting knocked up by a middle school soccer player, Angie had been thrown out of the house to spend the rest of her teen years moving from one foster home to another, always hoping against hope that her mother would at least come to her rescue.

She had miscarried on the streets, so of course, there was no baby. Surely that would make a difference. But evidently it didn't. Her parents never called. They never asked. When she was sixteen, she slipped away from school and took a bus back to her old home, ready to fall on her knees, if necessary, and beg for forgiveness, but they had moved away leaving no forwarding address.

She never saw them again, but she did eventually find out where they were living. Her father had accepted a job with Gates Rubber, working on the line, she guessed. He certainly had no skills for anything other than that. She had learned their whereabouts when she started at the Police Academy. One of her assignments was locating a missing person. She thought her parents qualified. They were as missing as anybody, and it really wasn't that hard to find them once you had all the right tools and knew how. But she didn't call them. She told herself she didn't need them. Still, when it came time to invite family to graduation, she had slipped their names into the invitation list to be notified.

Enrique's "Fuck!" broke through her indecision.

Getting up and slipping into a skirt, she tried to explain, "I better get it. It really might be them."

Enrique reached over to pull a sheet up over his nakedness and she heard him mutter, "Next time, we celebrate in my place. I don't have a fuckin' doorbell."

She had to laugh as she left the bedroom, "Enrique, you don't even have a fuckin' door."

"So what's left to steal?" he called after her.

Moving down the darkened hallway, she heard another knock on her chained front door. Running a hand quickly through her hair and turning on a table lamp, she called out, "Who is it?"

The doorbell rang again.

"I said, 'Who is it?'" she repeated.

Then she heard a familiar voice, "Angie, it's me, Seth. I'm sorry it's so late, but I need to talk to you."

"Seth?" she questioned, peering through the security viewer in the door.

"I'm sorry," came his reply.

Quickly unlocking the door, she threw it open in concern, "There is nothing wrong with Rachel, is there?"

Before he could answer, two men she'd never seen before stepped in to stand beside him.

Jay Acresti was preparing a late-night dinner in his small, but nicely efficient, bachelor's kitchen. The music of Carrie Underwood's latest country hit could be heard filtering through from the other room. Though the apartment wasn't nearly as large as the house he had shared with his ex-wife and daughter, he found it was exactly what he wanted and needed, and he was happy. It had been so long since he had been really happy and, for many years, he didn't understand why. Once he discovered the truth, his entire life changed. It had not been easy, and it had not been overnight, but the change was complete and irreversible. His new direction was more than just turning over a new page. It was writing a whole new book.

Graduation that morning had been a prime example. Good bye Jay Acresti, promising young attorney-at-law and hello Officer Acresti of LAPD vice.

A voice, from the next room, asking him a question brought him back to the present. Listening, Jay stirred the alfredo sauce a couple more whips, just to make sure it hadn't stuck, and then turned off the burner, and moved to the pasta that was steaming, ready to be taken up.

In answer to the question, he replied, "I don't know how I feel yet. I'm just glad it's over. So, maybe now, I can get on with living and not have to think about it every minute of every day."

Thinking about the last seven months, he laughed, "It wasn't as bad as everyone said it was going to be. Of course, I think it blew them out of the water that I topped out in fire arms, hand-to-hand, and cross-country endurance. Gotta give it to Utah, you can't grow up LDS there and not learn something. Double 'A' ratings straight across the board. That's got to stand for something. The others may gag on it, but it's got to stand for something."

The timer on the oven rang softly, and Jay moved into action.

"Okay, that's it. Everything's ready."

With an economy of motion, he efficiently retrieved some hot, steaming French bread from the oven, placed it on a platter, grabbed up the pot of fettucini, poured its contents into a colander over the sink, rinsed it, and then transferred the pasta into a waiting bowl. The rich steaming alfredo sauce went into the next bowl.

"You want to fill our plates in here, or eat like civilized people in the dining room?" he called into the other room.

The door to the kitchen swung open in response and Cameron entered. A good-looking Nordic blond with fine, almost delicate, features, Cameron reached across the counter to pick up the salad and the bread.

"You kidding? This is a celebration," he pointed out, as he pushed back through the kitchen's swinging door, and into the dining room. "So let's get started."

With a smile, Jay grabbed the other two bowls, and followed Cameron into the romantically-lit dining room that his lover had prepared for him. Setting his dishes down, he almost wanted to take Cameron in his arms and hold him, never letting him go, but he knew that would come later. For the time being, he settled for "Nice."

"So sit," Cameron ordered like a French maître'd as he expertly poured the champagne, first in Jay's crystal glass, and then, his own.

Jay couldn't help smiling as he slid into his place. He did that a lot now: Smile.

Cameron remained standing to propose a toast. When he had Jay's full attention, his blue eyes glistened softly as he held the lightly golden glass of bubbles out to the man before him. "Here's to your graduation.

To the courage it took to survive it. And most importantly, to all those things I feel and would like to say to you."

He extended his glass to Jay, but the pure ring of their glasses as they touched was lost when the doorbell rang.

CHAPTER V

The three-tiered room was filled with over two hundred young men and women already seated. Those who arrived late were quickly trying to find a place to blend into the group. All were equally subdued; all equally unsure why they have been brought together. Although extremely diverse in ethnicity, and dressed in three-piece suits to extremely casual, the group was unified in only one major aspect: their silence. Whether it is from the uncertainty of the situation or the obvious presence of the non-smiling FBI agents lining the walls, except for an occasional cough or the clearing of a throat, the room was unnaturally quiet. So silent, in fact, that when the hand of the large clock on the wall jerked forward with a click to one minute before the hour, everyone heard it.

Seth, Jay, Miles, and Angie had been some of the last to arrive, their plane landing a scant twenty minutes earlier. An FBI escort had been waiting, and quickly guided them out of the terminal, and into a waiting car.

They had been surprised that no other cadets from their graduating class were with them on the plane. Most of the two-hour flight was spent speculating why they were being flown to Denver, and Jay wondering if there was still any snow left on the mountains they might take advantage of before returning home.

Disembarking, they didn't even get a chance to pick up their bags. For some strange reason, they had been told to use the restrooms on the plane before landing.

Entering the lecture hall, they quickly made their way up through the tiered levels to slide quietly into a row so they could be together. On the speaker platform below, at the front of the room, two agents stood on either side of the podium, unmoving, facing the group. The silence in the room was almost unbearable. No one moved. All eyes were trained forward. Waiting.

The hands of the clock hovered for a long moment, before jerking into final position, straight up, with another audible click.

Still, nothing happened. Finally, Miles could stand it no longer, and leaned over to whisper to Seth in his not-so-quiet voice, "This is making me nervous. It's worse than waiting for the results of a VD test." Then he added with a smile, "From what I've heard."

A ripple of nervous laughter spread through the room. Seth couldn't help but smile. Jay, who had also been listening, had to swallow his laugh as it was cut short by the door, closest to the podium platform, opening. Bob Ryder entered, causing a collective shift in focus, and a visceral sense of the entire room having snapped to attention.

Ryder scanned the room for just a moment before stepping up on the platform and approaching the podium. He wasted no time in beginning.

"Good afternoon. My name is Robert Ryder, special advisory counsel to the President of the United States. I appreciate your being here on such short notice and under such unusual circumstances. I know what you've been through in the last twenty-four hours has smacked of subterfuge and cloak and dagger; rushed flights, the cancellation of plans and a total disruption of your routines, all with very little information as to why. I would apologize for that, but once you have fully been apprised of the proposition we are about to make to each of you, I'm sure you will appreciate both the urgency and secrecy."

Angie glanced over to Jay to catch his reaction and found he was looking to her for the same reason. Ryder's next statement pulled their attention back to the stage, and then, around the room.

"Now at this time, I would like this room sealed, and that includes every agent not specifically assigned to this project, either by myself or Deputy Director Tamwell."

Most of the agents lining the walls looked a little confused and surprised by this directive, but slowly made their way down to the nearest exits. The few remaining assigned agents efficiently closed the doors, locked them, and then, physically, blocked the access.

If anything, the removal of the agents made the cadets even more nervous; and now, everyone was looking to the others in their row seeking some indication that at least someone around them understood what was going on. Nobody did and, eventually, the murmurs calmed down. All eyes moved uneasily back to Ryder who remained at the podium, waiting. His eyes scanned the group before him, his head nodding imperceptibly when he knew he had their full attention again.

Leaning slightly into the podium, Ryder's next words seemed to be directed to each cadet in the room, individually.

"First, each of you is here because you've already passed an extensive screening process that's been going on for the last three months of your training programs. A screening process, I might add, that your instructing officers knew nothing about. As a result, what you, as a group, represent are the top-ranked police academy cadets from the entire western portion of this country.

That, in itself, is a big honor, and I congratulate you. And if you choose to accept the offer I am going to make you today, you will be linked up with your counterparts from the northern, central, and southern regions, making you a part of the most elite police force this country has ever known."

Unable to contain his pride at being one of the top cadets, Miles gave Angie a slight thumbs-up that made her smile.

"One that could alter the direction of law enforcement in this country, and possibly the world, from this time forward."

Ryder paused at this point, as though waiting for some sort of response, but there was not a sound in the auditorium, and the power of that silence was almost overwhelming. Miles, Angie, Seth and Jay found themselves, like the rest, leaning forward in anticipation of what was going to follow this pause. Seth suddenly had the uncomfortable image of lemmings leaping off a cliff and had to shake his head to regain his focus, but the thought still lingered at the edge of his mind.

"Okay, let's get down to it," Ryder began.

CHAPTER VI

On the steps of the capital, the press was swarming like flies over a dead body, their cameras and microphones jabbing and thrusting, in hopes of catching a tag line for their own evening news of a story ABC's Marshall Foster had already broken that morning. Marshall Foster, was, of course, already set up and on the air, so they were forced to try to catch what he was announcing and repeat it for their own coverage. Some just gave up, and linked into his broadcast directly, because they knew if they didn't, almost all their viewers would be switching to ABC anyway.

Marshall was in top form. "This country is still mourning, and they should be. Shari Benton and her daughter, Leah, were brutally murdered right here in the nation's Capital three months ago and, in spite of the constant video reminder every hour on the hour, in spite of the millions upon millions of dollars that have been contributed to Leah's World Foundation, in spite of the world conference last week on violence, the crime rate in this country has increased, not decreased, and as I announced this morning in an ABC exclusive, it's just been discovered that more than ninety percent of those new crimes were committed by repeat offenders. America is outraged. I am outraged. Our prison officials have denied releasing known felons back onto the streets to repeat their crimes but the statistics we now have prove that's exactly what they've been doing."

Marshall paused for impact before continuing. "Well, let me tell you, and this is a Marshall Foster prediction, unless our government steps in, and steps in sooner, rather than later, with some massive attempt to stop this rising tide of crime, self-protection is going to be the only way to survive on our streets, and that means more guns in more untrained gun-owners' hands. My sources have confirmed that the President has been in a closed session all day with select members of both the Senate and House, and that meeting, we understand, is about to break up. Although we have been told that no one will be allowed to comment on the proceedings, I think we, as Americans, deserve to know if this meeting is to address the violence in our nation, or not."

As if on cue, the crowd on the steps surged forward, as the President and his security detail made their way out of the huge bronze doors and hurriedly moved down the granite steps to perfectly-timed limousines that, just then, pulled to a stop at the curb.

"Mr. President? Mr. President?" the shouts bombarded the man. "Any comment? The repeat offenders?"

The President's detail moved through the crowd, parting it like chaff in the wind. In passing, the President did glance up once to flash that winning smile and waved. Foster was at the base of the steps. He was one piece of chaff that wasn't going to be easily blown aside.

"Mr. President," he shouted, the camera man behind him capturing the moment. "Is this really what you want to leave as your legacy to the world?" The President stopped abruptly as though considering.

"Marshall Foster, ABC News," Marshall identified himself smugly.

"I know who you are, Mr. Foster," replied the President, his voice level and without a smile.

"Then you know why I'm here," Marshall rejoined, as he rudely thrust his microphone into the President's face. "Any comment?"

The security team instinctively moved forward to knock the microphone aside, but the President waved them away and locked eyes with the reporter, fully aware that every camera on the steps was focused on this exchange.

"Let me assure you, Mr. Foster of ABC news," his voice slow and measured. "In spite of what you've been reporting, this administration does take the problem of rampant crime in our nation seriously, and a solution to that problem is already underway."

"What solution?" Marshall pushed back but found that the President was already gone and had, in fact, dismissed him with a mere sound bite and nothing else. "Mr. President? Mr. President?" he angrily called out, but the man was already been encased in his shielded, sound-proofed limo and was being driven back to 1600 Pennsylvania Ave.

Standing in the street and realizing that his cameraman was still broadcasting, Marshall wheeled to deliver his parting promise to the American people, "So, you heard it here. The President has a solution to all this crime," he waved his arms around to indicate the streets of Washington, "but, he was a bit sketchy on the details, which has been a running theme with this administration, don't you agree?"

"Well, I'm not letting him off the hook this time and neither should you," he challenged his audience. "You know what to do. Write your Congressman. Write your senator. Write the big man, himself. Demand to know what this solution is. He probably won't give you any more details than I got this afternoon, but trust me, I'm going to find out for you. If there is a solution, you as Americans have a right to know."

CHAPTER VII

Back in Denver, Seth wasn't listening to the newscast. In fact, he'd noticed when he first opened his door and clicked on the lights that there wasn't even a T.V. anywhere in the room. He could see where it had previously been, but now there were only a few loose wires and cables. It crossed his mind to question whether all the other rooms had also been stripped and why, but forced himself to concentrate of what Ryder had said in the meeting.

His first priority was to call Rachel, but he realized, glancing at the clock on the bedside stand, that he had been sitting on the edge of his bed, staring at the phone for at least thirty minutes, not really sure what he was going to do or say when he did finally call her. Finally? He didn't have finally. He had just a couple of hours before he had to give them his decision.

The meeting had ended over an hour ago, the message delivered, though still not absorbed. The President's advisor had left the chamber to stunned silence; nobody had moved or said anything for at least a couple of minutes. Even Miles, who could always be counted on to break the tension, just whispered a quiet, "Holy fuck!" before getting up and leaving, without even turning back to see if the others were following. No one else spoke. No one asked what anyone else was doing for dinner. No one dared think of anything except what they had been offered, and what it would mean to the rest of his or her life, and the lives of their families.

Seth had come back to his room and pulled the blinds. He didn't know why he had done that. It was still a beautiful day outside, the sun glinting off the snow of the peaks surrounding the city. Any other time he'd be like Jay, thinking about how to catch a few runs on the slopes Colorado was so noted for, but the blinds were closed and he had less than three hours to make his decision.

He couldn't do that without Rachel. Punching in her number, he listened to the soft ringing through the receiver and wondered if anyone else was listening.

"Hello?" her voice was soft and, for some reason, he almost cried on hearing it.

"Rache? Hon? It's me. Yeah, I'm fine...just a little dazed. You won't believe what this is all about."

In Angie's room, she was having less luck in reaching Enrique and although she had re-dialed every fifteen minutes, she kept getting the answering machine. The messages she left had grown increasingly desperate.

"Damn! Enrique, it's me. I need to talk to you as soon as possible. You've got the number, room 306. Something real big has come up and I need to run some things past you. I've got to make a decision and I only have a couple more hours. Where in the hell are you anyway?"

Seth found it was not that easy to explain to Rachel what had been offered; now that he was trying, he found he wasn't so sure himself. "It's hard to explain. It was all real closed-door. And Rache, I mean, top security. They even asked the Feds to leave. No, I'm not kidding. This guy, who was telling us about it, had the room cleared and actually posted guards on the doors. That's just it, I don't know. It's some sort of new program. They wouldn't tell us a whole lot, just enough to give us an idea of what we were in for."

Jay caught Cameron at his office. As lead designer at his own design firm, Cameron was always the first to arrive and the last to go home. Although he had never met her personally, Elise, Cameron's secretary, put him through immediately which always thrilled Jay. Cameron was equally exuberant when he picked up, but that excitement dimmed somewhat when Jay tried to explain what had been offered.

"I don't know," he tried to explain. "They wouldn't really say. It's kind of a blind grab." then laughing, he said, "No, not that kind of blind grab...very funny. It's hard to explain. From what I gather, it's evidently a lot of advanced training, a super crash course in some new way of handling crime."

"What do you mean?" Rachel questioned, as Seth stumbled over what he was trying to explain.

"Something about revolutionizing the whole process," he tried again.

"How?"

"I don't know. That's just it. You know how Miles used to kid that some of our lessons sounded like buying a pig in a poke? Very un-Jewish, but he was right. Well, this is that times five. We really won't know what we're getting 'til after we've got it."

When she didn't respond, he continued, "But it sounded...I don't know how to describe it, Rache,...it just sounded like maybe they really finally had a handle on the situation, and we were going to be the first step in making it happen."

"Then, what's the problem, Honey?" probed Rachel quietly, though something in her mind was screaming, Come home Seth. Now! But that wasn't what she said. Instead she heard herself saying, "Is the money that bad?"

Although Miles was dating Rhondene, in a situation like today, the only person Miles wanted to talk to was his mother. But he didn't want to scare or upset her, so, true to his nature, he was keeping the phone call light, just like he had done whenever he had called home from his tour of duty in the Middle East. Keeping it light kept everybody happy, and as long as everybody else was happy, Miles could survive.

"I'd be some sort of Supercop...a rich super cop, and I mean, real rich, mama. We're talking good money. Dealers on the corner hear about this and they'd all be applying."

"Are you ready for this?" teased Jay. "Two hundred and eighty-five to start. No. Thousand. Yes. Two hundred and eighty-five thousand...to start."

"What do you mean, 'start'?" gasped Cameron.

Rachel was just as taken back. "Are you serious?"

"With a hundred thousand-dollar bonus upon completion of training, and then planned yearly merit increases after that," Seth raced on in excitement.

"Two hundred and eighty-five. I don't believe it...that's more than... I can't even imagine it."

"I know," he laughed, "but they said it was because it was experimental and evidently only the top cadets around the country got invited to participate."

"Honey, with that kind of money, do you realize what that would mean? We could buy our own home. The baby could have a new home."

In her room, a frustrated Angie was still trying to find Enrique and time was fast running out. She tried another number. It was picked up almost immediately. Angie didn't even wait for a hello. "Hi, Kathy? It's me, Angie. Yeah. I'm fine. Just trying to get a hold of Enrique. Have you seen him around? No, just something's come up and I need to talk to him real fast."

In his room, Jay was laughing now. "Yes, I'll speak to you when I'm rich and famous," and then suddenly the laughter went out of his voice. "If I decide to sign on."

"What the fuck does that mean?" gasped Cameron. "If?" Cameron almost yelled over the phone. "Are you crazy?"

"No, I'm not crazy."

"It's a big fucking honor, or did you miss that point?"

"No, I know it's a big fuckin' honor, but come on, Cameron, I'm not like you. I never asked to be a pathfinder. I just want us to get back to some sort of normalcy. And...damn it, if I take it, I have to relocate."

That caused a silence on the other end and then, "Where?"

"They won't say where. Another one of those top secrets. I don't know, Cameron. You've got your job and you're all established. So where's that leave us? I...I don't want to, will not give us up."

"You won't be giving us up," assured Cameron, though he, truthfully, had never considered having to be apart from Jay or what that would mean to their relationship. He had met Jay three months after the divorce and two months after Jay had come out. Cameron hadn't been looking for any long-time attachments and definitely not to a recent breeder who hadn't yet discovered any of the hard realities of being gay. Jay was a romantic and looking for some fantasy life. Cameron was a realist, who at thirty-five had already discovered the pitfalls of trying to force straight ideals of monogamy on a gay relationship.

It was not that Cameron had a problem with committing, but all of his previous partners certainly had. Jay was talking love after their first night together, and Cameron had to admit there was something intrinsically exciting about being with a man who was just discovering how exciting his body could be.

But Cameron also knew he should have run for the hills after that first date. Jay was just equating his first real climax with Cameron as love. Women in romance novels might do that, but Cameron knew sex and love were not the same thing.

Cameron was the first guy Jay had ever really gone to bed with. Jay had never had his time of experimentation. He had never known the excitement of anonymous sex in dark rooms, the heat of multiple bodies rubbing against his, the hands groping, tongues flicking, and breath catching. And yet, a year and a half later, here they were discussing the ramifications of a new job on their relationship.

Jay was just as ardent as that first night, and Cameron had never been so in love. He had never even known it was possible.

Jay's next statement brought Cameron back to the man on the other end of the phone. "The three months of training will be bad enough."

Rachel was no longer so excited.

"Three months?"

"Starting tonight," Seth had to tell her.

"Tonight?"

"If I take it..."

"But you'll be here for the baby." It should have been a question, but she still wanted to assume.

"No, that's just it, we'll be in isolation somewhere, maybe in Europe. We don't know. They won't tell us. That's why I can't do this."

"But you've got to," Rachel heard herself saying. "It's too big an honor."

"We don't know that," Seth asserted, sounding like he was trying to convince himself as well as her. "It could be a bunch of crap. Besides, when has anything the government tried ever worked out like it was supposed to?"

But you don't think so this time, Rachel knew instinctively. She could hear it in his voice. "If it weren't for the baby, you'd go," she stated with sad conviction.

"No,...Yes...I mean, I just think it's all incredibly bad timing. Look, I'll tell them no and be home on the next flight."

"Don't you dare, Seth Slavin," Rachel heard herself saying with more strength and determination than she thought she had. "This is too important."

But Seth was equally adamant. "No, it's not. We're going to have a baby. That's what's important. And they're not even going to let us communicate with anyone for any reason during the next three months."

"Nothing, not even letters," Rachel faltered.

"No, God damnit! I wouldn't even know if you were all right. I couldn't handle that."

Rachel didn't feel like she could handle that either, but pulling from some inner reserve of strength she didn't even know she had, she was not going to let Seth know that.

"Seth, Honey," she pleaded. "Now listen to me. I'll be fine. I've got your mom, and God knows with her, this baby and I are going to have more attention than either of us can stand, so..."

"But," Seth tried to break in.

"I said, 'Listen'," she stopped him. "Hear me out. When you were in special forces, your mom and I didn't hear from you for months."

"And I almost died worrying," he reminded her and himself.

"So did I. So did we, but we survived," she answered softly, and then added with more strength than she felt, "and when it was over, remember you had all those letters stacked there just waiting for you. So you really knew what was going on...just a little late."

"But the baby?" he was pleading.

"Your baby will be fine, Mr. Slavin, and so will we."

"But, I want to hold you now," he whispered, and it tore her heart to hear his voice breaking, "...and I can't even do that."

He was crying softly now and it took every bit of effort she had to keep from breaking down herself.

"God, I love you," he cried, his voice so small and hurt.

Drawing in a deep breath to steady herself, she did the only thing she could do from this distance. She whispered, "Me, too, again and again, as the tears ran quietly down her own face. "Me, too.

CHAPTER VIII

It was late and the First Lady had already sent word that she expected her husband in her bed within the hour. She was like that. She knew that if she didn't occasionally remind him that he was only human, he'd work around the clock and nobody could be effective if they kept that up. So, on days like this when the President had been going non-stop since six that morning, and even his staff couldn't get him to call it a day, she would step in and send him a recorded message over their private line. She never named herself in case these somehow slipped into the wrong hands, but they almost always got her husband laughing and usually out of his office and on his way to her within minutes.

The messages were always worded differently. The First Lady prided herself on her vocabulary and her imagination, and they were never without humor. She used a secret code she knew would appeal to the man who was President but first, was her husband.

This particular message was, "Hey Cowboy, I'm tired of wasting my time riding this mechanical horse. I'm waiting for the real one...in bed. I've got the spurs, you bring the whip."

At his desk, the President had seen the flashing light, picked up, and listened. Closing his eyes, he caught himself almost laughing out loud at the image of his wife, not in bed, but giggling as she recorded this missive.

She would have had that twinkle in her azure-green eyes that always appeared when she was playing with him. He loved that twinkle. He loved those eyes. In fact, he'd fallen in love with his wife the first moment he saw her racing across the campus mall, her arms full of books, her auburn ponytail swinging in perfect time to the smooth bounce of her hips.

Dessa, for Desiree, had been named after a heroine in a country music song. Even though she accused her parents of having been drunk at the time of her naming, and probably also at conception, she actually liked the comparison. He couldn't get enough of her, even after all these years and after how far they had both come: she, from a small mill town in Pennsylvania; he, from a mining town in West Virginia. Unlike their closest friend, Ryder, the man, who would be President, and the woman, who would become First Lady, were born, not poor, but wanting. Both had determined, at an early age, that the only way out of their situation was through drive and education.

The President wanted nothing more than to drop everything and take the back steps up to her side, but he still had to finish with Ollie Misner, a rather unctuous, annoying brother-in-law of one of the President's chief fund-raisers. Burying him in a subcommittee of the re-election committee had been the President's way of distancing himself from Ollie, but unfortunately, this well-dressed though somewhat paunchy little man with a balding friar's circle of hair, managed to show up at end of day, an exhausted look on his face and an armful of documents ready for his Presidential signature. Most of the papers were just fodder for some paper shredder, but to Misner, they were his responsibility, and the President's signature, though not necessary, signified that his work was important.

Ollie Misner was one of those people who prefaced everything with a weary exhalation of breath as though it was his last, due to all the hard work and long hours he was putting in. In truth, he did put in long hours, but it was not because he had to, but rather that he chose to. The President guessed correctly that Ollie Misner lived at the White House because he didn't really have any other place to go.

"Just a couple more signatures for the campaign fund," Misner exhaled, as he pushed another two sheets in front of the President. "And then I want to update you on the inner office memo system I've implemented."

The President groaned inwardly at the thought of being trapped there while Dessa was waiting upstairs. His reprieve came the moment Joel pushed into the office unannounced; his arrival also shoved all thoughts of Misner and Dessa from his mind.

"It's time, sir."

"Denver?" The word was out before he even realized it.

"Just time, sir," responded Joel, a warning look in his eyes.

"Oh yes, of course," realized the President who then turned to Misner with a dismissive wave, "Ollie, look, we'll have to take this up tomorrow."

"But, sir, I still have..."

The President cut him off by rising. "Tomorrow. Make it tomorrow."

"Of course, whatever you say." Misner instantly began gathering up his papers and was backing to the door when a phone inside the President's desk began to buzz urgently. The President immediately pressed his thumb print on the lock, waited for the click, and reached in.

"Is this something I should be aware of? I mean, anything I could help with?" Misner stammered, as he noticed Joel electronically wanding the room for security bugs. "I mean, my security level allows me to..."

The President snapped his eyes towards the little man and repeated, this time angrily, "Tomorrow, and tell Mrs. Kline, no interruptions."

Ollie Misner quickly left the room and closed the door, but not before he heard Joel say, "Okay!" followed by the President's cautious, almost fearful query to whoever was on the phone, "Okay?"

In the outer office, the President's private secretary was still stationed and busy at her desk, even though most of her staff had left hours before. Though sixty-two years old, the impeccably-coifed, severely-groomed Mrs. Kline took her Oval Office gate-keeping duties seriously and worked harder and longer than almost anybody in the entire D.C. area; nobody questioned or even considered challenging her on that reputation.

The President's hours were her hours and she would not have it any other way. Looking up, as Ollie Misner left the Oval Office, she coolly wished him a good night and turned back to her work. She was surprised when she heard him say, "That last phone call cut me short."

She glanced at him curiously, "I don't know what you're talking about?"

Misner realized she was telling the truth. None of the lines on her desk were lit up, which meant it hadn't come through her com-board.

"That Joel kid, you know, Ryder's assistant, he just walked right in on our meeting," Misner protested. In actuality, his curiosity was peaked.

"Well, the President has given him 24-hour unlimited access to the inner office."

"Why?" Misner questioned, knowing full well he had to schedule his appointments days, if not weeks, in advance and, even then only got the latest time slots.

This time, he realized he stepped over this guard dog's line of comfort. Her entire demeanor took on a dismissive coldness he could almost feel.

"I'm sure if you want that answer, you'll have to ask the President himself."

With that, she turned back to her work.

"Oh," he said, "then could you reschedule for tomorrow and no interruptions?"

Ever efficient, Mrs. Kline did her best to keep her dislike for the slug of a man before her as she pulled up her appointment screen to reschedule Misner. "Oh, this doesn't look good," she advised. "The President's schedule is just blocked solid for the next few weeks. Tomorrow's completely out of the question. I could possibly pencil you in for Thursday at about this time, if that's okay."

"Thanks," he said, now to the back of her head. She had turned back to her work.

Misner mumbled his good-nights and started to leave, but turned back at the door. He had one more question he wanted to ask her, but knew he was treading on dangerous waters. There were other ways to find the answers.

The White House custodial staff was monitored twenty-four hours a day, seven days a week, because they worked twenty-four hours a day, seven days a week. While the majority of the heavy work was done at night or early morning, documents and memos were shredded around the clock personally by the individuals who created them; and for less sensitive or just scribbled memos, at a central location.

As Misner headed back through the half-lit halls to the campaign offices where he worked, he passed several small custodial crews working the hallways, polishing the floors and emptying trash. They always made navigating back to his cubicle difficult when he worked late. Tonight, surprisingly, he didn't mind. In fact, the sight of them brought a smile of satisfaction to his face.

In Ryder's office, carefully locked by Joel before going to the Oval Office, a security guard watched as a lone worker, listlessly went about his duties, emptying all the wastebaskets into a plastic bag. There was not a lot of trash. Taking a well-used cloth, he wiped the desks around the papers, being careful not to touch or move anything, picked up trash off the floors, and generally cleaned up the area. Satisfied by his efforts, he crossed back to the security guard, and went out into the hall, as another worker was allowed in to vacuum the carpets.

In the hallway, the lone worker, with his bag of trash, headed for the men's rest room, propped the door open, blocking it with his mop. Moving into the sink area, he emptied the overflowing paper-towel disposal bin into a second bag and, in one fluid motion, stuffed Ryder's small trash bag into the now-empty slot. Taking a paper towel, he quickly gave the sinks a swipe, and then threw that soiled towel into the bin, effectively covering any chance of anyone seeing the bag inside.

Satisfied, he swept each of the stalls, rinsed the urinals and wet-mopped the entire area with disinfectant. His job done in the men's rest room, he clicked off the lights and moved on to the women's rest room. He didn't even glance up as he passed someone heading for the men's room. He didn't want to know who secretly paid him to hide the stolen trash from Ryder's office.

There were three trash-strewn telephone booths at the darker edge of the dimly-lit all-night convenience store parking lot, located on the opposite side of the beltway from the White House. Even at this late hour, or early hour depending on your nighttime habits, all three phones were being used; the end phone by a nervous Ollie Misner.

"I don't know," he whispered with his hand cupped over the mouth-piece. "But whatever it is, it's certainly got his full attention.

Something to do with Denver. At least that's where the call was coming from. Then right away, he wanted me out of the office. Then it was just him and Ryder's ass-licker, that Joel kid."

Someone on the other end of the phone asked a question of him, and he glanced down at the manila envelope tucked into the darkness of the booth by his feet. "No, not that I can tell, just a few scribbled numbers, throw-away notes, and old correspondence. Yeah, they're here. Just don't pick them up until after I'm completely gone."

Another question, a quicker response from Misner. "No, nothing that makes any sense. Just scribbles, and the word Miami and Delaware and something that looks like MASC, or something like that. The rest of the letters just sort of trail off. You know how he scribbles. The only letters that I think I can make out are in a couple of words; one that's maybe feather or father, another that looks like fire or fine and there's something turtle. I don't know what any of it means. Maybe you can figure it out."

With that, Ollie Misner hung up and quickly got into his car and drove away. As soon as he was gone, Marshall Foster hung up his own phone and stepped out of the third telephone booth. Moving towards the street, he seemed to remember something, reached in his pocket for another couple of quarters, went into Misner's recently-vacated booth and picked up the receiver. Then evidently, thinking the better of it, he hung up the phone and started out, but not before reaching down, picking up the envelope, and stuffing it under his coat.

Crossing the street on foot, Marshall quickly turned into an alley, and made his way through the darkness to where an unmarked car was parked. The driver was waiting inside. The ceiling light of the van had been dismantled, so that opening the door would not send a beam of light into the darkness.

"Anything?" the driver asked, as Marshall slid into the passenger seat.

"I don't know," he replied, as he ran his fingers over the surface of the envelope he held, feeling the uneven surfaces of the documents stuffed inside. "Maybe, maybe not. A few key words to strike on: Miami, Delaware, FBI, Licking, fire and muski-something. I don't know."

CHAPTER IX

The cadets were all near exhaustion; the strain of the decision was evident on every face. Angie and Jay stood waiting with about fifty other cadets, and their luggage; their eyes looking at the door where the flow of cadets accepting the proposition had dropped to a few straggling individuals. They were asked to report at 0230, and the clock on the wall of the holding room had passed that marker seven minutes previously.

"What did Enrique say about all this?" Jay whispered to Angie, though his mind was more focused on Miles and Seth, who had not yet shown up.

Angie's response, "Who cares what that son-of-a-bitch says?" brought a smile to Jay's face, which broke into even wider grin when Miles suddenly burst through the door with an energetic, "Robo-cop is here!" This brought appreciative laughter from the crowd and hugs from Jay and Angie.

"You came," said a very-relieved Jay.

"Hell, yeah, you don't dangle that much money in front of this dawg and not expect me to be climbin' your pole." Then noticing, he looked around, and the smile left his face.

"Where's Seth?"

"We haven't seen him since he went back to his room."

"I knocked on his door on my way over," Angie offered. "He still hadn't made up his mind. With the baby and all, it's a hell of a decision for him. Not like me, who just has a 'sleaze bag' to consider."

"Oh, come on Angie, give your guy a break. Maybe he was working," offered Miles and heard both Jay and Angie respond in unison, "Enrique?"

Their laughter was broken by Jay's cry of excitement, "There he is!"

All three turned towards the door as Seth slowly made his way into the room, carrying his bags.

Miles instantly moved through the crowd to wrap his arms around his buddy, squeezing. "All right! The Four Musketeers ride again!"

Everyone joined in the hug, and then, Jay stood back and gently asked, "You okay?"

Seth really wasn't sure. All he could say was, "I guess I won't know until I get there. I don't think any of us will." None of them could argue that he wasn't right.

CHAPTER X

The plane banked to the left, still climbing. Seth sat alone in the darkness, listening to the roar of the engines as they struggled to keep the 747 airborne. Whether it was actually a 747 or some other plane, Seth wasn't really sure. Miles was much more knowledgeable about things like that, having flown more than all of them combined, but Miles wasn't anywhere around and neither were the others, as far as he could tell. They had been separated moments after they got off the bus that drove them out of the city.

Boarding the bus, it reminded Seth of a high school field trip, though the passengers were a lot more reserved. The bus was standard charter with elevated seating over the luggage storage below. As their names were checked, and double-checked, off a list by two officers at the door, they were issued standard dog tags and asked to confirm the information stamped into the metal. Holding the cool metal in their hands and rubbing their thumbs over the ridges that made up their names and numbers, Seth glanced over at Miles and knew that they both had the same sinking "what the fuck" feeling in the pit of their stomach. He could read the panic, bred from experience, buried there. He saw Miles rub his hand down over his eyes and knew exactly what he was thinking. *It's like being in the fucking armed forces all over again.*

It took every ounce of Seth's will-power not to bolt for the door and run from the building. He didn't, and neither did Miles. They didn't look at each other as they emptied their pockets into clear plastic bags and handed them over to the officer-in-charge. Only the dog tags, hanging like ice around their necks, were allowed to be carried onboard the bus. Everything else was stored below for later retrieval.

Although conversations were allowed, once they were seated, there didn't seem to be much to say. The four had found seats together, and there was comfort in that, as always.

No one knew where they were going, but Miles, who was good at sensing directions, leaned over to let them know they were heading south out of Denver. But where to?

"Hell if I know. Just heading south," he responded.

"Maybe the Air Force Academy," suggested Jay. "That's south of Denver and not a bad place to be stationed. It's got a huge campus with state-of-the-art equipment. They even have their own training field for pilots."

Seth was only half listening, staring out at his reflection over the passing black landscape, still questioning the decision he had made to even be on this bus. Hearing his name called pulled him back into the group.

"You think it's the Air Force Academy, Seth?" It was Angie who was asking.

"What?"

"Where they're taking us."

"I don't know," he responded, then considered, "I don't think that would be so bad though. At least there, I might have some way to get a message out."

"Yeah," she agreed. "Someone's bound to have a cell phone or something around there. It's not like it's the end of the world."

"No?" laughed Miles. "We're talking Colorado here. It may not be the end of the world, but you sure as hell can see it from here."

Miles was a born, and bred, city dweller and tended to get anxious in wide open spaces. Actually, more than anxious. He knew there was a word for that. Agoraphobia. He'd even looked it up in high school after the basketball team played some team out near Riverside. He played forward and had been excited, until he'd looked out the window and noticed, for the first time, all that wide-open, flat land flowing past his window. Miles and miles of it racing by, and suddenly, he felt a clutching vice grabbing at his chest. He could barely breathe. His hands were frozen to the seat in front of him. When they pulled into the other school's parking lot, Miles still could hardly breathe. As for getting off the bus, forget it. His coach thought he was coming down with the flu, and he went along with the diagnosis, but he knew that wasn't it. Now, here he was, in another bus, with Pike's Peak glistening in the distant and chilled-starlight emphasizing the complete lack of city lights spreading out before him.

"Shit!" was his verbal realization that he had better get an internal grip on himself; this made imperative by how little he knew about what they were heading for.

All conversation stopped abruptly around him. Mile forced himself to look out the window just as the bus raced past the Air Force Academy entrance and onward towards Colorado Springs. A disturbing and uneasy quiet settled over the entire bus.

Evidently, everyone had come to the same conclusion that the Air Force Academy was their destination. Now, everyone felt equally lost. Nobody spoke until suddenly, the bus began applying its brakes and slowed to a near stop about ten minutes later. The lights in the bus were extinguished, as if on command, and after some muffled communication between the driver and someone seated near him, the bus turned off the main road into an access feeder lane, leading to the cargo hangers of Peterson Field.

At that point, the cadets were asked to lower their window shades which, until then, most had even noticed. Seth and Jay, on the window seats, did as they were instructed; from that point on, everyone sat in the dark as the bus made several turns and, finally, pulled to a stop.

Fully expecting instructions that didn't come, Jay reached over to find Angie's hand and found hers reaching for his. No one said a word. Not even Miles.

After what seemed like an hour, but was probably no more than ten or fifteen minutes, Seth felt his spine stiffen as he heard a rustling sound coming from outside; actually, from the sides and roof of the bus, like canvas being draped over the entire vehicle. Miles reached across Seth to slip a peek under the shade and found only darkness. Hell.

Once the rustling from outside died out, a clunking sound from beneath alerted them that their luggage were being transferred. Somehow that sound was comforting in that it meant people were out there, people who knew what was going on. And if the luggage were being moved, then it wouldn't be long before they would be moved too. Someone in the dark whispered loudly, "Want to hear a ghost story?" and everyone laughed. It felt good to laugh.

Angie hadn't realized how tense she had become and welcomed the release of tension when, suddenly, the entire bus lurched and sank about three inches, almost making her scream. Other muffled gasps came from the darkness around her, and she could feel the bus being towed slowly across a smooth surface, followed by a not-so-smooth surface, before it came to a stop, rocking slightly.

The sound of pneumatic pressure being released signaled the opening of the front door of the bus, and the harsh brightness of a flashlight cut through the darkness that entombed them.

"Okay, soldiers, follow me and watch your step," came a voice from the silhouette holding the light. And then, the light was gone.

"They've got to be kidding," Seth heard Jay whisper. "I don't think so," came a reply from someone in the darkness, a voice they didn't recognize.

Jay felt Angie's hand pulling him up out of his seat and into the aisle. "Watch your step," she whispered.

"Wait a minute. My jacket." Jay's hands fumbled around in the darkness until he felt the fabric and pulled it to him.

Miles did not take his jacket off, so all he had to find was the candy bar he bought just before leaving the hotel. Tucking that into his pocket, he reached forward to feel for Jay and Angie in the seat in front of him, but only found open space. "Shit!"

Cautiously extending a hand out into the aisle, he waited until he found an open gap and then stepped into it, turning back to grab Seth's hand, "Come on."

He could hear Seth standing, and felt his reassuring touch as Miles held a place for him. Satisfied that they were together, they moved towards the front of the blackness.

Someone grabbed the back of Jay's belt to steady himself, and a voice whispered, "Sorry. Lost my balance."

"I know the feeling," he whispered back, tightening his own grip on Angie's coat ahead of him.

"Watch it, step down," came a voice, just to the front and side of him. Simultaneously, he felt Angie slowly lowering herself down, one step at a time. It was like being blind, reminding Jay of those haunted house mazes he used to love as a kid in Provo, Utah. Except in the haunted house there was at least some light; enough to reveal the scary things that were going to jump out at him. Here, it was absolute darkness. In fact, he didn't think he had ever seen such darkness before in his life. There was nothing his eyes could hang on to and try to make materialize. The only way to move was in unison with the person ahead, just as the guy behind him was following his every movement. If he moved left, so did his no-named caboose.

Seth thought they must look like a fucking long snake winding in the darkness and that wasn't a comforting thought. If there was one thing Seth hated above almost anything else, it was snakes. Having been raised as practically the only Jewish kid in southern Louisiana, he had been the butt of a lot of jokes and pranks, and most of them involved snakes. It stood to reason, as snakes were easy to come by in southern Louisiana, whether you had a practical joke in mind or not. Snakes were an everyday thing to contend with. You never stepped off your porch at night without turning on the lights and making a lot of noise. You never went to bed at night without looking under it, or at least Seth didn't. He knew too many people who'd been bitten for making that mistake. No, that was not exactly true; he had heard too many stories about people who'd been bitten. He'd seen his fair share of snakes in those swamps: cotton mouths, rattlers, copperheads, and even coral. But he didn't have to see one strike a second time to know he didn't want to get bitten.

His daddy, always the entrepreneur, used to like to tease the snakes, get them all riled up, then smash them with a shovel, and cut off their rattlers and their heads. Snake heads made good souvenirs for the tourist. The rattles made good wind chimes to keep the rest of the snakes away. Seth felt a chill matching his sweat trickled down his back, as he tried to shove the memories of his past into the recesses of his mind, where they belonged.

Suddenly, the man in front of Seth stopped. "There's a step," he heard and he repeated the warning to the man behind him. Now, at least, they were on level ground, or whatever the surface they were standing on, was.

"Okay, everyone freeze," came a commanding voice in the void. Everyone stopped moving, but remained linked to the person in front and behind them. "Now, raise your hands up in the air."

Tentative hands reached up into the darkness.

"Now, with your hands up, both of them, slowly take four steps to the left, or to the right. No talking. It doesn't matter which direction you choose, just move. Now, stop. If you moved right, take three steps slowly backwards. If you moved left, take three steps slowly forward. No talking."

There were muffled grumblings and shuffling, and "excuse me's" and "sorry's," but no one talked.

Seth had no idea where Jay or the others were at this point, and realized that that was the purpose of this entire exercise. Forced isolation. Conscious of hundreds of bodies surrounding you, but forbidden to communicate.

More position commands came from the voice in the dark, and with each, bodies moved silently past bodies, the only sound was the rustling of clothes brushing past other clothes.

"Now, slowly reach out your right hand until you feel the shoulder of a person before you," came another command. "Attach yourself to that person by that hand. Not both hands, one hand. If there is no one in front of you, move forward slowly until you find someone. Once you are attached and likewise feel someone's hand on your shoulder, squeeze your hand to let the one in front of you know that you are attached. Only then can you again start moving forward. If you find you've reached a person who is already attached, you must move backwards down the column until you find an unattached back. Take hold and wait until someone else attaches to you, then squeeze."

Jay never knew himself to be claustrophobic but something unnerving was certainly wriggling its way up his spine and into his shoulders, other than the hand that suddenly clamped there possessively. It was like being in a pit of worms, bodies sliding past bodies and, momentarily, he wondered if this was the sensation Cameron used to say you'd find in the gay bathhouse mazes. If so, Jay was pretty sure he was glad he had missed that step in his sexual education. Still, it would be something to remember to tell Cameron about, if and when they got back together. Wait a minute, why was he questioning Cameron's loyalty just because it was dark. "Stop that," he said, almost loud enough to be heard. *I'm not afraid of the dark. What the hell is there to be afraid of? I love the darkness. Yes,* he reminded himself. *You love the darkness when you know what's hidden in it. Here?* The question hung like a suffocating cloth around his face. He was finding it difficult to concentrate and realized he'd never been in a situation that was so completely disorienting.

"God, help me," he whispered to no one in particular. "Don't let me scream."

CHAPTER XI

Had anyone been able to see it at fifty thousand feet, the 727 would have appeared nothing more than a colorless shadow sailing through the moonlit darkness for a destination still to be determined.

Inside the windowless plane, most of the cadets were strapped in their seats, sleeping. Everyone fell asleep almost before take off. Whether it was from complete exhaustion, or reduced oxygen levels, or something introduced into the cabin air system, Seth would have probably questioned if he hadn't been fighting so hard to stay awake.

Angie slept, curled up, in what would have been a window seat had the plane had any windows. Unbeknownst to her, six rows back, Miles' lanky frame made do with an aisle seat. His head was thrown back and his mouth was open. The window-shattering snores his girlfriend, Rhondene, needled him about were destined to surface before long.

Further back in the plane, Jay lay awake. Groggy but not asleep. Small pen lights pierced the darkness as several soldiers moved down the aisles, surveying their sleeping cargo. When a soldier's beam struck Jay's open eyes, he blinked and asked, "Has anyone mentioned where we're going?"

"I'm sure they'll tell you when you get there," came the reassuring reply, followed by, "Here, take this." The soldier poured some water from his canteen into small paper cup, and offered it to Jay, along with a blue liquid capsule. Jay started to protest but instead accepted the pill and water.

"It'll make it easier," assured the soldier.

"Make what easier?" Jay tried to say, but his eyes were already closing and his mind was shutting down.

Seth watched the exchange from several seats back. *They are trying to put us to sleep, he thought. Shit, Jesus, what the fuck is going on?* The words ran through his increasingly incoherent mind. It was taking every ounce of his strength to remain awake, remain focused. He could see the soldier now moving up the aisle towards him. Seth didn't want to sleep though his body craved it with every breath he took. The soldier was getting closer now, the beam of his light moving from face to face. *I can't be caught*, Seth thought, as he closed his eyes to avoid being discovered awake by the beam of the pen light. He could feel the heat of the beam passing over his eyelids, and wondered what kind of light could be that strong. Then it was gone and a wave of relief washed over him. He was sitting with Rachel, on that first date so long ago, when he looked into those eyes, when he realized nothing was ever going to be the same again, when he realized nothing was going to turn out as he had planned. Only this time, he was asleep.

It was already mid-morning in Washington and the President arrived in the Oval Office at five-thirty before everyone except, of course, Mrs. Kline, the venerable keeper of the keys. Somehow, she always seemed to divine when he'd be arriving, and never failed to be at her desk with his coffee hot and exactly like he wanted; and with the materials and notes he'd need for his appointments, ranked and placed in his top desk drawer to be drawn out from top to bottom as his day progressed. This day was no exception, but the drawer was lighter. He had purposely cleared his morning calendar in anticipation of Ryder's return from Denver. Mrs. Kline, who, out of necessity, was privy to some but not all of the details of Ryder's mission, had informed him that Ryder's driver had picked up his passenger on schedule, and were en route. The President asked that he be sent in, the moment he arrived.

Then, it was time to wait, and the President had never been good at waiting. He was pacing when the intercom finally buzzed.

"Send him in," the President responded, without even waiting for the announcement.

The door to the Oval Office opened, and an exhausted but triumphant Ryder stepped in.

"Well?"

Ryder just smiled and nodded, closing the door behind him. "Phase One, done."

The President exhaled the deep breath he hadn't known he was holding, and turned away to look out over the White House lawn. Though glistening from the previous night's rain, everything within the iron fence still looked exactly as it had the previous day. Beyond the fence, the same held true. Traffic still jammed the street. Protesters carrying signs and banners, a recurring entitlement of citizenship, as usual blocked the sidewalks. Tourists moved excitedly amidst the crowds, cameras clicking, to document their visit for those back home. Yet, not one of them knew that this day would go down in history as bigger than 9-11 or the bombing of the Sears Tower in Chicago.

He didn't know what he had expected to see, but 'everything as normal' was not it. Somehow, he felt the world should sense a huge rip in the fabric of time, a splintering, an impact, something to mark its passing, a monument to the rest of the world that during the previous night, the first step in the extinction of the political dinosaur, known as democracy, had begun, not with a deadly racing comet, but old retrofitted 727s blasting into an uncertain future, but certainly a future that was better than what they had now.

CHAPTER XII

Seth awoke as the 727's wheels touched down on the tarmac, and the jet engines roared against the brakes and forward thrust of the plane. Though the cabin lights were now on, everyone around him seemed to be in the same dazed and lethargic space, not really sure where they were, or caring. The stale air of unwashed bodies had Seth shaking his head to get rid of the fog that still lingered behind his eyes. Rubbing his face to try to get some sort of feeling back to the numbness, his fingers suddenly stopped, and then, hesitantly, began skimming the surface of his face, not believing what they were sensing: the unshaved stubble of several day's growth.

How fucking long had they been asleep? Certainly more than one night. Seth couldn't deny that he was a rather hairy guy; "hirsute" as Rachel liked to joke as she ran her fingers down his chest, but this was ridiculous. He never found himself in the morning with a stubble like this. He had to have been asleep for a couple of days, if not more. Twisting in his seat, he saw others coming to the same conclusion.

Crossing his arms, he felt the lump in the crook of his arm. Pulling his shirt-sleeve up, the lump turned out to be a bandage, neatly applied. He knew, even before he removed it, what he would find; a needle-puncture mark. While he had been asleep, someone had hooked him up to an IV. Quickly pulling up the sleeve of the protesting cadet in the next seat, he found the same type of bandage.

"What the fuck?" he heard the startled cadet whisper under his breath, as his eyes opened wide in fear.

"Yeah, what the fuck," was the only response Seth could give him in return.

Lifting himself slightly up in his seat so that he could see over the rows in front of him, Seth looked for Miles, or Angie or Jay, and instantly spied Jay about fifteen rows ahead, his eyes equally scanning, trying to make a connection. Finally seeing each other, both held for a second, relief obvious on their faces, before nodding slightly and sinking back into their seats. They were not alone any more.

Jay was so relieved at seeing Seth, he almost cried. He was totally disoriented when he awoke, and his throat was sore and dry. It wasn't until he started patting down his pockets for a mint or a lozenge that he realized where he was, and that he had been sleeping. Or, was it really sleeping? He felt drugged, as if somebody had given him a pill, or something. He vaguely remembered that, but nothing else.

The young woman, sitting next to him, still had her eyes closed, as though afraid of what she might find when she opened them. He reached out to reassure her, but she instinctively jerked back at the contact, and Jay mumbled an apology before settling back into his seat.

They sat on the plane for at least thirty minutes; the actual time was hard to determine as all watches had been confiscated, along with everything else, upon boarding the bus in Denver. Surprisingly, nobody seemed to be talking. Jay heard a couple of soft murmurs, but no open conversation as one would expect from passengers waiting to disembark.

What he did hear in the silence, now that the engines had been cut, was the creaking of the plane, the shifting of metal parts, and the vibrations of sub-doors being opened, and the metal-on-metal 'thunk' of something that was hard to define, until he felt the plane starting to silently roll forward, and realized that they were being towed.

With no windows and limited cabin lighting, Jay felt like he was sitting mid-section in a low-tech space capsule, uniformly colored in army olive green. The air was stagnant with sweat and the closeness. At least turn on the fucking fans, he thought, and was relieved when they did just that.

A switch had been thrown somewhere, and fans over each seat began circulating fresh air. The lights in the cabin also brightened, and Jay instantly felt the mood-shift of those around him, as though everyone was drawing in a fresh breath of air after being submerged for weeks under water.

The young woman sitting next to Jay actually opened her eyes and took several deep lasting breaths, offered him a weak smile, then turned to look at her hands, as though seeing them for the first time. Turning her left arm over, the fingers of her right hand traced a path up to the bend of her elbow and circled the Band-Aid there.

Jay checked his own arm and, sure enough, he too had a Band-Aid.

"How long were we out?" whispered the woman.

"I don't know," Jay answered honestly. "A long time would be my guess."

He watched as she pinched the skin in the palm of her hand and stared at the crease she momentarily created. Then she reached for his hand and, after a momentary hesitation, he let her take it.

"I'm a nurse. Or was a nurse," she said, as she repeated the slight pinching of his palm just below the thumb. "We've been hydrated," she confirmed. "That means longer than twenty-four hours."

"What do you mean?"

"I mean, we could be anywhere. Absolutely anywhere."

Unconsciously, running her thumb slowly over her lips, she sank back into her seat, "I guess now all we can do is wait."

They didn't have to wait long. The voice of the Captain introduced herself, and immediately switched the feed over to another more commanding voice who didn't even bother to introduce himself. He just told them the sequence of events that were going to happen.

"The doors forward and aft will be opened and you must move to the exit nearest you to disembark. You have been asleep for a while so you may feel some discomfort standing at first. Although we want you to move swiftly, make sure you have regained your balance before disembarking. If you are having difficulty in regaining your balance, remain seated, and a steward will assist you after the plane has been emptied. The plane has been towed into a large military hanger. Upon exiting the plane, move across the hanger to and through the large yellow doors at the end for processing."

"Welcome to Camp UI which stands for Unknown Island. Unknown because it's of no consequence to you and your training, and at no time during the duration of your stay will you be given either the name or the coordinates of your current location. 'Island' because it might as well be an island as far as you are concerned. There is nothing other than this camp, and for the duration of your training, this is where you'll be. Anyone attempting to leave, or break out of the boundaries of this camp will be shot. I want this clearly understood so I will repeat it, 'Anyone attempting to leave, or break out of the boundaries of this camp will be shot.' Not arrested. Shot. Dead."

"Jesus, sounds like a fucking prison to me," came a whispered voice from somewhere behind Jay.

And then, to the shock of everyone on the plane, the voice replied, "It is a fucking prison, and everything you say, and everything you do, from this point on, will be and is monitored. You take a shit, and we'll know where and how much. The sooner you understand that, the easier it will be for you to adjust."

"And if we've changed our mind," came another voice from the back of the plane.

"There is no changing of your mind. The moment you stepped onto this plane, it was too late for that."

"Wait a minute, you can't do this," came another protest, this time louder.

"Yeah, we're Americans," came from another voice.

There was a long weighty pause before the voice on the monitor responded, and when it did, everyone on the plane could be heard drawing in a frightened breath.

"No," it began. "You are not Americans. Not any more. As far as you're concerned, there is no America."

Before anyone could say anything else, the heavy doors of the plane swung open, and a squadron of armed military personnel entered and moved into position around the doors. Nobody in the plane moved until there was a united audible click of live ammunition being chambered, and the soldiers commanded the immediate evacuation of the plane. No one stayed behind to protest.

The hanger was huge, stark, and militaristic. The plane they had arrived in was one of four parked within its cavernous walls. At one end of the hanger, groups of cadets in military fatigues were running in place, dropping to the ground, and rolling, much like football practice. Somehow, though, the intensity of the training unmasked the feeling that more deadly games were at stake.

Passing through the bright yellow doors under armed guard, the new arrivals found themselves in an equally large hanger, partitioned into multiple holding, processing, and rest rooms. Seth made it his first priority to find the rest of his group. Several planes had emptied their human cargo at the same time, so it was not as easy as he had hoped, but within twenty minutes or so, not that he had a watch to confirm anything, he found Miles and, together, they set out in search of Jay and Angie. Miles was the first to spot Jay, and pushing through the crowd, was also relieved to see Angie standing nearby.

Together again, all the questions they'd been afraid to voice earlier came out in a flood. Had everyone noticed the cadets drilling? Had anyone counted the number of planes that were unloading? Miles asked if anyone had noticed that in both hangers every window was boarded up and sealed, making it impossible to tell whether it was day or night outside. How many fucking days had they been asleep? Before anyone could respond, a surge in the milling crowd around them led them to the conclusion that their luggage was being delivered to the room.

The next half hour or so was spent searching through, literally, piles of luggage, and claiming their belongings. Luckily, finding a relatively clear and claimable space against a far wall, the group dragged their bags over to stack together. Sitting down on the floor beside them, they waited for their next instructions. While they questioned what was going on back home, surprisingly, no one seemed to want to question what exactly had or had not happened to them, as they slept through on the long plane ride from Colorado to this Unknown Island. Or what kind of training program this was they had signed onto.

CHAPTER XIII

Seth was the first of the four to be called for processing. Before he left, he suggested they meet back at their wall after the processing and compare notes on the experience. The rest unanimously agreed. From that point on, the four Musketeers were going to stick together through this program. There was safety, strength, and, Angie wanted to add, security in numbers. Seth's name was called again, and he quickly made his way out of the room.

Typical of most military processing, everything had to begin with paperwork: reams of forms, tests, and files that had to be filled out and completed.

Much later, in either another section of that hanger, or another hanger completely, Miles and Angie found themselves at the end of a maze of rooms, at two of over a hundred occupied war-surplus steel desks, struggling through their own personal ream of paperwork.

Seth, having been called in earlier, had completed his forms, and was being interviewed at that moment by a board of three examiners where he was asked everything from the first time he had masturbated to the due date for his baby. The questioning and cross-examining went on for at least an hour, probably closer to two, and reminded Seth of being deposed in a criminal case. Each question was asked again and again, in four or five different ways, worded slightly differently, as though looking for the crack in a person's life story, the lie that even he was not aware of.

In another part of the complex, Jay had already been stripped down to his shorts and positioned on an examining table, while a battery of doctors drew blood and prepared him for a battery of other tests to be performed.

At one point, he was sitting upright, strapped in a padded chair, dozens of electrodes attached to his skull. Momentarily, he feared they were going to subject him to electro-shock therapy; but when the switch was thrown, all he experienced was a mild tingling sensation along his scalp, and the strange feeling that the colors in the room had suddenly brightened and became more crisp. And then, it happened. Just a flash, but it literally took his breath away. It couldn't have happened, but it did. Although his eyes were closed, he had been able to see not only the two doctors standing in front of him, but the one behind him as well. "Jesus," he exclaimed. And then, it was gone.

"What just happened?" he asked, as they began detaching the wires.

The doctor, removing the two from just above his left eye, merely said, "Just another test."

"Did I just see what I thought I saw?"

"I don't know. What did you see?"

"I saw him," said Jay, swiveling in the chair to point at the doctor behind him. "I saw him." And then, for emphasis, he repeated, "Him, but I was facing you."

Angie had been through two review boards, and was now sitting before her third, trying to answer the same questions she'd been asked a dozen times already that day. She thought they would be easier to answer, but instead, they became less easy to articulate.

"No, I wouldn't exactly say I was a feminist, but then, I don't like labels. I'm me. That's the only label I need. If you want to know whether I can hold my own with men? Then my answer is 'damned straight!'"

Miles entered an examining room and began to disrobe as ordered, thankful that wherever they were, it was warm. He could see the air conditioner, recessed in the wall, was on, but not blasting; so he assumed that outside, the climate was moderate. He had stripped down to his shorts when he heard the door open behind him, and turned to face an attractive female medic who entered and crossed to a work station, her back to him.

"Please disrobe completely and face the table," she commanded.

Slipping his shorts down and stepping out of them, Miles felt an initial tinge of embarrassment, which had to come from his past and his mother's strict admonition that while God gave everyone a beautiful body, he did not approve of little boys stripping down naked in front of strangers. This trip down memory lane and the smile that had crept across his face were both wiped away when the attractive medic turned back to face him, popping on rubber gloves, and told him to bend over for a rectal exam. Miles groaned and felt his sphincter tighten into a knot at the prospect.

Jay rarely lost his temper but after several hours of being probed, touched, injected, and questioned relentlessly, he was tired and hungry. Yet, there he was, facing his fourth review board. Though he fought to keep his voice under control, he was suddenly angry, defensive, and fighting to stay seated before the three coldly-unsmiling men, sitting across the gray metal table from him. Jay could not believe the question he'd just been asked, or that it had not been asked before he got on that bus and took that drugged flight to God-only-knows-where. There was only one answer he could or would give them and he was angry enough now that he really didn't care whether they liked it or not.

"Gay. The answer is gay! So if that's going to be a problem, you had better let me know right now. That's who I am, and it's taken me a hell of a long time to learn to say it. Trust me, I'm not going back to pretending for anyone. 'Don't Ask, Don't Tell' is fucking dead." Suddenly, realizing whom he was addressing, he swallowed and added, "Sir."

One man on the board, a major by the muted insignia on his chest, glanced at the other two members, then made a notation on Jay's papers before continuing, "I see you have both the Navy Pistol Marksmanship Ribbon and the Rifle with Expert Device. What were your scores?"

"M-9, 230; M-16, 200; Sir," Jay responded, as he settled back into the less personal questions.

Later, back in the commons area, Jay, Angie and Seth regrouped as planned and waited for Miles. All were exhausted and quickly found spots to sit on the floor, their backs leaning against the wall, or their stacked luggage. They had been given a paper bag, containing a cellophane-wrapped turkey sandwich, an apple, a cookie, and a bottle of water. They made a place for Miles, who sank down between them to begin his meal.

"Damn, it's about time they fed us something. I feel like I've lost ten pounds," he complained, as he dug into his bag and ripped open the sandwich.

"I don't think they wanted to screw up our blood work," Seth commented.

"Well, shit, they got enough of that," Miles groaned between mouthfuls. "If I have to roll it up, bend over, or piss in a bottle for one more person, I was gonna bend one of them over."

"Jesus, and could you believe those psychological questionnaires?" added Angie. "I couldn't figure out where they were even heading, much less what they were trying to find out?"

Jay debated whether to ask the others the question that bothered him the most, but finally couldn't resist. "What did you think of the eye test?"

Angie responded first, "What the fuck was that?"

Miles whispered, "I don't know what you saw, but I think we're dealing with some really high-tech scary shit here, and I'm not so sure now I'm ready to be superman. Have any of you heard anything, or got any better ideas where we are? I hate these boarded up windows."

"Well, it's definitely the south," said Jay as he wiped the perspiration from his face.

"But south of what? Where?... Georgia? Florida? America?" Seth asked.

Jay just shrugged. "I don't know. If I could see some trees, I might be able to tell you, but this is like being in a cave. I see those clocks on the wall, but something tells me they run on their own time. It says 16:50 but that doesn't feel right. Something inside says it's morning."

"Well, at least we're together and your sweaty company is better than getting my butt reamed by that broad with the cold fingers."

All four began to chuckle at that.

"Yeah, she was kind of a trip," Seth commiserated.

"Least you got a broad," Angie complained. "Me, I got the old guy with stirrups and probes he'd pulled out of the freezer."

Their exhausted laughter was cut short by the sound of the door opening across the room, and the entrance of a Non-Com in brown khaki, carrying a clip-board.

Blowing a whistle, like a high school referee, to get attention, he made his way into the center of the room.

"Okay, listen up," he commanded, in a voice that was much deeper than his body-build suggested. "When I call your name, report to the barracks assigned, and pick up your schedule. Classes begin at 1830."

There was general grumbling among the exhausted cadets.

"Shit, you mean there's more?" whispered Miles to the others.

"That only gives us less than an hour," complained Jay.

The agent was already drilling down his list. "Barrington, Bravo-3; Jameson, Echo-24; Carlisle, Alpha-8,..."

Tired cadets gathered their bags and headed out as their names were called. Angie struggled up as her name was called.

"Castillo, Alpha-5."

"Well, see you around," she said, as the others reached out to touch her as she collected her luggage and made her way out the door.

"Marshall, Delta-4; Hadley, Lima-12;..."

"What did he say?" Miles asked as he jumped up hearing his name.

"Lima-12," Jay repeated, as he patted him on the back and watched him run for the door.

"Slavin, Juliet-14," came the next name from the Non-Com with the list.

Seth jumped up and quickly got his bags, but stalled a little until Jay's name was called.

"Elliott, Bravo-12; Snortland, King-15' Frazier, Tango-13; Acresti, Golf 5."

"That's me," shouted Jay, relief in his voice. He jumped up and grabbed the bags which Seth had already pulled from the pile. Together, they made their way out, as the agent with the list continued to spiel off names.

Outside, the afternoon sunlight actually hurt their eyes.

Jay glanced around, "Not a tree in sight. So much for locations. But it's definitely southern-something. The humidity is so high, it feels like the air is loaded with water."

Looking for a direction marker or some indication of where they were to go, Seth saw a marker on the corner of a building, which other cadets were reading. He moved in that direction.

"K barracks," he announced as he read it. "I guess I'm somewhere down here."

"Great," said Jay, "I'm G-5. The other direction."

Both stood looking, hesitant about parting. Finally, Jay laughed, "With our luck, it probably stands for the Jew and Gay barracks."

Seth reached out to touch Jay, as he adjusted his grip on his luggage, "Good luck, see you around. I hope."

"Me, too," said Jay, tossing his luggage over his shoulder as he trudged off in the direction he hoped the G-barracks would be.

Seth watched him go, then followed the signs in the opposite direction, and was led down a row of sealed barracks looking for J.

There were no sounds; no radios blasting, no talking, just other cadets, all in a hurry. Everyone seemed to be running, or walking with purpose, as though trying to find where they belonged, or being late for their next class or appointment.

Seth found himself beginning to instinctively walk faster as well, until he faced the J-barracks. Like everything around him, it looked deserted. Taking a deep breath, he climbed the steps.

Stepping out of the bright sun, it took a moment for his eyes to adjust to the interior. Although brightly lit, it was nothing like he expected. He was standing in a small central core from which long narrow corridors, almost like spokes, fanned out.

Finding the corridor to his room, he moved past the closed doors to #14 and knocked. When nobody answered, he opened it slowly, and found himself in a stark makeshift version of a Japanese businessman's hotel room: a narrow, 7-by-12, windowless room, barely large enough for a single cot, a desk, a chair, and a slotted wardrobe.

Stepping inside, Seth lowered his bag to the floor, only to find he couldn't close the door until he moved the bag to the bed. The door automatically swung shut. On its back, a sign said, "Keep Door Closed at All Times."

On the bed, a printed schedule rested on stacked sheets and wardrobe. Seth picked it up and got the first glimpse of what the rest of the day entailed. In hindsight, it was a day he should have enjoyed, because it was to be the last day for a long time that he would see the sun. Everything from this day forward would take place either at night, or in a windowless room. Not knowing it then, he thus merely focused on making sure he found his first appointment.

In a line with other cadets he didn't recognize, Seth moved past dutch windows, receiving regulation-training apparel: shoes, socks, underwear, slacks, and other items. At the last window, he was asked if he had any personal effects, or time-pieces, he had not turned in previously.

"No," he responded automatically, thinking he was speaking the truth. He hadn't considered his wedding ring as a personal effect, because it had become such a part of him. He had not taken it off since the day they married, not even during the war, or officer training; but he was asked to remove it now, and he reluctantly obliged, feeling more naked than he had ever felt before.

From that point on, a numbness settled over Seth. He wasn't sure whether it was from the strenuous daily schedule he found tacked to his door each morning, or the pills he was to take with each meal. The purpose of the pills was never disclosed, and "morning" was a relative term, as no sun shone in the sky when he went to classes or physical discipline. The only brightness he saw was that from the huge floating light balloons, hovering over playing fields and outdoor areas, like giant planets burning overhead.

It was a greater struggle for Jay being deprived of the sun. He had always been a sun person, a beach person, and he guessed the pills he was asked to take with every meal were to counteract his reaction to the sun deprivation. Whether they were working or not was still questionable. For days he'd been lethargic and exhausted. On the exercise fields, he had to fight to keep up, readjusting his body to the lack of light. While he looked for the others in his group, the only one he'd seen in over two weeks was Seth jogging around a track in what looked like exhaustion. He was part of a small group of other cadets, Jay assumed, but cadets he didn't remember seeing before, either from Denver or from their first day on the Island. It was funny, he had accepted that name as their destination and had tried to write his lover a description of everything he had experienced since his arrival, but it was pointless. Always, when he returned from class, all his notes would be gone, removed. Even when he took to keeping his private scribblings on his person, they would be gone when he awoke each morning. Nothing was ever said and he never protested, but after a couple of weeks, he no longer attempted to remember what he had been doing during the daily schedule. He had tried to stay awake a couple of nights to catch the mysterious person, or thing, who invaded his room every night and searched his body or did God-only-knows what other things to him. He didn't know why he slept so soundly, but it was more than exhaustion.

He once wrote a note on a sticker and stuck it to the end of his penis when he went to sleep. It had read 'Don't Touch!', and the next morning the note had been gone, but another attached. It read, 'Not interested', and then, there was a smiley face. From that point on, Jay stopped worrying about the midnight marauder as he began to think of him or her. He or she was obviously someone who had a sense of humor and that was somehow comforting. That was also about the time he realized he no longer came awake exhausted.

Seth missed Rachel more than he could imagine. But he was so tired every day that sometimes he had a hard time visualizing her. The Island was like a nightmare: grueling, exhausting, and never ending. He guessed everyone was experiencing the same routines he was, but that was just an assumption. No one else ever talked or initiated communication at meals. Schedules during the sunless days were never the same, but always exhausting: classes, drills, firing ranges, hand to hand combat, and forced marches. The nights were left for study, not from books, but from recorded instructions through ear phones that Seth put on as he lay down and listened to until he finally slept. How long he slept was an unknown factor. The lights were never turned off in his room; in fact, it had no switch.

At first, Miles would cover his face, but after several nights found it wasn't necessary. Coming back from dinner or final maneuvers, he'd crawl into the shower and stay until the water turned cold. Then he'd climb onto his bed naked, put on his headset, begin listening to the droning voice, and be immediately asleep. When he awoke, he was always refreshed, but he was never really sure what had awakened him, or whether it was morning, afternoon, or night. So much about the Island was really unknown and he guessed he would never really know or understand what was going on. *Just like Las Vegas*, he mused once to himself, *What happened on Unknown Island, stayed on Unknown Island.*

CHAPTER XIV

For Jay Acresti, the best part of every day was the two hours he spent on the firing range. No matter how varied the rest of his day was, the only constant was his firing round after round into targets, the first day shaped like bulls-eyes, and some days later, geometric shapes. Somewhere along the line, those geometric shapes became more homunculus, human-like, and ultimately, they were just images of people. The repeated firing routine was just that, a routine. No thinking, just firing. No fear or anger, just firing. No thought. Just firing. No hesitation, just firing. Paper targets of men, women and children flashed by and felt the instant rip of Jay's bullets. After a while, there was almost a sexual satisfaction, a stirring in the groin with each of these artificial kills, but even that disappeared, and Jay's sharpshooting became rote, as much a part of him as his breathing. One day, it occurred to him that on the firing range, his focus had become so complete that he wasn't even aware of the other cadets firing next to him. Suddenly the thought grew into the realization he couldn't remember the last time anyone at the firing range had spoken to him, or greeted him, or said anything to anyone. He wondered if the others in his original group were having that same experience.

Miles had always considered himself to be in good shape, but after several weeks in the weight room, he knew he was moving into the best physical shape he'd ever known. He understood it had to be the supplements he found on his desk in the morning that were part of his regime, but he didn't care. Whatever it was he was taking, his reflexes were quicker, his muscle mass was stronger, and his body fat was near zero. Yet still his instructors harassed him continuously to push harder, press more and more weight. He had worried that all the added mass was going to make his other physical activity more difficult, but on the field he was also running faster, had more stamina, and his endurance seemed to have more than doubled. He laughed to himself that if this regime kept up, he might find himself able to leap tall buildings, but so far that hadn't happened. Although that morning, with a running start, he had been able to scale an eighteen foot brick wall in less a second.

Angie had been kept so busy since her arrival that she hadn't really had the time to focus on anything except getting through the steps of her schedule and that was what she considered them: steps. Walking in the dark, she used to complain to herself. There was never any light, not real light. Long corridors of dark-vinyl plastic linked every building, lit only by long lengths of fluorescent tubing. After a while she began to notice a low pitched humming as she walked under the tubing. They flickered, maybe a thousand times a minute, but for some reason, she was aware of it, and could actually see it.

Aside from the usual field work and shooting range, Angie spent at least one additional hour every day in an isolation booth with earphones, pouring information into her head. The information had at first been routine historical facts, but over time the narration had begun to speed up, until Angie was no longer sure exactly what, if anything, was being transmitted. It all seemed like static to her. While the hour was not painful, she often found upon completion that her face was tight and her brows furrowed. She knew she hadn't been asleep, but if she couldn't remember anything she had been listening to, how the hell was she going to pass the tests she knew were eventually going to be coming.

Something was just not right. What did they expect of her? What was she supposed to do? What was happening to her at night? She suddenly found herself remembering a kid in her high school drama class. He was the best actor in the class, but he always panicked before auditions; yet he always got cast in the lead. Theater was the only thing in his life that he loved, but he was scared of it as well. He told her that he kept having nightmares about being in a play. He'd be on stage. The curtain would go up. The audience was there and he wouldn't have a clue what the play was, or even what part he played in it. He was sure that if he just ad-libbed long enough, someone else would come on the stage, and then, he'd know what part he was playing. But nobody came, and he wanted to get off of that stage. He'd start towards the door but just as he reached for the doorknob, the doorknob would begin to turn and he'd be suddenly terrified. But he didn't know what of. So he'd back up screaming, looking for an escape. All of the other doors were locked. There was only one big open window and he realized with amazing clarity that he was supposed to throw himself out of that window. And that's what he would do, screaming himself awake.

Angie wondered what had made her think of that kid. His name was Jamison. She hadn't thought of him in years. Not since she had heard he committed suicide, somewhere out in the Midwest when he was in college.

CHAPTER XV

Maybe Joel was being overly paranoid, but he didn't think so. His boss, Ryder, had agreed with him when Joel said he wanted to fly commercial into Detroit and take some other means of transportation to his final destination. Ryder had arranged to have a small private jet meet Joel on the tarmac upon landing in Detroit and take him to Columbus. He could have flown into Zanesville, but Joel thought arriving by private jet, though unmarked, might end up biting them in the butt, as his father used to like to say. Joel's father was a small town doctor, and never bought a car that wasn't at least a year old, not because he benefited from the depreciation costs, but because it sent a signal to his patients that he wasn't getting rich from their illnesses. Of course, he was getting rich, but buying a new flashy car would have been like rubbing it in their faces, and Joel's father was not going to do that.

"It could bite us all in the butt," he used to say, "financially, and socially."

Of course, Joel, in all his closeted gayness, wanted everything bigger and flasher. "Bright, Shiny Boy," his father used to call him. As a kid, if something was new, or flashy, Joel wanted it. But now he understood. The news would spread quickly of somebody flying into that small airport in his own private jet. The eyes of everyone on the field would be on him, and anonymity would have been impossible.

His final destination was Riverton, a small town on the eastern border of Ohio. He had to sneak into Ohio, get into Riverton, find who he was looking for, and without anyone noticing him. Normally that wouldn't have been a problem, millions of people flew every day and traveled wherever they wanted and nobody cared. At least, that was what everyone assumed.

The truth was an entirely different story. The Homeland Security mainframes cross-referenced everyone using a credit card, taking a flight, renting a car, or purchasing a movie. It was all random unwatched computing; source code racing after source code until a hit occurred. A person of interest doing something of interest, or something triggering some unknown link could cause that person to be moved from random data-status into a folder for further, closer study.

Since Channel 7's Marshall Foster had challenged the President on national T.V., every member of the President's staff had been targeted for deeper investigation. While the President could nullify some of the scrutiny as a matter of national security, Joel knew for a fact that he was Foster's best link to Ryder, and Ryder was Foster's best link to the President, or more importantly, to the President's mysterious unspecified plan for pulling this country out of its downward spiral.

Joel had relatives in Detroit: distant, maybe but still relatives. He had made a point of calling them a couple of times a week for the last two weeks, so no one would be suspicious if he suddenly flew into Detroit. Detroit was in Michigan and Michigan bordered Ohio. The assumption would be that he was visiting relatives. Of course the assumption would be wrong, but by that time, he would be already on another plane: a private one, headed for Ohio. He could have driven to Ohio, but time was running out. Information leaked daily from the White House. Foster's private sources indicated that while the newscaster was not even close to what the President had planned, but it wouldn't be long before the pieces began falling into place, and the entire project blew up in their faces.

The second leg of Joel's trip would be to Columbus, a much bigger airport, where he would not likely draw attention by his arrival. He could always pick up a car there. Joel hadn't reserved it, and would decide which agency to use once he arrived. He would also pay for the car in cash and was using a driver's license and credit card supplied to him by his boss that stated his name was Jerry Fuller, and he was a college student from Iowa State University in Ames.

The first leg of his trip to Detroit was uneventful. Stepping off the plane onto the covered bridge, nobody seemed to notice when he slipped through the service door and down the steps to the tarmac, where an Air Force jeep was waiting to whisk him around the perimeter of the terminal to a waiting, small single-engine jet.

Climbing aboard and ducking his head to enter, Joel found himself in a compact, four-seat cabin with a chilled diet cola and two packets of peanut butter and cheese crackers. *So much for sparing no expense,* he thought, as he buckled himself into his seat. The door to the cockpit was closed, sealing the entrance, and had not the access steps been pulled back into their place Joel might have wondered if he was alone.

Being an Indiana boy at heart, Joel would have liked to have seen the pilot and known that it wasn't just a robot up there getting ready to hurl him into the sky, but when no pilot's voice came on to say, "Buckle up," or "Welcome aboard," Joel settled back and started going through his papers, even though he had them burned into his memory already.

In all the years he'd been working with Ryder, this was his first really big solo assignment. The only reason he'd gotten this chance was because Ryder, himself, had been out of his office too many times and for too long, and people had started to ask questions that were becoming more and more probing. It was agreed that Ryder had to stay in Washington, at least for the time being, and be seen at as many functions with the President as possible, in the next three or four days to lessen any chance speculation about the project.

That meant Joel got the assignment: three days to find what he was looking for. Actually, who he was looking for? Or rather "whom" he was looking for, as his father, the English authority on everything grammatical liked to remind him. As a kid, his father's constant corrections used to drive Joel to distraction. No teenager liked to be constantly corrected by a parent, much less a parent who had to drop out of school in the sixth grade to support his own parents. His father hadn't gotten a chance to pick up his education until he was almost thirty, finishing high school, then college, then Med school.

In hindsight, Joel considered his father one of the greatest men in the country next to the President and of course, Ryder. His father was a self-made man in every meaning of the word, a millionaire multiple times over, and a major contributor to the President's re-election campaign. Medicine was not his only forte. He also served on the board of more than a dozen companies, and had two hospitals named after him.

That sort of influence had gotten his son his first Congressional page position in Washington. Then the work ethics and standards of reliability, which Joel had learned on his father's knee throughout his childhood paid off, and Joel had moved up the ranks into the inner circle. Although he was not officially or publicly out, Joel had no doubts that both his boss and his boss' boss knew of his private life.

The fact that his sexuality had never been a question made him love both men even more, especially Ryder. Joel never did anything to disappoint either man, and wasn't now about to let Ryder down.

Landing at CMH, Columbus Regional Airport Authority, Joel was met by another jeep and driven by another non-speaking military driver to a service entrance that led him up into the main concourse and terminal, where he made his way to the car rental desk.

After two hours of driving through rolling forest and farm lands, Joel slowed his car, as the small industrial town of Riverton appeared on the banks of the Muskingum River, which emptied into the mighty Ohio. It's weathered docks were lined by graying warehouses, mostly empty, with their broken windows long since boarded up.

Downtown Riverton, although no more prosperous, did share a certain charm in architecture that spoke of past decades of family run stores and theaters, of community shopping and commercial viability. Now, most of that was gone with the years of recession. What few old businesses and hotels remained competed for space with empty graffiti-streaked storefronts, x-rated arcades, and sex shops. Wandering vagrants and glazed-eyed teenagers sat in doorways, waiting for their next connection or customer, which ever the night brought first.

Joel began his search with a list of last known addresses but had no luck. It did prove, however, that the man he had been sent to find had not gone up, but had been caught in the downward spiral of Riverton's layers of depression and corruption that were more severe than even the decaying buildings along Main Street revealed.

The search was tedious and frustrating. He couldn't use any of the normal sources one would use in finding a missing person. He was not allowed to contact either the police or any social agency in Riverton. In fact, his directives were to slip into the town, find his target, and exit the city without any one of importance knowing who he was or for whom he worked.

Joel had worried initially that someone might recognize his picture from the papers. He had often appeared behind Ryder on press junkets. To counter this, he had taken a room for a couple of hours, dyed his hair a darker shade of brown, and changed to a pair of faded jeans and a worn flannel shirt. He stored his true belongings, and he hoped his identity as well, in an airport locker. He hated his hair. It had turned out more black than brown and didn't look anything like the color on the box. He actually sort of liked the jeans and shirt look, thinking maybe for the first time in his life that he could really pull off butch, if he wanted to.

Masculinity had never been his strong suit, but a good thousand dollar suit made almost any man look like a man, and his first three paychecks in Washington had been spent entirely on achieving that image. Now, the suit he had arrived in was stored in an airport locker, and he was about to play undercover in a town that had a really dark-side of its own.

He soon realized the chance of anyone recognizing him from a newspaper photo or magazine article was almost nil. From the looks of the people he passed on the streets, he doubted any of them ever read a newspaper, or subscribed to anything other than T.V. Guide or Entertainment Weekly. Still, he was glad he had taken the precautions. It showed he was organized and thinking of every possible eventuality.

The one thing he wasn't going to do was fail, not on his first assignment for Ryder. He didn't want to let either the President or his boss down, and it suddenly dawned on him, that he didn't want to let himself down either. That realization actually surprised him. His entire life he had tried to fit in, trying to keep others happy, especially his father. This assignment was a chance for him to prove something to himself. It took less than forty-eight hours to know he was failing.

He had just finished his second day of searching, and come up with nothing. He had eaten another greasy burger at Lum's Burger which sold only two kinds of burgers: with or without cheese, and it wasn't even real cheese. Joel didn't want to think where the meat came from. Disgusted with himself, and his complete loss as to what to do next, he headed back to his one-star Skyview Motel on the outskirts of town, uncharacteristically cursing to himself.

"Shit!" he heard himself say, as he started to get out of his car in front of the motel. For all Joel knew the man he was looking for was already dead, or had long since moved away; though he suspected the former was more likely than the latter.

Where do you go when you've fallen off the map, dropped off the radar? The last census put him in a run-down apartment in Riverton, he thought. What does that tell me about you? One, you were civic minded; at least more civic minded than most skidders. Most alkies don't register or even fill out the census form; they certainly never use their real names. You did. Two, you had a place to stay, at least for that period of time and three, you're human, so you had to eat and drink.

Joel had already checked every bar on the riverfront, the seediest part of town and probably the entire United States.

Nobody had recognized the photograph Joel showed hundreds of times a day. Of course, the picture was a twenty-year-old service picture, and the denizen of the bars in question could have been lying, probably were in fact, but Joel had presented himself as a relative looking for his lost uncle. Maybe he should have dirtied himself up a bit more, scuffed up the tennis shoes, and actually had a drink or two in each of the bars, but the truth was that even as an undercover agent, Joel had real issues with dirt under his fingernails, and drinking from glasses that still had finger prints on them was not his strong suit.

Okay, Joel determined. I can't go undercover unless I really am willing to get under that cover: lice and all.

So, it was decided. The next day, against every hygienic cell of his body's protest, he would return to each of those sleazy bars and get to know the drunken patrons. He "might" even slip down to the mission to eat his meals. It couldn't be any worse than Lum's.

No, not "might," he corrected. I will go down to the mission first thing tomorrow.

I don't really have to eat the food, just sort of move it around on my plate and look like I'm enjoying it, he reminded himself. I won't even comb my hair, and I'll say I slept on the street.

Daylight came too early, as Joel staggered out of his bed, slipped on his shoes, (God knows, he wasn't going to walk around barefoot in this motel room), and made it into the bathroom to relieve himself. There were no roaches that morning in the sink, which he took as a good sign, as he reached in to turn on the shower. Suddenly, he remembered that he couldn't shower and that depressed him because he never really woke up until he'd had his morning shower. He hoped his boss appreciated the sacrifices he was making for the cause.

Stepping out of the bathroom, he noticed a bad case of pillow hair, but decided, What the fuck! And resisted the urge to grab the gel and slick it down. Grabbing up his clothes, the same ones he'd worn since the day he arrived, he put them on the floor and stomped on them to make them look dirtier, which always guaranteed a new stain or two coming off of the carpet that looked like it hadn't been vacuumed since installation.

His first night, Ryder had stepped out of the shower and simply walked to his bed. Eight feet from one destination to the other and the soles of his feet were literally black from the passage. He didn't want to think what a forensic lab would find if he took a sample back for analysis. He didn't want to know. Realizing it was ten minutes to six, Joel picked up his clothes and shook them to make sure nothing had crawled in during the night. Then he dressed.

The morning was already hot. The steam, coming off the dirty converging rivers, formed fog banks that disguised the look but not the smell of the warehouse district. The bars he passed looked closed and empty, but he knew that they never closed and in truth, several men mentioned that after two a.m., buying three beers got you the right to sleep the night away at one of the small, dirty tables.

Joel made his way down to the First Street Mission. The queue was already out the door with men, women and children waiting in the urine-stained humidity for a chance to eat a meal. He found the end of the line and took his place behind two young women, both, he assumed, street walkers as well as junkies. Their banter, edged with desperation and frustration, was loud in the stillness of the morning, because the line was moving so slowly and keeping them from their work. It hadn't been a good night for one of the girls, though the other seemed to have faired better. Neither had brought in more than seventy-five dollars, and they couldn't go to sleep until they'd scored at least a hundred and twenty-five.

Joel thought about showing them the picture, but he decided against it. Both had already given him the eye and laughed when he blushed. One had even reached over to run her finger down his crotch.

"Interested?" she smiled revealing a missing tooth.

"Only in food," stammered Joel. "I've got my own troubles," he added for some reason.

"You new in town?" asked the other whore, eying him a bit more closely. "Cause if you are," she continued, "Mickey's always looking for new tricks, and the money's good. I mean, good for this shit-fuck town."

"If you're interested, you'll find him at the Crusty Crab, back table," added the first. "But tell him Erika and Robin turned you on to him."

Joel thanked them and said he'd consider it, but inside he was wondering if he had somehow forgotten to wash off the stamp that was evidently on his forehead that said, Gay-Boy.

The line moved into the building and Erika and Robin split to hook up with some of their friends, and Joel was left to soak in the steaming smell of unwanted breakfast and unwashed bodies. The combination was almost overpowering, and he could feel the remains of last nights Lum Burger raising up to make another appearance.

Pushing his way back to the door, he suddenly glimpsed the reflection of the man he had been looking for in the cracked mirror by the door. Stopping dead in his tracks, Joel turned to see the one whose reflection he had seen, and there he was behind the food counter, supervising the serving, and even dishing up hot cereal himself. He was much older now, at least fifty, but definitely the same man, the same strong features, the skin weathered by years in the sun and a hard life.

Without thinking, Joel pushed his way back into the food line, garnering grumblings from those who thought he was breaking in. He didn't care. He was just reclaiming his place, his rightful place, he thought. He grabbed up an empty bowl and plastic spoon and inched along the line until he finally stood in front of the man he'd been looking for, Joseph Redfeather.

The man's Native American heritage was obvious in the chiseled granite features that seemed to have been carved by centuries of warriors, and the pain of a youth spent unwisely. Yet his eyes were clear and as dark as the shadows of a canyon. They were the type of eyes that seem to see everything, Joel thought uncomfortably, as he stood before him. The man seemed to be studying him as much as he was being studied.

"Oatmeal?" came the deep voice.

Joel just held out his bowl to be filled, but didn't say anything. Joel could see that Redfeather's hands were strong and callused; the muscles of his arms obviously used to lifting heavier things than ladles of steaming food to the lost of the waterfront.

"You new?" Joseph asked, looking at him closely.

Again, Joel didn't know what to say.

"What say, you finish up that oatmeal and then, let's talk. I know some places you might find work, and maybe I can score you a bed for a night or two while you're here. At least, I can tell you what to steer away from."

"Thanks," Joel replied, and then moved on down the counter to find a seat where he could wait. Mission accomplished. He had found the man he'd been sent after. The missing piece to the puzzle, and Joel had found him.

He wasn't supposed to engage the target, just identify him and then contact Ryder. Ryder would take it from there.

So, Joel had to let Ryder know, but he couldn't pull out his phone here at the mission, especially not his phone: a special government release that made the latest cells out there look like play toys. Seeing his quarry move into the kitchen for another kettle of oatmeal, Joel took the chance to slip further back into the room, as though looking for a table, and then, slipped out a side door into the damp narrow brick bypass between the mission and the next run-down building. To his left, he could see traffic beginning to move on River Road; to his right, the bypass ended in an alley. Moving quickly in that direction, behind the mission building itself, he found himself in a slimy-wet alley strewn with the cluttered debris of poverty. A chill ran through him as he realized rats, half the size of cats, dominated here, challenging him with their eyes and their upraised posture, before recognizing him for the wimp he was and moving on, to scurry on clicking nails like so many giant ants swarming over the overflowing dumpsters ripe with the sour smell of rotting garbage, even in the cold.

Joel hated vermin of any kind and felt like his body was crawling with lice and every other imaginable corruption, but he had to make sure he was alone before he pulled the phone out.

An overwhelming sense of relief swept over him as he dialed Ryder's private line. The phone line opened almost immediately, as though, Ryder had been waiting.

"Randy?"

"I found him."

"I knew you would! That's why I sent you."

Joel felt his entire body flush. A rat perched on the overflowing dumpster directly opposite him, momentarily jerked his head in Joel's direction, causing Joel to freeze. It took a moment to realize his boss had asked him a question.

"What was that?"

"I said, how does he look?" asked his boss on the line.

"From where I sat, he looks made to order. Perfect."

"And you base that opinion on what?"

Joel suddenly recognized that the tone had changed and the answer he gave would either raise or lower his newly acquired prestige. He gave himself a second or two to formulate exactly the right answer; the truth as he saw it phrased in the manner his boss wanted to hear it.

"Well, sir, from what I can see, he's managing a food shelter on wharf street, feeding the homeless. He spotted me as soon as I stepped in the line."

"As a plant?"

"No, I don't think so. I think this man knows everybody on this street. Not just who they are, but what they are. And I get the feeling it's like family. I can call you back as soon as he's finished the line. He said he wanted to talk with me so I've got to get back in. He said he was going to try to find me a place to stay for the night. I can call you back after I've talked to him, and then, you can talk to him."

"No, I think you're the best bet we've got right now in convincing him. So level with him, and tell him that you represent the President of the United States, and that we'd like to talk to him. I'll fly out tonight and can meet you both in Columbus. Let me know if he agrees to the meeting. He's the key to everything."

"Yes sir."

"Joel. I'm depending on you. Hell, the whole project depends on you."

Sliding the phone back into his pocket, he stepped around the edge of the building and instinctively yelped. He was standing face to face with Joseph Redfeather. The man's towering presence made Joel take a step back.

"I thought I'd lost you," came the deep voice.

Joel looked down, avoiding the eyes, trying to think how he should respond.

"You know we do have clean bathrooms and even showers in the mission." Joseph spoke up. "You don't have to use the alley."

"I didn't know," stammered Joel, as he felt Joseph's strong hand on his shoulder.

"Come on let's go back in and get you something to eat. Then we can talk."

"I'd like that," said Joel, as he followed the taller man back into the mission.

CHAPTER XVI

Junisha Butler had known fear for most of her life, but the feeling pushing through her stomach, while nothing new, still set her nerves on edge as it had always done. Some things for a black woman never lessen with time, only the triggers that set them off. Tonight, sitting in the silent darkness, staring at the flickering screen across the small cluttered room, her right hand tightly gripped the remote; her fingers circling the mute button, ready to push it in an instant should the image she'd been dreading appear on the screen. In a more reasonable state of mind, she might have realized that the chances of what she feared, most even being reported as a late night, news break was less than a million to one, yet still she watched.

Some people lived lives of action, of changing destiny, of making something out of nothing. Junisha used to be one of those people, or at least she had a distant memory of being someone other than the frightened woman she now was, a watcher. As the saying goes, "Shit happens!" and some people just watch it happen. Junisha lived in dread of that happening, but had no control over stopping it. All she could do was wait until it happened, and that was what she was doing.

But until it happened, she divided her focus between the images on the screen, and the two children curled in sleep beside her on the worn, mottled sofa. This was their bed, and while she would have loved for them to be able to stretch out, the sofa was the only real piece of furniture in the front of the small tenement. She would remain sitting here, until she could go to her own bed. Besides, her children were so used to this nightly routine, they'd probably feel strange without their mother sitting vigil over their sleep.

Six-year-old Tamara tossed and mumbled something in her sleep, and Junisha quickly pulled the thin covering over the child and then, did the same for Robert Jr. who'd just turned ten, though he hadn't moved a muscle for at least an hour.

It was well past midnight the next time Junisha looked at the cheap plastic watch she had purchased for two dollars, because it had a button on the side that lit up the face in the darkness.

Darkness was a large part of the life of Junisha and her children; not perpetual, but habitual darkness.

A salvaged packing blanket tacked over the solitary front window was buttressed by stacked crates of discarded magazines and newspapers providing a bulletproof barrier day and night, protecting her small family against what went on outside the apartment. It was not paranoia that fueled the defense, but street-sense. Junisha knew from experience what went on outside the apartment.

No light must ever be allowed to escape through the window. She had learned that in the worst way imaginable at Cabrini Green. Lit windows provided targets, invited break-ins, and being robbed was the least painful thing that could happen in a break-in. It was a lesson learned when she was the age of the children beside her, another lifetime ago, but still as fresh and bleeding as it had been that night when three men killed her father and forced themselves on her. She was only twenty-six now, and already most of her past was a blur. That was probably for the best. Some things should not be remembered.

This night, this moment was all she knew, all she had the strength to control; though control would hardly have been a word she would have used had she even known what it meant.

Life had been bad enough when they lived in Cabrini Green with it's drug deals and gang fights as much a part of the day and night environment as the graffiti-streaked walls and chipped sidewalks. Back then she was part of that scene, it hadn't seemed so unusual. Now, in contrast, straight and sober, the blinders were off, and things were much worse.

She had no man, at least, not any more. When she stopped using, at first he'd been with her, hoping to make it work for both of them. But without drugs, they had nothing more in common, not even the two kids now sleeping beside her. So he'd left, first to make another connection, and then, permanently, when he couldn't pay for what he'd used. No one had ever come to tell her. No one had ever come to offer sympathy. She had seen his riddled body on a news-flash. He'd been shot down along with four other people in a drug deal gone bad.

She still missed him, but not as much as she had last year, or the year before that. The truth was on some nights she wished he had died sooner, because single mothers were given preference. He was still with her when they first applied for housing, before Cabrini Green had been torn down. A new North Tower Village apartments was going to built on the Cabrini Green rubble. Surely they could find a place in that new complex. So they filled out the forms but found, surprisingly, that no one gave her any hope of actually getting a new apartment. She had a man in the house, not a man who supported anyone, but a man. The fact that he was a junkie, a drunkard, and had never held a job didn't fit into the equation. He was still biologically a man, though he had been castrated by his own inadequacies. He had gotten himself killed, and by then, even with her new sobriety, it was too late for her to get help with relocation. The lottery had already been held, and she wasn't even in the running. There were cries of outrage and promises of help, but when thousands are displaced and only hundreds are re-housed, a mother with children no longer took priority. Children were like cockroaches to most city planners, continually bred by the least likely to support them. So Junisha, unskilled, untrained, and until now unmotivated, like all those other misfits who couldn't be placed, was forced to fend for herself and her children. "A day late and a dollar short," her grandfather would have said. It had been the story of Junisha's life. If she wanted anything, she had had to do it herself. Even with the children, she had never felt so alone.

She was lucky to get this shell of an apartment. It at least had running water and a flushable toilet. Many had settled for far less.

Outside the chain-locked door, she heard the distinct pop, pop, pop of single shots, and ducked instinctively covering her children, but her barriers held as tightly as her breath. Someone ran quickly past, outside in the hallway, and she could hear the metallic "clunks", as they took the metal fire-escape steps down to the floors below, two steps at a time. Others footsteps followed, running, chasing, cursing, then, more shots.

Junisha ran her hand over her mouth tentatively, holding her breath, wondering if this new barrage was the one she's been dreading. Reaching out again to reassure herself, she touched her two children, still safe, curled up in sleep. For the moment, they were oblivious to the violence beyond the chain-locked, battered metal front door.

Then, there was silence. She continued to sit and stare at the silent images on the flickering television. It must have been at least an hour later when she finally heard the sound she'd been waiting for, the key in the lock.

Slipping off the sofa, she reached the door just as it opened to snap against the limits set by the two security chains on the inside. A muffled curse, "Jesus Christ, open up!" challenged her as she fumbled with the chains.

"I'm coming," she answered as she pushed the door back against the pressure to give the catches a chance to release, "ease up!"

Finally, managing to undo both chains, the heavy metal door swung open, and fourteen-year-old Wayne Thomas, her oldest, pushed past her.

"Wayne Thomas, where have you been? You promised," she began as soon as he was safely inside.

Wearing his anger like a badge, Wayne Thomas didn't even bother to acknowledge his mother as he headed for the back of the apartment. Even though his baggy clothes couldn't hide his small and slender frame, he still moved with a practiced force much greater than his size. The back of his shirt was torn, but Junisha was too busy relocking the door to notice. That didn't stop her however, from continuing her reprimand. She knew he wasn't listening and that it was pointless, maybe even damaging, but still she continued.

"You were just gonna go to the store, not stay out 'til I'm worried sick. You got school tomorrow. How you gonna do that? Wayne Thomas, I'm talkin' to you."

Finally catching a glimpse of his torn shirt as it disappears down the hallway, "Wayne Thomas, what happened to your shirt? How I gonna get another one?"

She followed him back towards his closet-like bedroom, but Wayne Thomas had already shut the door and her out of his life. Still she pleaded outside the door.

"It's just you shouldn't ought to stay out so late 'cause bad things happen out there. That's all I'm worried about. I don't want 'em happenin' to you. I don't want 'em happenin' to you."

He, of course, did not answer, and she was left talking to a closed door.

"You got better in you, Wayne Thomas. We all got better in us."

She thought she heard a muffled "Fuck off", as she turned back to the living room to check on the other children one last time. Reaching for the remote, she clicked off the television. At least for tonight, she didn't have to worry about seeing her son's face on the screen. He was home. She could now go to sleep. Everyone was safe and accounted for.

Outside the heavy metal front door, the renewed sound of feet racing past in the corridors meant the darkness continued still, and would, even past dawn.

CHAPTER XVII

Rachel sat up in bed, glancing for the second time at the small calendar she kept beside her bed. In the six weeks since Seth had left, it had become a habit: twice a day, first thing in the morning and the last thing at night. Each day, she hoped against odds that this would be the day he'd call, or better yet, coming racing up the walk to sweep her into his arms. Of course right now, she was way to big to sweep. As Mama Slavin liked to put it, Rachel looked like a pretty balloon that was ready to pop. Rachel knew that Seth's mother meant it to be comforting, but the idea of exploding was not that appealing to Rachel in her frustrating condition. The baby was overdue, thirteen days overdue to be exact. Rachel was ready for the little alien inside her to make up its mind and let go.

Rachel really wanted to have this baby naturally, but at the rate this kid was growing, it felt like it would be ready for school before it popped out. The doctors had been forced to schedule a Caesarean in two days, so Rachel told the baby it had until then to get moving.

Lying back, Rachel reached over and picked up a book to prop on her protruding stomach, so she could read. Reading was about the only thing she'd found that took her mind off Seth, the impending birth or her mother-in-law, who meant well, but could drive a person crazy with her constant chattering.

The newscaster, Marshall Foster, was muted on the T.V. screen on the far wall, but she could tell by just glancing that it was another litany of gang violence and corporate fraud; another bank had been caught draining funds off of customer accounts and into the pockets of some of the biggest names in the financial sector.

The problem was that there was nothing anyone could do about it. Money was transparent. Its value could be wired from account to account with no one ever taking physical possession of the original funds. In this latest case, the funds just disappeared. The trial would last for years of course, and by that time, the initial investor's would be lucky if they saw five cents on the dollar.

Pushing herself up from her bed, Rachel slowly made her way into the kitchen to get another glass of water.

Looking for something to munch on, she opened the refrigerator door and pulled out a platter of left-over chicken. Mama Slavin did make good chicken. Rachel hadn't even taken off the tin-foil covering the plate when the first contractions hit. Doubling over, she cried out Seth's name, as the plate crashed to the floor.

#

Seth was sitting in class, when suddenly he looked up and around, as though someone had called his name. Shaking off the feeling that something was wrong, he fought to return his concentration to the class.

Another cadet was arguing, "But what's the point?" to which the instructor replied, "The point is everything. This is a class in theory. It's not that anyone's asking you to forget that you're Americans. In theory, I'm asking you to think, to analyze what you mean by the term and redefine it. Is it what you want it to be? Is it perfect? What would be the perfect state? If you had everything you wanted, in a perfect world, what would that include?"

"World peace," came a reply from the back of the room followed by a few groans.

"Okay, that's a start. Not very original, but a start. Now let's try to make it practical. Let's keep it local. Make it manageable. Right here, right now. And by here, I'm referring to your own communities."

In another class, the same topic was being discussed. This time, Jay and Angie happened to be together. "The perfect place, Utopia, What? What do you mean by that?" challenged the instructor.

Jay answered, "Freedom of speech."

The Instructor wrote this on the chalk board, but added, "We've got that. Give me things we don't have?"

Another cadet threw out, "Safety."

"Define safety," prodded the instructor.

"Just being able to walk the streets," came the reply.

"At night without fear," added another.

The instructor wrote all of this on the board as well.

Still leading them, "That's good. Now, how?"

It was Angie who answered, "Get rid of gangs for starters."

"And rapists," came another.

The answers now came rapidly and the instructor quickly wrote each down.

"Muggers."

"Murderers."

"Yes, why don't we outlaw murder," came a voice from another cadet.

Everyone laughed but the instructor. He kept writing on the board.

Jay added, "How about no more prejudice?"

"Define?" the instructor enjoined.

"Blacks, whites, reds, yellows, gays, straights"

"And don't forget about adding Jews, Christians, Atheists," shouted another cadet.

In another class, the discussion was growing with the same excitement, but this time it was Miles who was the most vocal. "Blacks, white, Jews, gentiles. Stop the hatred. Stop the prejudice."

"How?" the instructor questioned.

"End the fear," another cadet joined in.

"Define."

"Everybody's afraid," he responded

"Why?"

"'Cause it's crazy out there," Miles interjected. "People are crazy. You can get blown away for honking your horn."

In Seth's class, the discussion had moved on to laws. The cadet next to Seth was getting more and more frustrated.

"So what good are stricter laws, when we can't enforce the ones we've got."

"Explain."

"It's obvious. You know what I mean. A good attorney can get you off for killing your parents, even when you admit you killed them."

"Unless you're black," chimed in a decidedly southern voice.

"And whose fault is that?"

"Most of the time, the juries," Seth interjected.

"Then are you suggesting, that maybe, we ought to do away with juries?" The question was aimed directly at Seth.

"No, it's just that... Besides, that's not possible."

"Why not? It's not such an unusual idea. Singapore did it more than thirty years ago. They officially did away with the jury system."

A hush fell over the room.

"Why? Because it didn't work," the instructor continued. "It only worked for the rich. The ones who could afford the best lawyers. The ones who could find the biggest loopholes."

A young female cadet asked, "So what do they do without juries?"

The instructor held for a moment to make sure he had all of their attentions, "Judges hand down all the decisions. And the penalties are a lot stricter than those in our country."

"Yeah, but who wants to live like they do in Singapore?" It was the young female cadet again.

"Young lady, that country has the lowest crime rate, and the highest employment rate in the world. It also has one of the highest standards of education and living. I think you might find a few Americans who'd vote for a little of that same security."

"Yeah, but don't they cane people?" asked Miles, "you know, beat them, as a form of humiliation. That's barbaric!"

It was another cadet who came back with, "Not if it works."

The instructor stepped in with, "He's right and the question for you, for all of you, is not whether it's barbaric, but whether it works?"

Miles responded immediately, "No. It's wrong."

"On what do you base that?"

"I don't know. I just know you shouldn't go around beating people. You can't degrade human beings."

"But if it works, why not?" It was the same cadet.

Another joined in, "Besides, human beings are always degrading themselves."

This brought a laugh from the group.

Then the instructor turned to Miles. "First, I want to say that degrading people is not the issue, and I agree with you, it should never be used for any reason, but..."

"There is no 'but' in my book," Miles replied, surprised how angry he'd become. "There is never an excuse for minimizing one set of people, one race, one orientation, to make another feel superior, and trust me, I know what that feels like. It only breeds anger, resentment, and retaliation."

"Okay, here's your assignment, and it's an assignment for everyone in this room," said the instructor, as he scanned the class before him. "If caning doesn't work for you, what would? If racial profiling doesn't work. If nothing we've tried historically has worked, then by next class, I want each of you to create find something that does. I want you to create the perfect society for me. Not the houses. Not the jobs. I want new governing laws to live by, and keep them simple. I don't want one thousand different ways of interpreting it. Hell, that's what we have now. Don't let your morality, or humanity hold you back."

"How do you do that?" someone questioned. "I like to think of myself as human."

"No, you like to think of yourself as law-abiding. That's different. I'm just asking you to use your imagination."

The instructor looked at them, counting off on his fingers, "If we didn't have any of the laws we have right now, none, and there were no restrictions? And you were forced to start all over, start from scratch, what laws would you institute that would make this dream "Utopia" work?"

"And," he said, holding up one last finger, "here comes the hardest part. I told you I wanted it kept simple. I want all of your thoughts condensed down into one paragraph. One sentence if you can. Theory! Open your minds to any possibility. Don't limit yourself by saying, 'Yeah, but we couldn't do this.' In your new society, you are the one who decides. You are the one who makes the rules. You are the one charged with making it work. Nothing is out of the realm of possibilities. You just have to make it work."

CHAPTER XVIII

In Glendale Memorial Hospital, a scant mile from Los Angeles rustic Griffin Park, Rachel pushed back against the stirrups letting out another scream. Her face grimaced. She was soaked in perspiration. Mama Slavin stood beside her, holding her hand and for once, not talking. In fact, Rachel thought, the venerable authority on almost everything was close to passing out.

"Push," came the command from between her legs. "That's it."

"Yes, push," Seth's mother also squeaked out.

"You're doing fine," the nurse encouraged, wiping Rachel's forehead. "Just a little bit more."

Rachel felt her entire body convulse. Her teeth ground in intensity and her back arched from the muscles that seemed to want to rip her apart. She screamed again, and then, tried to focus. To concentrate, to get it over with. Gathering what little strength she had left, she pushed one last time. She suppressed the scream she felt rising from her throat, to focus all her energy on the life she now felt slithering out of her womb.

"That's it. That's it," exclaimed the doctor, and Rachel thought, "It better be, and it sure as hell better be better looking than it felt coming out."

A flurry of activity began happening just outside Rachel's view, and she suddenly realized she was holding her breath, waiting for that sound she had been told to expect. The baby's cry. *Where the fuck was the baby's cry? What's happening!* she wanted to cry out in fear.

And then, there it was: angry, piercing, royally ticked off at having been awakened so rudely, and as the nurse held it for her to see: wrinkled, red with a chock of black spiky hair, and definitely male. Rachel laughed, and felt Mama Slavin squeeze her hand, and whisper, "Look Rachel, I'm a grandmother."

#

Seth's small room looked like a cubicle in a library. He had a dozen books spread over his desk and bed, as he worked on his assignment. He started by studying Singapore's laws, then comparing them to his own, to England's, to Russia's, to Bali's, to Iraq's. He had never known there were so many different types of government; some blatantly barbaric, others completely fanatic. Some started out simply based on logic, only to become totally illogical through misuse. He was amazed at how many laws had been created to just interpret the simplest of truths, and how many times the legal system had been corrupted by lawyers and judges who just wanted to circumvent the very system they were sworn to uphold.

Fortunately, Seth had also found that there was a core belief, or better yet, a purpose, in the basis of all legal systems, and that fundamental truth would be what he would have to base his fantasy legal system on. One paragraph. One sentence. He still had a lot of work ahead of him and realized he wasn't actually sure how long he'd been working on the assignment. His stomach told him he hadn't eaten in quite a while, but he didn't feel tired. Maybe, he'd just grab an apple or something else off the table out in the lobby. The table had appeared several days before and was covered with bowls of fruit, cookies, and chilled water. But that could wait, he wasn't hungry enough yet to want to break his concentration.

Seth was reaching for another book, when something momentarily distracted him. It was as though he had heard something, but that was impossible. The room's walls were completely soundproof. He decided it must have been his imagination and went back to his research, but then, he heard it again, a soft knocking.

"Yeah?" he called, pushing away from his desk and crossing to the door. "Is someone there?" he asked, as he opened it to be blasted with a flurry of sights, sounds, and activity, and voices screaming, "Congratulations!"

He stood dumbfounded until he saw the banner hastily prepared that declared, "IT'S A BOY!!!"

Screaming himself, Seth leapt into the air as Miles, Jay, and Angie surrounded him, all bouncing like kids up and down, and pounding him on the back.

Miles quickly started pulling Seth towards the mess hall. "They're going to let you make one phone call. Come on!"

It didn't take any encouragement. All four raced for the connection. The phone call had already been placed and was being held by one of the camp directors.

"One minute. That's all," the director said as he held the phone out. The three side-kicks pushed Seth forward, and then, quickly sat down in a semicircle around him to enjoy the moment.

Seth took the phone and placed the receiver to his ear. "Honey," was all he got out before a beam of happiness spread across his face, even as the tears began to roll down his cheeks. Then the words were tumbling out of him.

"They told me. Are you okay? Yeah, me too. Look, I can't talk. I've just got a minute. I'm fine. I just wanted to say, I love you, and I miss you. Kiss him for me and tell him I love him. Oh, what's his name?" he suddenly remembered to ask. "Tell him his daddy loves him. Tell everybody else I love them too, 'specially Mama. Especially you. I've gotta go now. I love you. I love you."

The Director held out his hand, and Seth reluctantly gave the phone to him. Without ceremony, the Director hung up the phone and repacked the wireless into its case.

Seth found himself saying, "Thank you," to the man's back as he left the building.

All three bombarded him with questions, but the main one was, "What's his name?"

"Seth David. I'm a daddy!"

Angie threw her arms around him, and then, everyone hugged him and it felt just like old times.

"Someone in the kitchen made you a cake," Angie said excitedly, and then added laughing, "And as invited guests, we get to share it."

All four ran for the table.

"Sit," came Angie's command, which all of them did. The cake was obviously hastily made by someone not well-versed in the craft of cake making; one layer having already slid off center, but nobody minded.

"Jay, you cut. I'll just make a mess of it," Angie proclaimed. "Plus, I want a big piece. To hell with diets. I'll bet I've lost twenty pounds so far, and where in the hell have you guys been? I don't think I've seen anyone except Jay more than twice since we got here, and that's been in classes."

"They must have us all on different schedules or programs," concluded Seth, as Jay handed him his piece of chocolate cake.

Miles said, "Hell, I stopped looking for you guys after a while. I thought you had all dropped off the face of the earth."

Seth agreed. "I may as well have with the schedule I've been keeping. Do any of you have any day classes?"

"Who can tell?" responded Miles with his mouth full. "Shit, I haven't seen sunlight since we arrived. Everything's night, or those dark tunnels. It's really screwed up my clock."

Jay reached out to touch Seth and Miles, "So, how's it been going for you guys?"

"Who the hell can tell? With classes, and that constant feed in my ears," Miles complained.

"Did you guys get put into that robo suit?" It was Jay asking. "Like an exoskeleton? Said it would help me get used to the power, then told me mine will be internal."

"Yeah. What the fuck does that mean?" Miles asked.

"I don't know," Seth concluded. "I've gotten the same spiel, but no explanations. Just getting us ready, but ready for what? Every minute of every night it's something. They've even got me hooked up when I'm asleep. Subliminal something or other. It's funny. I don't hear anything except music."

Angie slid closer and lowered her voice. "Me either. Except sometimes, if I listen real closely between the notes I can hear a real small voice."

"You do?" Jay asked.

"Yeah, it's saying, 'Angie's horny as hell!'" Angie laughed.

They all laughed, and it was good to be back together again.

"Has it only been four weeks since Enrique," she moaned.

"No, just three," corrected Jay.

"Three?" Angie questioned.

"You're crazy! I thought it'd been closer to four. That's why I was so worried. I mean, the baby was due. But Rachel said the baby was two weeks late."

Miles slowly let his breath out as he considered, "Six weeks. I'm not believing this. She must have made a mistake. I've been keeping track and Jay's right. It's just three. Well, one over, twenty-two days. I've been checking the days off on my desk. Making a scratch every time we get down time.

The others slowly turned to him as each said, "So have I."

They all looked at each other uneasily.

Seth was the first to speak, and it was with disbelief, "No wonder we're so tired all the time."

"We've just been going by their clocks," whispered Angie. "How long do you think we've really been here?"

"Six weeks," Seth concluded. "Rachel wouldn't make that up, and if that's true, we're close to half-way through."

"Half-way through to what," Jay wondered aloud, "That's what I'd like to know."

CHAPTER XIX

At the elementary school two blocks from the projects, tall, battered chain-link fences supposedly protected the grounds and children from the dangers of the streets, but nobody in that area of Chicago was fooled. There were no safe places for children anywhere around the projects.

Inside the Principal's office, Junisha sat nervously on a long wooden bench under a cluttered bulletin board. The tile squares at her feet were cracked and in some cases missing. The reinforced windows with additional bars and mesh had been added in the years since Junisha had been a student there.

The smells were the same though—polish, disinfectant, and urine. The school had toilets, but no sane student or teacher would ever go into them. Students learned in the first grade to hold it, and if you couldn't, then you went outside behind the phys-ed building and did your business. But since the phys-ed building windows were always open year round, the odors permeated the halls, and after years made their way into the other buildings, and now to Junisha's nose. She felt her stomach roll at the bad memories of this place, and fear of what she was going to have to face today. She hadn't been told why she'd been summoned, but it couldn't be good. It was never good.

She noticed the shadow of a figure passing behind the frosted glass of the door of the principal's office, and then, the door opened and a tall, severe black man stepped out to face her.

"Mrs. Butler? I'm James Ready, the Principal here at Robert Taft Elementary." He held out his hand to perfunctorily indicate his office. "Would you please come inside?"

Junisha quickly moved past him to enter, and found her ten year old son, Robert James, sitting quietly, his face down, afraid to look up at her. Beside him stood two policemen.

"What'd he do?" she stammered in shock, then turned to her son, "Robert James, what did you do?"

Principal Ready moved behind his desk and retrieved a pistol from his desk. He slid it across his desk in her direction.

"Does this belong to you, Ms. Butler?"

Junisha could only shake her head in horror.

"Do you have any idea where he got it?" This from one of the police officers.

Junisha knew exactly where he had gotten it, but she continued to shake her head in the negative.

#

At the same time Junisha was being questioned by the police in Principal Ready's office in Chicago, Ollie Misner was finding himself in equally hot water. He'd just been coming out of a book-store on his lunch hour when Marshall Foster stepped in beside him and grabbed his arm in a vice-like grip.

"What you got?" was all the newscaster said, as he jerked Misner to a stop.

Misner was genuinely shocked and frightened. The two of them had never met openly in public. He could lose everything: his career, his reputation, everything, if anyone even suspected he was leaking information to the press. He tried to pull away, but the newsman wasn't letting go.

"What are you doing here?" Misner demanded. "Don't you realize what you're doing to me?"

"I don't give a fuck about that. We don't pay for nothing, and so far, that's all you've been giving us."

Misner tried to steer Foster out of the flow of foot traffic and into a more private corner. "Listen," he asserted, "it's all too close to the top. I can't help you. Now get away from me."

Foster leaned in, planting his arms on the wall on either side of Misner's head, and Misner could actually feel Marshall's breath on his face. "What are you saying? Are you saying we're not friends anymore?"

"I'm saying, you're going to make me lose my job," stammered Misner.

"Then I suggest you find us something. It's been over two months. What about Ryder?"

"He's in and out, mostly out. I already told you that."

"In and out, where?"

"I don't know. I do know he's been issued his own private jet. Maybe you can check that out somehow."

"See," the reporter smiled. "And you said you didn't know anything. The jet, that's something. Not much, but something." With that, Foster pushed away from the wall. "Keep in touch," he said, "or I'll do it for you."

With that, he stepped into the flow of shoppers on the sidewalk, and within seconds, he was gone.

Misner's legs felt like they were turning to liquid, and he had to force himself to remain erect. What had he gotten himself into? Taking a deep breath, he glanced both ways to see if anyone had spotted the confrontation and then realized that if they had, he could always make up a story or reason for the unexpected meeting. Feeling a little more confident, he stepped out of the shadows and made his way to his parked car.

Unlocking his car, Misner threw his newly purchased book inside and climbed behind the wheel. His breath was still coming in shallow bursts, and as he tried to insert the key, he saw that his hand was visibly shaking. So much for self-delusion. He was more frightened than he'd ever been in his life.

CHAPTER XX

Since the late night call about the baby, Seth and Jay found that their schedules were becoming more attuned, and several times a week, they'd end up in the same classes, but the classes were changing. In hand-to-hand combat, the training had always been both rigorous and specific, but it began escalating. Pairs were taught to square off and throw their opponent to the mat within two moves. It was a simple two-step process. Now, a third step was added. Once the opponent, the defeated one, was on the mat, the Guardian, a new designation for the one on top, would step in swiftly with an additional "coup de grace" shot to the back of the defeated one's head. So intent were Jay and Seth on making sure they completed the three moves within the time limit set by their commanders that neither questioned the moral implications of what they were doing, nor did they question why they didn't question. And neither noticed how much faster they were able to move, or exponentially, how much stronger they had become, or the shaved spot at the back of their head.

In the middle of the night, cadres of cadets would be awakened, to march in the darkness in closed formations, learning the intricacies of working together, even when they could only sense the others' presence.

Training for Angie was just as rigorous. There was no sexual discrimination on the Island. Angie liked that she was treated like a man. Yet, some remnants of her feminine side still slipped through, and she worried they could get her killed.

On the shooting range, she had been moving through the gallery, where human shaped cardboard targets popped out at her, and she had only an instant to choose whether to shoot or not. One target was of a little eight-year-old girl. Angie hesitated, and an instructor, she hadn't even known was there, stepped in beside her and smacked her to the ground with a blow to her back.

"You're dead."

"But," Angie stammered, trying to regain her breath.

"Look at her hand."

Angie rolled over to look at the cut-out of the child, and sure enough, the little girl had a gun in the hand down by her side.

"But," Angie stammered again.

"You're dead," shouted the Instructor again, as he pulled his own gun and literally blew the cutout's head away in a dozen violent shots.

Angie staggered back to her feet.

"Will we make that mistake again, soldier?"

"No, sir," she agreed.

"Because next time, it will not be my fist in your back, but six rounds of snubs tearing out your spine."

Angie understood and did not question. She would not make that mistake again. Sentiment had no place in whatever she was becoming and whatever that was, was growing stronger and quicker every day.

Classes had moved past theory to something more akin to rote. Drills were repeated over and over again.

"Murder?" the instructor asked in a quiet voice.

"Red," came the booming response from the cadets.

"Rape?"

"Red."

"Robbery?"

"Red."

"Protest March?"

"White," the response was equally loud.

"Prostitution?"

There was a hesitation, a smattering of both Red and White responses.

"Is there a victim?" the Instructor questioned. "No!" he answered his own question, then continued, "just two definitions—red or white. Right or wrong. Is there a victim? It's that simple. Two consenting adults?"

"White," the response was loud and unanimous.

"DUI?"

"Red."

"Child Pornography?"

"Red."

"Shoplifting?"

"Red."

"Religious Freedom?"

"White."

"Cults?"

There was a slight hesitation at this point, then one response of "White," soon echoed by the rest.

"Louder," shouted the instructor. "I want definite."

"White," the shout echoed through the exposed rafters.

"Graffiti?"

"Red."

"Gays?"

Again, the hesitation.

"Is there a victim?"

"What if it's children?" asked a cadet.

"That's not being gay," responded another cadet. "That's being a child molester. He said gay!"

The Instructor seconded the statement, "He's right, I said, gay."

"White."

"Profanity?"

"White."

"Drugs?"

"White."

"Selling Drugs?"

"Red."

Seth was on his way to classes when he passed by the physical combat course and saw Angie in hand-to-hand combat. In less time than it would have taken to call out her name had he dared, she had hurled the much larger man to the ground and placed a newly designed palm gun to the back of his head. It hissed, rather than shot. *Way to go, Angie*, he thought, as she turned to take on her next opponent.

Target practice had moved from reality to virtual. An electronically wired Jay, wearing an all-encompassing helmet, in his own electronically simulated world, moved through an empty warehouse space, wheeling, diving for cover, and firing left and right, as though under ambush. At one point, the thin steel cable attached to his back suddenly jerked him backwards, hurling him into the wall.

"You're dead," came a voice out of the darkness. "Now, get up and start again."

Rubbing his arm that was already beginning to swell from the impact, Jay readjusted his headgear and turned again to face the unseen adversaries.

Sleep was not easy for any of the cadets. Whether it was from exhaustion or from the artificially designated length of their days and nights, or from the constant input being poured into their heads at night, no one ever felt like they were truly rested. Miles probably wasn't the only one who began to sense rather than notice that their numbers were diminishing, that more and more cadets were beginning to show signs of their bodies breaking down. At first, it sometimes appeared as a slight twitch of the eyes, or the corner of a mouth, or the redness of shingles appearing on the arms or neck. Nothing was ever really said until noticed, and then, anyone showing symptoms of any kind were instantly rushed to the infirmary. The cadets were always assured that nothing was more important than health, but none of those affected ever seemed to show back up again. By the following day, most of those who had disappeared were completely forgotten. A cadet, now called a Guardian, might vaguely remember that another Guardian used to lie beside him in a shooting gallery, or be his counter in hand to hand combat, but just what that cadet had looked like would be somehow missing from his memory.

Miles' daily routine was varied, but getting more and more strenuous, though he had long since stopped thinking about it. After a six mile hike carrying over one hundred pounds, he and another cadet were sent into a mock city slum as a team. Their assignment was to stage a successful drug bust. Their opposition were other cadets and staff, dressed as derelicts and drug dealers. None of the participants were told whether their guns were filled with live ammo or blanks. They no longer cared. Everyone knew what his or her assignment was and that was their only focus.

Elsewhere on the base, Jay and another Guardian were challenged with moving through a shifting maze of corridors, with the understanding that both had to arrive at the other end dry. Moving through the sometimes darkened rooms, they were forced to dodge powerful water jets that shot out of the wall from various angles trying to strike them. Since there was no obvious assailant, they had to listen and sense where the jets would be coming from, and Jay was surprised that he actually could sense the water pressure building before release. He managed to make it through forty-three attempts to hit him. His partner was not as lucky, so both had to repeat the exercise, but this time with live steam and scalding water. Jay made sure this time both of them made it out alive.

CHAPTER XXI

In the hallway outside of Ryder's office, Joel was having to run to keep up with Ryder.

"We're going with Riverton, based on your recommendations."

"Jesus," cried Joel, "so in other words, if this goes down the tubes, I'm the scapegoat."

"No," laughed Ryder. "That will definitely be my honor. Is the money in place?"

"More than I've ever thought possible."

"Yeah, I know what you mean," Ryder agreed as he suddenly detoured into a restroom. Joel quickly made a U-turn and followed him in.

Glancing around, the restroom appeared empty, and Ryder quickly moved to one of a long bank of urinals to relieve himself. He continued talking throughout the process, and Joel, staying by the door, took notes as fast as he could.

"The Man wants to see a copy of the new laws and keep it simple. One page summary. Don't confuse the issue. And it would sure help if we could find another name."

"For the town?"

"No, for the project. Right now, it's still coded Singapore."

"Maybe you ought to put a plus on that and let it stand."

Finishing his business, Ryder laughed and quickly moved to wash his hands. Not even bothering to dry them, Ryder was already heading for the door, which Joel held open for him.

"Let's not worry about that now," he said, as he moved into the hall. "After the fact, nobody's going to give a damn about what we used to call it." Joel raced after him, narrowly avoiding another staffer coming from the opposite direction, obviously in need of his own kidney break.

Moving quickly to the other end of the urinals, this staffer was just unzipping when he heard a toilet flush in one of the stalls. Finishing his own business, he moved to the wash stands in time to say hello to Ollie Misner from public relations, hurriedly exiting a stall and rushing out the door.

Misner bypassed his own cubicle, passed through security, moved quickly down the steps and out of the gates. Barely glancing at the traffic, the nervous little press agent cut across four lanes, narrowly missing getting clipped by an elderly woman on her cell phone, who looked up just in time to slam on her brakes, and shout a profanity out the window. Ollie Misner didn't even bother to look back. He knew he had to find a secure phone, or at least one, that couldn't be traced back to him.

An hour or so later, the President's admin, Mrs. Kline, was going over her boss' schedule for the afternoon with him when the first indication of trouble came.

"Senators Dorman and Marshall at 3:00 here; Nancy Eskew of League of Nationalist Women Voters at 3:15 by phone," she pointed out on the schedule. "A Press photo for Boy Scouts of America at 3:30. Girl Scouts at 3:45. Special Olympics at 4:00. Chris is working out their release dates now."

It was then, she looked up from the schedule, "Oh, Marshall Foster of Channel 7 News called a couple of times."

"What about?" asked the President, not yet aware of what was coming.

"He said, he wants to know about some project called or coded, Singapore."

Now she had the President's full attention.

"He was very persistent," she commented, "but then he always is. I asked him if he was referring to the country and suggested he ought to get an Atlas, but he wasn't buying it. He said to tell you, he intends to go with the story with or without your comments."

"Good, then no comment." The President distractedly ran his hands over his desk as though trying to make sure it wasn't going anywhere. "Anything else?"

Mrs. Kline paused a second before answering. "He also wanted to know, and I quote, "Which city have you selected and what are the new laws going to be?""

"Shit!" swore the President. "Get me Ryder."

Ryder was there within three minutes, and Joel was with him. Mrs. Kline closed the door quietly behind them and took up her station at the desk.

Inside the Oval office, Joel scanned the room for electronic bugs and only after an all-clear signal from him did Ryder allow the President to speak.

The words burst out of him, "Marshall Foster at Channel 7 knows. Not a lot, but enough to get rolling."

"How?" questioned Ryder.

"How do they ever? This place is like a sieve."

"Well, we knew it had to happen," reasoned Ryder. "The city scopes out."

"And it's the best?"

"It's the only one that really fits, especially if we have to push it."

"So push it," demanded the President, then questioned, "what does this do to us time-wise?"

"Well, it sure makes it a hell of a lot more exciting."

"How long?"

"I can be there tomorrow."

Joel exhaled loudly enough for both men to turn and look at him.

"Sorry, I just realized I wasn't breathing."

Ryder laughed. "Maybe you better get used to the feeling, 'cause we're taking the world's biggest roller coaster ride, and I hate to tell you, we haven't even finished the track."

\#

On the island, if it was an island, Jay and Seth found themselves in the same rotation for what they assumed was a week, although they had no idea if two days or over a week had actually passed. Time meant nothing on the island with its perpetual darkness. The only light they had felt since the day they arrived were the artificial lights that burned down upon them at regulated intervals which signaled or rather triggered the need to sleep or to wake up, or to eat or to defecate. The only indication the men had of the true passage of time was by the growth of their beards as they shaved during their presumed daily showers. Like the plane trip onto the island, they used that bodily redundancy as their own secret attempt at still holding on to the outside world, and then, the outside world swept over them in full force the day the tents came down.

Seth and Jay, with at least two dozen other cadets, were coming out of a training class and double-timing it to their next. It was a mindless routine. The class buzzer sounded, and everyone stopped immediately whatever they were doing. The lights were turned off in the classroom. And everyone, including instructors, exited the room and the building, merging into the running line of other cadets racing down the dark unlighted walkways to their next building, their next class.

Jay mentioned to Seth the second day they were in rotation together that he felt he could probably run between classes with his eyes shut completely, and together, they decided to experiment. Jay was the first to attempt it. With Seth as his control in case he misstepped, Jay merged into the line of running cadets and unerringly made every turn and climbed every step, located their next class and even made it into his seat without ever opening his eyes. At the next class switch, it was Seth's turn at blind navigation, and he too was able to find his way to the next class. It was not just rote steps though, because sometimes new obstacles had been inadvertently left in walkways. Instantly Seth and Jay were aware of the differences and made corrections in their movements. It was exhilarating to both of them, almost like having a sixth sense, a bat's supersonic sense. During the week they were together, they tested it everywhere, often in the latter days never opening their eyes, even to select the food they were eating in the cafeteria.

That last day they both stopped instantly in the black corridor between buildings, at the ripping sound coming from overhead. Everyone else stopped as well and some even cried out. Fortunately, for

Jay and Seth, with their eyes closed, the shock was not nearly as great or painful.

The black tarps covering the tunnel-like corridors in which they had been running were ripped away by workmen on the outside. Almost every cadet, save Seth and Jay, ducked down, shielding their eyes. Only those two stood tall, faces thrown back, feeling the rush of warm fresh air washing over them, the colors of the real sun slicing through the darkness and their eyelids, triggering instantly memories of the worlds they had left behind. Rachel, the baby, Cameron, Jay's daughter Kaaren, everything. It was like emerging from a dream, or a submarine after years at sea. Jay and Seth slowly opened their eyes and both found their cheeks soaked with tears.

From that point on, the cadets took their food outside to sit in the sunlight...and with the sun they found the chance to re-establish old friendships. The instructors took these friendships now into account and purposefully scheduled group work based on those friendships. Seth found himself once again teamed with all four of his old friends from the police academy.

One afternoon, while the four of them were enjoying a moment together, Seth asked, how much of their training they remembered. The others thought that was a stupid question, but then, realized that most of what they had been through was a blur. Jay said, he remembered target practice, and then, suddenly he blushed.

"What?" asked Miles. "Why are you blushing?"

"Never mind," said Jay, still as red as could be possible.

"Don't give us that," egged on Angie, "now I want to know."

"So do I," added Seth.

"Okay, okay, but you guys had the same thing. It's just that with me, it was sort of my fantasy when I was still not out."

The others leaned in closer.

"Remember when we had that series of virtual shooting exercises, where we were in an empty room but through the goggles we could be taken anywhere."

All of them nodded.

"Well, the steam room with all those naked men, I think that was the hardest for me, because before I came out, that was my fantasy."

"Steam room?" questioned Miles and Seth at the same time.

"Yeah," answered both Angie and Jay, nodding their heads.

"It was distracting at first, all those naked men stepping out of the steam," laughed Angie.

"Tell me about it," Jay agreed, as he rolled his eyes.

"At least," he continued, "it was easy once you got past the initial shock to see the weapons."

"He means the lethal ones," grinned Angie, giving Jay a teasing shove.

"I never had a steam room," said Seth, with Miles shaking his head in agreement.

"You didn't?" This was from both Jay and Angie.

Miles looked at them and volunteered, "The worst for me was when I put the goggles on, and I was standing in the middle of this place, like Death Valley, with nothing for miles, only it wasn't really nothing. The enemy was buried just under the surface and could jump up and shoot me at any time. I didn't have any place to hide and was backing up, starting to panic when suddenly it was all gone."

"The place?"

"No, the panic. It was gone, and I was calmer than I had ever been in my life. Like I was on remote control, and I cleaned the area and never got even a scratch."

The others sat there listening.

"Why would they put me in a place like that? I never told anyone that wide open spaces always freaked me out as a kid."

"My fear was snakes. They had me walking through a swampy bayou with rattler and cottonmouths coming out of the water and slithering around my feet, and I had to focus on getting my targets. At first, all I wanted to do was back up and run, and then, like you, like some switch had been thrown, I was aware of the snakes, but the fear was gone. My focus was on the enemy."

"Whoa," whispered Angie, reaching out to touch Seth's arm.

"How did they know I was so afraid of snakes, or you, of wide open spaces? I never told anybody that?"

Jay suggested uneasily, "Maybe we didn't know we were telling them."

The others turned to look at him.

"Maybe at night, stuff wasn't just being poured into our heads. Maybe, it was also pulling things out."

Training was accelerated, as though the sun added a new element to the regiment, and it did. All four found that working in the sun actually increased their own individual strengths. Target practices were now held on brightly lit slopes, and the cadets wore specially designed sunglasses that not only cut through the glare, but enhanced their eyesight. The other unusual aspect of the glasses was that they also worked at night. Though no bigger than regular wrap around sunglasses, these solar-enhanced, powered glasses were specifically designed for the Guardians and provided the wearer with almost 20/20 color-accurate vision in the dark. The Guardians began wearing these glasses in all their training exercises and classes, whether in-door or out.

Once the sun was allowed in, the Guardians found that they began to act more as a unit than individuals, often standing at attention for the entire class and answering all questions as one.

On the fields, cadres of Guardians, including the Los Angeles team, moved on one-syllable commands as a precision unit displaying perfect unison and perfect timing. Even with their ever-present glasses nowhere in sight, they were all, as Jay and Seth had weeks earlier, able to move perfectly blind. There would not be a single misstep throughout an entire two hour exercise even with every eye closed.

CHAPTER XXII

Mayor Gerald Brandy of Riverton hadn't hesitated a moment when he received the call and was asked to pick up the Presidential advisor, Richard Ryder, at the airport, and he was secretly pleased that the advisor had asked for him by name and asked to meet him alone. That meant that even the White House understood who the real power broker was in Riverton, and as Mayor, he was going to do his best to milk the man out of every cent the government could send Riverton's way; that was his job, the one he'd been elected to do, and if standing out there in the chill and drizzle was the price he had to pay, then he'd pay it.

Mayor Brandy naturally assumed this unprecedented visit was a prelude to offering financial relief to the town before it was forced to shut down completely for lack of funds.

The Mayor had been rehearsing his speech from the moment he'd gotten the call and was even now anxiously re-running it over and over again in his head, revising it on each pass, looking for just the right word combinations to win his case.

It didn't help that he was getting cold and wet standing there waiting for the private jet. It was a miserable spring day, one of those that couldn't make up it's mind whether it was going to snow, or turn sunny. In another week or two, it would be warmer. *Everything looked better when it was warmer*, he ruminated before continuing, *as long as it didn't get too hot*, which it often did in Riverton. With the dual rivers moving slowly past, the humidity and mosquitoes could bring a sane man to his knees.

Maybe it's better they visited now, he reconsidered and then realized again why he had had this mental digression in the first place. There was no place to take shelter at the almost deserted airfield. No, not almost deserted, completely deserted.

The Riverton airport, which had never been used for much more than the occasional corporate or commuter flight since it opened, had been closed for more than two years. What was the point of keeping it open once the last major company in town, the Wurtham Box Company, had shuttered its doors and relocated to Xenia.

The airport had never had much of terminal. Inside, there were just a few counters, a couple of benches, and three snack-machines. Of course, the terminal was boarded up now. The benches had been sold for five dollars each to the downtown mission, the vending machines were carted away by their supplier. The only thing left was the old building's shell. Long ago, its windows had been smashed out by vandals and its walls were marred by graffiti.

Not a great introduction to one's city but Ryder had insisted on flying into this particular airport and no amount of arguing had dissuaded him, so here the Mayor was, waiting for the private jet he had been told to expect. He hoped the plane wouldn't loose a wheel landing on the cracked and weed-incrusted tarmac.

That would be just my luck, Mayor Brandy thought, as he shifted his rather barrel-shaped body and waited. He could almost see the newspaper headlines in his head. *PRESIDENTIAL ADVISOR KILLED IN PLANE LANDING AT RIVERTON AIRPORT. Mayor held responsible.* Hell, why not, he was blamed for almost everything else since the city took a nose-dive. What was he expected to do? He couldn't raise taxes. Nobody had any money in Riverton. He couldn't increase fines or penalties for the same reason. Nobody had any money to pay. Nobody had built a house in Riverton in ten years, and there were almost more houses empty now than occupied. Also without businesses, who was going to buy them? The last bank branch had closed six months ago and moved its minimal receipts over to a branch at a neighboring town twenty miles away.

What the hell was he expected to do? He had been about ready to bail himself when the phone call came from the White House, and so here he was, waiting for his last chance, Riverton's last chance.

Glancing at his watch, Mayor Brandy was about to conclude that Ryder might have changed his mind completely about investing in a town that was too far-gone to save. Then he heard it, the small Leer jet breaking through the overcast skies above him. It circled once, then came in for a surprisingly smooth landing.

So much for predictions. Mayor Brandy sighed a sigh of relief and put on his best smile.

"You should have seen Riverton, fifteen, even ten years ago," pitched Mayor Brandy as he drove Ryder around the city, being careful to skirt the seedier parts, which were becoming increasingly more difficult to avoid with every passing day.

"You couldn't have picked a better place to live, and the schools, right up there at the top. Oh, it had its problems, but nothing we couldn't handle. The town just kept getting bigger and better. That's how we used to promote it—Bigger and Better. The first part was true."

He let the statement hang there, waiting for a response. In fact, he would have liked any kind of response. Ryder hadn't said more than three words since their introductions at the airport. It had been just Ryder and his assistant, some young guy named Joel. The mayor wasn't sure whether Joel was a first or last name. Anyway, they'd all been together in the Mayor's car driving around for almost three quarters of an hour, and Mayor Brandy was running out of things to say. He'd driven them past the outlying farmlands, most of the fields lying fallow. Then there were two housing developments that had never been completed, sidewalks leading nowhere, three closed factories and an industrial park that had been proposed, but never built. But after a while, one failed dream looked just like another, so he changed his plans and skirted the more rundown sections near the waterfront and drove them down through the main streets of Riverton, past the overgrown, though still used, city park, and up to circle the courthouse and town square, which managed to hang on to the feel of Riverton's more illustrious past and probably a few of its ghosts. The library building, built in the 1930's by the Carnegie foundation, was an especially grand old building, though only opened now one day a week with a volunteer from the women's assistance league manning the desk.

With nothing more to say about the town, he found himself forced into its history, babbling about the Indian tribes that used to camp in the fork of the rivers. That was when he realized in embarrassment that he'd never really looked at his town as a stranger would and the longer he drove, the more depressed he became and the more he inwardly cringed.

Hell, this town is fucked, the Mayor almost said aloud, then found himself getting angry.

What the fuck? What was Ryder here for anyway, if not to bail them out. They expected bad. Maybe not this bad, but bad. They expected poverty. The entire country was in a recession; had been for over twenty years. If they didn't expect those things, then they were idiots, he thought, realizing he was getting defensive, protective of his town, and angrier by the minute.

"What exactly kind of financial grant are we talking about here?" he almost shouted to the men in the car with him, then lowered his volume and offered, as a way to get the conversation going, "You said, some kind of experiment."

Neither man answered, and the silence seemed to suck the air out of the car as it passed the "Whistling Pig" cafe and drive-thru, which was the only real diner left in Riverton. It offered fifteen to twenty comfort-food menu items and two daily specials to keep its doors open. And those doors opened early. The "Whistling Pig" also served up a pretty good breakfast if you didn't mind everything served up with a dollop of questionable grease. The coffee was fortunately, most agreed, strong enough to dilute or melt through even the worst case of cholesterol overdose.

"What kind of experiment," the Mayor asked more directly this time, trying to keep his voice under control.

Ryder turned slightly to glance into the back seat where Joel sat, holding a stack of file folders tightly in his crossed arms.

"It'll all be outlined in the meeting tonight, and I think you'll find our proposal extremely exciting.

"Proposal, hell, Son," laughed the Mayor, trying to sound light-hearted, yet serious at the same time. "It better be a whole lot more than that. As Mayor of this town, I can tell you financial aid had better be a big issue. And I'm talking an immediate infusion. Your team last week went over everything, and we haven't held anything back. There's not a person called tonight who doesn't know this town's so far underwater financially, we might as well bulldoze it right now."

He pointed out a strip mall in passing, "Oh, there's that strip mall I was telling you about, the new one. Opened three, three-and-a-half years ago."

Both Ryder and Joel glanced out the window at the passing site. The parking lot was partially full, especially in front of the grocery store as people did their last minute shopping before dinner. But even here graffiti marred the walls.

Mayor Brandy's voice continued his pathetic pitch as they drove past, "It was supposed to revitalize the area, but shit, half the promised stores never even made it to opening, and the rest are barely hanging on. Grocery stayed cause it's the only one in the area, but now they're threatening to pull. Vandalism's rising and the city can't even afford security for the parking lot."

In the mall's parking lot, one of the shoppers, Doug Browning, was helping his wife load groceries into their car trunk when the sound of an engine backfiring rang out. Both instinctively ducked their heads at the sound, looked in all directions for the source, and then, when no real sign of danger appeared, smiled rather sheepishly at each other and continued, loading the groceries as though nothing had happened.

Across the parking lot, the cause of the backfire, a lowrider, muffler hanging, peeled out of the parking lot and onto the thoroughfare forcing others to yield to its complete disregard for anything else on the road. The car's mufflers roared and its radio blasted ear shattering funk as it raced away.

Inside the car, fifteen year old Billy Harker and his friends, Tyler Parks, Harry Small, and Joey Wilkie shouted group "Fuck you's" at every car they passed. Of course, none of them used their real names with each other. Billy was Supernova Glide, or just Glide to his friends, and the others were Rebok, Nike and Addidas; four immortals who ruled the roads of Riverton, underage drivers always out to have a little fun and carve a name for themselves in Riverton's history.

Glide was the obvious leader in looks and height, if not brains. Although the four boys talked of girls, and even claimed success in that area, all four would have been pegged as losers anywhere else in the world, and had they not joined forces, probably even in Riverton. But together, they had become a force to be reckoned with.

"Okay, mother fuckers, get the windows down," Glide shouted out orders to the others.

Fifteen-year-old Addidas, in the back seat, was of course the first to comply. He would have done anything Glide told him to and later in life might actually understand his attraction. But for right now, it was just hero worship. Pushing his geekie glasses up off his nose, he whipped down the window in preparation.

"Mine's down," he cried, and then turned to his side-kick in the back seat. "Ready, Nike?"

Nike, who looked even younger than the rest and actually was only fourteen, rubbed his hands nervously on his thighs. His window was already down.

Glide was calling out instructions that were almost lost in the noise and cold wind whipping through the windows.

"Okay, they're coming up," he shouted.

"And don't miss like last night, shit-head," added Reebok, Glide's second in command from the front seat.

Nike reached down between his legs and pulled out his father's handgun and fumbled with the safety until it was released.

"Okay," Glide shouted.

"Slow down," Nike complained as he brought the gun up to window level.

"Shit on that," Reebok laughed.

Nike suddenly saw his target, and with his eyes almost completely closed from the fear and wind, fired five shots in a row.

Two of the three mailboxes alongside the road got a permanent reminder of their passing.

Squeals of laughter and forbidden excitement filled the car as it roared away and past the old, Welcome to Riverton, sign on the outskirts of the city. Mayor Brandy had been right. The weathered, bullet-hole laden sign did still say, "Bigger and Better."

That evening, Riverton's twelve council members and the Mayor sat at their horseshoe-shaped stations around Ryder who waited patiently at his own table in the center. He was waiting for each member of the council to finish reading the proposal that Joel had handed out, once they had all arrived and been seated. Joel had also placed a microphone before Ryder so that his answers could be clearly heard and could not be misunderstood. There were bound to be questions, and Ryder was prepared.

Joseph Redhorse, looking completely out of place, sat uncomfortably beside Joel near the chamber door. Since the proposal was only two pages long, Ryder could see the expressions, and then, fear, as they read. Several glanced up at Ryder periodically during their reading as though to confirm this proposal was to be taken seriously. Others finished and began rereading it again, this time underlining words, phrases, and entire paragraphs.

Mayor Brandy was the first to try to speak, but appeared not to know what to say, an almost complete loss of words, which was very unusual for the man.

"Uh, Mr. Ryder, I uh...well, nobody expected," he stammered.

"Not yet," demanded another council member waving his hand. "I'm not through."

Councilwoman Laverne Hardy was already standing, "This can't be done, can it?"

"Yes Ma'am, it can," assured Ryder in a quiet level tone.

Now, everyone was talking, "But it's not legal" "The government can't just take over." "This is our home."

"I understand your concerns," assured Ryder.

"Concerns, hell!" shouted Mayor Brandy. "This is outrageous. I was talking about a bail-out, not a complete take-over. And these laws, they're ridiculous," he said, waving the sheets around.

"It's an experiment," continued Ryder, his voice moderate and unemotional. "What happens here at Riverton will determine the course of this country's judicial system from this day forward."

"To hell with the judicial system," the Mayor continued, his face growing redder by the second. "What's going to happen to our people?"

Councilwoman Laverne never sat down. She leaned across her station and screamed at Ryder, "This is Riverton, not Los Angeles, not Chicago or New York. There I could understand, maybe, but here? Why here?"

This was the question Ryder had been waiting for. He almost wanted to thank the councilwoman, but realized she wasn't looking for thanks, but answers. Slowly pushing himself away from his table, he rose to his full height and began:

"Why Riverton? Because Riverton has boundaries. Your area and population are both small enough to monitor but not so small as to make the results questionable. And face it, the twentieth century didn't pass you by."

"But that doesn't mean...," came a protest, but Ryder cut it off with a raised hand.

"Let me finish, please. You've got all the problems of most urban areas: crime, drugs, violence, poverty, delinquency. You've got it all. Hell, you're the perfect American town. But America is not so perfect any-more and your town, like all the others you mentioned, reflect that. Well, that's what we're trying to address. What happens here in Riverton this year will determine what happens in the rest of the country next year."

The female councilwoman was having none of it and threw up her hands in despair. "Wait a minute. Wait a goddamned minute. This is insanity. Someone tell me this is a dream." Wheeling on Ryder, she glared, "You listen to me, Mr. High and Mighty, Mr. Man with the Credentials, I don't know who you think you are, but this council is made up of members of the business community, teachers, lawyers, and... This..." She threw the proposal sheets at Ryder, "This is ridiculous. Stupid. What's more it's frightening. No, terrifying, and it can't work. It's a pipe dream. As it is, our property values are already practically the lowest in the nation. Do you have any idea what's going to happen when this gets out? The bottom's going to completely drop out, and we're going to lose everything. Ruined. You just can't come in here and do that to people."

"I hear you. I understand your concerns, and yes, fears," replied Ryder as he stooped to pick the thrown papers. "As for property values, that's been taken care of. We'll be glad to buy your homes."

"Oh, sure," Laverne shot back, angrily sarcastic, "Thank you, at ten cents on the dollar and..."

"No, at twenty-five percent over market value," Ryder replied as he placed the papers back in front of the councilwoman.

There was a momentary stunned silence in the chamber.

"The whole town?" asked the Mayor in disbelief.

"We don't think it will be the whole town," replied Ryder

"Then you fuckin' don't know Riverton," the Mayor blasted. "Nobody, and I mean nobody's going to stay for this."

At that Ryder shrugged and sat back down. "Then, I guess, the whole town."

There was another stunned silence, a long one, until finally one of the less vocal of the council, an insurance broker from Farmers, a man, named Jason Rankin, asked, "Who's going to set the value?"

Councilwoman Laverne was back on her feet at the mere thought of the question. "Are you crazy, Jason? This isn't about money. This is ridiculous. I don't intend to sell, so I vote, No."

Several others chimed in as well with their No's, though with decidedly less enthusiasm and more than a few completely withholding their responses. Ryder didn't care either way.

"I'm sorry," he said, now standing to address the group, "I don't think you understand. What you have before you is not an option. I wasn't sent here to get your opinion, but to tell you what is going to happen."

Councilwoman Laverne was stunned, couldn't believe what she was hearing. "But you can't do that."

Another Councilman stood up beside her, "Uh, My name's Luther Frank. I'm a teacher here in Riverton, and maybe, I don't know everything about the law, but I do teach high school civics, and Laverne's right, you can't just do this."

"You'd be surprised, Mr. Frank, what you can do in a state of emergency."

"But we're not in a state of emergency," Laverne protested.

"But you are," replied Ryder with a momentary edge to his voice, which he quickly modified.

"Please, this plan is not a negative. I know it sounds that way right now, but we want, I want, what you want, to rebuild your city. Right now, it's bankrupt."

"Maybe I exaggerated," blustered the Mayor.

"Your books don't, and neither does your tax base. This is a town that was designed for more than one hundred thousand people. You have barely ten thousand left and with those you have forty-five percent unemployment and rising. You've been losing industries at the rate of eight a year and store closures at six. Your city government is barely functioning with mostly volunteers like yourselves, and your police force has been cut to a skeleton crew. Your board of education, not only have you had to close three of your schools, you've also had to lay off over sixty percent of your teachers, and you can't pay those you've kept."

Laverne was almost pleading now. "But this is our town. We love it."

"I know you do. The President of the United States knows you do. That's what we're counting on. Don't you see what you're being offered? Can't you see what the possibilities are? Riverton, Ohio can go down in history as the first city in the world to completely conquer poverty, eliminate crime, and raise the educational standards of its children to the highest in the world."

Everyone slowly sank back down in their seats. No one spoke for a long moment while they considered what had just been said.

Finally Mayor Brandy turned in his seat to face Ryder, breaking the silence, "How long do we have to decide?"

Ryder's eyes swept the frightened eyes of all those in the room before settling on the mayor's. "I'm afraid, the decision has already been made," he responded, as he began gathering up his papers. "Our task force has already started arriving and as of this evening, Riverton will be effectively quarantined until everyone has had a chance to choose whether they wish to remain or leave this community. Oh, and I might as well tell you now, to minimize any outside interference until we're completely set up, all internet and phone links, both cell and land, to any place outside of the immediate area have been cut as of fifteen minutes ago. So, I think that means we've got a busy night in front of us, don't we?"

Councilwoman Laverne slowly stood up and walked from the chamber, getting angrier and angrier by the moment, her speed increasing until she was practically running. Bursting from the doors of the courthouse, she stopped suddenly in horror.

The courthouse square was already filled with military personnel and vehicles. Sinking down on the courthouse steps, Laverne realized the invasion had already begun.

"Oh my God," she cried to herself. "We've got to get out of here." But it was basically a rhetorical statement. She didn't get up, or run for her car, or do anything except sit there and watch the camp being established on the courthouse lawn. Had she tried to drive out of the city, she'd have found that roadblocks were already being set up, with no traffic allowed either in or out of Riverton. But Laverne didn't know that yet. The hour was late, at least by Riverton standards. Nobody would notice anything until morning. By then, it would be too late. The town of Riverton was effectively cut off from the outside world.

Feeling an overwhelming loss, even greater than the one she had felt when her mother passed away the previous year, Laverne wiped the tears slowly coursing down her face, and then did what she always did when life seemed unbearable; she went back to work. Tonight, that work was in the council room. Slowly Laverne stood back up and returned to the council chamber.

CHAPTER XXIII

The next morning, the Riverton's council members were spread out across the courthouse steps to face the first onslaught of citizenry who were confused about the military presence in their town. The council handed out fliers that Ryder's team had prepared. His personal office team had taken charge the moment they arrived, under Joel's supervision. Within hours of arrival, they had set up temporary offices and command centers, both inside and outside the courthouse. The once-green expanse of lawn, in front of the courthouse, was teeming with activity, military activity.

Councilwoman Laverne was exhausted, but then, everyone from the previous night's meeting was. They had been up all night and were now running purely on caffeine and adrenaline. She heard one of her fellow members explain as he handed the local pharmacist a pamphlet, "No, we're not under attack. It will all be explained tonight in the high School gym. Everyone must be there."

"Why are they carrying guns?" came a question another council member had to answer.

Laverne had her own questions as the crowd gathered. In Riverton, nothing unusual had happened in so many years that anything out of the routine spread through the gossip grapevine like wildfire. She knew it wouldn't be long before half the town would be converging on the courthouse to see what was going on.

"I'm working tonight. What's all this about?" This question was directed at Laverne.

"Don't worry about that. All businesses will be closed. Everyone, and that means everyone, must be at this meeting," she said, as she handed out fliers to eagerly reaching hands. "This will affect you all directly. You must be there or at least have someone there to represent your family."

"I'm scared," confided an elderly woman reaching for a flier.

Maybe you should be. Hell, we all should be, thought Laverne, but she kept these thoughts to herself. The guns held at ready by the soldiers on the steps were loaded.

The soldiers at the roadblocks, set up several miles out of town, had all been hand-picked and were beginning to catch the morning influx of traffic which was light at first, but growing exponentially by the hour.

Several cars had pulled to a stop and were being turned back, but one car, driven by a resident, was trying to get back home.

"I've got to get through. I live in Riverton. My family's there." His desperation showed in the frightened look of his eyes. "What's going on? Has something happened?"

One soldier handed him a flier, motioned to the other soldiers to swing open the barrier that was blocking the road, and said, "It'll all be explained as soon as you get to town."

"But you didn't answer my question. Everything's all right, isn't it? My family? Are they all right?"

"Everything's fine," the soldier assured him. "It's just a military exercise. Your family's fine."

On the other side of the barricade, cars were also lined up with residents wanting to drive out of Riverton. Another group of soldiers was handling those residents.

"But I've got to get to Columbus, I've got meetings," said one disturbed Rivertonian.

"I'm sorry, sir. I'm sure they'll understand. Everyone is quarantined until further notice."

"What do you mean, 'quarantined'? Why? Oh my God, have we been exposed to something? Are we going to die?"

"No, sir," assured the young soldier. "I just meant that Riverton is under martial law for the moment, and that just means that until it's lifted, nobody can leave. I'm sure it won't be for long."

Handing the driver a flier, he added, "Now, if you'll just turn your car around, I'm sure you'll get more answers back in Riverton."

Back in Washington, Marshall Foster was not in a good mood, and everyone in the Channel 7 newsroom knew it. When he called a special meeting of his core team, they were all worried. Job security in D.C. news circles was solely based on how well you could dig the dirt, and lately, Marshall had been more demanding than ever.

Once they were all seated, he closed the door and turned to look at them, but it wasn't anger they saw in those eyes, just exhaustion.

"Okay, you've had two weeks," he began. "What have you got for me? And I don't want to hear you've come up empty handed."

Nobody spoke. In fact, most of them looked down at their laps like school children who'd been caught stealing.

"Jesus," Marshall said in disappointment. "Are you telling me, nothing?"

"Marshall, none of it computes," came back his lead researcher, a young black woman from Chicago. "We've run those words through every filter and every search engine we can and none of it computes. I mean, Miami and Delaware are city and state names, but where does that lead you? The letters MASC could be Mascot, or an acronym for a thousand things from Master of Applied Science to Maintenance Support Coordinators to Michigan Association of Student Councils. But none of it leads anywhere, and we're not even sure those are the letters. There was a coffee stain that blurred the letters. Even through enhancers, they were questionable. And forget it for words that end with feather or father?"

"Don't forget fire, fine, and turtle," scoffed another member of the team.

"Right. How many thousand uses do you want us to present to you on those words? They just don't link. They just don't lead us anywhere. I know you don't want to hear this, but we need more information. I'm sorry. That's just the way it is."

They waited for his outburst, but it didn't come. Finally he said, "Okay, I'll go back to my source. There's got to be something else. There just has to be." After a long moment, Marshall waved their dismissal.

Everyone was pushing back from the table when a junior staff member said in a quiet voice, "You know, Miami and Delaware are also Indian names, tribe names. And that may link into feather and turtle."

"Turtle?" asked Marshall focusing on the young man.

"Well, I mean, it's probably a long shot, but I put Miami and Delaware and feather and turtle into Dogpile."

"Dogpile?"

"It's a search engine I used to use in college and it came up with three of the four linked. Like I said it was a long shot, but I thought I'd just mention it."

"And?" Marshall asked impatiently.

"Oh, there was this Indian, Native American, called Little Turtle and he was some sort of great leader of the Miamis. That was the Indian tribe that ranged throughout the Midwest. Anyway, this Little Turtle helped to lead a force of Miamis and Delaware Indians to victory over two American armies in the 1790's."

There was a long moment when nobody spoke or moved in the conference room, then slowly everyone slid back into their seats.

"Why the fuck would Bob Ryder be making notes about Indian tribes?" It was the lead researcher who asked the question.

"Maybe we better find out," Marshall said. "What territories specifically did those Indian tribes live in? Where are they now? Do they have reservations?"

"Oh my God," one team member said. "We need to check and see if and when anyone from that tribe has petitioned for sovereignty, for the return of their native land."

"Their own laws, their own casinos," realized the lead researcher. "But why would the President care about Indian casinos?"

"He wouldn't," Marshall thought aloud. "But he might be interested in the fact that a reservation is governed by its own set of laws."

Abby's Bella Vita, an eponymous fixture in Riverton, was one of the few remaining beauty salons in town. Located across from the courthouse square, it had been the hub for local gossip since Abby's grandmother opened the shop in 1945 after the war. She had used the proceeds from a ten-thousand-dollar death benefit she received from the loss of her husband. She considered the swap a fair trade and a hell of a lot more stable.

"The first thing I ever got out of the asshole," she liked to say. Abby Senior was never one to mince words with anyone about anything, and the successive Abbys had followed in her footsteps.

This morning, the Bella Vita regulars were lined-up at the window, watching the activity outside.

Holding court as always, Abby Three, as she became known since her grandmother's passing and her mother's accidental overdose more than eight years ago. Forced to give up her place at the window, she focused on going over everything they all knew so far from the handout she had secured the moment she arrived for her first appointment.

Normally, the phone would have been buzzing off the wall, but since the phones weren't working, it felt as if one of the main arteries of the gossip train had been derailed, and Abby wasn't happy about it.

Even with the flier handout, the news coming in from each customer was more horrific than the last: Soldiers all over the place. They had guns. Loaded guns. And Mabel, one of Abby's regulars, who came running in for her monthly perm, said she'd heard there was some kind of leak somewhere, down by the docks...nuclear waste or something...and everybody had already been exposed. Contaminated.

Almost instantly, Abby started feeling faint. Her horoscope had said that this was not going to be a good day. Between sideways breaths to avoid the toxic chemicals she was slathering all over Mabel's head, she took a moment to pat her ample breast to see if her heart was racing any faster than before; it was. She would be lucky if she didn't have a heart attack before the meeting that night. But heart attack or not, she was determined to be there. Wild horses couldn't have kept her away. There was bound to be gossip.

#

At the mall, what business there was had ground to a halt as the soldiers moved from store to store handing out fliers to everyone, whether working or shopping there.

"Young man," an old woman in a walker asked, "are we being invaded?"

"No, ma'am," he reassured her with a smile. "It'll all be explained tonight at the meeting."

"But I don't drive at night."

"I'm sure you can find a way to get there. If not, give this number a call," he indicated a number on the sheet, "and we'll arrange to have someone pick you up. It's important."

"Are you going to be there?" she asked coyly as she ran a gnarled finger over his sleeve.

"Yes, ma'am," he said as he stepped away. "Everybody's going to be there."

#

Nike, when he wasn't shooting up mailboxes, or talking shit with his friends, worked as a bag boy at the grocery store at the end of the mall. Usually, he would look for any excuse to slip back into the stockroom to steal a few candy bars or cop a smoke; and today, he could have literally robbed the place blind. Nobody was paying attention. Everybody, clerks, patrons, supervisors, all of them were lined up at the front windows, watching the soldiers stopping everyone at the other end of the parking lot as they moved through the strip.

"Mommy, are those guns real?" asked a child. Her mother didn't answer but instinctively pulled her child tightly to her.

"What's going on?" someone else asked. "What are they handing out?"

"Maybe they're recruiting, or something," answered Joella, a rather pudgy teenage clerk Nike had already decided was ready for tapping. Since he was always looking for a way to get closer, he took the opportunity to slip in beside her at the window.

"Don't worry," he whispered into her ear as he slid up behind her. "I won't let anything happen to you."

With that he let his hand accidentally slide down to rest on her well rounded buttocks. Joella effectively used her elbow to knock the wind out of what she considered the runt of some subhuman litter.

Nike's gasp of pain was barely audible over the more urgent speculations at the window. The soldiers were moving in the direction of the market. No one knew whether to run. Should they pretend they were shopping, or act nonchalant about the whole thing? They ended up just remaining glued to the window, mouths hanging open, excited and afraid at the same time.

#

By three o'clock that afternoon, the line of traffic outside of town to be turned back had grown to over a hundred, including impatient truckers honking to show their agitation. One especially irate driver, Otis Tunker, a man known for having a short fuse even in the best of situations, was well on his way to exploding when it was finally his turn at the roadblock.

He shouted out his window to the young soldier blocking his way. "Fuck that, buddy, I've got produce here and it due today, so just get your skinny ass out of the way and let me through."

With that, Otis gunned his engine threateningly, thinking *ass-hole*. As he watched, the soldier slipped out of the truck's path, as expected.

What happened next, he hadn't expected. The soldier stepped up onto the driver's side running board, drew his gun and put it to Otis' head, holding it there calmly.

"Maybe I didn't make myself clear," he said, as he clicked a round into the chamber. "I asked you to turn this rig around."

Otis sat there, weighing the situation, nervous but not cowering. "You're bluffing, you little ass-hole," he challenged in his best beer-hall bravado.

The young soldier didn't say a word. He just blasted three huge holes through the roof of the cab of the truck; its noise was deafening in the enclosed space. He turned the gun back on the cowering driver.

"Jesus," was all Otis managed to get past his now stammering lips.

The young soldier slowly pressed his gun back to Otis' temple and posed a simple multiple-choice question. Only it wasn't really multiple, it was more of an 'either, or.'

"Now, sir, do you turn this rig around, or does this ass-hole dump your body at the side of the road and do it myself?"

Suddenly afraid to even move his head, Otis did cut his eyes enough to see his truck being surrounded by other soldiers, all with their weapons drawn.

What the fuck was going on? How had things gotten so far out of hand. Otis had never been really good at bar fights, more bluff than bite, and that was usually all it took. Nobody ever challenged Otis. Hell, this wasn't even a bar. He wasn't even drunk. It was broad daylight. What was going on? He had just been minding his own business, trying to deliver some potatoes and lettuce to Riverton, doing his duty. Now he had some little cock-sucker in a uniform holding a gun to his head, threatening to shoot him. Well, someone higher up was going to hear about this when he got out of here. Otis wasn't going to take this lying down. He had his rights. Otis' chain of fevered thoughts were suddenly jerked back to the present when he heard the gun, still pressed to his head, slid another round into its chamber.

"Jesus, man, whatever you want," was all he could muster, as he slipped the truck into reverse, and worked his way through a wide three-point-turn, and found himself facing away from the city. The soldier jumped off the running board of the truck and watched as Otis pulled away. Raising a hand in farewell, he shouted after the truck, "Oh, and have a nice day."

Several other drivers in line, having witnessed this confrontation, began maneuvering their cars and trucks into turning around. One of the drivers was Eric Toro, a Century One realtor from Monroe County, who had an appointment that morning with a couple in Riverton to list their house for sale. It was a last desperate effort on their part to avoid foreclosure. Eric didn't think it would work. Nobody was buying homes anywhere, much less in Riverton, but he'd do his best; or he would have, had he not been turned away.

Driving away, he kept glancing in the rear view mirror, questioning out loud to himself, "What the fuck is going on back there?" The road to Riverton had always seemed isolated, but now, even in the afternoon sunlight, it seemed to have more traffic than usual, and somehow that felt menacing. He flashed his lights at the oncoming traffic, wanting to warn them they were heading for a roadblock and a dead end.

It must have been a hell of an accident or something in Riverton to have everything shut down like it was, he thought, but then he questioned, *why hadn't he seen any racing sirens to the scene? And where was the highway patrol? What was going on?*

Seeing Shipman's Gas and Goodies coming up on the left side of the road, Eric clicked on his turn signal and slowed to make the turn into the dirt and chert parking lot. Shipman's was hardly more than a weathered roadside stand with doors, but it did have reasonably good coffee, and a bathroom that was legend for its filth and nastiness. Male commuters liked to joke that instead of going inside where the smell could be lethal, they'd just stand in the door, whip it out and aim across the room for the urinal. From the looks of the floor, it had not been a joke.

Pulling to a stop in front of Shipman's, Eric pulled out his cell phone and found it still didn't have a signal. Something had to be wrong with the phone because he had never had a problem before. Just his luck. Something big came up and his phone died. Maybe it was only calls into Riverton. On that thought, he dialed home, which was outside Riverton. The phone worked, but he hung up before anyone picked up. Shari, his wife, hadn't been all that pleased with him that morning; something about never listening, or spending too much time at work. He wasn't sure which. He hadn't been listening.

Well, if the cell phone wouldn't reach Riverton, there is always the old-fashioned way.

He got out of the car, not bothering to lock it, and went directly to the pay-phone hung at the side of the Shipman's front porch under an awning that was supposed to provide shade, but looked more like an umbrella whose spokes had been stripped of fabric. He was in luck. The phone did have a dial tone. Now, if he just had enough change to make a call. How much did it cost nowadays? He hadn't used a pay-phone in years. Fishing out coins, he held them cupped and ready in his right hand and read the instructions out loud to himself, "Dial the number first, then insert coins as directed."

That seemed simple enough. His clients in Riverton were expecting him. He had better let them know the reason for the delay. Dialing their number though, all he got was a busy signal. That didn't make sense.

This was a land-line. Surely their phone wasn't out as well. Dialing again, he got the same results, busy. Only the signal sounded more like 'out-of-order' than busy; more of a 'fuck you,' than 'call back later.'

Rolling the coins around in his fingers, he thought for a long moment and dialed again, but this time to another number he knew in Riverton. It was to an old poker friend he had known since high school who was now with the Riverton police department. Again, the same busy signal.

If he had been curious and a little concerned before, now it was becoming personal and personal worries were always a lot more frightening. Shit, who should he, or could he, call now?

Certainly not anyone in Riverton. That seemed pointless. Scanning through the contact numbers on his useless cell phone, nothing jumped out at him as worth calling, and then, it hit him. Knowing the number would not be in his personal cache, he pocketed the phone and flipped open the weathered pages of the phone book, dangling by a rusty chain, between his knees. Finding the directory he wanted in the first few pages, he ran his fingers down the numbers, until he found what he was looking for, and dialed. This time, it went through, and this time it cost him seventy-five cents.

"Hello, Highway Patrol?" he stammered, as soon as the connection was made, "Uh, I'm just curious, what's going on over in Riverton? Yeah, I know it's not your jurisdiction, but I was supposed to meet somebody there this morning, and you guys are not letting anybody in. No, I'm not joking. No, I mean, a roadblock. Some of your guys, or at least it looked like some of your guys and soldiers, with guns. No, I'm not kidding. Yeah. No. No, I've tried that. Everything's busy. No, I didn't try calling the phone company. I called you. The phone company doesn't set up military roadblocks, unless you know something I don't know. Yeah. Thanks. I'd appreciate that. Maybe they'll know. Yeah, I'll wait."

Put on hold, Eric fumbled in his pocket, and pulled out a crumpled cigarette, which he didn't light. He'd promised his wife he had stopped smoking, but she could always smell tobacco on his breath. Tobacco breath meant no sex, and he was newly married. Eric might not want to listen to her, but he would give up sucking on a grass product any day to spend the night sucking on something else. Still, he did miss the taste of a good cigarette and secretly, was already trying to find a way he could disguise the smell, if he really got desperate.

The voice on the other end of the line brought him back to the problems at hand.

"Yeah, but I thought police stations had rollover lines. Even in a town like Riverton, they wouldn't all be busy, would they? Yeah, maybe you better. I just think something bad's going down. You know, a feeling."

Whomever he was talking with obviously thought so too, and didn't waste any time in hanging up. At least, he hoped that was the reason for the sudden disconnection.

Back in Riverton's city hall, Ryder and Joel had turned the boardrooms, courtrooms and offices into their control center. Council members, who were not handing out fliers on the front-steps or town square, manned non-essential com-centers, installed by military personnel and technicians which bypassed the restrictions imposed on the other phones in the community.

In the Mayor's office, Ryder and Joel tried to get away from the noise, so they could focus on their own deadlines. Nothing was happening as easily as they had hoped.

"Are you sure it's big enough?" demanded Ryder. "It's got to hold everybody."

"It's the only place even close to big enough," Joel held up the sheets he had been working on. "There are a couple of elementary school gyms, but nothing of any size. The schools aren't all that big, and everything's been consolidated to save money. A couple of the old schools were sold off to businesses, but even those have folded. One was burned down."

"What about theaters?"

"I checked," replied Joel, checking his notes. "The last real theater closed a couple of years ago. The seats were all stripped out. The gymnasium we have is right now the best we've got to go, but it's got a lousy PA system: totally out of date. I'll try to have one thrown in with everything else coming this direction, but don't hold your breath for tonight."

"It'll have to make do. I can talk loud."

"Why would they let things go so downhill? It's a school, for God's sake."

"It's called the real world, Joel. Unlike in the government, if you don't have money, you don't buy new things. What about the Guardians? I thought they were due already."

Joel glanced at his watch before replying, "Between seventeen thirty and seventeen forty-five. They had to do some plane switching in Columbus. Riverton's airfield wouldn't handle our transports."

"Do they know the agenda?"

"They will as soon as they disembark," Ryder was assured. "One way or the other, we'll be ready for tonight."

We'd better be, thought Ryder, but he didn't say it out loud because Mayor Brandy had stuck his head in the door.

"Uh, guys, there's some problem at DQ-Charlie."

"What the fuck is a DQ-Charlie?" demanded Ryder.

The mayor blushed, "Uh, that's what we designated the roadblock on Old Town Highway. DQ for the Dairy Queen that used to be there."

#

The sun had another couple of hours in the sky, but the shadow of the moon was racing it for dominance. Evidently, nobody noticed time was running out. The roads in both directions were still congested. Several highway patrol cars from Monroe County, having cut across fields and taken every back roads they could find, finally managed to force their way to the front of the stalled line, but that was as far as they got. Soldiers and several highway patrol officers on the Riverton side of the roadblock were holding them back and refusing their demands to pass through. The exchanges had already gotten ugly by the time the Riverton Police Chief's car came racing up to the barricade, throwing gravel as it stopped. Joel and the Chief of the Riverton Police Department, Hank Williams, 'so named because he was born the year, the month and the day of the great country singer's death', got out. Tall, lean, and lanky like his namesake, Hank was nervous but trying to remain calm. Waving off the guards at the barricade, as he approached, he stepped around the blockade to address his friends from the Highway Patrol.

"Tyler, how's it hanging?"

"Hank, don't you 'how's it hanging' with me. What's all this about? Those fuckers over there won't let us through."

"Sorry about that, I meant to fill you in. Civil defense, they're using the town for a test for a couple of days. Germ warfare training, that sort of thing. I'm not real sure myself what it all entails."

"But they're not letting people in or out," Chief Tyler protested.

"Yeah, well, that's what it would really be like. You ought to see what they've done to the square. Hollywood make-up artists putting blotches on people, making 'em look real sickly."

"But they've got guys, like over there," he said pointing, "dressed as highway patrol officers. That's against every rule in the book."

"Costumes, just costumes," volunteered Joel. "Badges are all fake. Movies do it all the time."

Chief Tyler, who had known Hank Williams since they were both kids, kept his focus on his friend. Something seemed wrong. "When did you find out about all this?" he questioned.

"Couple of weeks ago. I didn't think it was going to be this big."

"Why'd they pick you?"

"Don't know," Hank answered, "but they're paying enough for a couple of new squad cars, fully equipped, so we figured we'd go along for the ride."

"Shit," whistled Chief Tyler, looking past Chief Williams, as though he could see around the many curves into Riverton. "This ought to be something to see."

"Maybe tomorrow. These guys, they're playing it for real today. They say they'll shoot anyone who tries to get in or out." Both old friends laughed at that, though neither quite knew what they were laughing about.

#

At seventeen twenty-seven, that same afternoon, two small planes landed in tandem on the tarmac of the shuttered Riverton airport. Both planes barely had time to stop before twelve troopers, in silver and maroon uniforms, leapt out of each and made a dash for the waiting buses. Seth, Miles, Angie and Jay were among those in the first uniformed group to hit the ground.

Inside the first bus, they quickly and silently moved to their seats and watched, as their planes took off to be replaced almost immediately by two other planes flying in to land. One of their instructors from the island swung himself onto the bus as it started to pull away from the field. He stood, his shoulders rock-solid and level, at the front of the bus, totally unaffected by the jolts and bumps of the uneven road. His muscled legs absorbed the impact as though he was sliding on smooth ice.

All eyes were on him as he spoke. "Okay, team, this is it. Welcome to the future."

CHAPTER XXIV

For almost an hour before the time specified on the handout fliers, the citizens of Riverton began showing up at the school, slowly gathering near the open doors of the high-school gymnasium, their nervousness and fear clearly visible. Nothing like this had ever happened to them. It was almost like their town had been turned into a concentration camp. How could this happen? This was America. Soldiers couldn't just come in and take over a town. But they had. And now, here, its citizens stood, like cattle, afraid to move forward and afraid of the consequences if they didn't. This was a town unused to fear. Kevin King, the local postmaster and a royal pain in everyone's ass, arrived five minutes before the appointed time, and moved through the crowd with all the righteous anger of Riverton's Guardian.

"Get out of my way," he yelled as he pushed his way up to the open doors. Then turning back, he raised his hands and a hush fell over the waiting crowd.

"Well, don't just stand there, like fucking sheep," he shouted. "Let's get in there and find out what this shit is all about once and for all." With that, he turned and entered the building and the crowd erupted in angry agreement as everyone fought to be the next to stand tall before the invaders.

Inside, a dozen Guardians, including Angie, made sure each person was being handed a sealed packet.

"Please remember," she said to each recipient, "these packets are to remain sealed until further notice. Do not open them until instructed to do so."

"And what if I fucking don't give a shit what you say and open it any way."

Another Guardian turned slowly to the protester and remarked with eyes that could have bored a hole in steel, "Trust me, I don't think you want to try that. Not today. Not now."

In the center of the gym, a portable stage had been assembled with a podium, several chairs and a microphone. A government camera crew was still working to set up video equipment in front of the stage. Ryder stood by the stage, while Joel checked last minute details. Scanning the audience, he noted, "Not bad, should be close to three quarters, maybe more." Then noticing, he added, "What's with the segregation?"

Joel glanced down the left side of the gymnasium where the attendees, most of whom were black or ethnically-mixed, stood boisterously waving to draw others of their color to join them on their side of the court.

"It's the west side of town," Joel observed. "A lot more resistant there to us being here. That turnout is only half of what it should be. They think tonight's a white thing and doesn't involve them."

Ryder merely said, "Let's do a sweep of that neighborhood tomorrow first thing, and round up any that missed tonight. We may be doing this a couple of times before we get them all."

"How soon do you want us to start? Hold for stragglers or set a precedent?" Joel questioned as he watched the crowd becoming more and more agitated.

"Let's give 'em a little longer. The more we reach tonight, the less chance of problems tomorrow," Ryder decided, then turned to another aide holding out a mobile-con unit to him.

"Ryder," he barked into the receiver, then listened for a moment, visibly stiffening.

"No," he stated in no uncertain terms. "No exceptions. Not until I give the word."

At the roadblock outside of town, Arnie Barker, a twenty-four-year-old Texan, recruited into the Guardians in Denver the same day as Seth and the others, had been put in charge of the roadblocks. Hanging up the receiver of his field unit, he turned back to Marshall Foster and his Channel 7 News team.

"I'm sorry, sir, it's as I told you. No exceptions."

"But I'm the Press," demanded America's number one journalist, "and this badge says, I can go anywhere I damn well please. Now, get out of my way."

"I'm sorry, sir," Arnie apologized in his best Texan drawl, "but my orders were..."

"To hell with your orders," Foster cut him off.

"My orders were to 'shoot' you if you tried to get past," continued the young man facing Marshall.

At that, every soldier within visual range, unslung his weapon. This mass movement and the staccato clicking release of their safeties effectively cut off Foster and his crew's protest for the time being. Even Foster was at a loss for words, which was totally unlike anything he had experienced before in his life.

Reluctantly, he motioned his crew back into the news van. Once they were inside, and the doors were closed, they saw the soldiers lower their rifles and return to a more relaxed stance.

Foster slowly turned to his crew waiting nervously in the back of the van. "They're bluffing," he challenged, then turning to his driver, he ordered, "break through that barricade."

"What?" shot back the incredulous driver.

"You heard me! Gun it!"

"Marshall, are you crazy? Those are government soldiers out there. They've got guns."

"Since when did a dumpy, little town like Riverton become off-limits. Bullshit, something's up, and I intend to find out what. Now, goddamnit, do as I say, or I'll do it myself."

Before the driver could even say, "Count me out," Marshall kicked his driver's foot aside and gunned the gas pedal himself. Unfortunately, or fortunately for the van's occupants, the gear was not engaged.

Outside, in one mass move, every soldier wheeled and took aim at the news van.

"Shit!" cried the driver, as he tried to duck and cover his head.

"Fuck, those guns are real," yelled the cameraman, throwing himself down to hide behind the seats.

Foster was angrier now than he had ever been in his life. Nobody had the right to keep him from anything he wanted, and right now, he wanted to show those ass-wipe teenagers with guns that they didn't scare him. Smacking his driver on the shoulder, he yelled, "They wouldn't dare shoot. Hit it!"

The driver's hands were shaking so hard, he fumbled twice before he got the van thrown into gear.

"Go!" screamed Foster, and the engine roared. Instantly, all eight soldiers opened up, blasting away at the tires of the news van.

Inside the van, Foster's camera crew were still screaming before they realized the shooting had stopped, and they were unhurt. Foster, pulling himself out from beneath the dashboard, was furious and leapt out of the van, spewing venom and threats even before his feet hit the ground.

"You fuckin' stupid shits! You'll pay for this! Do you know who I am? I'm Marshall Foster, the number one newscaster in this country and..."

Suddenly, his voice stopped in his throat. Every soldier's rifle had been raised, and Foster could clearly see the infrared dots peppering his chest and heart, and one dot was even circling his groin. He glanced up into the inscrutable face of Arnie Barker in time to hear him say to his squadron, "Anybody here impressed?"

There was a resounding "click" of new bullets being loaded into chambers, and Foster slowly backed up to his van and got in. "Let's get out of here," he heard himself saying.

"How? We don't have any tires left," whined the driver, still frightened.

"Drive on the rims, I don't give a fuck. Just get us out of here."

Back in the gymnasium, the mood of the crowd hadn't grown ugly yet, but when Ryder headed for the stage, all bets were off. His voice swept a reluctant hush over the audience.

"Ladies and gentlemen," he began, making sure his focus was directed equally to both sides of the room. "My name is Richard Ryder, and I'm here representing the President of the United States."

"Big fucking deal," came a voice from the back of the gym, but Ryder ignored it.

"What I have to say to you tonight will have a major impact on your lives, your town, and your country."

And then, he began to methodically lay out the plan for the crowd. Literally, months had gone into the preparation of this presentation: what words would be used, what sequence would be followed, continuously simplifying, detailing and clarifying. At the last minute, Ryder had decided on his own to eliminate the first-half of the presentation and cut straight to the chase.

The first-half had dealt with the history of Riverton and the surrounding county, its indigenous peoples, and those who came after, and while that history was the groundwork upon which the entire project was based, it was only the door. The people facing him that evening, however, only cared about what was on the other side of that door. As Ryder spoke, his words were met with curiosity and mumbling, then stunned silence, and then, sudden gasps. The deeper he got into his presentation, those gasps turned into rumbling waves of disbelief, then verbal fear, and finally, anger and helplessness.

The entire audience had gotten the message; nobody in that room doubted, from that very moment on, the lives they had always known, prior to this meeting, no longer existed. In fact, they had just been given a blueprint for the destruction of everything they had ever known, and if they were to believe what was being said, it was already happening or it had already happened, and they were helpless to do anything about it.

Still, some were not going down without a fight. Kevin King, the postmaster, was one of the first to leap to his feet in outrage and stormed to the microphone to square off with Ryder.

Waving the information sheet he had now been allowed to open, he screamed, "This is a bunch of crap! You can't just buy towns!"

Ryder's voice cut him off, "Yes, sir, you can, if it's bankrupt, and Riverton was bankrupt. Is bankrupt. There are government bailouts, and there are government buy-outs. This is a buy-out, and Riverton is now officially government property, like a national park, only with more restrictions."

"But we live here," Kevin shouted back, to the crowd's angry agreement.

Ryder raised his hands to try to restore order. Once they had calmed down, he continued, "Yes, you live here, and we hope you'll continue to do so."

The Postmaster angrily began waving the papers in his clutched fist, screaming, "With these rules?"

"Yes, with those rules. You have been asked to become a part of an experiment."

"I wouldn't call being invaded being 'asked,'" came a shout from a man in the crowd, whose voice was so loud he didn't need a microphone.

"But that is the express purpose of this meeting tonight. You *are* being 'asked' to join us. We are giving you the opportunity. If you choose not to, you may leave at any time, but if you stay, you will be living under a new set of laws."

"I'm an American citizen, and I know my rights," shouted a woman grabbing the microphone from the Pharmacist and pushing him aside, "and you can't just..."

"Yes, ma'am, we can," interrupted Ryder, "because if you chose to remain in Riverton County, you will no longer be living in America, and you will no longer have those so-called 'rights', at least in the legal sense."

"That's not possible," cried another voice from the crowd, which sounded more frightened than angry.

"But it is," Ryder assured them. "You see, as of eight forty-five this morning, Riverton County, your county, officially seceded from the United States of America."

The entire audience was now on their feet, but after the initial gasps of horror and disbelief, most were still too stunned to say anything. All eyes focused on the man before them.

"I repeat, this is a government experiment. You are being asked to become a part of it. To live by these rules. To give up certain 'inalienable rights.'"

"Like the right to bear arms?" came a question from an obvious veteran. He was missing an eye, and one side of his face looked like it had been melted by napalm.

"That's right," Ryder replied. "Guns are outlawed: All guns. Except for the police, and they have been specially trained. No weapons will be allowed in this community, in this country, and that's what Riverton has become—its own country."

"But how do I protect myself?" asked one man who appeared more politically bent to the right, than frightened.

"You don't protect yourself. That's the responsibility of our police, and this police force has been specially trained for civilian protection. They are now your Guardians. In fact, that is what they are called, The Guardians."

"But I'm a hunter," another irate citizen shouted from his side of the room.

"So hunt," smiled Ryder, with his hands outstretched in a giving manner. "We never said you couldn't own a weapon, a fine hunting rifle or pistol."

Murmurs of approval greeted this statement, but turned into yells of protests on the next.

"You just can't keep it at home."

Raising his hands to get order, he continued, "Any time you want to hunt, or go to the firing range for target practice, you simply check your weapons out from a convenient storage control center and return it immediately upon completion of the activity. It is true that there is a limit to the type of weapons that may be owned, and as much as I hate to say this, men, you're going to have to start giving Bambi a chance."

This brought a surprising ripple of applause.

"So there'll be no more Uzi's, machine guns, or similar rapid-firing assault weapons allowed for any reason."

"But that's not fair, I'm a collector," shouted one irate gun owner.

"Not anymore," Ryder responded pointedly. "At least, not a weapons collector."

The meeting was going a little better than expected, thought Joel about a half hour later. Of course, he wasn't really sure what he expected. In Los Angeles or New York, Ryder and all of them would be dead by now, having been overwhelmed by irate citizenry. But here, in Riverton, Ryder had been right in speculating that the people were so beaten down by everything that had gone wrong in their community, they didn't have much fight left in them. Only a couple of the more irate citizens had tried to leave and been forced to return to their seats, and only one of those had become so vocal, he had to be restrained. Other than that, Joel was feeling pretty confident that this plan was going to work.

The next hurdle was taking everyone through the rules of the new Riverton, and of course, several people were already lined up at the microphones to protest, but their protests were more in the form of questions than actual hostility. Ryder was a master at answering questions.

"There's a very good reason why we listed them that way. Because in America," he waved his hand, as though to indicate some place out there, not here in Riverton, "they seem to have forgotten that with every right, there is a responsibility. Liberty is a partnership. So, what do you get if you stay in Riverton?"

Everyone quieted down and Joel could see them visibly leaning forward.

"One, you get the right and the responsibility to live safely in your community without the fear of violence. Think of what that means. You have the right to walk on your streets at night, sleep with your windows open, your doors, or leave your car unlocked without fear; that's our goal. Wouldn't you like to see that happen? Think back to that time, if you're old enough to remember it, when it was actually safe to live in your city."

Some of the older audience nodded, remembering.

"Two," Ryder continued, "you have the right to raise your families, but along with that comes the responsibility for them."

"Three, the right to a quality education for everyone, and the responsibility to see that that right is never jeopardized by violence, vandalism, or disruptive behavior."

At that, Joel could hear a smattering of applause from the otherwise silent crowd.

"Four, you have the right and responsibility to work, to have a meaningful job and be paid for it. A full day's pay for a full day's labor, and the benefits that come with it. That, of course, eliminates the need for unemployment, and except for extremely special cases, that also eliminates disability. We expect everyone, who decides to stay in Riverton, to work to make this community the thriving metropolis we think it can be."

"Our goal is 98% employment within six months, and I know that sounds ridiculous, considering the high rate of unemployment you're now experiencing, but we have new companies already lined up and committed to moving into the area."

"Look," he explained, "I could go on through this entire list, but you can read it yourself. Discuss it among your friends. We'll be holding meetings every day, and there will be someone here to answer your questions twenty-four seven, but it all boils down to this: How much are you willing to give up to gain back some of the American dream?"

In Chicago, Junisha Butler was worried about keeping her family alive. She was about to begin her nightly ritual and turn down the volume on her battered old television when she caught Channel 7 Late Night News. Marshall Foster and his co-host, Lisa, were discussing his breaking report on some town somewhere called Riverton.

Foster was already in full steam, " ...with the entire county cordoned off and all communications in and out stopped."

"And you're saying, they actually opened fire on you and your crew," chirped in his co-host with a flip of her hair.

"Yes, and without the slightest provocation. Soldiers opened fire and practically destroyed our new van."

Behind them, Junisha could see a picture of that news van. It didn't look so bad to her, until she noticed the close-up of the tires. Hell, flattened tires were the norm in her neighborhood, but evidently not where Mr. Foster lived.

"What has been the official response so far?" came Lisa's concerned and perfectly timed response.

The camera pushed in for a close shot of the good-looking Marshall Foster. "According to a spokesman for the White House, no one is allowed in or out of the area in question until further notice. A series of tests are being conducted..."

The sudden sound of gunshots in the streets outside her own apartment distracted Junisha from the rest, and she quickly reached out to make sure two of her three children were still sleeping safely beside her on the sofa. For once, her older son was also home, though not asleep. He stood at the window, looking out at the night through the ragged slit in its padded storage blanket covering.

Marshall Foster's voice continued to drone on, but Junisha missed whatever it was he said next. In truth, she didn't really care. The only world she cared about was in the room around her.

CHAPTER XXV

At the 'Whistling Pig', the day following the meeting at the gym, the diner was packed with not just the regular crowd, but also with more than two dozen stragglers who felt the need to be with others after the meeting the previous night.

Abe Johnson, a former press operator at the Wurtham Box Company, was in his regular seat at the Pig's lengthy breakfast counter holding court. But most eyes were on the television set hanging on the wall over the service window. It was set for the morning news.

Throughout the siege, as they referred to it, television had remained their only one-sided contact with the outside world, the normal world. And it was terrifying to everyone in Riverton that the previous night's programming had gone on as usual: no special announcements, no alerts, nothing.

It was like being in the midst of a tornado, desperate for help, and finding out nobody even knew you were in trouble. Abe had several friends who were ham operators, but quickly learned that the ham and two-way radio operators' equipment were confiscated within the first hour of the invasion, even before the soldiers arrived in town. That meant there had to be an advance team already stationed in Riverton before the soldiers arrived; traitors in their midst who had mapped out every person with the potential to warn the world of the attack on their city, and had rendered them harmless. Everyone in the diner had an opinion on these possible traitors and who they could be until Dessi, the Pig's short-order cook, who actually knew something about short-wave operations, having been in communications in Vietnam, reminded the diners that it didn't take a traitor to hone in on ham operators, just a military receiver. Of course, that observation put Dessi on Abe's short list of traitor suspects.

Bea, the younger, stockier and slightly prettier of the two morning waitresses, could hardly focus on her work as she poured coffee into half-empty cups. Jerking her head towards the television newscaster, and at the same time, almost pouring scalding coffee into Abe's lap, she said, "Look at that. Last night, nothing, and this morning, we're all over the news, but nobody knows anything. God, what I wouldn't give for an inside line to the Enquirer. I'd be rich."

"You'd probably also be dead," remarked Abe, then added, "hey!" as he pushed her hand away and slid back to avoid the overflowing cup. Having thus saved his private jewels as he liked to refer to them, he warned everybody, "I don't think they're fuckin' 'bout this. You see those guns last night?"

Natalie, the Pig's other morning waitress, was setting down Old Walter's daily order of 'double low stacks, hash browns crisp, and bacon burned.' He also liked his coffee hot, no cream, no sugar. He was called Old Walter because he was, but the name originated when he was a four; his mother, not the most imaginative of women, had named Walter's new baby brother Walter as well. Evidently, she had done it to piss off their father, a man named Hiram, or maybe she was throwing something in his face or telling something to the world nobody cared about hearing. Either way, Hiram split. No one else named Walter ever stepped forward to fill the void, and Old Walter had been Old Walter ever since. Now seventy-two, the old man barely looked up at the intrusion of the waitress. He was too busy jawing with his cronies, Bertie and JJ. All were retired. All were over seventy. And all were opinionated as hell. Eating at the Whistling Pig was a daily ritual, and had been since its previous owner, and the one before that. If one of these old guys didn't show up, the others would automatically know he was dead.

At that moment, Old Walter was in the midst of making another point. Natalie could always tell he was making a point when he punctuated each word with a jab of his finger.

"But nobody's...asking...the big...question," the old man jabbed. "The twenty-four-thousand-dollar one. At what price??? Looks like to me, we're giving up everything."

Natalie couldn't help butting in as she replenished Bertie's plate of biscuits for the second time.

"What are we giving up?" she asked. "I mean, think about it. What are they asking you to give up? The right to kill somebody? To steal from somebody? Old Walter, you don't do that anyway."

JJ, forever the pessimist and the reactionary of the group, grabbed a biscuit off the protesting Bertie's plate and proclaimed, "Well, I'm sure as hell not stayin'. If they'll buy my place, I'm gone. I'm up to here with this town." He made a slash mark with his biscuit in the air at eye-level.

"JJ, this town is up to here with you," laughed Old Walter, making a slash mark two feet over JJ's head.

Then all three men were laughing and stuffing their mouths with Bertie's biscuits.

"Up yours," mumbled JJ, as he tried to swallow and lick his finger at the same time. Bertie just pulled his plate of biscuits away from the other two. No wonder he always had to get it refilled.

Miriam Toking, Bertie's wife, was sitting at the next table. Usually she pretended she wasn't paying attention to anything the men were saying at their table; and in most cases it was the truth. She seldom interjected with an opinion in anything, but on this particular morning, she did.

"Well, I like what they're doing with the schools. I only wish they had done this when our kids were younger. It just makes good sense. Running classes from seven-thirty 'til six-thirty, just like work hours. We could have left for our day's work at the same time and all been home at the same time every night."

"With the shifts I work, fat lot of good that's gonna do me," remarked Natalie in passing, on her way to get Miriam another donut to dunk in her coffee. Natalie was a single mother of three.

Miriam came in every morning with her husband but she never sat at the same table with him. She said it was his chance to be with the other old farts, and her chance to some peace and quiet, while enjoying a couple of those fresh doughnuts Natalie slipped her every morning.

Natalie knew the real reason for Miriam being there was to keep an eye on Bertie after his last heart attack.

Topping off Miriam's coffee and slipping her a second glazed doughnut, Natalie glanced towards the T.V. set and said, "I don't think they thought about someone like me," to which Miriam responded, "I think they're just trying to make sure at least one parent's at home when the kids are."

"Like I said, I don't think they thought about someone like me."

Not everybody's marriage in Riverton had lasted as long as Miriam and Bertie's.

Abe was shouting again from his counter seat. Natalie couldn't tell whether he was shouting at the television or something someone said. Could be either, or both. It wasn't her problem; Abe was sitting at Bea's counter. Just one of the perks of seniority.

Abe was holding up the yellow sheets of paper everybody had been given at the previous night's meeting.

"Bullshit! These laws aren't laws. They're a prescription for disaster. Did you see what they say about drugs?"

Everyone had, of course, but he said it anyway, "They're legal."

If that pronouncement caused a stir the first time Abe shouted it at the Whistling Pig, it caused a lot more than just a stir in the Riverton Middle School gymnasium later that morning.

Nike, always the center of attention if he could arrange it, was one of the first students to line up at the microphone to ask questions of Miles and Seth, who had been assigned to explain the new rules of the experiment to the students.

"Come on, man. What does it mean, legal?" laughed Nike, fanning more than a few catcalls and derisive disbelief.

Although the school's principal standing behind Miles looked nervous, Miles was very clear in his answer. "Just what it says. As long as you're fifteen or over, what you do with your own body is your own right."

At least half the student body raucously cheered at that announcement, while the other half seemed stunned.

Miles continued, "So if you want to buy drugs that's your right."

More cheering, glad handing, and high-fiving erupted through the bleachers.

"But along with that 'right' comes some responsibility."

This came from Seth, stepping in beside Miles. "That's the sticky part because, while it's not against the law to buy and use drugs," he said, "it is very much against the law for anyone to sell drugs."

"Shit," Nike complained, "I knew there was a catch."

"No catch," replied Miles. "As long as you are over fifteen, you can buy whatever you want at your local drug store for your own personal use, and that means for you personally to use. And you can buy it at a price that's about a tenth of what it would cost you on the street."

Cheers erupted again throughout the gym. Billy Harker, a.k.a. Glide, standing and waving his arm, shouted from the bleachers, "How about meth, or coke?"

Rebok followed his lead. "Or heroin?"

Seth raised a pointed finger and directed it to the two vocal boys. "Whatever you want. The way we look at it, if you're stupid enough to do drugs, then that's your problem. But it's no longer going to be this community's problem. So there's not going to be any more slipping around and playing cool. You can do drugs whenever you want in the privacy of your own homes, or the homes of your friends. That's up to your parents. But, and I want you to understand this, you can't get trashed out in public places where your smoke or your limited capacities might cause harm to yourself or others. And if you are stupid enough to OD, you just OD. Nobody's sending for an ambulance to bail you out. There'll be no paramedics to hold your hand or keep you from strangling on your vomit."

The crowd noise had grown considerably less rowdy. "You're on your own from now on if you use drugs."

"And don't even think of being caught driving," added Miles, "or doing drugs with a minor. A minor has been redefined as anyone under fifteen years of age. And most importantly, don't, I repeat, don't ever be caught selling drugs, or buying them for someone else, anyone else. There will be no sharing of drugs, or drug paraphernalia. If you've got a problem, it's your problem. And if you get into trouble with that problem, you pay the price."

At the Riverton High School, where Jay and another Guardian were speaking, the students were much more racially mixed and openly hostile. These students didn't bother even going to the microphones that had been set up. If they had something to say, they shouted it.

Jay was trying to explain, "And that means no more gang colors, and no more graffiti. Marking is vandalism, the destruction of property. And you really don't want to do that under this new system."

At that, someone in the crowd shouted a loud "Fuck you" and the rest of the students began chanting. Jay noticed that the teachers, although they tried to quiet everyone down, were really helpless in the situation.

Jay simply raised the volume of his microphone and continued.

"And no weapons in school. That means guns, knives, chains, mace, or anything else that could be considered a weapon."

One thick-necked six-foot gang member jumped up at that point and began humping the girl in front of him. Most of the other students went wild and some shouted at Jay, "What about that? His body's a lethal weapon."

Jay only smiled and said, "I'm sure it is but if you're caught with any other type of weapon, you'll be taken from school and punished according to the new law."

This brought even more jeers of laughter, with students mooning the stage, begging to be spanked.

One especially angry young woman with the mouth of a sailor shouted, "What you gonna do, motherfucker? Expel us?"

Jay just shook his head. "No, under the new law, you break the rules and we terminate you."

That response brought even louder pandemonium with laughter and jeers of "I'll be back."

#

Meetings were being held everywhere for the next couple of days in Riverton with Ryder, Joel and the Guardians splitting up the task of making sure the town understood exactly what they were committing themselves to if they stayed in the experiment.

At a local business association luncheon held monthly at the Whistling Pig, Angie had been assigned to address the group. Although normally everyone ordered lunch during these meetings, on this occasion, aside from cups of steaming hot coffee and a couple of ice teas for the transplanted southerners, nobody had any appetite. The membership of the business association of Riverton had shrunk over the previous four years from over two hundred active members to less than fifty; and of those, only twenty-five usually bothered to show up. On this day, Angie faced forty-nine members.

Angie stood at the front of the room in her Guardian uniform addressing the crowd. Prior to her being introduced, the old juke-box, that usually could be counted on to fill the banquet room with original oldies like *Wake up Little Susie, Dream* and *Rockin' Robin*, had been unplugged for the occasion. Evidently that was a big event in itself. In all the thirty years since it had been installed, an antique by any standard, the glass and chrome-domed Wurlitzer had never been unplugged before. Although the restaurant had changed hands many times over the years, the instrument, with its keys to a world of past memories and better times, had never been unplugged. There was even some fear that it might never start again when reconnected. "That would be a really bad omen for Riverton," said a worried Stanley Harbuckle, the current owner, as he stood back and surveyed the lifeless machine. Angie could tell by the look in the man's eyes that he wasn't kidding. Almost everybody gathered in that room saw that machine as Riverton itself.

So, standing at the lead table, she got right to the point.

"I don't have to tell you how much money is lost each year just to vandalism alone. You're all business people and I'm sure you have your own horror stories, but just as an example, last year in Riverton, your schools spent over $100,000 of your limited budget on just repairing destroyed or stolen property in the school buildings. It's been so bad in Riverton, you've had to close down two of your high school campuses just because you couldn't afford to make repairs. Think how that multiplies over this entire community. That's lost revenue, wasted revenue. This program will effectively stop that waste immediately."

"And think about the cost to your businesses. Petty theft, shoplifting. Think how much that is costing each of you on a personal basis. I wager that a twenty percent loss in inventory wouldn't be too far off base for most of you. Just think how much more profit you could make if we stopped this type of behavior completely? And the other side of that coin is how much savings you could pass on to your customers if your prices aren't having to be jacked up to cover the costs of shoplifting. And that's exactly what you've been doing, what you've had to do to survive. You know it and we know it.

"Well, what we're offering is an entirely new way of doing business, ethically, responsibly, and financially rewarding for everyone concerned. This program doesn't take anything away from you but gives you back the dreams and goals you had when you first chose Riverton as the place to open your business."

"But I've run out of money. It's too late," said Doug Browning, the owner of the last dry-cleaner in town. "Maybe three years ago it would have helped, but it's too late now. I can't afford to stay open."

Angie smiled at him. "See me after the meeting. In fact, any of you in a similar situation, stay after and let me explain our new incentives to keeping your businesses open. I'm not talking charity or free hand-outs, but I am talking financial incentives and low, low interest loans to get re-established and help you grow your new business, and in turn, help you grow your new town. Any more questions?"

Some of the other groups Angie faced during those weeks were not as easily placated.

At RAM, the Riverton Ministerial Association, held in the basement of the Bethel Baptist Church, all religious leaders and denominations were represented except for the priest from Saint Andrews and the rabbi from Anshe Emes synagogue. Somehow, they had not been informed of the hurriedly-called meeting.

Angie and Miles were the ones sent to answer questions.

"What about abortion?" The question hung there expectantly, all eyes on Angie as though she would have to be the one to answer it. So, she did.

"Except in specific, medically-approved cases, abortion will not be permitted in Riverton."

Sighs of relief spread through the room.

"But what about a woman's right to choose?" asked the Presbyterian minister.

"Under our new laws, everything is predicated on *No Harm*. In abortion issues, in *Right to Life* issues, the question becomes, '*Whose right—the mother's, or the child's?* While a mother may have the right to abort, she does not have the right to take a life. And life is defined as a viable, healthy embryo."

"What about rape victims? Or incest?"

"Rape and incest are termination offenses."

"What about teenagers accidentally getting..."

"Knocked up?" asked Miles. "You, as parents, better make sure that doesn't happen unless you want another child in your home. There are no easy passes. If your child is old enough to be sexually active, you need to take steps to make sure there are no unwanted pregnancies."

"And," added Angie, "you better find out who your children are hanging out with because the parents of both the mother and father will be responsible for that baby until the parents have finished high school and are working, whether the couple are then together or not. Also, be aware that any male or female, regardless of age, who fathers or mothers more than two out-of-wedlock or financially unsupported children will be sterilized since they obviously aren't capable of protecting themselves."

The thought of male sterilization had several of the ministers crossing their legs. The next topic had them on their feet.

"Since sex seems to be of such interest to your gentlemen and ladies of the cloth, we might as well make sure you understand that in Riverton, under the new laws, prostitution is now legal."

There was a collective gasp.

Angie jumped in with, "It has to be. It's a victimless crime. As long as the woman or man is of age and agrees willingly to provide that service..."

The Pentecostal minister beat the Baptist to the floor.

"You mean, men? Homosexuals too?"

"Victimless crimes," reminded Angie.

"But they're preying on our children," cried a member of the Four Square ministerial staff.

"That's not homosexuality," Miles clarified. "That's child molestation. They are not the same thing."

"But you're condoning this evil in our community."

"The morals of this community are your concerns," Angie said. "The legal system is ours and we intend to control it."

"Prostitutes swarming the streets?"

"No," Miles assured them. "Right now, you've got prostitutes and pimps working most of your downtown streets, especially around the wharves. Well, under our system, that's all gone, especially pimps. There are no more pimps. Prostitution is governmentally controlled. It's legal...and it's taxed...treated like any other business with the added requirement of weekly medical check-ups."

"And now, we're talking about only one street instead of blocks," Angie told them. "One street on the outskirts of town. Several buildings have been set aside specifically for this business, and anything else dealing with the selling of sexual materials like bookstores, adult videos, and things like that."

"But we're not talking about creating a red-light slum," said Miles. "This street will appear like any other nicely maintained row of houses."

"In fact, many of them are rather charming Victorians," chimed in Angie, "and the activities and number of women and men working there will be strictly enforced and controlled."

The Pentecostal minister was outraged. "We won't stand for it. God demands we reject fornication. Or do you reject God? Or is protesting evil against the law now too?"

"Of course not," assured Angie. "You can protest all you want. You can march. You can picket. You can rail against anything you want, just as long as you don't destroy any property, vandalize, or unduly disrupt business by blocking access."

#

That night in the Riverton Council Chamber in City Hall, special phone lines had been set up for the Guardians and designated staff to be able to contact family and loved ones to help mitigate some of the misconceptions about the takeover in Riverton. The phone lines for the rest of the community would be opened only after the new law had taken effect.

Seth's first call had of course been to Rachel.

"Seth, are you okay?" were the first words out of her mouth. "I've been watching the news and am terrified. Are you okay?"

"Honey, I'm fine," he cut in. "I'm all right. Yeah, we've got reporters swarming all around the roadblocks, but everything's fine here."

"But I heard...the contamination"

"There's no contamination. It's not anything like that. It's just the experiment."

"What do you mean, 'experiment?'"

"I can't say anything just yet, but Rachel, if this works like we think it will, it's going to change everything."

"Seth, baby, this is scaring me."

"Rache, please, just trust me."

"But what do you mean, it's going to change everything?"

"I mean, everything, Rache. And I'm going to be stationed here a long time. We can get a house and you and the baby can..."

"Not here in Los Angeles?"

"I know that's what we talked about, but...I can't explain it now, but you'll love it here in Riverton. It's beautiful and it has four seasons and we can get a house, a real house with a yard and..."

Seth noticed the signal that his time was almost up. "Look, honey, just trust me. I'm running out of time on this call."

"What do you mean you're running out of time? I don't understand."

"We just getting set up now and things are still pretty unsettled right now. No, not dangerous, just changing. I can't explain it all now...but in a couple more days, everyone will know, then we can make some plans of our own, and I'll have more time to talk. I love you."

The line went dead before Rachel even had a chance to respond.

#

About a mile away in one of Riverton's older subdivisions, Doug Johnson stepped out on his screened porch to bring a coat to his wife, Doris, as she watched yet another neighbor's moving van hurriedly closing its doors. The evacuation had been going on since midnight when the prices had been set on homes going up for sale. Vans and trucks had been rounded up throughout the county, and others had been requisitioned by the invaders, as Doris referred to the Guardians. In their neighborhood alone, almost every other house was being abandoned and the sound of moving furniture, cursed frustrations, and trucks moving in and out of the area had been almost non-stop.

"It'll be okay," Doug said, as he wrapped the coat around her.

"But Doug, everyone's leaving..."

"Well, we're not. This is our home. I don't care what they're paying. This is our home."

"But nothing's going to be worth anything with all those empty houses," Doris said, not for the first time. The worry was etched on her face. "What's this place going to worth then? I just can't stand it, we're going to lose everything."

"No," her husband assured her, gently brushing a strand of hair out of her eyes. "Maybe, at first, it'll look like that, but I don't think so in the long run. If this thing works like they say it will, I should be buying every one of these houses myself, right now."

#

Outside of town, as the first loaded vans were processed out and allowed to cross through the roadblock, leaving Riverton, representatives from almost every news media service in the country were swarming over the deserters, trying to get interviews, as the Guardians tried to minimize the congestion. It was a madhouse of confusion.

One frustrated ex-Rivertonian shouted to the reporters and cameras from his car window, "They're crazy in there. Want to do away with all the laws, and start over. We're getting out."

Another older couple whose car was pulling a small U-Haul loaded to the brink, slowed when a reporter waved them over. Cranking down the window of the driver's side, the elderly woman driver shyly responded to the shouted questions, "Well, it just seemed a good time to go. My James," she indicated her husband sitting in the passenger, looking dazed, "hadn't been able to find work there anyway, so when they offered to buy us out, it wasn't a hard decision. We have children and grandchildren in Xenia."

"Is anyone being threatened in there?" came the unmistakable voice of Marshall Foster, and she looked up and smiled in recognition. "Oh, good heavens no, not that I know of. Everybody's been real nice. It's just sort of scary with all those soldiers and nobody knowing what's really going to happen."

This wasn't the answer Marshall was expecting, and he quickly turned away to search for another sound-bite more appropriate to the broadcast he had already planned in his head.

#

At the Riverton County Jail, handcuffed prisoners were being loaded into a bus with bars on its windows. Uniformed Guardians were assisting Chief Williams and his one remaining deputy in handling the twenty-four prisoners who had been temporarily housed in the Riverton jail, awaiting trial.

As the last prisoner stepped up into the bus, the Chief waved to the driver his okay, "That's the last. Get 'em into Columbus. They're expecting you. Tyler's not happy about it, but is expecting you."

Both he and Deputy Minkus watched as the bus pulled away. Homer Minkus, who was just six months away from retirement, had been kept on when others on the police force had been laid off. Since then, Hank had been secretly paying Homer's salary out of his own pocket. If Homer had known about this special arrangement, he would not have accepted it. Homer Minkus was nothing if not a proud man. Nobody who knew about the arrangement would ever break Chief Williams' trust.

Homer turned to one of the Guardians standing behind the chief and asked, "Okay, so what do we do now since we've dumped all our outstanding citizens on our neighboring counties?"

The Guardian simply shrugged and began rolling up his sleeves, "We start cleaning up those cells for other uses."

#

In Los Angeles, Rachel sat nursing her baby as she watched the news broadcast from Riverton. Mama Slavin sat beside her. Neither woman spoke as the camera moved in on a large press conference being held by Ryder on the Riverton courthouse steps.

A voice, easily recognized as belonging to Marshall Foster, whispered over the proceedings.

"For those of you who've just tuned in, this is our first live broadcast from within the town of Riverton."

Rachel scanned the screen for a glimpse of Seth, but the focus was solely on Ryder, who was speaking now from a podium set up on the courthouse steps.

"The legal changes are major. In civil and business lawsuits, we will follow the lead of Singapore and have the attorneys present their case in front of a judge for a decision."

"But in matters of capital offenses, when 'right' is more than a legal definition: murder, stealing, DUI, hit and run, child abuse, molestation, vandalism, assault, and battery, in cases like that, we're no longer going to go through lengthy and costly court battles to prove what we already know."

"Now, what I'm going to say next will probably be the hardest thing about this entire experiment for you emotionally to accept, because it seems to strike against everything you've ever been taught about being an American. But, once you experience the reality we anticipate, and get past the verbiage, I think most Americans will see its wisdom."

"In capital offense cases, if you are caught red-handed, you will no longer be 'innocent until proven guilty.' If our police, now named Guardians, can prove without a reasonable doubt that an individual is guilty, then that culprit is removed immediately from the legal process."

A flurry of flashes and shouting began all at once.

"What do you mean by removed?" It was Marshall Foster pushing to the front. "What exactly is the punishment for those crimes? You know, selling drugs, murder!"

"Just like Singapore," replied Ryder. "Death."

Rachel and Mama Slavin both sat up, leaning in, not believing what they were hearing. Rachel instinctively pulled her baby closer to her.

On the screen, everyone was vying for the next question, but the anchor from Channel 7 was not giving up the floor.

"But you said, 'immediately'. Are we talking, without a trial?"

"Yes, that's exactly what we're talking."

Another reporter pushed past Foster and shouted, "What's that going to prove?"

Ryder paused before answering, the cameras pushing in on his face, "It sends a message loud and clear. Don't commit a crime in our community, or you'll pay the consequences."

The press conference was being televised live, not only nationally, but around the world. Because Junisha's only safe contact with that outside world was through the medium of television, she was watching as well. Old reruns of *Jerry Springer* and *Maury* had been interrupted as she heard a reporter from California stating, "Mr. Ryder, as an American citizen, I consider this an outrage. I'm not a criminal and I don't commit crimes, but..."

"Then you'll have no trouble living in Riverton," interrupted Ryder, "because these laws do nothing except remove that criminal element from our society, once and for all. Why pay eighty-thousand dollars a year or more to keep them in jails just so we can release them to go back and repeat the crimes they got arrested for the first time, and that's what happens in ninety percent of the cases."

"I know the statistics, as well as you do," responded the reporter. "And I know that there are some fruit-cakes out there who will take what you're proposing seriously."

Ryder interjected, "This is not a proposal."

"Yeah, well, that remains to be seen. You mentioned a statistic, a ninety percent recidivism rate? What about the other ten percent who learn from their mistakes, turn around and lead productive lives after prison? What about them?"

"They committed a capital crime, so they only killed once, only raped once, only held up a grocery store and robbed once. Well, in Riverton, that's enough. One strike and you're out."

"So you get rid of all the presumed criminals, what are you left with?" came another question.

"A safe place to live," Ryder replied. "A safe place to raise your children."

Junisha, sitting alone in her dark, barricaded living room, grasped at the word 'safe' and clung to it like a life-line. Waves of fear washed over her at what she was considering, but the words 'safe' and 'children' kept her mind racing in spite of those fears. She could feel the fine line of perspiration that had broken out on her face as she considered the possibilities. Junisha never had possibilities before. Maybe she didn't now, but the man had said, 'Everybody was welcome' and she and her kids were an 'everybody.'

The last thing Junisha heard before she got up off the stained sofa was 'And it all starts first thing tomorrow morning.'

She thought hard to figure out what she had to do next.

CHAPTER XXVI

The experiment officially began on a beautiful spring day as the snow cover melted to just patches and the first flowers beginning to push through the winter frost in shades of green. The temperature was in the mid-fifties, and there was a smell of freshness, of new birth, in the air. The sun dispelled the morning mist that rolled off the Ohio. A few cargo boats passed on the opposite side of the river from the town and its deserted docks. Buoy markers stretched down the center of the channel to avoid unwanted landings until shipping regulations for Riverton could be finalized. Since hardly anyone had used those particular docks for more than fishing in over two years, the markers were mainly to keep away unwanted protesters or reporters.

At the roadblocks leading out of town and at two designated exit roads, both lanes of both roads were filled with moving vans heading for some other life outside of Riverton.

After the press conference the day before, reporters and their crews had been again escorted from the city, to give Riverton's first day of the experiment some privacy. When Marshall Foster shouted that 'privacy' smacked of 'lack of transparency,' Ryder agreed. The first day of living in the new Riverton was an internal affair, but he did promise a second press conference in two days.

Undeterred, the Channel 7 team and a dozen other news outlets had set up at the crossing, documenting the mass exodus from the President's great experiment.

In the suburbs, most of the residential streets looked almost deserted with only one house in five showing any sign of life. Only a few cars traveled the streets. The only people walking were parents with their elementary school children clutching books, and dog-walkers clutching plastic baggies. It was the lack of sound that was perhaps the most frightening. It was almost as though nature was also waiting to see how this first day would end.

At the town's only remaining grammar school, composed of grades one through eight, Principal Mary Hewgley greeted the students as she had for over thirty years and assured parents that everything was going to be fine, and the children could be picked up that evening at six rather than the customary two-thirty.

The presence of two Guardians, flanking the front door, did very little to mitigate parental concern, but they trusted Ms. Hewgley. She had been a fixture in Riverton since most of the parents and their parents had been students, and if she said, everything was going to be all right, they believed her. Ms. Hewgley never lied and would never have done anything to put one of her charges in danger.

At the high school, which handled grades nine through twelve, the excitement was much less subdued. In fact, that sense of bravado and entitlement, that infected teenagers everywhere, was ramped up to fever-pitch at the prospect of some outside authority trying to change their right to be and behave however they felt. Even the Guardians and metal detectors at every door didn't quell their boisterousness, but instead caused another sort of roadblock; however, nothing compared to what was awaiting them in the halls.

All lockers were to be opened by the assigned student under the supervision of the Guardians.

"Wait a minute, you can't make us do this," protested one student to Jay who had been assigned to the school.

"Open it now, please, or I'll rip it off its hinges," was Jay's reply.

The student, a lanky kid with a bad case of acne and a scratch under his left eye, reluctantly dialed his combination. "Shit," was his only comment and that was under his breath. Obviously, not a gang leader, just a hanger-on.

Completing the combination's back and forth swirls, the kid stepped back and let Jay have the honor of swinging open the door. The inside face of the locker had been decorated with nude playboy photos, which were typical and not very current. Ignoring them, Jay, wearing protective gloves, began pulling things out of the locker and handing them to the student to hold: a sweatshirt, several books, a packet of condoms, two magazines, a small tin of rolled joints, a small packet of powder-like substance, and a knife. Jay removed the knife and threw it into a collected pile of other confiscated weapons on the floor of the hall.

"Knives are considered weapons," explained Jay. "Other than that, have a good day."

The student couldn't believe the Guardian had just gone past the drugs and not said anything. Then, Jay turned back.

"Oh, those drugs. You plan on using them all today?"

The lanky kid didn't know how to answer the question and finally managed to stammer out a, "No... No."

"In that case," Jay said, as he came back to confiscate them, "new rules, only enough for the day."

With that, Jay threw the cocaine into the pile of weapons and opened the tin of joints.

"One or two?" asked Jay.

"Uh...two," came back the confused reply.

Jay extracted two rolled joints from the tin and handed them over to the boy who almost was afraid to reach out and take them. "Go ahead, they're yours," Jay smiled, as he pressed them into the kid's hand, then threw the rest away.

Down the hall a little further, Seth, who had also been assigned to this detail, was emptying another student's locker and noticed the carved initials, C.W., in the metal.

"Those yours?" he asked the student holding the combination lock.

The kid stammered out a denial, "Uh, no, man."

From his list, Seth noted that the kid's name was Carl Williams. "Well, Carl, they're yours now. Fix it."

Carl looked even more confused until Seth handed him a can of spray paint that matched the original color.

"And while you're at it, you might as well get the outside looking good too," Seth smiled, and patted Carl on the back. "I'll check back later to see how it looks."

Classes that day were much more subdued than anyone could ever remember. Those students who weren't in the halls quietly repainting their lockers, were in class actually listening, or at least, sitting quietly in stunned silence. For many of them, this was the first time they had ever really sat quietly in a classroom.

As for the teachers, it was a revelation, and frightening. They could actually teach, but that meant they had to actually have a lesson plan prepared to teach. It had been so long since many of the teachers had done more than monitoring duty, making sure nobody killed anyone in their class. Now that they were expected to teach, a few couldn't even find their textbook guides.

If the majority of students and some of the teachers were having to adjust to the new guidelines, a few students faced even stauncher restrictions. Upon entering the front doors, they were ushered into the boy's or girl's locker rooms, under appropriate Guardian supervision, and required to strip out of their street clothes and into gym clothes that were provided. Each student was given a folded sheet of paper explaining the new dress code, and what they were expected to wear the next day.

Changes in Riverton that morning weren't limited to the schools and students but were being enforced throughout the whole of Riverton as well.

On the streets of downtown Riverton, the vagrants and the homeless were being rounded up by a Guardian task force under the direction of Joseph Redfeather, and escorted onto waiting buses.

One thirty-five-years-old vagrant whom Joseph knew only as Lyle, looked fifty and had the eyes of a man who was already dead. Yet still, something about losing the last place in the world he had called home, scared him, and he began to resist.

"Where are you taking me? I don't want to go," he screamed as he struck out at the Guardians.

Joseph quickly stepped in front of Lyle, and motioning the Guardians to step back, tried to get his attention.

"Come on, we're not going to hurt you. You know me. I would never hurt you."

Lyle's eyes cleared for just a moment, but still it wasn't enough to calm his fears. Backing up, he started to cry again, "No. Stop it. I don't want to go."

At this point, two Guardians stepped past Joseph and restrained the frightened man.

"Don't hurt him," the Native American heard himself saying.

"We won't," one of the men assured him. "We just don't want him hurting himself."

Returning his focus to Lyle, the Guardian said, "I know you don't want to go with us. I can understand that. But you can't stay here either, so that kind of puts us in a bind."

"You'll go with me?" Lyle pleaded with Joseph.

Joseph Redfeather extended his hand and let the frightened man grab hold and cling to it.

#

Back at the high school, the bell had already rung for second period when the last group of so-called students straggled in. While the initial screenings had gone without much of a hitch, this group promised to be a little rougher. They represented four separate street gangs, at least, in their own minds. Most were just an annoyance to the city, and a costly annoyance at that, smashing home and car windows, all in the darkness of night, so no one could prove who they were.

They were all dressed in gang colors and all walked with the same 'don't fuck with me' swagger.

Stopping just outside the front door of the school and seeing the newly installed metal detectors, the brighter of the gangs realized that they were going to be caught with their weapons if they went into school. They came only to show the authorities that they were not like the rest of the town, intimidated into obedience. They came dressed in their own flagrant gang colors, bandannas and arm-bands, boldly stating for everyone to see that they couldn't be forced into anything, and nobody was going to suppress their right to remain who they were. They found their protests limited to vocal taunts rather than the usual brick-throwing or vandalism. They were testing the waters, so to speak, and if this worked, they would escalate their individuality and prove their superiority. Of course, they didn't think in those terms or with that much foresight. The truth was they didn't intend to get arrested by the new goons surrounding the front door, until they found out how they would be treated. Something about the new police force, and that was what they were in spite of what they called themselves, made the gang leaders nervous.

So after shouting loud obscenities to those students who had capitulated and entered the school, they turned, as one, to leave but found themselves face to face with a string of Guardians who had come up behind them, blocking their exit. The leader of the Guardians, a burly black man, took command.

"You don't want to do that," said Miles. "You know your mamas wouldn't want you standing out here, shouting all that shit, and then going home. This is a school day, and school's that direction." He pointed, in case any of them had any questions, in the direction he intended them to go. "So unless you can prove you're over eighteen, you belong in school."

"What if I can prove I'm over eighteen?" demanded one gang leader, a tough with spiked hair.

"Then you're trespassing on school property, and trust me, you don't want that to be the case. We have rules about trespassing. New rules."

The group standing before him knew better than to ask what those new rules were. They could tell by his eyes that they didn't want to know.

"Now, I'm only going to ask this once, and once only, and I expect an answer, 'Are all of you over eighteen or under?'"

The group before Miles had become strangely subdued. Several nodded imperceptibly, while most just glared at the Guardians.

"And those colors," Miles continued, referring to the bandannas and arm-bands, "I thought we told you about that. No gang colors, no gangs. It's kaput. Now, face the wall, hands behind your heads."

Most of the gang reluctantly did what they were told, but one greasy-haired punk decided to make a show of resisting.

"Make me, ass-hole," he managed to get out before one of the Guardians cut off his show and slammed him into a nearby wall, face first. Holding his bleeding nose and lip, he started to protest again.

"Don't be stupid," Miles warned. "We don't want to hurt you, but we will."

Jerking a handkerchief from his pocket to staunch the bleeding, the kid slowly turned around to join his friends facing the wall with only one of his hands behind his head.

A crowd of students who were on the soccer field gathered behind the school fence, having heard the commotion, and now, could barely control their jeering as they watched the gangs being forced to comply like everyone else.

The Guardians ignored the gathering crowd and kept to their task, frisking each gang member. They did not seem really surprised to discover hidden within the clothing, eleven knives, four guns, various quantities of drugs and hallucinogens, and two three-foot lengths of chain.

Dumping the items on the ground at their feet, Miles then ordered the young men to strip.

"What?" came the almost unified disbelieving response.

Holding out gym clothes, Miles repeated his command, "Strip! And then, put these on. You read the guidelines, no gang colors. And if you can't read, you should have gotten someone else to read it for you."

The gang looked both angry and embarrassed, faced with disrobing in front of a large group of students who were now laughing at them through the fence. A dozen eyes darted to Miles and the other Guardians to see if there was any negotiating room, or the possibility of calling their bluff and fighting their way back into control. The eyes that stared back at them were unflinching, warning: Don't even think about it.

Finally, several of the less aggressive of the gang members slipped the bandannas from their heads and the colors from their sleeves. The others slowly followed suit. No way were they going to strip completely. At least in that, they could still maintain some of their hard-earned self-esteem. One ended up having to take off his shirt and was promptly given a gym shirt to cover his scrawny chest.

"That's better," smiled Miles, "and we're going to go easy on you today, 'cause this is the first day and you obviously didn't understand the rules. So get on into class, and," he indicated the weapons on the ground, "don't bring this type of shit back here again, because this is a school and we're playing a whole different ball-game."

With that, Miles turned to leave and, behind him, the gang leader with the spiked hair suddenly slipped a long needle-thin stiletto from his hair and struck out at Miles' back, screaming, "I'll show you ball-game, motherfucker!"

Miles, even though his back was completely turned away, reacted instantly, thrusting his arm behind him to stop the deadly strike in one lightning-fast hand move. Slowly turning to face the stunned youth, Miles twisted the stiletto away from him, snapping the punk's arm in the process and throwing him screaming in pain to the ground. It didn't stop there. Instantly Seth placed a knee on the screaming and writhing youth's back and pressed a small cylindrical-shaped object into the back of the punk's neck, causing a slight 'sparking sound.'" The screams were instantly cut short and the twisting body slumped into stillness.

His friends and the other gang members first reacted in violent verbal protests, but it took less than a minute before the 'fuck-you's' turned into silence as everyone there came to the same realization that their friend on the ground wasn't moving any more.

"Whoa, you knocked him out, right?"

Miles turned to look at the acne-scarred youth who had spoken. "No, he's dead. Anyone else want to try taking a weapon into that building?"

Several of the watching students behind the fence who had made it past the security check glanced at each other, and then, slowly slipped nail files and other forbidden objects from their pockets and dropped them to the ground.

But not all were so malleable. Jorje, the leader of the Red Cutz, a marginally delinquent Hispanic gang, had spent his entire life, all of seventeen years, getting to his position of leadership and wasn't about to give it up without a fight.

"Fuck you, nigger," he shouted defiantly. "You're the one who's dead."

With that, he and several others of his gang began backing up, then turned, and raced out of the school grounds, back into their territory.

Neither Miles nor any of the other Guardians followed or even made an attempt to stop them. Today, there was no law against running away or refusing to go to school, so they just turned back to the ones still standing before them and motioned them through the metal detectors and into the classrooms.

CHAPTER XXVII

Outside the Riverton police station and jail, the bus, carrying Lyle and the other street people who had been picked up, was being off-loaded. Some were so confused they had to be carried off the bus. Lyle did not fall into that category, but he was certainly scared and ready to fight anyone who came close enough to touch him.

"I didn't do anything. I was just sleeping," he protested to anyone who would listen, but soon realized nobody was listening. Frantically searching for a way to escape, all he could see was a cordoned line of Guardians blocking every escape route.

"Just move it inside," said the rough-looking Guardian closest to him.

"I don't think so."

"Well, think so. You either go in on your own two feet, or we'll have to carry you."

Then, a younger, less aggressive-looking Guardian interjected with a smile, "He's serious about the carrying, and I really don't want to have to do that. Him," he said, cocking his head to the rougher Guardian, "he's built like a gorilla. You know, sloping head, hair on his back. He could throw you up over his shoulder and wouldn't feel a thing. Me, my back's been giving me fits. I really don't want to have to do any lifting today. Okay?"

This moment of unexpected levity confused Lyle even more, but for the younger Guardian, it had had its desired effect. Lyle was no longer pulling back. He wasn't moving forward, but he was now looking at the Guardians, who he had considered his captors, with a little less fear in his eyes.

"What are you going to do to us? In there?" he asked the younger Guardian.

"I'm not going to do anything to you, and neither is anyone else in there," the younger Guardian said, indicating the open door of the jailhouse. "They're not going to lock you up, or anything like that. They're just going to feed you, then talk to you."

The thought of food made Lyle's mouth water and it felt like a betrayal. But when the Guardian reached out his hand to him, Lyle stepped back to show his independence, but because he had no other choice, he skirted the offer of assistance and joined the other dirty, frightened vagrants moving like concentration camp victims through the open doorway.

Inside the building, the line moved down a long empty corridor and the smell of new paint and plaster still so strong that it was almost overpowering. It did at least cover the layered noxious body odors of those walking through. It had been a long time since Lyle had smelled clean, and that smell of paint reminded him of better times when he wasn't what he had become.

The corridor ended in a large open holding area where rounds of tables and chairs had been set up. Along one wall, a buffet line had been set up and the aroma of more than a dozen steaming choices stopped Lyle in the doorway. He was looking at more food than he thought he'd ever seen. *Surely this wasn't for them, he thought. It couldn't be.*

Joseph Redfeather stepped out from behind the food table.

"Okay, you all know me. I think I've met and talked with everyone here at one time or the other. So I want you to listen to me for a second. Nobody's going to hurt you. We just want to get you fed and then talk to you. But I'm asking you to shower first. I promise the food will still be here when you get back."

Lyle's mouth was already watering and nobody else in line wanted to take a chance on leaving the food.

Slowly, nodding in understanding, Joseph picked up a large platter of biscuits from the table and held them out to the men and women facing him. "I'll tell you what you can do. I realize most of you haven't had breakfast yet, so if you want to pick up something just to tide you over until after the shower, we've got hot biscuits straight out of the oven."

Everyone swarmed the platters Joseph held; some taking two or three. Lyle had his hand on a second biscuit but put the second one back when he heard Joseph say, "There's plenty to go around and there will be more when you get out of the shower. I promise. Okay? Now, ladies on the right, gentlemen on the left. You'll find soap, towels and clean clothes to change into after the shower. Once you've cleaned up and gotten dressed, then come on out here and eat. I know some of you probably had a rough night, so take your time. I've had hot coffee put in the dressing rooms, so grab a cup or two if that'll help clear the cobwebs. I want you thinking straight when I start explaining the new rules."

"What rules?" asked Lyle, turning back.

"Don't worry about it now, Lyle," soothed Joseph. "Just get yourself cleaned up and have a good hot meal. Then we'll talk."

Washing away the grime of months of neglect, Lyle stood in the steaming stall as the hot water cascaded down over his head to streak in dark rivulets down a body he hardly recognized any more. Ribs stuck out where there had once been muscle. His arms and shoulders were crusted with scabs and dirt that had gone so deep that they had stained his skin. He almost threw up the biscuit he had just hurriedly eaten. What the fuck have I done, he thought, as tears coursed down his cheeks to be washed away by the hot water. Grabbing a cleaning brush, resting just outside the shower, Lyle pulled it into the shower and began scrubbing his alien skin until it almost bled.

Afterward, dressed in clean jeans and a shirt that had been provided, Lyle made his way back into the dining area and found that Joseph Redfeather had not lied. There was even more food than before. Still, not knowing where his next meal was coming from, he began hurriedly stacking his plate to overflowing, even slipping an extra apple and a banana into his pockets. He debated grabbing a few more but didn't want to do anything that might get him thrown out before he could finish his meal. He'd been thrown out of the Mission twice, both times for being overly drunk.

Being drunk was a normal state of his being for Lyle, and yet he didn't consider himself an alcoholic, just a drinker. To make him forget, to keep him mellow. But sometimes it didn't work, like the two times he was thrown out of the Mission. Those times, the cheap wine didn't make him forget.

It was all there right in front of him, just like it was yesterday and not ten lost years ago. He raged at what had happened, and what it had done to him, and he wanted to hurt everybody around him, and probably would have if Joseph Redfeather hadn't dragged him outside and talked him down. Joseph was the only person who knew Lyle's story. It had spilled out of him like spewing vomit, and Joseph had just listened, just listened. It had been the first time in so long anyone really had listened that Lyle never forgot it and would always be indebted. It didn't solve his problems and he had one other episode of raging out of control, but that time, he sought out Joseph to stop him before he hurt somebody he didn't want to hurt.

Now, choosing a corner table where he could be by himself, Lyle ate, hunkered over his plate as though afraid someone was going to steal his food.

He ate quickly—a habit learned from years on the streets. No one could steal food you had already eaten. When finally, his plate was clean, he looked up and back longingly at the serving table. Although he was no longer hungry, his survival instinct made him want seconds. But another part of him, like a caged animal who had been beaten too often, was afraid to tempt fate. When another man went back for more, he waited to see the Guardian's reaction, and when none came, Lyle quickly darted back to the table to fill another plate, but this time, with things he could hide on his body. Even with the apple and banana already secreted there, he thought there was still plenty of room under his new clothes for other things to eat later. The very thought that he was thinking this surprised him. 'Later' was a concept Lyle had lost somewhere out on the streets. Everything on the streets was just surviving the immediate.

After everyone had eaten, they were given a chance to return to the clean restrooms to relieve themselves. This was a luxury most people of Riverton took for granted, but not these wanderers of the street who were used to urine-soaked alleyways or equally dingy back-room johns.

It was a good psychological move on Ryder's part. He firmly believed anyone could become a productive part of the Riverton team if the town could re-awaken each one's individual humanity. In this case, it was hopefully a full stomach and a clean bathroom.

Lyle followed the others into a large, newly-painted holding room, filled with brightly colored metal chairs, looking like pieces of candy facing a slightly raised platform and a speaker's podium at the front of the room.

Lyle slid into the back row, true to his nature, not too close, but close to the door. It hadn't escaped his attention that in spite of all the colors in the room, the sunlit windows high in walls, were barred, casting striped shadows across the upturned faces.

Some of those within the room had refused to shower or take advantage of the clean restrooms and no amount of coaxing would get them to reconsider. Others, though showered and fed, rocked in agitated anticipation of god-knows-what their minds had construed, babbling to themselves like the mental cases they actually were, shouting bursts of obscenities periodically in angry nonsensical challenges. Others, like Lyle, looked much better for the soap and food and sat quietly, actually listening.

Joseph Redfeather stepped to the front of the room and greeted each person by name, even though some of those present were incapable of returning the greeting or even recognizing that they had been addressed. Of the thirty-five people assembled, Joseph turned his focus on ten he hoped he could reach, Lyle being one of them.

He ended his presentation with, "so here's how it stands, you have two choices. One, you can stay here. And I mean, here. We have jail cells that are being converted into rooms, but they are rooms you have to rent, and you rent them not with money, but by work."

"What kind of work?" asked an aging prostitute named Maggie, who had dropped so low on the social scale that she couldn't even afford a cot on the money she could charge, and had been forced to service the few tricks she was able to round up in her living room; a filthy alley behind Al's bait shop that always smelled of rotting fish and sludge-streaked water.

"Nothing you can't handle, Maggie," Redfeather assured her. "Cleaning graffiti, working in the parks, I don't know what you'll be doing, but if you're able, you'll be working, three days a week to start, with training classes and counseling the other two. Weekends, you're restricted to your cells until we're sure you can stay sober and clean. There will be no drinking, and no drugs. Not at first and not in here. This is your chance to get clean. You'll be fed, and you'll have a safe place to sleep every night, but the choice is yours."

"What's the other choice?" asked another of Riverton's substrata.

"We drive you to the outskirts of Riverton, actually about ten miles out and turn you loose."

"That's it?" asked Maggie.

"That's it. Once you've been driven out of the city, if you try to come back, and we catch you on the streets again, you'll be terminated. It's as simple as that."

"Like that kid in the school yard?" came a hushed question. Everyone in Riverton, including the vagrant population, had heard about the student in the high school yard, and even if they didn't know the accurate details, they all understood now what terminated meant.

"Just like the kid in the school yard. So think about what I'm offering you. What we're offering you. You decide to stay, and I'll be here to work with you. You decide to go, then I say, 'God Speed', and wish you well. The choice is yours."

CHAPTER XXVIII

Later that evening, well after dusk, Doug Johnson decided to drive over to Ace Hardware to pick up a hinge for the front door he had been promising Doris he'd replace. Actually, he agreed to go just to cut off her incessant nagging. Doris liked to nag, until she got her way. As she liked to put it, 'A squeaking wheel gets the oil.' Doug wasn't sure how that applied to anything, and often thought he'd ask if Doris was saying she'd gotten as round as a wheel, but even though he got some satisfaction thinking these thoughts, he knew he was never going to say any such thing.

He and Doris had been married twenty-three years and her nagging was just part of the whole parcel, and he was actually quite fond of the parcel. He even asked her if she wanted to go along for the ride, but he knew she'd say no. Doris hated hardware stores about as much as Doug hated Abby's beauty salons.

Doris was perfectly happy to stay at home and clean the kitchen if it took her mind off all the good neighbors she had lost over the last two weeks. So Doug had left, and Doris had worked methodically, as always, turning her domain into what she liked to brag was the most spotless kitchen in Riverton.

It was the popping sound that finally captured her attention. At first, she thought it was coming from within the kitchen itself, a bottle cap maybe that had exploded, but then she realized that the popping was coming from outside the house. Not able to see anything in the darkness from her kitchen window over the sink, Doris dried her hands and made her way slowly down the hallway toward the front of the house and the picture window in the darkened living room. What she saw in the reflection of the scattered street lights drained the color from her face.

Dozens of teenagers, wearing gang colors, were running through the streets, yelling and screaming, smashing windows of the deserted houses, and tearing down mailboxes. The deserted house directly across the street from Doris' white-shingle bungalow was already smoking from a fire that could be seen blazing through the broken front window.

Doris raced for the hall phone to dial 911, but not having her glasses, she clicked on the living room light, never realizing that the sudden brightness would act like a beacon in the almost deserted community.

"This is 911. What is the nature of your emergency?"

"They're burning the neighborhood," she cried into the receiver. "You've got to help me. Send help." Then, she heard her own front door being assaulted and screamed again and again.

#

Ryder was about to call it quits for the night when Joel ran in to his office in the courthouse.

"They're rioting on third and Maple."

"Who?"

"Gangs."

A dozen patrol cars raced into the area. The street looked like a war zone.

Several houses were fully involved, flames leaping through the roofs. Street lights had been shot out, and gang members raced down the streets hurling fire bombs, flaming arches in the darkness erupting on porches and through front windows.

Angie was in one of the patrol cars and was out with service weapon drawn before her car had even stopped moving.

Instantly drawing a bead on one gang member running with a lighted fire bomb, she dropped him with one quick shot. The struck teenager crashed to the ground and became a rolling fire-ball himself, but Angie already had her bead on another member racing towards her, brandishing a weapon. This one was dropped by the Guardian standing beside her.

Evidently, two deaths in such short order was more than the street thugs had bargained for, so they started racing for the other end of the street with the Guardians giving chase.

Too late, most of the gang realized that they were being cut off by Guardians coming in from the other direction. Caught between both sides, five or six continued firing and were mowed down where they stood. The three remaining finally threw down their empty weapons and held their hands up in surrender.

"Jeez man, okay. We quit," one of them shouted as the Guardians surrounded them.

"Too late," was the last thing they heard before three Guardians opened fire all at once, then moved in on the now dead bodies to make sure they were dead.

Sirens filled the air and fire trucks started arriving, but the fire men were torn between the grisly sight of dead bodes lying in the street and putting out the fires they'd been called on.

Angie was walking back to her car when she first heard Doris' muffled scream. Backed by her Guardian partner, she rushed in the direction of the scream, just as Jorje, the leader of the Red Cutz, stepped out onto the porch, holding his gun to Doris' head.

"Hold it right there, Motherfuckers," shouted the seventeen-year-old, "One move and she's...."

Without blinking an eye, both Angie and her partner fired their weapons, both bullets striking the gang leader in the head simultaneously, smashing him back against the Johnson's front porch, his own gun discharging next to Doris' head. She too fell to the gore covered floor.

Angie and her partner instantly raced for Doris' side, turning her over, their fingers instantly tracing through the blood to where a bullet had grazed her scalp.

"Get an ambulance, she's bleeding," Angel's partner shouted to two other Guardians running up to assist.

Angie, kneeling beside the fallen woman, began applying pressure to the graze wound at the scalp line, while trying to talk the panic out of the terrified woman's eyes.

"It's okay. You were just grazed. It'll burn like hell, but you'll be fine."

"You shot at him. He was holding a gun to my head, and you shot at him. I could have been killed," stammered Doris amidst sudden sobbing.

Angie quickly pulled out a handkerchief and expertly used it as a compress. "Yes, you could have, but you weren't."

"But you could have hit me."

Angie paused for the briefest of moments before reapplying her pressure. "No, I don't think so."

CHAPTER XXIX

The Guardians' attack on the Riverton gangs made national and international headlines.

The New York Times led with 'RIVERTON RIOTS SPELL DOOM TO PROJECT!' In bold, twenty-four point type, while the *Chicago Tribune* blasted an equally large '11 DEAD ON FIRST DAY OF UTOPIA.'

The Washington Post led with a headline condemnation of the President, 'THE BIG FAILURE,' while the *Atlanta Journal-Constitution* was a little more supportive with 'RIVERTON 1, GANGS 0.' *The Dallas Morning News* made no bones where their loyalty lay, 'Riverton's Alamo takes no hostages.'

Every television newscast was focused on Riverton and the killings, the 'murders', as the right wing was now calling them. In Los Angeles, Rachel had been trying to reach Seth for hours, and all lines into Riverton had been busy. Still she continued, punching re-dial over and over again as she continued to watch the coverage. The volume was down, but the reports out of Riverton were so horrifying, she couldn't turn them off.

Marshall Foster has been broadcasting for twelve straight hours, repeating over and over again the blood bath of Riverton's first day of independence. It sounded like a war zone.

"...With eleven confirmed dead, all under the age of eighteen, not twenty-one, as we were first informed. And this exclusive Channel 7 information comes direct from our sources in the Red Cross, who, as you know, are the only ones allowed into the city at this time. According to Richard Ryder, director of the project, resistance from the criminal community was anticipated and the Guardians' training quickly brought these pockets of resistance under control."

"Rachel?" Seth's voice was suddenly on the line and Rachel quickly muted the voice of Foster.

"Seth? Are you all right?"

"Sure, Honey, I wasn't even there. I was assigned to the schools."

"What happened? Those were kids that were killed. They're saying under eighteen."

"Honey, they weren't kids. They were gang members with guns, burning houses and shooting at people. The press is just making a big issue of it," he assured her, then promptly changed the subject. "Oh, honey, I can't wait until you get here. You're going to love it. I've found the most perfect house with a backyard and ...."

"Seth, what are you talking about? Children were killed. You don't just kill a dozen kids and then talk about houses."

"Yes, we do," Seth said, in a flash of anger. It was a tone Rachel had never heard in his voice before; a defiance she found both frightening and somewhat appealing.

"How many people were killed in Los Angeles last night?" he challenged. "Do you even know?" he continued. "What's wrong, Rache? Is the world only indignant when it's somewhere else? Or is it so common place in L.A., it doesn't even make the news anymore?"

Suddenly calmer, she heard him take a deep breath, probably surprised at his own anger. "I'm sorry. It's just that we're the big story right now, because we're trying to fight our way out of a system of behavior that is destroying the rest of the country."

She could hear his anger escalating again. "So please excuse us, if we don't just stand there with our fingers up our asses when kids point guns at us, when we fight back, because they are burning down our homes, and that is what they were doing. Did the press report that? They weren't playing baseball, or standing on the corner doing doh-wap. They were attacking, because they thought they could get away with it. Well, not anymore."

Rachel could almost feel the wave of anger subsiding again, though she said nothing and only listened.

"Honey, I'm sorry. I didn't mean to yell at you, and it wasn't you I was yelling at. It's just that we're tired and under a lot of pressure. The whole world is watching, and we're trying to do something we believe in."

Rachel paused for a few seconds before she could respond, and Seth thought maybe she had hung up on him.

"Rache?"

"I'm here, and I didn't mean it to sound like I was attacking you. It just all sounds so bad from here."

She could hear him laugh, but it was not a laugh of amusement. "When has the news ever told you the good parts. Yes, there are problems and will probably continue to be problems because this is all new, but as bad as it may sound, as bad as Marshall Foster may like to paint us, Rache, it's the beginning of something wonderful, unbelievable. Please just trust me. Wait until you get here. Wait until you see what's being accomplished. You've always trusted me before. Please just trust me now, and wait."

"I will, honey. I will," she promised as she hung up. Secretly though, she wondered if the man on the other end of the line was the same man she had married. It was the same feeling she had when he came back from Desert Storm, and that had turned out all right. She'd have to trust that this would turn out okay as well.

Turning off the television, she decided to wait and see for herself, and trust him like she had always done.

#

The next morning at the Riverton High School, kids were again arriving, but this time most gang colors were gone. The metal detectors and Guardians were still very much in evidence, but this time, the processing went a lot smoother than the previous day.

Raymond Alvarez, a young teenage boy with the required spiky hair of rebellion, seemed to be the only student that morning who was still wearing his gang colors, though he tried covering them up by wearing a coat that was heavier than the warming weather dictated. Letting other students move in front of him, he finally chose to make his move at getting into the school without being noticed. With his head ducked down, his eyes on the ground, he started to move through the metal detectors, but it didn't work. The young blond Guardian at the door spotted him immediately.

"Whoa there," the Guardian said, as he put a restraining hand on Raymond's shoulder. "You can't go in there wearing those colors."

Raymond was instantly defensive. "Jeez man, it's all I've got." And it was true. "Everything's colors."

The Guardian pulled out a gym shirt and handed it to Raymond with a smile. "Then you better be buying some others then."

Now Raymond was angry and embarrassed, "And how do I do that? Ain't got no money, and ain't got no one to ask for it either."

The Guardian stood for a long moment sizing up the teenager before him, then said, "What's your name? Not your gang name, your real name."

"Raymond." It came out quietly, as though it left a bad taste in his mouth.

"Well, hi, Raymond, my name is Jay," said the Guardian extending his hand. Raymond took it before he even realized what he was doing. The Guardian named Jay gave it a firm shake and then said, "I'll tell you what we're going to do. I want you to see me right here after school, and I'll write you a credit for some new clothes down at the Mall."

Raymond stepped back from him with a look that was a cross between disbelief and the knowledge of how ugly charity handouts could be. Jay recognized it immediately, having been once on the receiving line of charity himself, so he was quick to assure Raymond, "Don't worry, you get to pick them, and they'll all be brand new, no hand me downs. You can even pick the store, your choice, just like everybody else, just no gang colors."

He stuck out his hand again to Raymond, "Have we got a deal?"

Raymond reluctantly took the extended hand again, and realized this was now the second time he had ever shaken hands with anyone in his entire life. It felt sort of grown up.

While the school day would eventually start with homeroom, where the roll would be called, the decision was made that any announcements for the first few weeks would be made with everyone present in the auditorium until the students had a clear understanding of their new schedules and the disciplinary changes in force.

On this particular morning, the students were noisily taking their places, shouting out to friends and generally behaving as young delinquents normally do. The difference was that when the opening period bell rang, everyone quieted down. It was a major difference. Of course, several Guardians were stationed around the door, but mainly, the room was managed by teachers, hurrying students into bleachers, and shushing them when they thought they were being too rowdy.

Paul Frank, the assistant principal and a sociology teacher, approached the podium. Aside from a general restlessness, Mr. Frank had their attention.

"As you are well aware, the school day has been extended until 6:30 P.M. each day..."

A few groans were heard.

"...And that means every student will be expected to be on this campus from 7:30 in the morning until that time. New class schedules are being passed down the rows right now, and I want you all to make sure you get a copy. It's your responsibility to get a copy and keep that copy."

The schedules converged on the students from all directions, with those who hadn't yet gotten theirs, waving their hands to get the attention of someone who would give him or her a copy. Nobody shouted, and other than an occasional, 'He doesn't have one, or we need more over here,' everything moved rather smoothly and none of the teachers could believe it. In just one day, this wasn't the same student body. It was like someone had replaced all of their loud, obnoxious problem students with clones, responsive clones.

"Now, if everyone has his sheet...I know it looks confusing, but you will understand in just a second. It's color-coded. What does that mean? Well, it's simple or at least I hope it is. If you are in the 9th grade, a freshman, you only look at the blue lines. If it's in blue, it's yours. Not green, not red, not black. Just blue."

A murmur rippled through the bleachers like waves on a lake, as students ran their fingers along the blue lines. "Sophomores, 10th grade, you're Green. Juniors, Red. And seniors, that leaves you black. A few "Whooo's," like ghosts spread through the crowd, gaining tittered responses.

"Now, there may be some of you who will look at this sheet and not see any colors, period, and that's okay. Just see me after assembly and I'll personally mark your schedule; no big deal."

Okay, now let's look at these schedules, and I want to explain why it's arranged the way it is. The first-half of each day will be spent on getting back to the basics. What does that mean? Starting from scratch, finding out how far along you are in each discipline like reading, writing and arithmetic; and learning to get along in this world, which in your case means getting along with your fellow students. If you find all of this a big boring mess and you could care less, I only ask that you keep quiet and let the others learn. If you want to sit there in ignorance, picking your nose, though it's socially uncouth, that's fine. Just don't wipe anything on your desk and be respectful of the others in your class. What you do not want to do is disrupt the class or keep anyone else in the class from learning. That is harming that person and we all now understand the penalty for harming another person.

"You're also going to be learning history. You have to know where we've been to know who you are and the part you are right now playing in the history of our new country."

Thus, the school day started, and because new multidisciplinary teachers had been brought in to supplement Riverton's teacher base, every student in grades nine through twelve started with basic English and communication skills: spelling, nouns and verbs, adverbs and adjectives, even diagramming. Those that could not read, or read below grade level, were instantly spotted and quietly offered special attention. Every attempt was made to keep them with their peers.

It would be nice to say the new system caught on with amazing success. Nice, but not accurate. Most of the students were not interested in learning anything. In fact, some even slept, or pretended to sleep, but with the Guardian in the room, they weren't acting up, and teachers were able to focus on those students who were willing to give the new system a try.

In one classroom, while the teacher had students reading from the text book, Seth had noticed a gangly black student sitting at the back of the room, frustration and anger radiating from his body. The young man's constantly moving fingers flipped his text book open and shut with agitated snaps. Open, he'd glance at a page and run his finger under a word, then slam his book shut and grip the book, like he wanted to throw it against the wall, until he put it back on his desk and again repeated the single word search of understanding.

Glancing around to see if the teacher was looking and seeing that she was focused on other students, Seth edged up behind the student, pulled a comic book out of his coat and quietly dropped it on the student's desk. The kid jerked upright and turned to glare at Seth, ready to fight at the supposed insult.

Seth just shrugged and whispered, "It worked with me. That's how I learned to read." The kid continued to glare at the large man towering over him, then slowly turned his focus back down to the image of Spiderman swinging through the sky high above the streets. Without glancing back at Seth or even acknowledging him, the young black man slowly raised the cover, and leaning over his desk began to slowly make out the words in the comic book. Seth secretly smiled to himself. He knew what it was like to finally feel a bit of success.

Several hours later, after lunch, which was provided free to all students, history classes began. Buffalo horns were passed from student to student while the teacher explained how a fort used to stand right where the city courthouse now stood. Pictures of famous Indians lined the board. Several of the students were actually interested, but most of the students still looked at the teacher like he was crazy. They would continue to do so for several weeks to come, because progress with students is often a very slow process. Some of the changes, however, happened more quickly.

CHAPTER XXX

That night at the mall, Raymond Alvarez and one of his friends, an equally tough young man in a stained, cut-off tee-shirt, stood in front of the Under Twenty-One, the only really hot store to shop for anything if you were under 21 or wanted people to still see you that way.

The store had a few customers, and the clerk at the counter was busy, so at first he didn't see the two obvious gang members stepping inside the shop. Had he noticed them, and if he had been a policeman, he'd have said they definitely looked suspicious. But he wasn't a policeman, and these weren't the first two gang members who had stepped into the store that evening.

When the clerk finished up with his customer, he noticed the two young men and smiled.

"Hi, can I help you?" he called out.

The two facing him didn't seem to know how to respond for a moment, and then Raymond, putting on his best, I could care less machismo pulled a piece of paper out of his pocket.

"Maybe, maybe not. They said this was good here."

The clerk came out from behind the counter, and approached the two young men, glancing at the proffered slip, then smiled, "Sure. It's good for a couple of shirts and a couple of pants, and within reason, anything else you need. Kind of a swap. You leave those clothes here, and you get to pick what you want."

"Yeah, sure, from where?" Raymond was still not buying the sell. Nothing was ever free in his world. The clothes were probably old stock that nobody in their right mind would be caught dead wearing. "Where do you keep your rejects?"

The clerk smiled. "This is Under Twenty-one, we don't do rejects." Sweeping his hand to indicate the entire store, he added, "Be my guest."

Raymond's comrade suddenly remembered he had a slip too and pulled it out. "That go for me too? Anything I want?"

"Just so it can be worn to school, and it isn't gang colors."

Raymond began shaking his head and backing up towards the exit. "This is all bull-shit," he hissed. "What do I want your clothes for? I like what I got."

The clerk looked him over and then commented, "Well, except for the shirt, you could probably keep the rest. Just grab another. We've got a store full."

Then, he leaned in confidentially, "But if I were you two, I'd go back there and try on some of those new Wrangler stressed jeans. I mean, you're already here, and they just came in and everyone's wearing them in California."

Raymond glanced towards the back of the store, still torn, but his stained tee-shirt friend had already made up his mind and was moving towards those Wranglers.

While the progress with the students may have been described as slow but steady, the same couldn't be said for the renovation of the downtown area. It was much faster. Cleaning up mortar and brick was much easier than cleaning up ingrained attitudes and opening minds after years of mental neglect.

In just over three weeks, Riverton's downtown was beginning to take on a new shine. Graffiti was being removed daily by teams of street people, including Lyle. It was exhausting work; a lot of scrubbing and a lot of painting, but Lyle seemed to enjoy the activity and it wasn't long before he had begun to put on some much needed weight and regain his old strength.

Of course, giving up drinking had been the most difficult part for Lyle, and he knew, even if nobody else did, that he hadn't really given it up completely, in his mind. Liquor was readily available. It was his own body, and it was his choice what he wanted to do with his body. So it was his decision to go faithfully to AA meetings every morning and evening, and then close himself up in his small cell every night, cutting himself off from all temptation. His daily reward, aside from a clearer mind and healthier body, was treating himself to something new for his living space, to celebrate that he had been able to abstain for another day and night.

Lyle took great pleasure in finding things that, like himself, he could rejuvenate into something beautiful and useful. His favorite things were flowers, which he found peeking out from fields of weeds, gasping for light and air. He'd move them, roots and all, into pots he scavenged and nurse them back to life.

#

At the middle school, Billy Harker (aka Glide) and his friends had become bored with all the restrictions they faced in school and decided it was time to retest their limits. It began with a chalk-filled eraser hurled at the blackboard in Ms. Burgess' math class. This move brought squeals of laughter from the other students and a squeal of surprise from the startled Ms. Burgess. Then, this was followed by a yelp of pain as the Guardian, who had been sitting in the back of the room, knocked the perpetrator, Rebok, from his desk with a well-placed swipe of a club-like hand. Rebok was so dazed by the blow, he wasn't able to pull himself back into his seat. Nobody in the room, neither his friends nor his classmates, attempted to help him, or even look at him as he lay there on the floor. The class just continued around him.

Two weeks later, the Notorious Four, as they now dubbed themselves, tried again, this time as a group. "Safety in numbers," they felt, rough-housing as they moved between classes, slam-banging each other into lockers. Other students scattered, or if forced, started to push back. Almost instantly, three Guardians were there, breaking up the disturbance. No one got backhanded this time. Instead, Billy and his friends were put to work scrubbing graffiti off the school walls under the watchful eye of the Guardians.

CHAPTER XXXI

Riverton had been under its new regime for almost five weeks when historians would later say, 'the tide turned.'

It was mid-day at the roadblock, and like everything new and out of the ordinary, the few cars and moving vans that were still moving out had lost their appeal to the dwindling press. America's attention span was incredibly short. With no more attacks in Riverton, and murders becoming more prevalent everywhere else, newscasters were forced to turn their attention closer to home. Even the attacks on the President had lost their ability to draw a viewing audience. The President was almost a mythical figure to most of the country, and nobody felt they had a real say in what went on in Washington. Most felt they couldn't even control their own lives. Re-runs of old sitcoms seemed to have more relevancy to those in Middle America. It wasn't as though Riverton was another 9/11. Nobody was going to go to war over Riverton. In fact, most of the photographers left seated in the shade of the trees, lining the road, were free-lancers hoping to capture something worth selling to the bigger news outlets. This was going to be their lucky day.

It had been so long since anything other than supply trucks and military equipment had been heading into Riverton that the sight of the lone moving van, coming in that direction, got the attention of the soldier at the gate.

Stepping out of his kiosk, the Guardian in charge started waving the driver back and finally flagged the car down.

"Hey buddy, whoa, whoa. You're going in the wrong direction."

The driver of the van, Mr. Charles Tan, a Chinese-American from Fresno, rolled down his window and peered up into the face of the border guard.

"Hello?" he said in perfect English, smiling broadly.

"Hello, yourself," laughed the Guardian, making sure his smile included the man's wife and children who were anxiously leaning forward to see the man with a gun who had stopped their car.

"Anything wrong?" the father asked.

"Uh, nothing except you're going in the wrong direction. You want to go the other direction," he said, pointing in the direction the car had just come from.

"No," came the reply from the man and his wife.

"We want to move to Riverton," she said calmly, pointing in that direction. "We're highly educated. My husband is a doctor, an MD, and I am a teacher. We want to help your community."

The soldier appeared confused, as did the other soldiers who had moved closer out of curiosity. The lead waved them back and switched on his field phone.

Turning his back to the car and its occupants, he said, "Sir, uh, we've got a family here that I'm not sure what to do with. No sir, no problem, they...they just want to move in. Yeah, moving van and everything."

It took a few moments for the person on the other end of the line to understand. The phone was then apparently handed over to someone much higher in the chain of command, because when the Guardian heard that voice, his posture snapped to attention and he almost saluted.

"Yes, sir. Yes, sir. I understand, sir. Right."

The soldier hooked his phone back onto his belt and turned back to the driver.

"Sir, uh, I'm sorry it took me so long." Waving for the gate to be lifted, he continued, "If you'll just drive on down this road here about three miles, you'll come to the courthouse parking lot. You can't miss it. It's on your right-hand side of the road. Pull in there. Somebody will be waiting to help you get signed up and all."

"Thank you," smiled Mr. Tan, echoed by the others in the car.

Then confirming, Mr. Tan asked, "Three miles? You said, three miles?"

"Of course, he said three miles," Mr. Tan's wife interjected, before the soldier could respond. "Three miles."

"On the right," the soldier saluted the reprimanded husband adding, "uh, welcome to Riverton."

Every camera at the roadblock was on that van as it pulled through the barricade, headed for Riverton and every television set in the country.

#

At the courthouse, Ryder, Joel and more than half of the staff raced out of their offices and into the almost deserted parking lot, all eyes turned towards the soon-to-be approaching car and the future it held for Riverton.

"Now, don't scare them," Ryder warned those around him who were almost vibrating with excitement. "This is what we've been waiting for. It's just an everyday occurrence, the first of a thousand more. Don't fuck it up, please!"

And nobody did.

That night, Charles Tan and his family were the lead story on every news station, especially Washington's Channel 7, where Marshall Foster was never adverse to mixing his personal opinion into the nightly broadcast.

"...The Mayor of Riverton issued an open invitation today to anyone wanting to move into their community. So far, the grand experiment tally stands at 989 exits and rising, with only one entry request, and that from a former Singaporean resident," reported Marshall, as Charles Tan's picture flashed on the screen behind him, "who evidently doesn't find living in a police state all that different from good old home. Well, I hate to tell you, Mr. Charles Tan, true Americans don't give up their rights that easily, even with the doubtful promise of a safer place to live."

Marshall would have been shocked to find out just how wrong he actually was.

The next morning, Charles Tan and his wife registered their three children for school. By noon, Guardians were checking through dozens of trucks, vans and cars, all loaded with people, heading for Riverton, people who were willing to give the new community a chance.

By five o'clock that afternoon, as the stream of traffic grew, the waiting line at the roadblock was backed up at least a mile, and those waiting for entry were being swarmed by T.V. and news reporters.

"Where are you from?" a reporter asked one middle-aged couple.

"California, Van Nuys," came the reply.

"And you're moving here?"

"Damn straight," shouted back the husband.

"Why?"

"Have you been to California lately?"

Closer to the roadblock, Marshall Foster was doing a live remote, trying to win back some of his prestige after the previous night's faulty prediction. With him was Mike Moritz of the Washington ACLU.

"And so it appears that for today the tides have changed in Riverton, but according to Mike Moritz of the Washington ACLU, it doesn't matter which way this tide runs, Riverton is going to end up beached. Is that a pretty fair description of what we were just talking about, Mike?"

"That's so right," answered Moritz, in a gravelly voice, sounding very wise and all-knowing. "It is sometimes hard for me to believe the, I don't want to call it ignorance, but it certainly is naiveté, of some of these people we've seen here today. It's the same sort of blind following that leaders like David Koresch, Jim Jones and others generated."

"Only this time, it's for a town, a philosophy, not a man."

"Exactly, Marshall, but what everyone fails to realize is that in America, the very nature of 'rights' is that they cannot be 'given up.' And organizations like ours are here to see that those rights are protected, whether the American public realizes it needs them or not. Trust me, the legal battles have just begun in Washington."

About a hundred feet away, twenty-seven-year-old Keats Leigh, NBC's rising young star on the political news scene, was busy capturing her own sound bites. Clearly determined to beat Marshall at his own game, Keats used her hard-earned political savvy and undeniable good looks to circle ahead of the Channel 7 News team and garner her own sound bites.

Pushing her microphone through the car window of an obviously Hispanic family, Keats hoped to get either a usable quote, or, at least, a jump in her viewership because of her inclusiveness. The driver of the car, a proud Chicano man, was moving with his wife and three children to Riverton.

"Aren't you worried?" asked Keats.

"Why should I be? My family does not steal. It does not murder. My wife and I, we work hard. Why should we worry? Maybe, for once," he said, stroking the soft brown hair, of his youngest daughter, "we get to stop worrying."

Thanking the man and wishing him luck, Keats turned to look for another sound bite. She moved in on the next car in line, driven by a young professional-looking woman with an infant car seat in the back.

Inside the car, Rachel saw the reporter coming, and turned away, making sure her window was up and her doors locked. The last thing she wanted right now was to be interviewed. The truth was that she wasn't sure how she felt about Riverton at this moment, or if she would be staying.

When the car in front of her moved onto an access lane, a rather nordic-looking Guardian motioned her forward, and as she approached she rolled down her window.

"Just follow the crowd," he said to her, "and park on your right at the courthouse. They'll explain everything when you get there." He was already turning to the next car as he said, "Welcome to Riverton."

Rachel called out after him, "Excuse me. I'm looking for my husband, Seth Slavin. He's with the Guardians, and I..."

A sudden smile crossed the soldier's face as he turned back to face her. "Seth?"

Before she could answer, he asked, "You, Rachel?" and then seeing the baby, he beamed, "and that must be, Oh my God, Little Seth. You guys are all he's been talking about."

Excitedly thrusting his hand out to her, he apologized, "Oh, hi, I'm sorry. I'm Hovig Kolizarius. Seth's a friend."

Rachel couldn't help smiling at his enthusiasm or his strong handshake.

"Nice to meet you, Mr. Kolizar..."

"Hovig. Just Hovig. I work with Seth at the high school and he didn't say you were coming this week. I thought it was next."

"I wanted to surprise him and..."

"Oh my God, he's going to die," laughed Hovig, clapping his hands excitedly. You won't believe the house he's found for you. Oh, jeez, that was supposed to be a surprise."

Rachel was laughing with Hovig now, and feeling much more relaxed.

"I promise, I won't tell. You don't know how glad I am to meet a friend of Seth's. I didn't know what to expect."

"Oh, you're going to love it here. My fiancée's coming out next week."

"We'll have to get together."

"You got it, but first, let's get you hooked up with the Slavinmeister." He was now pointing, "Just follow the crowd, but take the first turnoff to the right." He stuck a colored pass under her window wiper, "This, will get you into our back parking lot. I'll try to track him down and have him meet you there. Oh, welcome to Riverton!!!"

Moments later, Seth burst out of the back entrance of an administration building, barreling down the steps, apologizing to those who ducked out of his way as he headed for the parking lot, his face beaming with excitement. Not seeing Rachel, he looked at the long line of traffic, moving at a snail's pace, past the entrance into town and unable to wait for her, he dashed past the guard at the entrance to the employees parking and down the line of slow-moving cars, searching and calling her name.

In her car, Rachel was so focused on trying to find the turnoff Hovig had mentioned, she heard Seth's voice before she realized he was the man rushing down the line of cars. In that moment, every doubt she had disappeared. Every fear she had built up in her nights alone, that somehow her husband had changed, disappeared as the tears streamed down her face. Stopping the car, she leapt out and in the time it took to call his name, they were in each other's arms, both trying to bury themselves in the other's body, oblivious to the smiles and stares of the people in the cars around them.

"Oh, God, I've missed you," Seth whispered over and over again, his face buried in her hair.

In his own van, the Chicano man smiled at his wife and nudged her, "I think he knows her."

His wife just gave him a playful hit, as her husband pulled his car around Rachel's idling vehicle. He also gave Seth a thumbs up sign as he and Rachel ran back to claim their vehicle.

CHAPTER XXXII

As they drove into the employees' parking lot, the guard gave Seth a welcome salute as their car passed. Rachel was driving because Seth had jumped into the back seat, not wanting to wait any longer to finally touch his infant son.

With the car parked, Rachel showed Seth the workings of the baby's car seat and released their son into his father's waiting arms for the first time. She then busied herself getting diapers out of the back of the car, knowing Seth needed these few moments alone with the baby.

When she looked up, Seth was gently rocking his new son, humming into his tiny ear a song that Mama Slavin had always said was Seth's favorite. Rachel didn't think she had ever loved her husband more than at that moment.

After the humming came baby talk, "Yes, you are a big boy, a itty-bitty big boy."

He looked up from his son to Rachel, and she saw the tears in his eyes, "Oh God, he's so little. Look at those fingers, and toes. I can't believe you're here. I didn't think I was going to be able to stand it until next week."

"Me, either," Rachel reached out a hand to touch him to make sure he was really there at last.

"Oh," he remembered, "Cameron got in last night. He and Jay are staying..." he suddenly caught himself, "uh, right near...uh....someplace I want to show you, after we get you checked in."

Then, for the first time, noticing the baby's colorful, stuffed diaper bag hanging from Rachel's hand, he asked in all seriousness, "What's that?"

Rachel burst out in laughter, "Oh, have you got a lot to learn."

She wrapped her free arm around her man, and together at last, as a family, they climbed the steps to enter the administration building.

While Seth had spent a great part of the last month in this building, to Rachel it was all a new experience. She found herself in a long corridor leading to the assembly rooms, bustling with Guardian activity. Crisp uniforms and smiling faces were everywhere and lots of organized activity. Rachel was reminded suddenly of the year the Chinese hosted the Olympics, everyone moving in sync, no wasted effort, like bees in a hive, or foraging ants. Maybe it was the uniforms, the fact that everybody seemed to look the same, and then, she realized that the uniformed Guardians were not the majority, only the most striking in their similarity. The rest were just citizens, dressed as casually or professionally as in any workplace; all working at their assigned tasks and seeming to enjoy being a part of something so new and revolutionary.

Seth appeared to be well-known by everyone, and he introduced Rachel and the baby to almost every single person they passed. There were too many names for Rachel to even begin learning, but she liked the fact that as busy as everyone was, every single person took the time to return the greeting, welcome Rachel and/or compliment the baby. And the greetings seemed completely genuine, completely heartfelt. Having the Guardians' families join them was a top priority for all of them. Only then would they really be a complete community.

When they finally reached a family restroom, where Rachel could change the baby, she had a chance to ask, "Do you think Angie's anywhere around?"

"I don't know. They change our assignments all the time," he replied, as he gingerly took the soiled disposable diaper she offered with a smile.

"What have you been feeding this kid?" he asked, as he opened the lid of the garbage can with his foot and dropped the baby's poop into the container.

"Just mama's milk, and if you think this is bad, your mother informs me that this is nothing compared to when we start him on real food."

"Maybe it's something I'll get used to after it becomes routine."

"Trust me, you'll get used to it. We don't have a choice." She completed the redressing of little Seth, and finding him just as cute as ever, handed him to his father so she could go wash her hands.

"Angie?" she reminded him of their interrupted flow of conversation.

"Oh, she could be anywhere. Depending on the day's assignment. We're all moved around a lot so we can get familiar with every aspect of what's going on. I hope she's out front. That's where we have to go next."

He held the door, and let Rachel step through before him. Then, he again took the lead heading for a double pair of doors across the work room.

Going through those doors, Rachel found herself behind a long row of desks being manned by civilians wearing *Welcome to Riverton* badges. A large sign above the door reaffirmed that sentiment as well, '*Welcome to Riverton.*' Families who want to move into the community must go through an interview process and moving past the interviewers, Rachel heard snatches of conversations.

"...A welder, that's good. There's a list of businesses hiring in your packet, but keep checking the number listed, because we're getting new businesses coming in at the rate of one or two a day."

And another, "...No, they're not free, but housing in Riverton is quite reasonable, and we do have several plans to help everyone become a homeowner."

"Retirement is fine, but we want to keep everyone active in the community, so Riverton has a very extensive volunteer program. I'm sure you'll find something that interests you and helps the community as well. Yes, it's required."

At one desk, although Rachel didn't know her yet, a rather quiet, actually frightened-looking, young, black woman sat before an interviewer.

"Junisha. Junisha Butler," she heard the woman say.

Rachel noticed that the woman's two younger children were sitting quietly by the desk, but her older child, probably a teenager, could barely conceal the anger that raged just below the surface at having been forced to come here.

When Seth moved off to get some paperwork, Rachel found herself listening to this interview a little more closely.

The woman, Junisha, was calling off names as the interviewer filled out the paper work.

"Chicago. Wayne Thomas, he's fourteen. Robert James, ten, and the baby, she's six, Tamara."

"And work experience?"

Junisha almost ducked her head as though avoiding a blow.

"I, it's been a while. There just weren't any..."

"Training?" the interviewer probed.

Again, Junisha had to shake her head and Rachel could see the woman's dreams of security for her children disappearing with this one interview.

"But I'll do anything," she pleaded.

"You understand, Mrs. Butler, there are no welfare programs in Riverton, and everyone has to work."

"I'll work," she cried. "I'll do anything. Anything. Please. This is for my kids. I don't want 'em runnin' with gangs. They're not going to have a chance unless... On the T.V., you said anybody..."

The older son, Wayne Thomas, suddenly stood up, the anger he had been holding back, finally spilling out. "I told you, fuck this. Now, let's go."

His mother, desperately wanting to be heard, screamed, "No!!!" causing those around her to look up. Junisha didn't care. She reached across the desk to grab the interviewer's hand.

"Please, just a chance," she pleaded.

Wayne Thomas wanted to take a swing at his sniveling mother, "Well, I ain't stayin'."

But Junisha wasn't listening. This was her only chance, and she knew it.

"Please, don't make us leave. A chance. That's all we want. It took everything we had to get here and we can't go back. Please give us a chance."

The interviewer, a rather severe-looking woman, whose name tag identified her only as Laverne, pulled her hand slowly back and reached for some other papers.

Junisha, in tears now, almost missed what the interviewer said next, "Mrs. Butler, I have no intention of turning you away. Anyone who is willing to abide by our laws, and work to make this community what we think it can be is welcome."

Junisha sank back into her chair, tears streaming down her face.

"We will need your signature on this," the woman said, indicating a form lying before her. "It'll cover your children, since they're all minors."

Junisha quickly reached to sign the form.

But Laverne held out a restraining hand.

"No, ma'am, read it first. These are important. They're the rules, rights, and responsibilities you're agreeing to if you move to Riverton. Then, if you agree to those rules, you can sign, but you are signing for your children as well and they will be bound by these rules, just like you will be. I'll give you as much time as you need to read through this page. Then, if you agree with them, you can sign. Then, we'll see if we can't find you a place to stay until you get yourself settled."

Seth's return with Rachel's own folder took her away before Junisha signed, but Rachel knew without even looking Junisha and her family was staying in Riverton. Rachel turned to Seth and the baby, as he said, "Sorry, I had already done most of the paperwork. They've even got some positions available in social services you might be interested in, once you're ready to go back to work. Oh, Rachel, you're going to love it here. It's fantastic and the people..."

"What's that sheet of paper everyone has to sign?"

"Oh, this," he searched through her folder to find hers. Finding it, he handed it to her.

"Just an allegiance statement, Riverton rules, responsibilities that type of thing."

He handed her a pen, but she waved it away as she read the paper. It didn't take long. It was only one page. But it was long enough for her to know. "Seth, I can't sign this."

"Sure you can. It's just a formality," he protested, seeming surprised.

"Seth, it says we agree to give up most of our basic rights for the good of the community, this community."

"Honey, I know what it says, but trust me, you're not signing your life away. It gives you, us, a new life."

"Seth, I cannot believe you."

"Honey, please," he pleaded, as he pulled her into a quieter corner of the office. "I need you. Give it a chance. Just think of it as...like living in a foreign country, where the laws are a little different. But you only have to obey them as long as you want to stay. No one is forcing you to do anything, and no one can make you stay. You can always catch the boat home, but I love what I'm doing here. I love what we're creating. Please, just give us a chance."

Rachel held for a moment, considering, her hand moving up to cover her eyes as though she had the beginning of a headache. Seth could only stand there. He was afraid to even touch her. His whole life depended on the woman before him.

Slowly, Rachel's hand slid down to cover her mouth and her eyes looked into Seth's, and she could see the desperation there. So much depended on what she would say next.

Taking a deep breath, she heard herself saying, "Well, it sure as heck doesn't look much like the Italy I remember."

Reaching out, she pulled the pen from Seth's shirt pocket, and signed her name at the bottom of the paper.

The rest of the checking-in process went smoothly. Seth, true to his word, had already filled out most of the paperwork, and the interview was less than five minutes long. Rachel looked around the room for Junisha and her family, but they were nowhere to be seen. She hoped she would get a chance to see the young mother again, and hoped life in Riverton would work out for her. Actually, she hoped it would work out for the both of them.

CHAPTER XXXIII

Once they were finished with registration, Seth took Rachel and the baby back to the car. After Rachel had secured the baby in his baby seat, Seth held the front-seat passenger's door open grandly for Rachel to enter. He even buckled her seat belt. Then, he drove his family to their new home.

It was on a beautiful tree-lined street with large mown front lawns, flower beds waiting for spring blooms and classic craftsman cottages with large beamed front porches that wrapped around both sides.

The one which Seth pulled her car into the driveway of was the most beautiful of all. Rachel sat for a full minute, just staring at it through the car window, wanting to remember this moment, this feeling of complete disbelief.

"I hope you like it," Seth said. "If not, we can always..."

She didn't hear the rest. She was already out of the car and releasing the baby's straps.

"Come on, Ikey. Let's see the new house Daddy got us."

Stepping up on the shaded front porch, the first thing Rachel wanted to try out was the porch swing, but she resisted the urge. Seth had already unlocked the mahogany double doors, with beveled glass inlays, and stepped back for Rachel to enter. Handing him the baby, she did. Stepping into the fieldstone foyer, she looked across the open empty expanse of the beamed and alcoved living room to the beautiful tree-shaded backyard beyond. A ceiling-high fieldstone fireplace, flanked by high dark-oak book shelves, dominated one wall, and she could see the fireplace was open to another room which she already knew would be equally as impressive. The house was unbelievable, and she reached back to grab Seth's arm to make sure she wasn't actually dreaming.

A big smile grew on his face, and Rachel caught herself laughing in excitement.

"It's perfect," she was squealing, and Seth, standing there holding the baby, looked happier than she'd ever seen him.

"I just put down a deposit on it, to hold it, hoping..."

She was already running to see what other room the fireplace serviced. "Oh Seth, it's beautiful. It's perfect."

Seth beamed down at the baby in his arms and cooed, "See, she likes it. Daddy did good."

From the other rooms, he could hear Rachel running ahead, and from the sound of her exclamations he knew she had fallen in love with the house the same way he had when he first saw it. It was meant to be their home.

Later that night, before a totally unnecessary, but very romantic, blazing fire in the fireplace, they nestled in each other's arms on blankets spread on the floor. Their clothes were strewn all around them and the after-glow of their lovemaking blended perfectly with the sparks and radiant colors of the fire reflecting around the empty room. Both were almost asleep after hours of getting to know each other's bodies again.

The baby, lulled by the warmth and flickering flames, was also fast asleep in his car seat beside them.

Rachel rolled over to press herself against the length of Seth's body and said, "Do you hear that?"

"What?" he asked.

"The birds, they're singing. I never knew birds sang at night."

She was right, over the crackling of the fire the song of birds could be heard in the moonlight outside the windows.

Seth smiled and kissed her upturned face, "We've never had our windows open before at night. Simple things like that, you tend to forget."

If they had not been so sated and oblivious to much more than each other's body, they might have heard a car moving slowly past their house.

Jay was driving with Cameron, visiting for the first time from Los Angeles on a temporary pass, riding in the front seat. Miles and Angie were in the back.

"I still think we ought to pound on the door and surprise them," Cameron said, as they passed Seth and Rachel's old craftsman.

"And you've got a sick sense of humor," teased Jay.

"That's why you all love me."

Miles suggested that they give Seth and Rachel at least one night to themselves, "'Cause we're all going to be busy helping move them in." Then he laughed, "Can you believe it, they've got the fire going. It's almost summer and they've got a fucking fire going?"

Cameron slid over to put his hand on Jay's leg. "I think that's romantic."

"They could have a heat stroke," Miles continued.

"Or conceive another baby," suggested Jay.

That's why Angie leaned forward excitedly, "Oh my God, wouldn't that be fantastic. We could call it Riverton, for its place of conception."

"I think Seth'll have his hands full just getting Rachel adjusted to living here," Cameron said as he glanced out the window and looked at the darkened houses passing by.

Angie was still excited. "I can't wait to see Rache and the baby. Auntie Angie... I like that." Then, reaching out to nudge Cameron over the front seat, she added, "Come on, Cameron, now that she's come in, you've got to take the plunge too."

When Cameron didn't respond, Jay put his hand on Cameron's hand reassuringly, "Don't press him. I've been doing enough of that myself. I'm just glad he's here now."

"So what's going on there in LA that's so important?" asked Miles, totally ignoring Jay's suggestion.

"I don't know," replied Cameron. "Same old same old. I've picked up some new accounts that..." Suddenly, he stopped and swiveled in his seat so he could face everyone in the car. "Okay, the truth of the matter is that this place sort of scares me. I don't know, it looks normal enough, but..."

"We're not exactly talking about the Stepford Wives here," Angie protested.

"I know, but... doesn't it all sound a little Orwellian? Big Brother watching and all that."

"But it's not like that. I told you," said Jay.

"It's hard to explain," Angie reached out to touch Cameron's shoulder. "I don't even know if it can be explained. It's just that things are much simpler. So much easier."

"You'll just have to judge it yourself," suggested Miles.

"What do you mean, 'easier'? 'Simpler'?"

Jay thought about how to answer, "That's really harder to explain. Maybe it'd be easier to show him."

This brought a laugh from the back of the car.

"Show me what?" asked Cameron.

"Just an example of how all of this plays out in every day life. Different?" Then, glancing at the back seat through the mirror, he asked, "What do you think, guys?"

"Go for it," came the excited, laughing reply.

"Go for what?"

"You'll see. You'll see." This was followed by more laughter.

#

The car drove through the silent streets toward the outskirts of town, finally turning on a rather pretty little lane, leading to a neatly painted, but quaint little four-story hostel with gingerbread trim wrapped by a large verandah. A sign at the entrance to the drive, proclaimed, The Wyndergarten Hotel.

The only sign of any street activity at this late hour was two men picketing in front of the building, carrying placards that read, "God is watching Riverton," and "Sodom and Gommorah."

Inside the car, Jay smiled at Cameron and announced, "This is it."

"What?" Cameron asked.

"You wanted to know how Riverton was different," said Angie. "Well, this is as good a place as any to get you started."

Cameron was still not seeing anything, as Jay pulled around behind the house, and then waited for a car to pull out from an underground parking garage beneath the house. Once the way was cleared, Jay drove down the ramp himself.

If the underground parking below a quaint looking hotel wasn't enough of a surprise, the fact that the parking lot was practically full really began to confuse Cameron.

"Don't tell me this is the hot spot in town," he heard himself saying.

"Something like that," Jay teased, as he finally found a parking spot.

Angie started laughing excitedly and Cameron found himself laughing with her, but not knowing what he was laughing about.

"I don't understand any of this," Cameron finally admitted, "but hell, it must be something to get Angie's motor running like that."

They all piled out of the car and followed Angie to the elevator where a uniformed doorman stood, holding the door for them.

"Good evening, Ma'am, Gentlemen," said the doorman, "welcome to the Wyndergarten."

The elevator itself was as quaint as the hotel and barely had enough room for the four who were now squeezed inside. The doors shut, and it groaned as it rose slowly up into the lobby area.

Cameron quipped, "Oh, whoopee, a Riverton thrill ride! Magic Mountain, look out!"

The rest were still laughing when the doors opened. They stepped out into the hotel's quiet little lobby and made their way to the quietly dignified desk clerk behind the counter.

"Good evening. Is this a group or are you singles?"

"Just showing a new friend around," said Miles.

"By all means. Do you need any assistance?"

"No, he's been here before," Angie said referring to Miles.

"Then, have a good evening. Tickets are one-hundred dollars each. Will that be cash or credit cards?"

Cameron didn't have a clue what was going on, but each of the others reached for his or her wallet, so he started to reach for his own.

Angie dropped her credit card on the counter first and announced, "I'll spring for it." She then elbowed Miles, "But I hold the tickets."

At Cameron's confused look, the clerk questioned, "Sir?"

"I'm okay I guess," shrugged Cameron. "I'm just along for the ride and at a hundred bucks a pop, it sure as hell better be worth it."

Jay smiled at the clerk who was running the card, "He's new in town."

After signing, the clerk handed Angie the four tickets and buzzed them through a hidden door, behind a sliding bookcase, leading to dimly lit hallway. Once inside, with the bookcase door securely closed behind them, Miles opened the door at the other end and music swept over them, filling the darkness.

Stepping into the small empty room beyond, the competing sounds of hot jazz and contemporary rock could be heard coming from behind the two closed doors, now facing them.

"Left or right," asked Miles.

"Let's start right," suggested Angie. "Sounds like the music's better."

They opened the right door, and Cameron followed them into a bustling nightclub filled with hot jazz, good drinks and men and women enjoying the music and getting to know each other. Some were dancing. Most were talking. It looked like almost any other small club except the women were all fairly attractive and all wore the same rather revealing shifts.

"You are fucking kidding me," Cameron laughed, finally understanding.

"Nope," said Miles, "and it's all legal and taxable."

"With set rates and weekly medical checkups," added Angie.

Cameron couldn't believe it. He was standing in the midst of a legalized house of prostitution.

One couple was sitting at the end of the bar. He was rather quiet-looking and slightly overweight. She was a strikingly attractive thirty-year-old brunette. Cameron saw the man shyly hand the woman his ticket and she smiled at him, took his hand and led him out of the room.

Jay whispered in Cameron's ear, "The ticket's good for an hour upstairs or you can just come here for drinks, decide not to go with anybody, and they'll give you a full refund when you leave."

"And they know about this? The city?"

"Of course they do," Jay responded. "Who do you think gets the money? It's not a crime anymore. It's just regulated."

Angie joined in with, "When we first got here, the entire downtown at night was a circus of two-bit hustlers, junkies, and pimps."

"Now, it's all strictly controlled by the city," added Miles, "and confined to the Wyndergarten. No more pimps, no more street hustling. Prices are regulated by the house. Limits as to what the ladies will do or not do are set by the ladies beforehand, not their customers."

"And it's far enough away from the residential areas to give some sense of privacy," added Angie. "And it's not only for men."

On Cameron's look and Miles' laugh, she explained, "You guys are not the only ones who need to get their rocks off on occasion."

Grabbing Cameron's shoulder and turning him to face two men standing by the bar, she proclaimed, "They're for me, or other discriminating women with good taste."

"Good Lord, they're gorgeous," volunteered Cameron.

"And straight," Angie laughed, as she gave Cameron a hug. "Hands off the merchandise."

"It seems awfully unfair to me," he laughed with her.

"Frankly, I like the music better in the other half," whispered Jay in Cameron's ear. "I think you will too."

Angie and Miles stifled a laugh as Jay led Cameron back into the entry hall, and this time, opened the left door. The music was indeed hotter, and so were most of the men and women enjoying it. Couples sat holding hands at the bar or in padded leather booths around the room. Glistening bodies danced in the disco and neon darkness, and most of those dancing were with a partner of the same sex.

The bartenders, with their bare chests and tattooed arms, could have literally stepped out of a *Tom of Finland* fantasy.

Angie nudged Cameron and whispered, "Your mouth is hanging open," and Cameron swallowed, realizing it was true.

Later, back in Jay's car, Cameron started asking questions as soon as they pulled out of the underground garage and onto the street.

"It's just that sex between consenting adults is not a crime," explained Jay.

"The key word there is 'consenting'," added Angie.

Cameron noticed the picketers as they drove past, "I see, not everybody is so open-minded."

"No, not everybody agrees with everything that's happening, but that's okay. There's no law against protesting, it just has to be done in an orderly fashion. No destruction of property. No physical abuse and no interruption of business."

"So what do you think?" asked Miles, slapping Cameron on the shoulder.

Cameron was silent for a moment, not really sure what he thought. "It's funny," he finally said. "I don't know what I think. I mean, I've always said it ought to be legal. You know, consenting adults, no harm, no foul, but now all I'm thinking is," he paused and turned to face Jay in the driver's seat. "If I catch your ass in there just one time, especially with Mr. Tattoo behind the bar, I'm gonna have your balls for lunch."

Miles and Angie burst out laughing in the back seat, and Miles reached up to slap Cameron on the shoulder again, "Wow, you know with you two, it's hard to tell whether you're really pissed, or making a pass."

Everybody was laughing then, but Jay knew Cameron was not kidding, and that jealousy made him as hard as a rock. Like Rachel and Seth, it was their first night back together again as well, and their quick tryst in the shower before picking up Miles and Angie was nothing compared to what he had planned for the rest of the evening.

CHAPTER XXXIV

It was amazing what the influx of businesses was doing to the downtown streets of Riverton. In less than three months, by mid-summer, the filth and graffiti were completely gone, replaced by clean, shining new store-fronts.

All along the avenue, crews worked to set young trees into freshly created holes in the repaired sidewalks. Some of the stores were already open and doing business while others were still in the process of stocking merchandise. A flurry of activity surrounded each of the trucks being off-loaded.

Lyle had been assigned to one of the new merchants and was helping unload new merchandise for the store. Crossing back to the truck for another armload, he was momentarily distracted by a tree being lowered into the ground in the park across the street. He smiled in appreciation and wondered if they were going to plant flowers as well around the base of the trees, and in thinking so, suddenly grew excited and could hardly wait to complete his day's assignment and get back to the shelter. He wanted to talk to Joseph Redfeather.

Although Lyle didn't know it, Seth and Rachel were also watching that same new tree being lowered into the ground. Seth loved showing Rachel their new town and the park with its benches and play-area was its center. The baby slept in a sling close to Rachel's heart.

"You can't imagine how much all this has changed," Seth explained. "I mean, it was like a cesspool when we first got here. Look at it now. It's alive."

Rachel looked at all the activity and she smiled at Seth's enthusiasm, but in her eyes, Seth could still see she questioned the dreams of Riverton.

"And more businesses are coming every day. And it's the same thing at the Mall. And people wanting to move here, waiting to use these businesses and start a new life."

Rachel held up her hand, trying to think how to put into words her reservations. "Seth, Honey, it's wonderful. It really is, but all it proves is that with enough money to throw at it, you can do almost anything. And this is government money. Nobody else has this kind of money."

"You don't understand," he tried to explain. "Yes, it's taken a lot of money. But then, a lot of money is being saved. And if everything goes as projected, the city should break even in about two years, have paid all this money back, and be working in the black in three. Show me where that's possible anywhere else."

"But it still all boils down to money," she protested with more resentment than she meant.

"No, it doesn't. Think of all the money that's been thrown down the drain, year after year, trying to put Band-Aids on gaping wounds. Rachel, you and I both know none of them addressed the real problems, giving people a feeling of worth, of security, of belonging, of being safe. That's what is working here. Look at those people there. Can't you feel it? You've just got to. They're part of something living, something growing, not dying."

"Okay, okay," Rachel surrendered, "I will open my pores, and soak in all this new-found freedom, but if you don't mind, it'll have to wait until after your son and I have had a change in habit. It's hard to concentrate with a loaded diaper under your nose."

Seth knew he had been coming on too strongly, but he was desperate for Rachel to love Riverton and its vision as much as he did. His life depended on it. If Rachel moved back to Los Angeles, he'd have to move back as well, and Seth wasn't sure he would be able to do that.

Helping Rachel get the baby out of the sling and onto one of the new Victorian-styled benches where she could begin changing him, he apologized, "I'm sorry. I just want you to like it here as much as I do."

"I know," she said, "and I'm trying, but Honey, do you remember last year when we decided to go see that Disney film that was being re-released. You know, Cinderella and we were the only ones without children. Through the entire movie, the parents kept trying to make sure their kids loved it as much as they had when they were kids. They talked all the way through the movie so their own kids never got a chance to really enjoy it. Well, I kinda feel like those kids. Just give me a chance. Let me find out for myself. If it's all that great, you won't have to tell me, or sell me. I'll know it."

Reaching out to touch him, she added, "I love you and I know I'm gonna love it here too, but you know me, I always like to do things myself." Then, she added with a smile, "But I will let you carry the twerp for awhile. And does this town of ours have a good Chinese restaurant? I'm starved."

#

The name of the old Jere Baxter Elementary School had been changed to the Riverton Elementary School to match its fresh new colors and state-of-the-art equipment. The office was bright, colorful, and welcoming, but it still intimidated Junisha as she stood at the counter enrolling her two younger children, Robert James and Tamara. The school secretary, Agnes Harmon, a retired elementary school teacher herself, had come out of retirement to fill the position, wanting to see for herself how this new regime was going to work out. Besides, what else was she going to do with her life since her husband of forty-five years, Ernest, had passed. Never having any children of her own, the generations of children she had taught were her only legacy. She had watched the slow deterioration of the Riverton educational system, from a place to teach to merely a place to placate parents, and to keep unruly children from harming themselves until they again became the problem of their own families.

Agnes had been 'old school.' In spite of all the latest rules and regulations, and they changed with each new fad, she herself had kept her classes under her control, teaching what she knew best: reading, writing, arithmetic, and structure. She had been considered a relic. Parents complained that she was too strict, too demanding, and too out-of-date, but since Ernest was then the principal and her husband, nepotism won out, and her class remained her private domain. Ernest had no choice but to follow the latest regulations, but he allowed her to keep to what they both knew was the only real way to teach. She had been proud to see many of her students move on to successful college careers, returning often to thank her for teaching them how to study.

Once Ernest died, his successor, a liberalist, quickly spotted the rebel in his midst and forced her retirement. Of course, that liberal lasted only two years before being fired for inappropriate behavior with an underage high school drop-out.

After the invasion of sanity, as Agnes liked to think of it, she volunteered to help out at her old school and, after meeting with Ryder, was welcomed into the fold.

She glanced up at the woman standing before her and liked the determination she saw in those dark eyes. The woman was frightened. Agnes could see that, but she had not been too frightened to uproot her family and bring them by bus from Chicago. That took real guts, and Agnes admired guts.

Helping Junisha fill out the registration forms, Agnes couldn't help noticing Junisha's oldest son, Wayne Thomas, sitting slumped in the corner, making a deliberate show of 'not giving a shit.'

Junisha interrupted her thoughts. "Robert James, he's ten and Tamara, she's six."

"I'm almost seven," interjected Tamara.

"Almost seven," corrected Junisha, stroking her daughter's tightly braided hair.

Agnes smiled and asked, "Address?"

Junisha seemed to hesitate at this, not really knowing how to answer. "Uh, you see, right now, we don't..."

"We live in a jail," blurted out Tamara.

Junisha, embarrassed, quickly tried to cover, "No, Honey, it's not really a jail."

"Well, it's got bars," said Robert James, wanting to be included.

Agnes looked down at both the eager children and smiled, "That must be a real adventure for you, but your mama's right. We don't have any jails in Riverton anymore."

Junisha felt a wave of relief at the kindness.

"Besides, it's only temporary," she said to her children, and then looked up into the eyes of the secretary, "'til I get myself some work and you know, find..."

Agnes quickly put her at ease, "Well, I'm sure you'll have your own place before you know it, but for right now, we'll just list Hudson Station. I kind of like that name. Samuel Hudson was one of the founders of the old Riverton, and he was a great-great uncle or something of my late husband's. I'm glad they kept that name."

Finished with the forms, Agnes came out from behind the counter and gathered the children around her.

"Now, are you guys ready to meet your new teachers?"

Both children instantly chimed, "Yes'm," with Tamara adding, "is she nice?"

Agnes laughed and promised, "They're both the best."

Turning back to see whether Junisha wanted to join them, she saw Junisha shake her head 'no' as she ran her hands over her poorly fitting clothes, self-conscious about how she looked.

"School's out at six, Mrs. Butler," Agnes offered. "You can pick them up on the front steps on nice days. If it's bad, they'll be in the auditorium. That's that door right over there," she said, pointing. "Of course, we'll have their teachers with them until you arrive."

She then remembered and looked down at Robert James, "And I think your class has a field trip planned next week on a boat."

"A real one? On water?" asked the excited child.

"On the great Ohio River," replied Agnes, as she walked the children down the hall.

Junisha raised her hand hesitantly to wave good-bye, but the children were too excited to even notice, as they followed Agnes out of the office. She could hear Agnes' voice continuing her discussion of the trip until her voice faded away. The last thing she heard was 'Did you know that,' and she thought she heard Robert James' awed, 'No.'

Wayne Thomas' mocking voice forced the smile off of Junisha's face. "Gimme a fuckin' break. Are you going to stand there all day?"

The middle school office was not nearly as hospitable. It still had its old name and appearance, much closer to what Junisha remembered about her old Chicago school, minus the graffiti. Wayne Thomas was even less cooperative here than at the elementary school. An assistant principal, a man whose name tag identified him as Van Martin, appeared much sterner than Agnes, and Junisha thought that was probably better. He did help her fill out the paperwork.

"Wayne Thomas. He's fourteen," Junisha supplied.

"Grade?" Mr. Martin didn't even look up.

"Eighth," she answered, "though he been havin' problems."

Finally the man looked up and focused on Wayne Thomas.

"What do you go by, Wayne or Thomas?" he asked to which Wayne Thomas replied with arrogance, "Bingo, that's my name."

The assistant principal just looked at him for a second before saying, "Well, we're going to have to change that. Don't have any street names here, so what's it going to be, you got two choices or both if you want. What's it going to be? Wayne, Thomas or Wayne Thomas."

"Like I care," was the only response he got, and it was true. Wayne Thomas was beyond caring about anyone or anything except himself. At fourteen, back in his projects, he had finally been accepted into the BC's, after years of degrading disrespect, a hazing that had lasted more years than it should have, all because he backed away from a fight when he was nine. The kid had been older and bigger, and Wayne Thomas did not know he was being tested. In momentarily backing up those three steps, he'd been knocked down in the projects to just short of a faggot or pussy-boy. It had taken more than four years and two shootings to gain back what he has lost. And then his fucking mother had moved them all and everything he had worked for so long, was gone. It wasn't going to happen. He wasn't a pussy-boy any longer. He was a BC to his soul and nobody better forget it.

At Seth's house that night, a small welcoming party was going on. There was still no furniture, but the gang didn't mind and were sprawled on the floor enjoying the fast-food entrees. It was a comfortable feeling with everyone talking at once while Cameron kept the baby entertained.

"How much longer are you going to be able to stay?" Miles asked him, as he reached out to tickle the baby's stomach.

"Two more days and then it's back to good old L.A.," Cameron replied.

"You know, I don't miss it at all," Miles said seriously, "I thought I would, but I don't."

"What's to miss?" inserted Jay.

"Oh, I don't know," responded Cameron, "how about people, plays, movies, concerts, nightclubs, major sports, culture, but who's counting."

Jay slid over beside them. "We'll have those here," he said, "just give us time. Maybe not major sports, but..."

"Okay, if I have to give up one, I guess..."

"But the rest, it'll come."

"In how many centuries? I'm not that young anymore."

Seth responded from across the room, "I don't think it will be all that long, really. There's already talk about building a performing arts center."

"Well, when they break ground, let me know."

Jay started to respond, but Angie broke in with, "I'm still hungry. Who wants ice cream?"

"I do," came the unanimous response.

Rachel got up to help her, "I think I put the toppings in the refrigerator."

In the kitchen, Angie was pulling out three different flavors while Rachel was finding twice that many toppings.

"Well, what do you think?" asked Angie.

"What do you mean?"

"The house? I knew you'd love it the minute Seth showed us."

"Oh, the house, it's wonderful. Unbelievable, if you want the truth, but I just wish, uh..."

"And this town? Have you seen the town?" asked Angie excitedly. "Can you believe it? It hasn't even been two months. I don't think I've ever been so excited about anything in my entire life."

Rachel found herself taking a step back away from Angie, unsure of even why she was doing it, then realized she recognized in Angie that same fanaticism she had seen in Seth.

Changing the subject, she asked, "So, what do you hear from Enrique?"

Angie, matter-of-factly shrugged, as she picked up the containers of ice cream, "I don't. Truth of the matter is, outside of bed, we didn't have a whole lot in common." Then, she suddenly smiled at the memory, "But God, he sure knew how to push my buttons in bed, the stupid shit!"

She was laughing as she carried the ice cream into the living room. Rachel followed with the bowls and toppings.

CHAPTER XXXV

Over the next couple of weeks, everyone in town was settling into the life patterns of the new Riverton. Junisha found that she loved her classes as much as her younger children loved theirs. Having never really been able to focus on learning, she now found that every day opened new doors in her mind, and all of it was geared to her being able to support herself and her children. Her eldest, Wayne Thomas, was still fighting the Riverton rules and restrictions, but at least his rebellion was limited to verbal and not physical abuse, and he knew the consequences of crossing the line in the classroom. Junisha knew he would eventually come around. He didn't have any other choice. Junisha also began to believe again, in herself and in God. Taking the children back to church suddenly became important to her and she found herself praying to a God she had long ago dismissed as uncaring and unreachable.

Rachel and Seth focused their first weeks together on getting the house ready for the arrival of the moving van. Together, they picked the paints and wallpaper, and worked together creating their own special home for their baby. She was also pleasantly surprised at how well-stocked the Riverton stores were, and how many new stores were slated to open in the coming months. It really was hard not to be caught up in the excitement you could feel in the air. *It must be like the settlers felt when they opened up a new territory*, she thought, on more than one occasion.

The day the moving van arrived, Rachel supervised the gang in unloading their furniture from Los Angeles. Cameron had left for Los Angeles, but everyone else was there to help. It was good to be surrounded again by all her old friends and her own furniture.

That night after everyone had left, and the baby was asleep, she and Seth continued to unpack the last of the boxes. Suddenly between boxes, he looked over at her, and she looked back at him. He smiled, as he toyed with the top button of his shirt. She smiled, and glanced towards the bedroom, then back at him. Instantly, they were both up and racing for the bedroom, shedding clothes as they ran, seeing who could get naked first. Their laughter carried throughout the house. Their house. Their home.

The next morning, as she kissed Seth goodbye on their front porch, she saw the love in his eyes and made a decision.

"Seth, I think I want to go see about that job tomorrow," she said.

"You sure?" he asked.

"No. But I think maybe that's what's bothering me. Not being involved like the rest of you."

Seth gave Rachel a big hug, and Rachel looked out over the quiet town and knew she should have been at peace. But in spite of everything, she wasn't.

It had to be her problem, she thought, not theirs, so at nine-thirty Rachel reported to the social services office in the municipal building. She found the place busy and congested with too many people working in too small a space. Some of them were even forced to set up their applicant processing stations in the lobby.

Ilona, the head of the Riverton Social Services, was a bright young African- American about Rachel's age, and the minute she heard Rachel was asking for her, she appeared and reached over the counter to take her hand.

"Hi," she said, with a beautiful smile, "I'm Ilona Striker."

"Rachel Slavin."

"I know. Seth told me all about you, and you don't know how glad I am to see you finally here. Where's the baby?"

Rachel found herself liking Ilona instantly, which was not Rachel's usual mode of trust. She couldn't help volunteering, "Seth found a sitter. It's my first time away from him."

"Oh, you should have brought him," Ilona said, as she led Rachel behind the counter and back to her office.

"Come on, it's a little congested in here," she smiled, then laughed, "a little, my God, we're falling all over ourselves."

Once in the office, Ilona closed the door and cleared files off a chair to make a place for Rachel to sit.

"I'd like to say things are not usually this cluttered," Ilona said with a laugh, "but I'd be lying. We've been in the process of moving for the last two weeks. Process, not actually moving. They're going to tear out some walls and give us about triple the space, but until then, it's make-do time. Unfortunately, not everything's on computer yet, so we all tend to keep the files we're currently working on close at hand; not very efficient, but we manage."

"It doesn't look that bad," Rachel said, looking around.

Ilona laughed again, and it was a throaty, warm laugh. "I like you. You said that with a straight face. It's terrible, but, we make it work. Well, how do you like Riverton?"

"Interesting," was all Rachel could manage to say.

"Said like a true diplomat," laughed Ilona with real sparkle in her eyes. "But, god, I know what you mean. I call it *Riverton Shell Shock*. It takes getting used to. Some can't. Most of this department, including my old boss, left with the first wave."

"Left?"

"Like rats from a sinking ship."

"Why'd you stay?" Rachel asked, really wanting to know.

Ilona didn't answer immediately as though she was trying to remember. "I don't know. I thought about it. I was scared at first. I mean, everyone else was leaving, but when I started looking, I found I really didn't have anywhere else to go. And you know when you're caught and not left with many options, you kinda swallow and try to act like things are normal. At least, that's what I did. So I just got up that next morning and came on into work, just like I always had. Four of us showed up. We just kind of sat around that first day in shock and pretended we had things to do."

"Next day, they called us all in, you know, Ryder, the head guy, and he thanked us for staying, and then, sat us down and explained the new directives. And you know, they sounded so logical the way they were explained, I guess from that point on, I stayed, because I thought they might work."

"Do they?"

Ilona didn't respond right away, and Rachel liked that pause, as though she wanted to be honest, "Who can tell anything in such a short time? We've had our moments. I mean, there have been a lot of changes. A whole lot of changes. But from what I can see, all of them have been for the better."

"But what do you do? I mean, what are all these people here for? I thought Riverton did away with all assistance programs."

"No, not really. Just redefined them. No more free giveaways. Oh, we make sure everyone has food, but it's based on service. You work, you eat. You contribute, you eat. You don't, you end up on a bus with a one-way ticket out."

"But what if you can't work? What if you don't know how to do anything?"

"That's unacceptable. Unless you're dead, or in a coma, you can always do something. What you can't do, we'll train you for. And there are plenty of jobs, all levels. I couldn't believe how many there actually were when we really started looking at just cleaning up this town."

"But who's paying for all this?"

"Right now, the government," Ilona was quick to say, "but, and this is a big *'but'*, it's payment for services rendered. They would have to pay someone to clean up this city anyway, so now they're paying in food, training, and housing. So, instead of somebody just sitting around drawing the dole, everybody benefits. If things work as they predict, pretty soon this entire community, Riverton, will be self-supporting, paid for by the businesses who benefit from having a steady workforce supply and customer base."

"The businesses?" asked Rachel.

"Well, that's not actually how it works. It's not the businesses alone; it's everybody. Taxes."

On Rachel's look, she laughed, "Ooooo, evil word. Except maybe not in this case. Twenty-eight percent across the board: rich, poor, business owner, or worker. And that, with what's saved on nuisance costs, like vandalism, shoplifting, and stuff like that, it's all supposed to work to end up with a balanced budget."

Noticing Rachel didn't look convinced, she added, "Look, I don't know how else to explain this, it's just different. I know not everything is going to be that easy to swallow, until you look at the whole picture. Here in this office, we find jobs, we train, we find housing, child care.

It's a whole new way of thinking. Everybody works or everybody goes to school, so they can work. You know something, these new businesses, those hiring, they're paying good wages, better than good. I've lived in Riverton all my life, and trust me, nobody has ever paid this good. Maybe it's because they have to be fair. They're held to the same rights and responsibilities as everybody else. And, get this, when they're looking for workers, nobody's asking us if our candidate is black, white, red, yellow, male or female."

"But that's always been the law," Rachel reminded her.

"Yes, but not everybody followed it, and trust me as a minority, I know that first-hand. Well, here all hiring is color-blind and gender-blind, and if you're qualified, you've got as good a chance at the job as anybody."

"Qualified. That's the catch, isn't it?"

"Not if we do our job right. It's our job to make sure everyone is qualified to work. It helps that the losers are gone now, the dead beats. People who stayed in Riverton, or chose to move to Riverton, did so because they want to have a chance at a better life. We're part of making sure they get it. I think it's exciting."

"So I keep hearing."

"Well, it is, and we need people like you who can help mold this process and make it work more efficiently. Rachel, I know you're not convinced. But haven't you ever wanted to make a difference? A real difference?"

Rachel found herself nodding.

"Well, now you can. How many times in your life do you ever get a chance like this?"

Cameron tried to fly to Riverton every other weekend and since the airport had reopened, it made travel between Los Angeles and Riverton easier to manage. One night after their third round of love-making, Jay ran his hand down Cameron's still glistening chest to see if any part of him was willing to go for round four. Cameron smiled at the touch and whispered in exhaustion, "You have got to be kidding."

"I don't want you to go," Jay said, as he rested his head in the crook of Cameron's neck and breathed in the smell of him.

"I know, Hon, but it'll only be a couple of weeks, and I'll be back."

Jay leaned up on his elbow and looked down at his lover, his finger tracing slow patterns on his chest, "But that still won't solve anything. It'll still be only a few days. Why don't you take a chance and just do it? I make enough to support us."

"I like to make my own money," Cameron asserted quietly.

"I know that, but with all the new companies here, they're going to need advertising. You always said you wanted to start your own company. Well, now you can."

Jay slid into Cameron's arms, and both were now looking up at the moon-cast patterns on the ceiling. Neither spoke for a long while, just enjoying the feel of each other's body beside him. Finally Cameron heard Jay say, "I've been trying to get Erika to move out here with Kaaren. She can always find a job and..."

Cameron sat up and tried to make out Jay's features in the shadows. "Are you serious?"

"It's just safer here. There have been three robberies in her apartment complex already this year and with me not there, I just..., would you mind?" he asked, without turning to face Cameron.

Cameron slowly rolled over on top of Jay, staring down into his face. "Of course I don't mind. And Jay, you never have to question that. You know how much I love Kaaren, so I think it's a great idea and I'm glad you want her here, but I can't see Erika buying it. I think she's going to be a very hard sell."

"Like you," said Jay, wrapping his arms around his lover.

"I'm not trying to be difficult. It's just that it's so, so unAmericanly perfect. I mean it's like everything everyone's always wanted, handed to them. I keep waiting for the other shoe to drop."

"It's not going to drop. Trust me."

Cameron slid off Jay and reached for his cigarettes, until he remembered he'd given them up more than two years ago. Why did he want one so badly now?

"You just have to stop being such a skeptic," Jay said.

"Jay, someone has to be. My God, to hear you guys talk, Jesus is building his own private tabernacle on Main Street, and God walks down the streets every morning blessing everybody."

"We're not that bad. We just like it here. It's everything we wanted. Everything they promised."

"Who?" asked Cameron. "Who promised?"

"In training."

"What are you talking about?"

"It's what they talked about in training. The whole purpose for this."

"What was that training like? You've never said."

Cameron could feel Jay shrug, "I don't know. It wasn't so bad. Not nearly like they said. In fact, all in all, it was pretty easy. They took over some base on some island, at least we all thought it was an island. They never would tell us exactly where we were, and we exercised a lot and had classes and they fed us good food."

"What kind of classes?"

"Just classes. We were so busy, I don't remember."

"What do you mean, you don't remember?"

"There was just so much going on all the time," Jay tried to explain. "I don't remember, and thinking about it gives me a headache."

"What does?" Cameron asked in concern.

"Trying to remember. Weird, huh?"

Jay laughed, but Cameron did not think it was funny and pulled his lover closer to him in the darkness.

CHAPTER XXXVI

Rachel had been working with Ilona in the Social Services office for over a month and found herself getting caught up in the new way things worked in Riverton. The first difference was that she could bring her baby with her to work and keep him by her desk. At first, she thought the confusion would totally disrupt the baby's routine, but found little Seth loved the noise and being fussed over. Also, he slept like a puppy in his bassinet by his mother's feet. Ilona had offered to set up a baby bed, but Rachel knew, that until the office was enlarged, space was at a premium, and truthfully, she liked being able to look down and see her baby, and know he was safe. Everyone was excited this morning, because Marshall Foster was supposedly in town, or was going to be, doing a documentary on Riverton. Rachel was surprised to find out she was also excited, excited to show off her town. She had actually begun to think in terms of Riverton as her town.

Ryder's press conference at the roadblock outside of town was being overrun by news teams from every part of the world, all voicing their objection to Foster being allowed to enter, while they were not.

Ryder was trying to explain, "We had another board meeting last night, and while we would like to have an open-door policy, this is a new process for everyone, and we have so much to do, that we really can't afford the disruption. So, it's been decided that we were going to allow Mr. Foster of the Washington ABC affiliate to be that one team. The footage will be shared."

Arnie Becker of CNN, protested louder than anyone else, "ABC is a major network and is biased. You've heard their reports. We, at CNN, report on what we see. We do not judge. CNN should be the one allowed in, and we already have the capabilities and history of sharing with other networks. Just look at the last wars."

Foster was already nudging his team towards the barricade. "This is not a war," he sniped.

"But you're treating it as one," Arnie shot back. "Like we're the good guys, and those in there are the bad."

"That's not true," barked Foster.

"Yes, it is true," Arnie said forcefully. "You have slanted your stories and used every opportunity to try to shoot down this project and the President."

CNN pushed their advantage. "We promise. We'll let our listeners decide. We don't editorialize."

Foster saw his exclusive slipping out of his grasp and wheeled on the CNN representative, "Fuck you."

"Nice," came back Arnie, "Great diplomacy. Ever think of going into politics?"

"Arnie, I understand your frustration with our decision," said Ryder, "and you will get your pass."

Marshall Foster was furious. "You said our report was going to be exclusive," he challenged Ryder.

Ryder turned slowly to face the reporter, and everyone instantly quieted down, but hundreds of microphones were thrust out to catch what was going to be said. "Yes, but that seems to present a problem. The team we allow to go into Riverton today will have to share their information so that everyone can get the information at the same time. As the gentleman from CNN just pointed out, you're not all that good at sharing."

Marshall started to protest, but Ryder raised his hand and cut him off. "At least, not until you've already aired it."

Foster's mind was racing, trying to save the situation. It was true. He never passed on new items until after he had gotten maximum mileage out of them, first on his channel, specifically his show. In fact, he never passed on information at all. If they wanted to copy his newscast, or pull from his transcripts, he didn't mind, but only after he had gotten it out first.

"But," he heard Ryder say, "everything you shoot, everything you see or say will be linked through our office directly to every other news team out here. CNN will also be providing the same service. Arnie, I'm going to ask CNN to focus on Riverton industry and redevelopment. Marshall, you'll be assigned to report on our educational system."

"What about interviews?"

"You can talk to anyone over fifteen, as long as you don't disrupt any classes, or instruction. You are to be observers. I will be glad to answer any questions you may have later."

"I'll bet you will," muttered Marshall under his breath, as his team followed their van through the barricade.

The CNN team quickly joined them in passing through the barricade with Arnie Becker thanking Ryder for the chance to bring Riverton to the American people. He was surprised when he heard Ryder say, "That's okay, Arnie. We're very sympathetic to the American people. Remember, we used to be them."

While the CNN team was being taken on a tour of downtown Riverton and the Riverfront area, Marshall Foster and his cameraman were taken to the high school, where the principal led them on a short tour, and told them they could videotape almost anything they wanted. Since all the classroom doors were reinforced glass, seeing inside the classroom was not difficult. The school was uncommonly quiet, and Marshall's cameraman whispered that it was almost spooky. If it hadn't been for that unforgettable smell of polished wooden floors and pencil shavings, "you'd almost think you were not in a school," he said.

In one classroom, the teacher was sitting at her desk, and the students were all busily working at their own desk, heads bowed over papers they were working on.

"This is a set-up, right?" said Foster with disdain.

"Excuse me?" The principal seemed honestly confused.

"A set-up, a press shot?" supplied Foster. "Good PR. Looks good for the public, but phony as shit."

"I don't understand," the principal questioned, as he looked through the glass to see what Marshall was referring to.

"Everyone busy at work."

"They're just taking a test. I can take you to any other room you want."

"Yeah, I'll bet you can. So explain this, for the camera. What in hell's a Guardian doing in there?"

The principal glanced back in the room and realized for the first time that a Guardian was indeed sitting next to a student in the rear of the classroom.

"Oh, him," the principal said.

"Yeah. Him."

"I didn't realize he was in there. We have Guardians all over the school, but I'd appreciate if you'd not tape him with this particular student."

Foster wheeled to his cameraman and said, "Full coverage. I want everything." The cameraman wheeled to focus on the boy at the back of the room.

"No, you don't understand," protested the principal. "Please, we'll show you anything you want, but uh...that student, that particular one, he's had uh..."

The camera was now focused on the principal's concerned face. "Well,...a lot of problems at first, former gang member, and uh, pretty much fought us the entire way through. Turns out, he has difficulty reading. In fact, couldn't. He's dyslexic. Now, we have special classes, and he is in that program, but he was resistant to leaving his peers, and we could understand that. So that Guardian you see there volunteered to read the test questions to him and write down his answers. It turns out the student's got a phenomenal memory, and with our buddy program in the afternoon, that's where another student reads his text to him, he's jumped from failing to a B+ average. Anyway, I just think we ought to get his permission before we present on national television that he can't read."

Marshall glanced back into the room. The Guardian was writing down another one of the student's answers. Both were being very quiet in their work. Back outside the door, Foster tapped his cameraman on the shoulder and pulled him away.

"Thank you," said the principal. "Let's see what Ms. Francis' class is doing. She teaches Biology."

At the Social Services office, Junisha was assigned to Rachel three weeks after she started. The young, black mother looked better fed and less overwhelmed by life than when Rachel first saw her here. There was something about Junisha that fascinated Rachel.

"I've been working on the park crews and like that pretty much," offered Junisha, as she sat across from Rachel. "But I don't see that leading anywhere. I don't mean to be ungrateful, I was wonderin' if you had something that might get me into more money?"

"Well, we've got lots of training programs," offered Rachel as she reached for the brochures.

But Junisha wasn't looking for brochures. There was something more pressing on her mind.

"I've got to get a place of our own. I mean, the jail's fine, but I want my kids to be proud of where they live. I know the teachers have all been real nice, and they don't tell anybody, but kids, they know. I think my youngest even tells 'em. She thinks it fun living down there, but time's gonna come when she's gonna want to do better, and I want to do better."

Rachel put the brochures back on their shelf and sat back down in front of the young mother.

"I understand," she said, and the truth was, she actually did. "Why don't we talk a little, so I can get to know you better, find out where your interests lie, and what your qualifications are."

"I don't have any qualifications," Junisha said, with a show of her former hopelessness crossing her face.

"Nonsense," assured Rachel, as she reached for Junisha's hand. "If you've raised three children as a single parent, and haven't run off and deserted them, you've got qualifications. Don't let anyone tell you differently."

CHAPTER XXXVII

That night, almost everyone in Riverton, like the rest of the country, was glued to the Channel 7 newscast. Rachel, Seth, Angie, and Miles sat on pillows on the floor watching. The living room sofa that Seth had ordered was, according to Rachel hideous and was thus sent back. Its replacement, Rachel's choice, had arrived in the wrong colors, and also returned. Since Riverton didn't have its own furniture store yet, everything had been done over the internet, and both Seth and Rachel agreed picking furniture over the internet sucked. However, a new sofa was due within the week, and God help anyone who delivered the wrong piece of furniture.

"Shhhh," Angie shushed, "he's on." And then, there he was. Marshall Foster smiling that trademark smile, but as soon as his bubbly co-host asked him about his visit to Riverton, his face lost its usual brashness, and he seemed to have to weigh everything he said.

"Okay. I have to admit my first day in the Riverton school system was impressive. Disconcerting, but impressive."

Behind him, a video montage of clips from his day at the school played, edited to punctuate the points he was making.

"First, the school year is twelve months long. Classes are held Monday through Friday, starting at seven-thirty a.m. and ending at six-thirty p.m. Classes are fifty-five minutes long with the first five hours covering the basics. Afternoon classes are spent on cultural enrichment programs: drama, art, music, dancing. There is a comprehensive sports program, as well as computer and science labs that stay open for those who want to work on their own. It's almost unbelievable, but almost any elective activity a student could want is available, as long as their regular assigned homework for the next day is completed. And to make sure that is done, there are special tutors and study halls set aside specifically for those needing help. Most of the tutors are teachers, but some are older students, and we even saw a few Guardians volunteering during their off-hours. According to the staff of the elementary, middle, and high schools, and the parents who are picking their children up in the evening, the consensus appears to be unanimous that the new Riverton system is working better than anyone expected. Teachers like Cindy Rhodes from Minneapolis don't seem to mind the long workday."

Cindy's face appeared full-screen and Rachel recognized that the interview was being taped on the front steps of the middle school. In fact, she remembered having seen the teacher in the grocery store over at the Mall, but did not know what she did. She looked to be about thirty with eyes as blue as cobalt, and a softly plump body, that men find appealing.

"It's a long day. I won't deny that," she was saying to the camera, "but we get time to get our paperwork done. Most importantly, they let us teach. Do you have any idea what it's like to be able to actually do that? To teach?"

At that point, the picture of Cindy froze on the screen with Marshall's voice interrupting.

"But just so you don't think everyone's sold on this Utopia, there are some who are not so happy about the changes."

The screen now cut to the blurred face of a man who obviously didn't want anyone to know who he was. Even his voice had been distorted so that what he was saying had to be printed on the screen below his face.

"The problem is we don't know whether we can complain or not. I mean, they say we have security, but they did away with tenure. That's right. There's no more tenure. So what security does that give us? If we don't keep right on top of things every day, we could be out. So I mean, why go into teaching if they're going to run it like the real world?"

Foster actually smiled as he came back with, "Imagine that. If you don't keep up, you might have to go back to the real world. I think he was talking about us, folks. Well, evidently not everybody minds taking that chance. According to J.D. Summers, Superintendent of Schools, the office has been inundated with over fifteen thousand applications in the last month from teachers wanting to join the Riverton educational system."

Lyle, with Joseph Redfeather's help, had been transferred to the Riverton Greens Project, tasked with reclaiming and revitalizing the city's parks and playgrounds, as well as the median strip between the inbound and outbound lanes to the city. Another park was being designed and created, down by the wharf area where prostitutes once plied their wares.

Lyle loved his new assignment. At last, he was doing something with his hands, creating beauty instead of destruction.

He loved even the most mundane tasks in planting and landscaping, because he believed every living thing deserved a chance to thrive, except weeds, of course. Lyle knew that weeds, if left to run rampant, would eventually strangle out the life of whatever was around them. There were people like that. Lyle knew that because he had been one of them.

Rachel watched Lyle weeding one of the tightly packed circles of color in city park. It was her lunch break, and she always took the baby out for his noon feeding, and to give herself a chance to relax and breathe in the freshness of the air. She liked watching Lyle work.

"They're really looking good now," she said, as she looked for a park bench in the shade.

Lyle looked up and smiled.

"Is it that time already?" he asked.

"Like clockwork," Rachel smiled, as she pulled Seth's son from the bassinet, then reached for his bottle.

"I brought an extra sandwich in case you're hungry," she added.

"Naw, I appreciate it, but that's okay," Lyle turned back to his work to avoid her eyes.

"Oh, come on, you've got to be hungry, and besides it gives me a chance to say thanks for keeping my restaurant looking so nice." She was pointing to his flower beds.

Lyle shook his head and smiled, then dusted himself off and shyly moved over to sit on the other end of the bench from Rachel.

"I am kinda hungry. They've got stuff so we can fix a lunch, but I had some things I wanted to try with one of the flower borders, and I went off this morning and forgot."

"Tuna or egg salad?" Rachel asked, as she looked into the baby bag.

Lyle shrugged, so she just reached in and handed him one, then pushed an extra drink over to him.

"Thanks," Lyle said, as he opened his sandwich and took a bite. Egg salad. He loved egg salad. "It must be nice to get to have lunch with your baby every day."

"It is," she answered, as she slipped the bottle's nipple into the baby's waiting mouth. "They said I could bring him to the office, but it's hard to get any work done that way. So, I figured if part of my job is recommending the city's child-care program, I better put up or shut up. It's really not bad. They don't mind if you pick him up for lunch."

"That's nice."

"And it takes some of the guilt away. Jewish mothers are full of guilt."

Balancing the baby and the bottle, Rachel reached into the bag again and pulled out her own sandwich. Partially extracting the sandwich, she took her first bite, and then settled back, enjoying the quiet.

All three focused on their meal, and it wasn't until she was burping the baby that she said, "You seem to like what you do. How did you get this job?"

"I asked to try it out. I mean, I was on one of their work details, and I saw this park across the street, and I thought it could use some help, so I asked, and here I am."

"So this is what you want to do?"

Lyle smiled and said, "Yes and no. I mean, I like what I'm doing, but I want to do more. I think I'd like to start my own business. You know, have my own nursery and provide landscaping design, that sort of thing."

"Sounds good to me. Why don't you?"

"Don't know how. It's just a dream. Spent a whole lot of my life living and not much of it learning."

"Well, we'll have to do something about that. If it's okay with you, I could do some checking for you. I work right over there in social services. Maybe there's a work-study program or something. You know, where you can learn and get hands-on experience at the same time. It's worth a shot if you'd be interested."

Lyle smiled at Rachel, then looked away shyly. "Good sandwich."

To avoid boredom and to minimize routine, the Guardians' assignments rotated regularly between school patrol, community watch, night call, and office. They were scheduled three twelve-hour days with two full days available to take off if they wanted. In most cases, the Guardians chose to report at least one or more of those days because they were invested in the growth of Riverton and didn't want to miss a single moment of its emergence.

Nighttimes however, if they were not on night patrol, they could be found either with their families or, if single, out with the rest of the young people of the community enjoying being young.

Angie and Jay loved going to Oil Can Harry's, a new country and western bar that had already become a favorite of almost everyone.

Sitting in their booth, watching couples two-step or shadow around the dance floor, both sipped chilled beer from ice-frosted mugs and felt that life couldn't get much better than this.

"So what do you hear from Cameron?" Angie asked, as she put her mug down and drew little circles in the frost on its side.

"He's fine," Jay replied, turning back from the dance floor. "I miss him, but he's got a lot going on right now."

"You two set any time frame?" she pried.

"No, I'm not pushing him. He's still not so sure he wants to become a Stepford Wife, and it's something he's got to decide for himself."

Both were silent for a long moment, both now drawing designs in the frost of their mugs. Finally Jay looked up and said, "Angie, can I ask you something stupid?"

"Sure, but if you want to know why some dicks bend to the left and others to the right, I don't know."

"No, I'm serious," Jay said, as he slid over to be closer and to be heard above the music that was pulsing with a new Carrie Underwood hit.

"Serious and stupid. I'm all ears."

Jay seemed to think a moment, formulating in his mind how he was going to ask his question. Finally, he took a deep breath and looked up at Angie. "I told you this was going to sound stupid."

"I think we established that."

"Okay, here goes."

Angie waited, but what she got was not what she had expected.

"What do you remember about our training?"

Taken completely by surprise, she thought at first he was joking, but could see by the look on his face that he wasn't.

"What do you mean?" she questioned for clarification.

"You know, the training course at where-ever it was?"

"It was training, and classes, and marching, and never enough sleep. That's what it was. Hell."

Jay laughed and agreed. "Yeah," he said, as he reached for his mug and drained the last of the brew. Then, without looking at her, he asked, "Do you remember any of the classes?"

"Come on, Jay, what's to remember? And who'd want to? We're supposed to be having fun here, and you're giving me a damn headache."

The music changed and everybody was moving to the floor for the Electric Glide. Angie couldn't help noticing that one of the guys was unbelievably good-looking.

Grabbing Jay's hand and pulling him out of the booth and towards the dance floor, she whispered, "Oh God, would you look at those jeans. No, don't. That's the guy I want to take home tonight. He's mine."

Jay laughed, as he followed obediently. "Okay, I promise I'll stay on my best behavior. Tonight, I'll let you be the trashy one."

Angie laughed with a throaty laugh, "Aren't I always." Then she slid them both into the line right behind Mr. Perfect.

As soon as the music started, so did Angie, and she was hot on the dance floor, giving a new sexy definition to the art of country dancing. It might as well have been a mating call. Mr. Perfect and half the other men in the club couldn't help but notice.

Jay wasn't a bad dancer himself. In fact, he found several women, not so subtly, moving closer to try to make contact.

CHAPTER XXXVIII

Life in Riverton returned more or less to normal over the next four months, and even Rachel found herself enjoying the newness of it all. Also, it helped that what happened in Riverton on a daily basis had ceased to be the focus of national attention. People still moved out, but many more wanted to move in. The line of those awaiting admittance would have stretched on for miles had not a 'number-and-date system' been put into effect. This gave those waiting a chance to find a place to sleep, rather than waiting on the side of the road for days at a time.

Neighboring towns began to flourish with bed and breakfasts, and hospitality inns became major tourist offerings and financial windfalls for cities almost as destitute as Riverton had been.

Of course, not everyone could or would be accepted into the Riverton community. Anybody with a criminal record, unpaid child support, or even outstanding traffic tickets was rejected as these showed a basic disregard for the law. Anyone caught bringing weapons or drugs into the community would consider themselves lucky to make it out alive.

Housing and business acquisitions were top priorities for the continued stability of Riverton, but quality of life entered into every equation. Riverton had a finite number of square miles within its borders, a finite number of homes that could be built. Green space had to be honored.

Seth and the other Guardians took their turns on patrol rotations, but on his days off, Seth stayed close to home and his family. He liked the fact that when he drove into his driveway at night, neighbors actually waved at him.

Moving vans were still a common sight throughout the city, but almost all of these were of people moving in, not out, and each new resident did so only after he had signed an agreement that he understood and would abide by the clearly-stated laws of the new country of Riverton, and that failure to do so, would have immediate and irreversible consequences.

Junisha was going to classes three days a week, catching up on all she had missed growing up. It was not easy, but she found encouragement in the evenings when she realized she could actually help her children with their homework assignments. She still hadn't decided what job she wanted to move into even though Rachel had been meeting with her weekly to show her new options. Junisha wasn't sure she wouldn't mess up somehow, the way she used to do, and destroy this chance for her family.

Of course, it didn't help matters that Wayne Thomas was still angry and resistant to anything that had to do with Riverton. She knew his teachers were good, and she knew they were trying everything they could think of to bring him around, but she had overheard one teacher saying that some students are just not cut out for Riverton.

Junisha had been called to the middle school office three times already; and each time, it had been because of something her oldest son had done that was not acceptable. She realized after the second time that it was like he was playing the Riverton system, always pushing the limit, but never stepping over it. He might yell or curse at a teacher, but he never hit one. He didn't do his homework, but he always showed up, even if he slept through the entire class. His disdain was palpable, and he was beginning to garner a following of sorts. She had never met them personally, but had seen Wayne Thomas waving off a scraggly group of white kids when she picked him up from school. She didn't know what was going to happen to Wayne Thomas, or to her, when it happened, but she thanked God every night that her two youngest were flourishing in Riverton. Tamara and Robert James had truly come alive and looked forward to each new day with an excitement that would not have happened had they still lived in Chicago.

Marshall Foster's reports on Riverton had dropped from daily to weekly, and generally, had gone from attacks to actual reporting. One week, he and his news team taped Rachel and the other social workers as they dealt with their clients in the Social Services office.

He had also done a report on the country music night that Jay and Angie hosted at the Senior Volunteer Center. The night he was there, the two Guardians were teaching the seniors a line dance called, "Popcorn." Seth and Rachel were manning the refreshment stand, and Miles was even doing his part, guiding a woman in a wheelchair through the moves. She clapped to the rhythm. It looked like something that had been staged, but in truth, it wasn't. The senior dance was a bi-monthly affair and probably one of the most popular events held in Riverton. Everybody attended, whether they were senior or not, and it had turned out to be a great place for families to get acquainted and have an evening out together. Best of all, it was free.

Another week, Marshall and his team focused on the new court system in Riverton. He had thought that trials were one of those things thrown out with the new Riverton laws, but found that it was business as usual at the courthouse with the hallways lined with attorneys and their clients, waiting for their chance in court. The difference was, explained one attorney, that the only cases now tried in Riverton were corporate or contractual in nature. Felony or indictable offence cases were handled outside of the court system.

Although he could not tape the proceedings, Marshall was curious enough to slip inside a courtroom to hear some of them. The look of the courtroom seemed the same as anywhere. Two attorneys argued before the judge while their clients sat at separate tables, listening. No one else was in the room, which made Marshall feel very uncomfortable. He had been told by Ryder that he was welcome to walk into any courtroom, as long as he respected the privacy of the participants and didn't document anything in writing or by recorder.

One attorney, in the requisite gray suit and tie, was saying, "It's simply a contractual difference of opinion."

The other attorney, his clone in attire but obviously representing the other side of the question, waved his hand and stated, "But a difference that has cost my client a great deal of money, your honor. The work was completed under the logical assumption that..."

"I object," interrupted the first attorney. "The term, 'logical', is open to many definitions."

The judge, an older gray-haired African American woman with wise and penetrating eyes, slammed her gavel down. "Overruled!" she roared.

"But your honor," protested the attorney again, "'Logical' can mean different things to different people."

The judge leaned across her desk and shrewdly pointed a finger at the objecting prosecutor, "Not in my court, Mr. Johnson. In my court, 'logical' means 'logical'. And if you can't define it to your satisfaction, I sure as hell can."

Marshall slipped back into the hall on that comment and found, he had a smile on his face.

It was almost nine o'clock and darkness had fallen over Riverton. Junisha's two younger children were playing on the bed they shared, as Junisha stood in the doorway of the apartment, waiting. Of course, her apartment was really still a jail cell, but Joseph Redfeather had found some curtain material with matching bedspreads to help make the space less institutional. The squealing youngsters, who had decided that bouncing on a bed was more fun than sitting, had loved the room right from the start.

"Hush down now, you hear," she said, then reminded them again that others in the building were trying to sleep. "You two go brush your teeth and get ready for bed. I'll be right back."

She watched them race for the family restroom she'd been assigned, then glanced again at her watch and moved down the hallway past the game room where several other people were sitting and talking, or watching television.

One of those watching television was Lyle. He noticed Junisha and started to smile, but she was too preoccupied to notice and continued on down the hallway.

Stepping outside into the warm summer night, Junisha moved to the edge of the steps and looked out into the darkness.

"Something wrong?"

It was Lyle, and his voice startled her.

"I'm sorry, I didn't mean to scare you," he quickly apologized. "I'm Lyle, Lyle Garrett. I've got the next...uh, place, you know, living quarters, next to yours. We must work different shifts. Sometimes, I see you getting your kids ready for school in the mornings, and I've seen you in the dining hall. I don't mean to meddle. It's just that you looked like you could use some help or something."

"No, I'm fine," she lied, then added as Lyle turned to go back inside, "thank you, though."

"You know," he said, turning back to her, "you've got some real good kids there. I've watched them playing with the others, and they play real good. And I like hearing 'em laughing when you read to 'em at night. I don't mean to listen. It's just that the walls are so thin, and anyway, you must be a real good mother."

"Wayne Thomas hasn't come in yet." It was out of her mouth before she even knew it.

"Which one's he?"

"My oldest. He's just fighting it so, us being here. If I could just get my own place, then maybe, he'd start minding."

Again, she looked out into the darkness hoping to see her son coming across the parking lot. Lyle stepped in to watch with her.

"You want I should go look for him?"

"No," Junisha sighed. "I got a feeling, he don't want to be found and that's what scares me."

For a small-town country oasis, the music was hot and the line dancers, not bad at all. Jay, in his tight western attire, moved with the best of them, and several women had their eye on him.

Angie, also out of uniform, was watching from a standing bar when a good looking man of about thirty-five, stepped up beside her. He watched her, watching Jay.

"You with him?" he asked quietly.

Angie turned toward the voice, and instantly liked what she saw.

"Jay? No. He's already taken."

"In that case, the name's Jerry," he smiled, extending his hand.

She liked his smile.

"Angie."

Indicating the dance floor, he said, "I saw you out there."

Angie smiled back. "I know."

Jerry suddenly blushed, and Angie didn't think she had ever seen anyone look so loveable.

"Sorry," he stammered, "never was much good at being subtle. My students tell me I telegraph exam questions a mile out."

"Students?"

"I know it's hard to believe, but beneath this rugged manly exterior, hides a closeted suit. Riverton High, English Lit. You?"

Angie thought for just a moment before she answered. "I'm a Guardian."

This was obviously not the answer Jerry had been expected and as he had warned, he really wasn't very good at hiding his surprise. Exhaling slowly, all he could manage was a quiet, "Wow."

Angie never took her eyes off his face. "So, cowboy," she posed, "is that a goodbye... or let's find out?"

Jerry found her eyes and then laughed, "I'll make you a deal. I'll stay off my soap box if you stay off yours."

He extended his hand in truce, and as luck would have it, the music changed the instant she reached out to shake it. Taking her hand, he turned it over in his own and ran a thumb over her palm.

Looking down at their hands, Angie found it suddenly hard to speak. "Are you asking me to dance?"

Jerry looked up with a twinkle in his eyes, "With you pretty lady, I think it's anything you want."

Angie burst out laughing as she followed him onto the floor.

"'Pretty lady', give me a break. Is that the best line you've got?"

"Well, isn't that what all good cowboys say?" he laughed as he swung her into the whirl of dancers.

At the bar, Jay watched them pass and heard Angie ask, "So just how good are you?" Jay didn't hear the cowboy's response, but Angie's sudden peel of laughter from the far side of the dance floor brought a smile to his own face.

CHAPTER XXXIX

On the outskirts of town, nobody paid much attention to the young, black teenager who made his way through the condemned and cordoned-off streets of old Riverton's only remaining housing project, scheduled for demolition. Wayne Thomas was on a mission. He'd been told by a reliable source that what he wanted he could find on this side of town. The rest of the directions had been sketchy at best, and he'd spent the better part of two hours just moving slowly up and down deserted streets, looking. Both sides of the dimly lit streets were lined with collapsing houses and duplexes with sagging porches and boarded up windows. Only one streetlight was still working, as the rest had all been shot out. This just felt right to Wayne Thomas, and he slowed his movement and kept his eyes open.

A dazed junkie staggered out of the darkness into the light of the solitary streetlight, then stumbled across the deserted street and up the walkway leading to one of the small houses. Following the junkie's movements, Wayne Thomas smiled as he recognized the thin slice of light coming from beneath one of the blackout shades. Bingo!

Instead of climbing the porch steps and knocking on the front door, the old junkie cut around the side of the duplex to a small window that even from where he stood, Wayne Thomas could see the window was barred.

Fumbling in his worn pockets, the old man finally found a handful of wadded bills, and satisfied, began to pound on the window.

Behind the glass, the shadow of a man appeared and the window was jerked open about three inches. Inside, Wayne Thomas could hear the sound of laughter over a blaring T.V. All he could see from his vantage point was the inside man's hands, but the gruffness of his voice was unmistakable.

"What you want?"

The Junkie backed up a few steps, then pushed his money through the bars. "You know, man."

The man behind the window took the offered money, counted it and then reached below the sill and withdrew a packet of something that he shoved out to the junkie.

The junkie grabbed the packet desperately, then began to protest, "Wait a minute, I gave you more than that. Two... two..."

The man behind the window was already slamming the window down. "Fuck off!"

The junkie wasn't that easily frightened away, especially where his next high was concerned. He began pounding on the bars; the sound echoing down the deserted streets.

"I gave you more! I gave you more!" he pounded.

The window suddenly jerked open, but this time much wider. Three men stood there with what looked like a full arsenal pointed squarely at the junkie, who quickly ducked his head and dropped to the ground.

"I said, fuck off," shouted the first man, "before I blow your fuckin' face off."

Scrambling to his feet, the junkie scrambled away, as the men behind the window laughed and slammed the window down.

Scurrying back across the front yard and into the darkness, the cheated junkie ran straight into Wayne Thomas hidden in the shadows.

"Watch it, man, 'fore I kiss your ass with my foot," hissed Wayne Thomas, as he tried to push the old man to the ground, but it didn't work out that way. The junkie didn't go down. Instead Wayne Thomas found himself flat on the ground with the junkie's foot planted squarely on his chest. The junkie was a large black man, and the gun he was now holding was pointed straight at Wayne Thomas' face.

"Beat it, asshole," the man, Miles, whispered, "before I break both your legs and send you home to your mama in a plastic bag!"

Wayne Thomas didn't dare even breathe. Even though the large black man stepped back, his gun was still aimed squarely between his frightened eyes.

"You heard me," Miles hissed. "Get the fuck out of here!"

Wayne Thomas didn't wait for any other demands. He leapt up and ran faster than he had ever run in his life.

Miles watched him go, the anger in his eyes slowly dimming, then turned, and walked over to a battered dry-cleaning truck parked at the curb.

Pulling off the hidden camera and dirty, dreadlocked wig, Miles asked the man who rolled down the window, "You get all that?"

"Didn't miss a thing," Seth confirmed. "From start to finish."

"Then it's good to go. Let's do this thing," Miles said, as Seth stepped out of the truck and went around to open the back door. Three other Guardians in full body armor jumped out, weapons held at ready.

As if signaled, another armored truck pulled silently around the corner to join the first surveillance truck. Six more Guardians were out almost before it stopped. All of these were also heavily armed and shielded.

Seth looked up in time to see the Channel 7 News truck coming from the other direction. It too rolled quietly to a stop. Moving quickly to this van, Seth made sure he kept on the far side of the vehicles as he motioned for the driver of the News van to roll down his window.

"I don't like you guys here," Seth whispered to the news team, "but my orders were to let you document. Just don't compromise my men or get yourself killed."

"We'll stay out of your way." The voice from the darkened interior was unmistakably that of Marshall Foster.

"You better," warned Seth, "because if this goes down badly, you're on your own. Those men over there," he jerked his head towards the Guardians lining up, "are the only thing I care about."

"Understood!"

From inside the van, Foster watched Seth walk away and then turned to his camera man, "Okay, let's go, but be careful. It's just supposed to be rousing some squatters, but squatters can have guns. I don't want to end up with either you or me dead here."

With that, he threw open the sliding door and quickly jumped out followed by his cameraman and his sound guy who was actually a young woman named Kat. Katherine, as her parents preferred calling her, was a recent USC graduate with a degree in television journalism. Through connections, her uncle had helped Marshall out when he started at CNN, and Kat had secured this primo position on Marshall's news team ahead of dozens of more experienced applicants. For once, nepotism for Marshall had paid off. Kat had proven herself to be very good at what she did and more importantly, during the six months she had been part of his team, had never once complained about the long hours or ever let him down getting the sound bite he needed.

Kat jumped out of the news van, ready for business, right behind Marshall, even before Marshall's favorite cameraman. Marshall's driver wisely decided to stay behind the wheel with the van's engine running.

Seth's men were already fanning out across the front yard of the duplex. His hand signals said, "Keep low and surround the house."

Foster found himself ducking down even lower than he already was and his eyes scoured the area for anything possible he and his team could jump behind for shelter if the need arose. The yard was almost barren and Marshall realized how incredibly exposed his team really was. To make matters worse, they weren't wearing body armor like everyone else in on this operation.

He was debating telling his team to move back when he heard Seth's whispered directive to another one of his Guardians, "Cut their power."

The Guardian silently disappeared into the darkness along the side of the house.

Miles, by this time, was climbing back out of the surveillance truck, dressed in protective clothing over his undercover disguise. He quickly moved into place and tapped Seth on the shoulder.

"Ready?" Seth asked

"Ready."

Raising his tear gas launcher, Seth whispered into the headset, "Okay, cut it!"

The lights in the house suddenly went out. At the same time, Seth shot a tear gas bomb between the bars of the front window, shattering the silence with the sound of breaking glass and screams of alarm.

Grabbing his microphone, Miles yelled, "You, in there, in the house! This is Guardian Force One. Come out with your hands up!"

Foster and his news team were almost up even with Seth and Miles when the front of the house literally seemed to explode with gunfire.

Everyone ducked, but Kat wasn't fast enough and took a bullet in the chest, which literally hurled her backwards to lie a mangled lump next to the broken sidewalk.

At the first sound of shots, Foster and his cameraman had frantically dived over a ragged hedge row into the next yard. It was only as he was trying to catch his breath that he realized Kat wasn't with them.

Burrowing back through the hedge, he could see her body lying exposed on the barren front yard. Everything was silent. Nobody from the Guardians had fired a single shot. In fact, it looked like every one of them had pulled back to behind the armored truck. *What the fuck?* Marshall almost screamed. His mind raged, *I thought you were an elite fighting troop and Kat is still lying there and nobody's making a move to save her.* And then, he began calculating his own chance of surviving if he made the attempt.

Behind the armored truck, Seth was on his headphones, "Report in. Casualties?" He seemed relieved at the report.

Miles pointed to the front yard, "Looks like one of the news team got hit."

Seth didn't even glance in that direction, but simply took off his headset and reached into the back of the truck and pulled out an M72 LAW (Light Anti-Tank Weapon) rocket launcher. Miles efficiently and quickly helped him load it.

At Miles' signal, Seth moved to the front of the truck and leaned over the hood to aim.

Four houses away, Wayne Thomas watched everything in complete fascination. This was better than fucking sex he thought as he felt his dick swelling in excitement.

Suddenly, the men in the house let loose with a barrage of gunfire, spraying everything they could see. Bullets nicked and pinged into the truck, one rapid-fire digging stitches across the dirt and weeds of the front lawn and up over the hood of the truck. One spray of bullets tore ragged holes not six inches from Seth, who never even flinched, but kept to his task, slowly pulling the trigger. The rocket exploded into the front of the house with such ferocity that flames and glass shot out of every window. At the same time, every Guardian rose up and began mercilessly blasting away at the house.

One flaming drug dealer leapt from a shattered front window, only to be blown back towards the inferno by the in-coming gun blasts.

Then, as quickly as it started, it stopped and the only sound was the angry jungle roar of the fire eating through the remains of the house and its occupants. Marshall Foster was still having a hard time catching his breath. It had all happened so quickly and the devastation was so instant and complete. But that didn't stop him from quickly turning to his cameraman to make sure he had gotten it all on tape. The cameraman was equally stunned but that hadn't stopped him from documenting every moment of the confrontation.

It was only after he was certain no one else was going to come racing out of the fire that Marshall finally remembered and ran to the side of his fallen team member. Kat's prone blood-soaked body cast black fire shadows on the ground all around her. As Marshall rolled her over, it was his anguished face captured at that exact moment that would become the image everybody remembered of what would soon be known as the infamous, 'Riverton Massacre'.

CHAPTER XL

The next morning as Rachel stood at the kitchen counter staring in disbelief at the television screen, Marshall Foster relayed over and over again the events of the previous evening.

"The most ruthless, bloodthirsty disregard for human life this reporter has ever witnessed."

Then came images of the fiery explosion and the inferno aftermath which was even more horrifying. The bullet riddled body of the flaming man being hurled back into the fire filled the screen. This was followed by the Marshall's own heroically painful attempts to save the life of one of his news team.

Rachel was stunned and unable to move. The camera swept the devastating scene and there were Miles, Seth, and several other Guardians she recognized, all caught methodically putting away their equipment as the fire trucks and ambulances moved in. The fire still raged in the background and you could hear the walls collapsing. But their job was over and no matter how forcefully or angrily put the questions by Foster on the scene, none of the Guardians even acknowledged that the man was even there.

The video ended with stunned firemen and rescue workers moving through the smoldering debris, pulling out bodies. The last image was of filled body bags lying scattered all around the small scorched yard.

"Unconfirmed reports put the death toll at nine in this outrageous attack. In addition to the injury of one civilian, our own Kathleen Norris, Channel 7's audio engineer, an innocent bystander, was caught in the cross-fire in the initial attack."

With practiced concern, Mark's co-anchor, Lisa, asked, "Has there been any determination yet as to how many of the victims were men, women, or children?"

Foster's face filled the screen. "We're still waiting. Three of the victims were reported to be women, but that is unsubstantiated. The number of children, if any, has not been released. I'm sure you can appreciate how difficult identification has been with the intensity of that inferno. This is Marshall Foster, reporting live from the Riverton massacre."

Rachel felt like her legs were going to give out. The only thing that kept her from sinking to the floor was the baby's soft hand-patting on his high-chair tray for another spoonful of food.

"Seth? Seth?" she called, her voice catching in her throat.

Seth didn't seem to notice as he came into the kitchen still buttoning the shirt of his uniform.

"Good morning," he said cheerfully, as he reached over to nuzzle her neck before moving in on his son.

Rachel pulled away from him, actually pushing his hands away.

"What happened last night?" Rachel demanded.

Seth seemed confused by the question. "Uh, nothing much, just work."

"You blew up an entire house with nine people in it, and it was just work," she yelled, surprised at her anger. "Wasn't there any other way?"

"I don't understand. What do you mean any other way?"

"I mean, couldn't you have talked to them? Couldn't you have reasoned?"

"Rachel, 'reason' means there is something to discuss. There was nothing to discuss. They were selling drugs. They were shooting at us. They broke the law."

Turning to nuzzle his son, he said, "Hey there, big man. How are you this morning?"

The baby, of course, opened his mouth in a big smile.

Seth kissed the baby again and then, turned back to Rachel, "I'm starved, Honey. What's for breakfast?"

Rachel just stared at him in confusion and fear.

"Seth, nine people. Nine people were killed. Wasn't there any other way?"

"What do you mean? I don't understand."

"I mean, couldn't you have talked to them. According to the news, you just... My God, how many of those people in that house were kids?"

"You mean, kid kids or punk kids. I don't know. They were shooting at us. I didn't have time to find out."

"But you, you could have..." she stammered.

Seth reached out to her. "Honey, they had guns and they were selling drugs. Either one of those is a capital offense in Riverton."

"But to blow them up?"

"That's what a 'capital offense' means." It seemed very rational to him. "Now maybe next time, after this, there won't be a next time."

"Seth, that's crazy," Rachel protested again.

"I don't understand what you're so upset about? It's not like it was surprise. We told them, 'Don't.' We told them several times, 'Don't.' We told them what would happen if they did, and they still did it anyway. So we responded. What are laws for, if nobody's going to take them seriously?"

Suddenly both turned to a news flash on the screen, accompanied by a siren. Foster was holding a sheet of paper and was even more somber than before.

"It has just been confirmed that three of the victims in last nights slaughter were indeed children, ages three, five, and six. I repeat, the..."

Seth was now the one to sink down into his seat by the table.

"Children? I... We... I didn't know," he stammered, his face ashen.

"Would it have made any difference?" Rachel asked, her voice bitterly sarcastic. "Does anyone really care anymore?"

"That's not a fair question, Rachel."

"Oh yes, it is," Rachel shot back angrily. "It's the question everybody should be asking. You said it yourself. They broke the law. What do you guys call that? 'Red?' Well, what about killing those kids? What color do you give that? Red? White? What about 'Gray', goddamnit?"

She wanted to throw up at that moment, and her breath was so ragged, she thought she might pass out.

"The frightening thing," she finally managed, "is that even if you had known about the children, it wouldn't have made any difference, would it? Not in Riverton."

When Seth didn't respond, she continued. "Absolute rules don't leave room for gray. Between 'Right' and 'Wrong', what ever happened to 'Maybe'?"

When Seth, Miles, Jay, and Angie met that afternoon after their rotation, they met in a bar. It didn't help. The atmosphere there was just as somber as everywhere else that day in Riverton. The deaths of the children had tainted the town and everything it stood for.

They sat around a back table, away from the door, their second pitcher of beer already half-gone. It wasn't helping. They were still speaking in hushed tones.

"Look," Miles offered, "we knew from the beginning that eventually something like this was going to happen."

"And we knew the news was going to have a field day when it did," Angie added.

"What did they expect was going to happen?" Miles added. "What did they think we were talking about? That when push came to shove, we'd revert back to the old ways and simply slap everyone on the hand and say 'bad boys'?"

"No," jumped in Angie. "Because in Riverton, it's like Singapore, only one huge step forward. Singapore Plus." Angie reached out to touch both Seth and Miles. "In Riverton, we stop it once and for all. You guys did nothing wrong."

"She's right, you know," Jay added. "They were breaking the laws. The laws are simple. Simple enough that even an idiot can understand them. And they broke those laws."

"They were selling drugs," Angie reminded Seth.

"Those kids weren't," whispered Seth as he looked up into all of their faces.

Nobody could argue his point. Finally, Angie squeezed his hand, "Seth, nobody wanted that to happen. But it did. And it doesn't change the facts."

Pulling his hand away, Seth said what they all had come to realize. "On paper, it's one thing. In theory, it's one thing. But when it actually happens, it's another."

Miles was suddenly angry, and Seth's logic and questions just fueled that anger. Getting right down into Seth's face, he shouted, "Don't you fucking think they knew that, Seth. Why do you think they hand-picked us? Why do you think they gave us all that training? Why do you think we're being paid what we're being paid, or living in all these nice houses. It's because we've got the responsibility. We were chosen, because they knew we could handle it."

Leaning back, he continued in a softer tone, "And by handle it, I don't mean just the easy stuff. I mean the hard stuff." The anger was now gone, but the determination was in his voice. "And we can handle it. We're working on a dream here, a revolutionary new form of government. And we're the ones, the Guardians, who can make it work. We've got to make it work, because deep down in each of us, we believe in it. And we know that if we fail, Riverton doesn't have a chance. And if Riverton falls, so does America."

Seth was not the only one having doubts that morning. The President was on the phone with Ryder the moment the story hit the news. Several of his aides, including Misner and representatives from the military, were also in the room.

"I told you having the press there wasn't a good idea, in fact, a damned stupid idea," he shouted at Ryder.

"It wasn't a stupid idea, sir. If we want to make our point, the public has to know."

"But blowing up a house full of people? They're playing it up like the Holocaust."

"Sir, we knew from the beginning something like this was going to happen. That was the whole point. To establish new rules, new laws. Well, those laws were broken."

"If this is going to work, we have to uphold the laws. Last night we did. That was the point we both agreed on, Mr. President, from the very start."

The President knew he was right. Ryder was only implementing a plan they both had discussed a thousand times.

"On paper, it's one thing. In the paper, it's another," the President groused.

"Sir, I understand, but I need you to also understand. The story may be shaking up Washington, but it's not doing a whole hell of a lot of scaring anywhere else."

The President swiveled around in his chair and looked out over the White House lawn at the people protesting on Pennsylvania Avenue or, more to the point, not protesting on Pennsylvania Avenue.

CHAPTER XLI

Within two days of the shooting, the roads into Riverton were literally jammed for over eight miles with cars and moving vans wanting to relocate into the safe city. Concession stands and portable restrooms had to be set up along the way for slow-moving travelers, and Guardians were back again barricading the roads, letting only a few cars through at a time. If congestion had been bad before, it was impossible now. People were getting numbers for processing, but only those able to be processed that day were allowed to remain in line.

Rather than cars moving up onto the roadblock, the processing team moved down the row of cars. Even with a staff working three eight-hour shifts a day, some of the new applicants would still have to wait at least a week for consideration. That meant finding somewhere other than on the road to wait. Another pressing challenge was that Riverton itself was eventually going to run out of immediately available housing.

"I'm sorry, sir," came the standard border Guardian's response. "They have sent word we have to shut everything off for today. They just can't process any more. You will be given a number and a time that will give you first priority."

"But they will open again?" everyone wanted to know.

"Yes, sir. They're doing their best to welcome everybody."

"Can I request political asylum and get on a shorter list?"

"Excuse me?"

"Asylum. Isn't that what it's called when you're afraid for your life?"

"Sir, you're driving a car with American license plates. Who are you afraid of?"

The man's answer struck at the heart of the entire Riverton experiment.

His answer was, "Who am I afraid of? Who can tell anymore? Everyone."

It would take another week or so for families already settled in Riverton to see their lives return to a tenuous normalcy. Nobody was sure it would last, but they were liking it while it did.

For the stores that had moved into the town, business had increased considerably. It was hard now to find a parking place at the strip mall, and plans were already underway for another enclosed mall to be built on the other side of town. New home buyers meant new people, new jobs, and new money.

At the grocery store, Jeffrey Sutherland, a new Rivertonian resident and young architect with New York City credentials, had just loaded his car and was backing out of his parking space when he accidentally smashed into the side of another car passing by. Both car alarms began screaming.

Inside his car, Jeffrey's face flushed in terror.

"Oh God, no. No, no," he cried, leaping out of the car just as the other driver was climbing out of his. The person whose car had been hit didn't seem nearly as upset as Jeffrey. But Jeffrey knew the accident was his fault.

"I didn't mean to. I'm sorry," Jeffrey started pleading.

"I'm okay," the other driver assured him. "What happened?"

"I didn't see you. I didn't look. Oh God, I didn't look."

Just then, both drivers looked up and saw the Guardian crossing the parking lot towards them. It was only then the other driver realized why Jeffrey was so terrified.

"Hey man, it's just a car. I'm okay and you're okay. You've got insurance, don't you? You do have insurance, don't you?"

The Guardian suggested they both shut off their car alarms which both of them quickly did.

"Okay, that's better. Now, what happened?"

Jeffrey started crying, "I didn't look. I mean, I thought I did, but I didn't see him. I'm sorry. I didn't mean to break the law."

The other driver was also pleading. "Hey, wait a minute. This isn't one of those laws, is it? 'Cause, it was an accident. Nobody plans something like this. I mean, it's not like he was trying to do something deliberate."

"Relax," the Guardian reached out to rest a hand on Jeffrey's shoulder. "Both of you, relax. Accidents are accidents. They happen. It's not our concern. As long as you've both got insurance, then you can fill out the forms and be on your way." Both started nodding in unison and scrambling for their information.

The Guardian watched and understood their fear, but wanted to assure them, "Hey, guys. This is your city. We're not here to frighten you. We're just here to protect you. Are both of you all right? Do you need an ambulance or a tow or anything?"

"No," both said at once, heads shaking in the negative.

"Good, then have a nice day. I'm glad nobody was hurt. It doesn't look too bad."

Both men watched the Guardian walk away and then, quickly exchanged insurance information. Though the other driver drove away, Jeffrey sat in his car for another twenty minutes, tears streaming down his face.

Surprisingly, once the new rules of Riverton were fully understood, citizens seemed to relax, even though they now understood the new regime was going to impact every aspect of their lives, from kindergarten to death.

At the elementary school, games that had always been played for simple entertainment were now used to teach the rules of Riverton to kids from an early age.

Angie watched a class of elementary school children playing during recess. A circle had been formed and they were playing what appeared to be a game of Drop the Handkerchief, except in this case, the child who was 'it' dropped a dollar behind one of the other children. The chosen child quickly scooped up the dollar and ran after the child who was 'it.' If he caught the child, he handed him back the dollar saying, "You dropped this." All the first-graders in the circle cheered at this point and the caught child said, "Thank you," and then started around the circle again looking for someone else to drop the dollar behind.

This time, the child dropped the dollar behind Tamara. She was too slow to react and her brother, Robert James, grabbed it for her and holding her hand, gave chase. They, of course, did not catch the child in time, so both of them took the dollar over to the teacher who had been watching.

"We found this money and it doesn't belong to us," they sang out in unison.

"Thank you. That's very good," the teacher replied. "Now, which one of you would like to be 'it'?"

Of course, both instantly wanted the opportunity, but Robert James let Tamara have the honor, and she beamed as she skipped around the circle. He knew she'd drop it behind him anyway, and she did.

Some lessons, of course, were harder to learn, especially in the older grades.

At the high school, the bell rang to end second period, and the hall was suddenly flooded with students, all hurrying to their next classes. None of them seemed to notice the wallet being kicked along by scurrying feet.

Joshua Granger, a Riverton junior and first-string football player, was taking his books out of his locker when he turned and saw the wallet. He knew what he was supposed to do, but old habits were hard to break. Besides, he was short on cash. Checking to see that no one was watching, he quickly crossed to where the wallet laid next to a wall and bending down, picked it up. Tucking it casually inside his pants pocket, he started down the hallway past the principal's office and then, cut down a back stairwell. He didn't even make it to the bottom of the steps before the pain hit. His screams were so loud that every other student within hearing quickly wheeled in that direction. Then everybody began running towards the stairwell.

They found Josh crying and rolling around at the base of the stairs, frantically trying to shed his pants that were literally smoking.

At first, the students on the stairwell began to laugh at what they thought was a ridiculous sight. Josh was almost completely naked from the waist down. But the humor of the situation quickly turned to alarm as Josh continued to writhe. Another student, a neighbor of Josh's, quickly stepped forward to try to help his friend whose upper thigh was now blistered and boiling as though acid had been poured over it. Grabbing the shed trousers and trying to push them away, the student suddenly found his own hands stinging and blistering.

"Get water!" he shouted. "Somebody get some water!"

Somebody else shouted, "Get the principal!" but the principal and Miles were already pushing their way through the back of the crowd and down the steps.

"Stand back. Stand back," Miles said, as he knelt beside the crying boy. Then he asked, "Okay, what you been up to, son?"

"Nothing, man," protested Josh. "Jesus, help me."

Miles reached down and turned the boy's tear streaked-face toward him. "I'm asking you just one more time. What did you do?"

"I told you," Josh again protested, trying to look away from the penetrating eyes.

He heard the principal's voice somewhere off to his side, "Josh, answer him. This isn't a game."

As another wave of pain swept over him, Josh finally relented, "Okay, okay. I found some money."

"And...?" Miles asked.

"I took it. Okay, I took it. Jesus, this stuff's acid. It's burning right through my leg. Help me."

Miles slowly stood up. "No."

The student who had moved in to help couldn't believe what he'd just heard and said, "Shit man, he's still blistering. You gotta do something."

"No, we don't."

The principal stepped in beside Miles and said in a loud voice that everyone could hear, "If he'd been anywhere other than in this building, Josh would have been terminated on sight. Maybe he won't forget this the next time he decides to steal something that isn't his. Maybe none of you will."

"You set him up," came the angry voice of another student.

"No!" Miles answered in contradiction. "This young man set himself up. It was just a training exercise in honesty, and he lost."

"Now, hurry up or you'll all be late for class," the principal reminded everyone.

Miles looked down at Josh and said, "When you think you can walk or crawl, there'll be a nurse in the infirmary."

"And I'll be in my office," added the principal. "This is not over. Your parents will need to be informed."

Everyone slowly dispersed and headed for their classes. Josh just laid there crying. He was in real pain, afraid to touch his blistering leg, and knowing if he did, the flesh would probably start to fall off. The bell rang for the next class and Josh had never felt so frightened or alone in his entire life.

"You gonna try something stupid like that again?" came a voice from the top of the stairs. Josh looked up and saw the Guardian, Miles, standing there.

"No, sir, never again."

"Good."

With that, Miles came down to sweep the crying young man up into his massive arms and carry him to the infirmary. The purpose of the exercise was to make a point, not scar a boy for life. But then, if he didn't learn his lesson, the alternative was death, and death had a way of permanently scarring everyone involved.

The students were not the only ones learning to survive or thrive in Riverton.

A late-model car pulled quickly into an open parking spot in front of one of the new shops that had opened in what was now known as 'Old Town Riverton'. It was a beautiful boutique specializing in women's clothing, jewelry, and reeked of high-end class. All of this was lost on Robert Tarmac, a well-dressed man, who rushed into the store asking to speak to the manager.

In the private manager's office, Robert's wife, Rene, a beautiful young woman with the features of a model, sat crying under the watchful eye of the store manager, a rather nervous Herb Winston, who was one of the first store owners to immigrate into Riverton. He had come from Atlanta. There was also a Guardian in the room. It was Jay.

Robert rushed to his wife and wrapped an arm around her protectively.

"What's going on?" he asked. "Honey?"

Jay stepped forward, introduced himself, and then explained, "Mr. Tarmac, your wife was caught shoplifting."

"You can't be serious. Why would she want to do something like that? We've got... she's got... enough money. She can buy anything she wants."

When neither Jay nor the store manager responded, he turned to his wife with an incredulous, "Are you crazy?"

Herb Winston tried to assure the couple. "I'm sure we can work something out. I don't want to press charges. The Tarmacs have been good customers of mine since the day I opened this store."

Jay raised a hand to cut him off. "I'm afraid that's not an option. Shoplifting is stealing, and your wife has been caught on the store video camera stealing a pair of earrings."

"Oh God...," was all her husband could say, and by the way he said it, Jay knew this was not the first time for the beautiful Mrs. Tarmac.

"Now, I want both of you to listen to me," Jay explained. "According to the new laws of Riverton, you have two choices. One, you can move out of Riverton or..."

"I can't move. Everything I've got is invested here," stated her husband in no uncertain terms. "My business is here."

"I just said that was an option, but you might want to consider it. The other option is you stay. But if your wife is caught stealing again, she will be terminated."

The woman's quiet crying instantly turned into a wailing keen.

"Wait, uh, this is crazy," Robert desperately pleaded, pulling out his wallet. "What was it? Wasn't it just a pair of earrings? We're not talking grand-theft auto. We're talking about twenty-five, fifty, maybe a hundred dollars?"

"No," said Jay sternly, "we are talking about stealing. That's against the law in any form."

"Okay, okay, okay," Robert's mind was already racing. "What if I get her into psychiatric treatment? See that she gets therapy?"

"That might be wise, but it won't change the decision," Jay explained, then turned to the now sobbing wife.

"Mrs. Tarmac? You have officially been given your first and only warning. If you are ever caught stealing anything again, you will not have the option again. You will be terminated."

Two days later, Robert Tarmac drove his BMW out of the city and past the roadblocks. His wife sat in the front seat, her head bowed. A moving van trailed the BMW. Since theirs was the only vehicle moving out of the city, Guardians had to walk in front of them, clearing the road for their exit. Reporters swarmed the car, but neither Robert or his wife took their eyes off the road ahead, and neither spoke to the reporters or to each other.

CHAPTER XLII

Over the next few weeks, progress was made on many fronts, especially at the elementary school level. Teachers routinely began suggesting, as their students filed out for recess that they leave any money they have on their desks so they wouldn't risk losing it on the playground. The students, who did as requested, always found their money exactly where they had left it when they returned to their class.

In the high school, Jenna Jared was running late for class. She was always running late for class. "It's in my genetics," she always explained, "the Jareds will be late for their own funerals."

On this morning, it wasn't her funeral she was running to, but a calculus class, and Jenna actually liked calculus. Grabbing the proper books and papers from her locker, she slammed it shut and tried to beat the bell to her class. She didn't realize she had dropped her wallet until she reached her class. In truth, she didn't realize until she reached into her book bag for her completed homework and discovered the wallet missing.

Raising her hand, she said, "Miss Johnson, I dropped my wallet somewhere. All my money for the week is in there."

The stick-thin Miss Johnson, in her always-sensible shoes, was at the blackboard writing assignments, but turned back reassuringly, "I'm sorry, Jenna. But don't worry. I'm sure it'll turn up. They always do. Now, if everyone will open your books to page one thirty-four, we'll begin."

The class all opened their books and after a moment's hesitation, so did Jenna.

As the bell rang to end the class, and students poured again into the halls, Jenna retraced her steps back to her locker, searching the floors for the missing wallet. At the locker, she turned in her combination and threw it open, but her wallet was not there either. Slamming the locker, she searched the floor around the locker. No wallet.

Frustrated, she turned, angry with herself for being so stupid for losing it, and feverishly trying to figure out where else she could have dropped it. She had almost convinced herself that she might have left it at home when through the racing students who were all hurrying to their next class, she saw it.

The wallet was resting on the window ledge and all the money was neatly placed back inside it. Snapping it up, the relieved Jenna hurried on to her next class and never thought about it again.

Jenna's brother, Rick, sixteen, wasn't in school that day. Normally, that would have been reason for someone at the school to check on him, particularly after it had been determined he was a user of a wide array of drugs. Rick was allowed, as an adult over age fourteen, to make his own decisions, and his decision was to keep using.

He staggered to the pharmacy every afternoon to show his ID and lay his money down on the counter. Although the druggist, Dr. Sam, knew the young man on sight, and had known him since he was a baby, he, nevertheless, as required by law, always checked Rick's ID against the computer list that was updated weekly.

"How many hits you taking a day now, Ricky?" he asked.

Rick scratched at a scab on the back of his neck trying to think. "Three, maybe four. Not many."

Rick never looked at the druggist. He never did.

Dr. Sam talked as he filled the prescription.

"You know, there are programs to get you off this stuff when you're ready," he said. "Longer you wait, the harder it's going to be though." Even though he was required by law to make the offer every single day, the old man actually cared about Rick. But Rick had long since stopped listening.

"Just fill it, please."

The druggist counted out the money and returned the rest to Rick.

"Five dollars and forty cents. Put the rest of this in your pocket," he said, as he tucked the money into Rick's shirt pocket, "so you don't lose it. And get off the streets before you take any. Okay?"

"Yeah." Rick was already heading for the door.

"See you tomorrow, then," Dr. Sam called after him and hoped he would see him.

Since the program had been put into effect, six teenagers had died from using. Wasted away, not eating, no intervention, no treatment. Somehow that didn't seem right to the druggist, but then, he had no idea how many kids had turned away from drugs once they realized that what they did with their own bodies was their own business, and no longer associated drugs with rebellion, just stupidity.

Rick was standing outside the drugstore window looking confused and unsure where he was going. Dr. Sam prayed silently that he would turn around and come back inside to ask for help. But Rick just walked away, mumbling as he left.

Dr. Sam could only watch him as he went, then turned back to his other customers.

One of the closed high schools had been opened as a job training center. As the town grew with more and more industry moving into Riverton, the need for skilled labor was an ongoing concern. Training was based on the skill-sets required by the industries as well as the fundamentals of communication, both verbal and written.

Junisha loved going to the training center, and as soon as the children were safely ensconced in their classes, she devoted as much time as she was allowed to learn everything she could to prepare herself for the job market.

Since one of the companies that had moved to Riverton was Apple, everyone hoping to work in the assembly division was wearing a lab coat, gloves and hair-net as their teacher instructed them on a range of topics form the dangers of contamination to quality control. Junisha thought the white lab coat made her look like a doctor's assistant, and part of her would have liked that.

Lyle worked every day in one or the other of the new parks and green areas springing up around Riverton. His specialty was roses, and he was working in the John F. Kennedy bed when Junisha came up. She loved to watch him work, and he tried to arrange his schedule now so that he would be working in the park nearest to her school when lunch came.

She still wore her lab coat, but she had pulled the hairnet off and stuffed it into her pocket. She carried a sack lunch. Lyle smiled at her, wiped his dirty hands off on his trousers, and joined her as she laid their lunch out on a picnic table. This routine had started almost a month ago. Unless he was scheduled somewhere else, then he would be waiting for her. His heart swelled every time she came into the park. He knew she felt the same way. Neither had ever put their feelings into words. It was not the time. He was still working on recovery, and she had three children who were her first and foremost concern. Lyle liked that about her. In fact, Lyle liked everything about Junisha. He didn't think he had ever really been around a good woman, a good mother; certainly not in his life, his old circle of the 'vaguely remembered'. Everything about Junisha was a new experience. He had to monitor constantly his thoughts and his words, because Junisha brought out something he had never experienced before, respect. No one had ever expected anything out of him, much less shown him respect. Junisha did, though it was never said, but he knew. He knew without a shred of doubt that he would never do anything to harm her or her children. He loved her children, especially the little ones. Wayne Thomas was a harder nut to crack. Still so angry. Still ready to strike out at the slightest thing. It was more than just teenage hormones. Getting laid wasn't going to help Wayne Thomas. Wayne Thomas was a ticking bomb ready to explode.

Sitting in school was torture for many kids but for Wayne Thomas, it was a blood-boil. He hated the teachers, the rules, and every 'cock-sucking mother-fucker' student who gave in so quickly and easily to authority. None of them would last a day on the streets of Chicago, New York, or LA, the only real places for a man to live. Wayne Thomas considered himself a man. He had been in fights. He had scored a hit, though the sucker somehow lived. All the better, he thought as he waited for the final bell. He could go back and finish the job as soon as he got out of Riverton. A 'Baron' finished a job and that's who he was, a 'Baron', even out here in *bum-fuck* Ohio. You didn't lose your family name or your friends just 'cause your bitch of a mother tried to pull you away. She was just a cunt like all girls. Actually, Wayne Thomas didn't really believe this. It was just something everyone said. He actually loved his mother though he would never admit it. Not that he needed her. He didn't need anybody. She was just nice to have around as long as she didn't mess with his life. Like now. Like moving here. Like expecting him to just roll up into a ball and accept it. He was a man now. Even in Riverton, fourteen, and he had the body hair down there to prove it. He had even fucked a girl, but he really didn't like to think about that. It hadn't been what he expected. She was just too big down there. It felt like poking a bowl of warm pasta. She just lay there like she did for all the brothers. All the brothers said she was great, so naturally so did Wayne Thomas, but secretly he was angry at the girl for not being good for him. He would kill her too when he got a chance.

The bell rang.

The time at school in Riverton hadn't been a complete bust for Wayne Thomas. He had managed to hook up with a few just as unbalanced as himself. Not that they talked that much in school. It was more a case of passed glances, challenges, the slightest jerk of the head, and sub-rosa hand signals just below desk level. He was gathering an army of followers, just a few right now, but it was a start. For once, they were following him. He was the leader. They were under his command, and it was up to them to do what he wanted; and waiting outside the school that evening after school, he was going to see how well his new family responded.

He was leaning back against a wall as he waited, looking like the street tough he had always wanted to be. Then he saw his team approaching.

Wayne Thomas pushed off the wall and began to walk away from school. Glide and his friends rushed to catch up and fall into step behind him.

Glide patted the bulge under his sweatshirt and said in a hushed, excited voice, "We got them. My dad kept a couple hidden in the basement."

"Ammo?" Wayne Thomas asked, expecting only one answer. At Glide's nod, Wayne Thomas smiled for the first time in a long time. "Then we're in business."

Nike was so excited, he was almost skipping to keep up. "Holy shit," he kept repeating at intervals as the gang turned into an alley and disappeared into the shadows.

CHAPTER XLIII

Chester Hillmore had always been a BMOC, 'Big Man on Campus', ever since his college varsity days. Now at 55, it was more BMIR or 'Big Man in Riverton'. Chester was old blood, the great-great-great-grandson of one of the original founders of Riverton, back when the town was little more than a collection of cabins on the bend of the Ohio. The original Hillmore, a bookkeeper from Philadelphia, had made it as far west as the Ohio River before his feet and his wagon gave out, and he started to build a cabin. His industrious wife, a round little woman named Doe, became known for her cooking. Soon the cabin on the Ohio River became a docking place for crews and settlers moving farther west. These first two settlers planted the seeds of what would become the Town of Riverton, and its sense of industry would be continued by their sons and grandsons. Somehow, though, in those generations leading up to Chester, that talent for making money had been lost.

Being a Hillmore, of course, meant that Chester didn't really need to work, but his teenage son, Angus, was going to be hard pressed to even make ends meet if his father kept living up to his current lifestyle.

Of course, when the great exodus occurred in Riverton, Chester and his family stayed put. He was a Hillmore. Where else was he going to go? Now that the town was prospering, and the few businesses he held onto were beginning to show a profit in spite of his neglect, he bragged how he had made the right decision. He and his wife, Reba, were always invited to all of the best parties in Riverton.

One such party was just winding down. Guests in nice evening wear were making their way across the lawn, still festooned with colored lights, to their cars. Valet service had not yet come to Riverton, but it would not be long. The host and hostess waved their good-byes as they watched their guests depart. The only two left standing in the dew were Chester and his wife, Reba, continuing the argument they had started hours before.

"Good night," called the hostess, which was her way of saying, "stop arguing and go home, please."

It didn't help. Chester was drunk, and Reba was a harpie. They'd be there all night unless something was done. The host and hostess went back inside and turned off the lights to the lanterns, leaving the two combatants momentarily stunned, and forced to find their way to the car in the dark.

"You had to keep talking, making an absolute ass of yourself," Reba picked up where she had left off as Chester fumbled for the keys to the car. "And that joke about the three-legged hooker. God, where do you come up with those?"

"Will you just shut up and get in?" was Chester's only response, shouted at the top of his voice.

"Shut up yourself, and give me the keys. You're too drunk to drive," Reba shouted back.

"Oh, get in. I wouldn't let you touch this car, much less drive it."

"Asshole!" Reba shot back. "Mr. Big Salesman of the Year. Yeah, right. The truth is you're the fucking low man on everybody's totem pole."

Chester got in and only clicked her car door open after she pounded on the window.

Reba reluctantly slid into her seat, and tightened her seat belt. She wasn't through. "Honest to God, I don't know why I even bother. I work all year playing kiss-ass to these people and in one evening, you manage to make us look like laughing stocks."

Chester had heard all of this 'ad nauseam' and had had enough of both that evening and his wife's mouth. Angrily, he slammed his foot down on the gas, causing the car's tires to squeal in protest as it fishtailed onto the road.

Reba grabbed the dash with both hands and screamed, "Will you slow down for Chrissake? You could hurt somebody."

But Chester wasn't listening. Wanting to drown out her harping, he reached for the car radio with one hand while using the other hand to careen the car around a corner where it immediately jumped a curb, sideswiped the rear end of a parked car in a driveway, swerved back onto and across the street, narrowly missed two other cars daring to use the road and finally came to rest in the front lawn of another house.

Inside the car, both Chester and Reba were momentarily sobered. Both air bags had deployed on the first impact.

Lights came on in the surrounding houses and people in bathrobes and pajamas began appearing on porches.

"Great, the laughing stock of the entire town, you ass-hole!" Reba shouted as she fought with the air bag to get at the visor mirror to check her makeup before getting out.

Chester looked into his rear-view mirror and saw the lights of a police car pulling up.

"Great, just what we need. The fucking police," Chester swore under his breath, then turned to Reba and warned, "You. Mouth shut!!! Let me handle this. I don't want our rates to go up."

Miles slowly got out of the patrol car with another Guardian and together, they crossed to Chester's car and peered in.

Chester was forcing the air out of his air bag as he rolled down the window and smiled at the silhouette behind the flashlight sweeping his car. "Evening, Officer."

"Will you shut off the engine, please?" Miles asked.

Chester quickly reached around the air bag, fumbled for the key, and finding it, turned off the engine. He hadn't even realized it was still racing, only held in check by the brake he'd practically shoved through the floor. "Jesus, I swear to God, I don't know what happened. I was turning the corner back there and all of a sudden there was this noise and these damn airbags came popping up and I couldn't see a thing. Don't think for moment, Hank at the BMW's not going to hear about this. It's a wonder my missus and I weren't killed. Whoooeee, will you look at this mess? Of course, until my insurance clears all this up with the dealer, I'll pay for everything," he added magnanimously. "Nobody'll be out a penny."

"Have you been drinking, sir?" This time it was the other Guardian who asked the question.

"Well, maybe just a few," Chester confessed in his best 'good old boy smile', "but that didn't have anything to do with this. You'd think there'd be a law against faulty..."

"There is," interrupted Miles. "It's against the law to drive while under the influence."

"Look, yeah, I know, but uh... it wasn't that many and uh... look, I'm with Hillmore Minerals and, you know, really don't want any publicity. How about you and I working something out?"

"I don't think so, sir. You could have killed somebody, driving like this."

Reba chimed in with, "I told him he should have let me drive." Miles shined his flashlight on the woman. As she flipped up the visor mirror, having finally gotten the lipstick off her front tooth, she smiled at him.

"That's right, ma'am," he said before turning back to Chester. "You should have listened to the missus."

Before Chester could even respond, Miles reached through the window and put the cartridge gun to Chester's neck and pulled the trigger. Chester jerked once and fell sideways into Reba's lap.

"You should have listened," Miles said softly to the now dead man.

Reba looked down at her husband in confusion and disgust. She never could stand to be touched by the man and now here he was with his head in her... And then, it hit her. Reba always had been slow. But not any more. Screaming hysterically, she was trying to push Chester's now-dead body off her lap and throw the car door open at the same time. By the time someone threw a coat over the still-screaming Reba as she crawled crab-like away from the car on her hands and knees, it was more than her makeup she had to worry about. Reba had soiled herself.

By that time, Miles and the other Guardian were already heading back to their patrol car, leaving the body for others to clean up.

Although it was late, lights were now on at every house on the street, and entire families in various forms of sleepwear quietly gathered to peer into the car.

Reba's screams turned to sobs and then, full blown hysteria.

CHAPTER XLIV

Foster and Mike Moritz from the ACLU decided to meet with Harlan Serle, the Senior Senator from Virginia, somewhere away from Capital Hill, somewhere they could be afforded some privacy. The meeting place turned out to be a backer's home in a gated community in Alexandria. The three men sat on a deck overlooking a rustic lake popping with dusk biting bass.

The three men sat with untouched cocktails in their hands, all momentarily savoring the colors on the water and the peace and quiet of their surroundings.

Finally Marshall broke the silence, "Senator Serle, the way Mike and I see it, you've got enough support to force this issue. With your party's push and the coverage I can give you, you ought to be a shoo-in for the nomination."

"That's the way you see it, huh?" replied the Senator, never taking his eyes off the lake.

"Yes, sir," jumped in Mike. "Your stand on civil rights has been a matter of public record."

"And it's a well-known fact that your relations with the President have never been more than strained at best," added Foster.

Senator Searle looked down at his drink and almost chuckled. "We hate each other and no bones picked. But I'm a politician, boys, not a fool." With that he drained his scotch with the ease of a seasoned drinker.

Marshall was leaning forward now, almost challenging the Senior Senator, "You can't mean you go along with this Riverton scheme? Look what it's doing to this country. It's destroying it."

Searle turned to face his challenger with years of wisdom behind his words. "You boys in the media have missed the point. This country is already destroyed. And as far as everybody out there is concerned, that son of a bitch is trying to save it."

"People are getting killed in Riverton," Mike said as he waved the latest headline at the Senator.

"You guys don't even read your own press," the senator said as he jerked the paper out of Mike's hand. "People are getting killed everywhere. Forget the fucking headline that's just to sell papers. Look at this," he said, pointing down to a lower column. "Thirteen Killed In Drive-By-Shooting. Thirteen, for crying out loud! And this," he was now turning the paper and reading random headlines, "Elderly Woman Beaten In Robbery Attempt. Third Child Missing In Three Days. Hit And Run. And mind you gentlemen, these didn't even make the front page because this is Washington, and we're involved in much headier matters than trying to save the lives of the people we represent."

Then, he slapped the paper back in Mike's hand and said, "My glass is empty." Mike ran to the bar to fix the Senator another drink, hearing Marshall say, "But Sir, you can't mean you're just going to sit there and ..."

Mike returned with the drink and the Senator thanked him before continuing. "That's exactly what I mean. The time of political rhetoric and god almighty spin is dead. Because people won't listen to it any more. They wanted action and they got it. Right now more people want to move into that place, than out. Property values and employment are up through the roof in Riverton. You look at the map of this great country of ours and you tell me one other place in that entire landscape, hell, let's make it the whole world,... You tell me one other place that can match that progress."

"But it's wrong," Mike protested. "Gut-down, you know it's wrong."

"Son, I don't listen to my guts and I'm not naive. In Washington, something is wrong until it's proven to be right. And at this moment, I've got five cities in Virginia that want to secede from the Union and join the Riverton Experiment."

"I'm sure they do," Mike said, his ACLU dander rising, "White people. That's what this is all about. White's fear of blacks, Mexicans...."

"Who said anything about minorities?" protested Senator Searle.

"Look at those headlines," Mike grabbed the paper again. *Gang Shootings In Washington.* "It doesn't have to say black or..."

"Then if they're the ones committing the crimes," shouted Searle in sudden anger. "Then yes, if they are the ones committing the crimes, I say, let's clean house. I tell you what, boys, and I hate to admit it, 'cause I had my heart set on being President, but I wouldn't go up against this incumbent at this stage in the game if my life depended on it. It'd be political suicide."

"But someone has got to do something," demanded the voice of the ACLU.

"Why?" Searle shot back, "So, all the other ACLU's out there whose money comes from defending the indefensible, can keep their jobs?"

Moritz angrily gulped down his drink and poured another. "The ACLU does not make their money on the defending the indefensible. We defend the under-represented."

"Well, answer this for me. What happens when you no longer have the under-represented to represent? Do you know how much money we'd save each year if we just got rid of our prison system? Seventy-billion, plus. And welfare, don't get me started. Eight times that, at least. And I'm talking yearly. Think what that money would do for our economy, our budget."

"Yeah, but at what cost? If America became Riverton, we'd have to spend all of that and more just on national defense, because we'd become a sitting duck for every other nation in the world."

"Maybe, but somehow I don't think so. Either way, I'm not running against the incumbent. What's the old saying, 'Build a better mousetrap and they'll come.' Well, he built one and everybody's stampeding for it. What a fuckin' revolutionary idea-the elimination of crime."

Searle slowly looked out of the water catching the last rays of daylight and toasted the President in absentia with his martini. "You son of a bitch, why in hell didn't I think of it first?"

In Riverton, life still had its challenges. While Rachel was settling into her job, Jay and Cameron had been going back and forth on whether Cameron was going to be moving to Riverton. Their last phone conversation had ended up with both men yelling at each other and then, hanging up.

"I don't know what I'll do if he decides to stay in Los Angeles," Jay confided to Angie as they did their nightly rotation on patrol.

"What do you think you'll do?" she asked, as a friend.

"He's got everything back there, his business, his condo, his friends, and all I have to offer is me."

"Well, maybe that's enough."

"I want to think so, but maybe not. Cameron says everything is moving too fast. He never wanted to get this serious and me, I never wanted anything else."

"He'll come around," offered Angie, and she really hoped that was true. The alternative was that they would break up or worse, Jay would decide to give up the Guardians and return to Los Angeles. For selfish reasons, she didn't want that, and deep down in some part of her mind late at night, she secretly questioned whether leaving the Guardians was even an option.

Wayne Thomas wasn't making the progress Junisha had hoped for and was, in fact, staying out later and later. While Riverton had no curfew, Junisha felt she, as head of her household, should have one, but every time she tried to assert some authority over her oldest son, it ended in his pushing past her and disappearing sometimes for days.

Junisha and Lyle usually ended up waiting on the steps of the housing shelter until after midnight.

Junisha stood as soon as she saw Wayne Thomas coming up the walk. "Where have you been?" she demanded, and got his usual reply.

"Out."

Junisha suddenly found herself slapping him and crying in frustration, "Don't give me 'out!' It's two o'clock in the morning. Where have you been?"

She slapped him again, and would have done it a third time had not Lyle gently grabbed her hand and stopped her.

"It's just your mama's worried, son," he offered as a way of explanation. "She doesn't want you getting into trouble. This is a new chance for her and you kids and..."

Wayne Thomas lashed out at Lyle with, "Who the hell asked you? We don't need you messin' in our lives, and I'm sure as hell not your son."

Momentarily stunned, but not surprised, Lyle quickly countered, "No, I'm sorry, of course you're not. But I was just trying to..."

Wayne Thomas shoved past the man, warning, "Just get out of my face... the both of you."

Junisha watched after him, then slowly turned into the comforting arms of Lyle.

"What am I going to do, Lyle? What am I going to do?"

Lyle didn't know how to answer, and then, slowly it dawned on him, maybe he did. "I think I might know someone," he offered.

Two days later, Rachel walked up the front steps of the middle school school. She waved a greeting to the Guardian at the door, then passed her book bag through the metal detectors, collected her stuff, and turned to face the surprisingly quiet hallways. The silence almost stopped her completely. She knew Miles had talked about it, but experiencing it first hand was something else. It seemed almost unnatural.

Heading for the Guidance office, she introduced herself and was shown into a small counseling room where she could wait while her subject was summoned.

She was going through his file again when Wayne Thomas was ushered in by the assistant principal who gave the boy a stern warning to behave before leaving. As soon as they were alone, Rachel stood up and offered her hand.

"Hi, I'm Rachel Slavin. I'm a friend of your mother's."

Wayne Thomas ignored the hand but did speak, "I know who you are."

"Good, why don't you have a seat?"

Reluctantly, he slid into the chair provided, but did so with an attitude that relinquished none of his power.

"So?"

"I work with you mother," Rachel explained, "and she's worried about you."

Wayne Thomas got up and started for the door dismissively, "She don't need to be."

"Wayne Thomas, please sit down and talk to me."

He remained standing.

"Fine, stand, I don't care. I just want to help."

Wayne Thomas crossed back to the desk and leaned into Rachel's face. "Look, lady, I don't need your help."

Rachel tried not to instinctively lean back and break eye contact. "That may be true, but your mother does. She's doing so well in her classes and her new job. And she's so proud of what she's accomplished, what you children have accomplished. And she's right to be proud. Your brother and sister are doing beautifully. I know you must realize how hard she's worked to get you here and make this work."

"Well, I never asked her to."

"Look, I've got an idea," Rachel suggested. "I've been able to locate a house. It's not big, but it's clean and in a good neighborhood. How would you like to be the one to tell your mom about it? I can stop by on Saturday and we can all go look at it together. If she likes it, it's yours. You'll have a home."

Wayne Thomas just shook his head and crossed to the door, pulling it open. "Bitch, you don't understand, jack-shit. My home's in Chicago."

Rachel made one last attempt. "Wayne Thomas, will you at least tell your mama about the house and ask her to give me a call?"

He stood at the door for a moment, considering, then said, "Sure. Why not." And then, he was gone.

Rachel was on the way to her office when she saw Lyle working on his roses in the park. When he saw Rachel Lyle quickly dusted off his hands and crossed to her.

"Ms. Slavin?"

"Hi, Lyle, how's it going?"

"Just wanted to thank you for getting me into that class."

"How's that working out?"

"Great...and the people at the nursery have been checking up on me. You know, here in the parks and in class and they say with a couple more months of training, I've got a full time job."

"That's wonderful," Rachel said. "And I'll let you in on a secret. They've been telling me the same thing. The owner of the nursery has been really impressed. He says you're a natural with plants and told me he thought you could make flowers grow in a desert."

Lyle beamed at the compliment. "Well, I've got you to thank for that."

"Don't be silly. You've done all this yourself, and I couldn't be prouder. You're my biggest success story."

"I like that," he smiled. "I've never been anybody's success story."

"Well, you are now," she laughed, and gave Lyle a hug.

Hearing a car horn honking, she turned to see Jay's car pulling up to the curb with Cameron hanging out the window to wave.

"Hey, hey!" he yelled. "Look who's here from Tinseltown."

Rachel was so glad to see Cameron and quickly returned his wave. Then, turning back to Lyle she explained, "Old friends from Los Angeles. I've really got to go. But keep me posted. Okay?"

"Sure enough," Lyle said. "And thanks again."

He watched as Rachel ran to the car and gave the blond man a hug as he jumped out to hold the door for her. She climbed into the front seat between the two men.

As they pulled away from the curb, Cameron said, "Let's do lunch."

"I've got to get back to work," Rachel protested.

"Come on," Jay pleaded. "This is a celebration."

"What for?" she asked, looking from one man to the other.

Cameron swiveled to announce, "Well, if the mountain won't come to Mohammed, then Mohammed's gonna have to come to the mountain."

"And that means... What?"

"It means, life's too short to be lonely, so if my heart's here," he reached across her to place a hand on Jay's arm, "then, that's where I ought to be, too."

Rachel heard herself screaming in excitement, and then, she was kissing both of them on the cheek.

"Whoa, I'm driving. Remember."

"Sorry, but you are so right. This is worth celebrating. My treat."

Rachel's treat was one of her favorites, a new vegetarian restaurant aptly named, "Simply Sprouts."

As the three were being seated, Cameron whispered, "This wasn't here before, was it?"

Jay laughed. "No, it's new. Everything's new here."

"We certainly have a lot more restaurants now," Rachel agreed as the waitress handed out the menus. "And more are openings every day. We've got Chinese."

"Taiwanese," added Jay.

"Mexican,"

"Good Mexican," Jay added.

Rachel agreed. "Good Mexican, and Armenian," then indicating the restaurant they were in, she added, "vegetarian."

"Plus," Jay laughed, the most important thing, "a new McDonalds and a Burger King. Two Burger Kings."

Cameron feigned a fainting attack. "Oh, no, tell me it isn't true," he cried, grabbing his chest. "The big times. Two BK's. I must have died and gone to heaven."

Rachel laughed with the two men and added, "and that doesn't count all the Mom and Pop places that still fry everything when you want a grease fix."

"I can hardly wait," laughed Cameron.

Jay was suddenly serious. "Neither can I."

Cameron reached out to touch Jay's arm. "I had to come. Who else is going to take care of you and make sure you eat right and all that."

Rachel looked at Jay and asked, "Haven't you been eating right, Jay? You should have called us. We've always got an extra place at the table. You know that."

"I've been eating fine," protested Jay, waving a dismissive hand.

"Well, something's not been right," Cameron said. "Anyone who can't remember half of what he does during the day, and gets headaches if he does try to remember, is going to have a physical."

"I've had a physical," protested Jay.

"Well, you're getting another one, and this time I'm going to choose the doctor."

Suddenly turning for support, Jay noticed Rachel staring at them, tears glistening in her eyes.

"Rache?" There was a touch of alarm in Jay's voice.

Rachel could barely answer but when she did, it sent chills down Cameron's back. "Jay's not the only one. Seth gets headaches too."

CHAPTER XLV

Later that evening, Rachel was feeding the baby when she heard the front door open.

"Hi, honey, it's me," Seth called from the front of the house.

"Back here, up to my elbows in strained carrots," she answered as she spooned another mouthful into the baby's open smile.

"Sounds delicious," he said, as he entered and kissed both of them on the head, though with Seth Junior, he was careful to avoid the sticky reaching hands.

"No, no, no, little man. Only Mommy gets carrots. I'm meat and potatoes, myself."

Crossing to the refrigerator, Seth pulled out a bottle of wine and poured two glasses.

Rachel, noticing, smiled her thanks and then, remembered, "Oh, I saw Cameron and Jay today."

"Cameron?" Seth said in surprise as he brought her her glass.

"The one and only. He's taking the plunge and moving to Riverton." Seth was genuinely excited. "All right!" he toasted. "Now I won't have to stare at Jay's mopey face on patrol."

Rachel wiped her hands and the baby's face, and then took a sip from her wine glass. "He's all yours now. I'll clean up and get started on dinner."

"Fair deal," Seth said, as he picked up his son and raised him over his head.

"Watch it daddy. We're talking stewed carrots here."

Carrying the baby tray to the kitchen sink, she methodically rinsed it off, and then, grabbed a towel to dry it. As she was sliding it back onto its track in the baby seat she was also working up the nerve to ask Seth what she'd been planning to all afternoon. She had rehearsed it in her mind a dozen different ways and all of them seemed easy, but now, with him standing before her, she realized she'd have to work her way into it.

"Seth, one of the reasons Cameron has moved here is that he's kinda worried about Jay's health."

"Why? Jay's as healthy as a horse except for all the whining and complaining about Cameron not moving here. Now that that's solved, he'll be fine."

"I'm just saying, he was worried. Jay has evidently been having headaches and some sort of memory loss."

Seth stopping playing with the baby and turned in real concern. "You're kidding?"

"No. Evidently Cameron was noticing it more and more, the more he asked Jay about what it was like at Guardian training."

"Funny, I never noticed it, but then we never talk about it."

"Why not?"

"I don't know. No reason to, I guess."

Now came the question she'd been waiting to ask.

"Seth, how come you never talk about the training with me?"

"I have."

"No, you haven't."

"Then maybe you never asked."

"Yeah, Honey, I did, but you never answered."

"Of course I did. Why wouldn't I?"

"I don't know. That's way I'm asking. What was your Guardian training like?"

Seth looked at Rachel in confusion, and then, putting his son back in the bassinet, he crossed back to where Rachel stood, still not answering.

Rachel asked again, "What was it like?"

Seth took another long moment as though scanning his memory, "I don't know. Just like cadet training at the Police Academy, only harder. Lots of exercises and classes and I don't know, stuff like that."

"What sort of special training did you have?" Rachel asked pointedly.

Suddenly Seth winced and furrowed his brow as though in pain, and he was suddenly angry. "Jesus, honey, I don't know. What's with the questions?" Completely agitated now, Seth started pacing the kitchen as though he was a caged animal looking for a means of escape.

"Seth, look at me," Rachel pleaded. "What's going on? Seth?"

"I, I, I," his voice had become almost mechanical.

"Seth?"

Seth didn't move. In fact, he didn't even look at her. His focus was on some spot on the wall, and he seemed frozen to it, except for his hands which now began to clench and unclench.

A chill suddenly ran up Rachel's back, and she realized she was afraid, but she wasn't sure exactly what of. Quickly grabbing up the baby and holding him close to her, she edged her way to the door. *What the fuck is going on,* she thought. And then suddenly Seth's hands stopped moving and though his back was to her, Rachel could see the tenseness leave his body. His shoulders relaxed and his composure returned.

Turning slowly to face her, Seth's face was again all smiles. "Look, I've got to get out of these clothes and into a shower. Then how about some food?" he asked, as though nothing had ever happened.

"Seth?" Rachel asked, barely able to make her voice work. "What the...?"

"What?" he asked laughing. "You look like you've seen a ghost."

Crossing to her, he leaned over and kissed her on the forehead. It took every ounce of Rachel's courage not to back up.

"Okay?" he asked.

"Sure," she said, then watched him leave the room and her held breath came out in a jagged gasp, "Fuck!"

The next morning, Rachel left the baby with a neighbor and drove to the Riverton Administration Building, as the old courthouse was now called.

She moved purposefully up the steps, through the doors and into the busy hallways. She knew precisely where she was going, and whom she had to see. John Ryder.

Cameron may think Jay needed a doctor, but Rachel wanted to go straight to the source of the problem.

Joel, Ryder's assistant, looked up with a smile as she entered the office. "Hi. Can I help you?"

Rachel didn't even bother replying and smashed straight into what she hoped was Ryder's inner office.

It was.

"Wait a minute. You can't go in there." Joel jumped up and tried to pull her back.

Ryder, who was on the phone at the time, looked up in surprise.

Grabbing Rachel's arm and trying unsuccessfully to usher her back into the outer office, Joel kept insisting, "Excuse me, ma'am. You can't just..."

Rachel beat off his hands and would have done worse if Joel hadn't taken a step back. Wheeling on Ryder, she hissed in a barely controlled fury, "What have you done to my husband?"

Joel tried again to reach for Rachel's arm. "I'm sorry, sir, she just..."

Rachel threw off his grasp again, but never took her eyes off of Ryder. "I said, what have you done to my husband?"

The stunned Ryder, realizing he still had someone on the phone, said into the receiver, "Look I'll have to get back to you on that. Evidently, I have a situation here. No, I don't think that will be necessary. I'll just talk to you later."

The phone hung up, Ryder stood and extended a hand to Rachel.

"My name is Robert Ryder."

Smacking his hand away, Rachel said, "I know who you are."

"Then that puts you at the advantage. Won't you have a seat, Miss...?"

"Slavin. Mrs. Seth Slavin."

"Mrs. Slavin?" He looked at Joel to see if the name meant anything to him, and it didn't.

"Sir, if you want, I can get security," Joel offered.

Ryder just waved Joel off, and said, "Well, Mrs. Slavin, you still seem to be at the advantage. What can I do for you?"

"I want to know what you've done to my husband."

"I don't understand." And he really didn't.

"What have you done to him? He's not the same," she explained, as the tears began sliding down her face.

Ryder slowly started to get up. "Joel, maybe it would be best if you escorted Mrs. Slavin to someplace more..."

"Don't patronize me, you son-of-a bitch." she shouted, anger beating tears. "He went to that damned Guardian training, and now, he's changed."

Both Joel and Ryder glanced at each other, suddenly understanding.

"Thank you, Joel," Ryder said in a soft voice. "I think I can handle it from here."

Joel closed the office door as he left.

Ryder moved behind his desk and indicated that Rachel take a seat. "If you'll please take a seat, I think I can answer your questions."

Ryder turned to face his computer screen and began calling up Seth's name, "Slavin, Slavin, Slavin." Then finding it, "Oh, yes, here he is. You must be Rachel. How's the baby?"

"You don't give a damn about how my baby is!"

"Of course I do. You have to understand I have over three hundred men and woman in the Riverton Guardians, and I haven't had a chance to meet each of them personally, but I can see from your husband's records that he's an excellent performer."

"You mean he doesn't cause you any trouble."

"No, I mean he's up for a merit raise for outstanding service to the community."

"You mean, killing people. What did you do to him in that camp? What did you do to all of them? They can't remember. And if they try, they get headaches."

"I'm sorry. Do they want to remember?" Ryder asked, as he leaned toward her across the desk. "Does your husband?"

"No. And that's what's so infuriating. He doesn't give a damn. My Seth would have cared. It's like you've wiped part of his memory away. That's it, isn't it? Some sort of brain washing?"

"Mrs. Slavin, Rachel, each of our Guardians was hand-picked."

"I don't give a damn about hand-picked."

"Well, you should. Being chosen to be a Guardian is a great honor."

"Not to me," Rachel shot back.

"Well, it should be. The entire well-being of this community rests on the men and women of the Guardians, on your husband. They alone protect all of us, acting as law enforcement, judge, jury and even, on occasion, regretfully, executioner. Normally that would be too much responsibility for any one person, but for this experiment to work, our Guardians had to be... more. So, we metabolically eliminated their burden of conscience. Temporary conscience that is. They have been programmed to respond to emergency situations instantly, without any second thoughts, and with deadly accuracy. Once the situation has been handled, they forget any of the situations that might burden them emotionally or keep them from continuing in their duties. It's for the wellbeing and good of everyone."

"You've turned him into some sort of fucking robot," Rachel cried.

"Nonsense, he's just as human as you and me. He's just been physically enhanced and mentally trained to focus on the protection of what is good and right in this community. At all other times, he should be just like he always was."

Ryder pushed back from his desk and stood up. "Now, since Riverton is still experimental, I'm sure you appreciate the fact that this conditioning is not something we wish to advertise."

Rachel remained seated. "I'll bet you don't. Did you even give them a choice?"

"Of course we did. Every Guardian here signed a consent form."

"But did they know what they were signing?"

Ryder sank back into his chair. "Yes, it was explained to them in detail, complete detail." Then, he added with a smile, "Of course, since part of the process was the removal of any memories of their training, I doubt any of them will remember it now, but yes, they all volunteered for the program."

"My Seth wouldn't have done that," Rachel knew.

"Well, he did," Ryder answered, "and I can show you his consent form if you like. All of the Cadets signed one, and they signed it because they believed in what we were doing. Your husband obviously still believes in what we are doing, doesn't he? That's true now, isn't it? Your husband believes in this program, doesn't he, Mrs. Slavin?"

"But you did that to him too, didn't you?"

"No, we didn't. Oh, we did intensify their desire to make it work, but their belief in what we were doing came from their own being. He's still the same man he ever was. Maybe you just didn't know him as well as you thought you did."

CHAPTER XLVI

That night, the lights were on throughout the house, but the angry voices were coming from the upstairs bedroom.

"I don't believe you, and frankly, I don't care," Seth challenged as he pulled away from Rachel. He was trying to dress and using that as an excuse to stay away from Rachel, but she was dogging him in determination.

"Seth, listen to me. He admitted it. Ryder admitted it. He said you were programmed. That means brain-washed."

"Oh, come on, Rachel, do I look like someone's who's walking around like a fucking zombie?"

"Yes, sometimes. Like when I ask you about some of the things you do during the day."

"And I don't remember. Honey, it isn't that exciting."

"Seth, you killed thirteen people in one evening and didn't remember."

"Of course I did," he almost screamed. "You don't forget a thing like that."

"But it didn't bother you."

"You mean, just because I kill a snake that's getting ready to strike at my family, I should then get down and cradle its slimy little body, and say, 'Oh, I'm so sorry.'"

"These were not snakes."

"Yes, they were!" he yelled at her. "They were the slime that's ruined everything for everybody in this country. But not here in Riverton."

Seth grabbed his coat and started down the stairs to the front door. "We're going to be late for Cameron's party."

Rachel charged after him, "Fuck Cameron's party. This is about us. You. How did they train you? What are your guidelines? If I pick up that poker and take a swing at you, do you automatically go into killer mode and shoot, or is there any part of you left that says, "Hey, maybe this person is just kidding, maybe they're sick, maybe there is another way, or maybe this is your wife?"

Seth wheeled back, "I like my job. I feel good about what I do. Can't you just for once be thankful for what we've got? Do you have to keep prying into this to satisfy some theoretical what-if? Just name me this. Name me one time since you've been here, when you've found anything you couldn't do; one time where someone stopped you from doing what you wanted to do? You can't, because the laws don't affect you. You don't break the laws in the first place. Our laws are for law breakers, and they are very simple, and yes, they are sometimes unforgiving. But because of those laws, for the first time I feel it's going to be one hundred percent safe for my family out there. You want to know what they asked us? They asked us how much we were willing to give up to make sure our families were safe. Well, trust me, there wasn't a whole hell of a lot I wouldn't have given up to know that you and the baby were never going to be being mugged, raped, beaten, or killed."

With that he stormed out the door. "I'll be waiting in the car."

#

The celebration was already underway by the time they arrived. 'Welcome Cameron' signs festooned the walls, and the wine was already flowing.

"We'd about given up hope," Angie said, as the brought another piping hot tray of store-bought hors d'oeuvres from the kitchen.

"I knew they'd come," toasted Jay, hugging Cameron.

"Well, we almost didn't," Rachel said angrily, as she poured herself a large glass of wine.

Seth ignored the comment and popped a beer from the cooler.

Angie pulled Cameron from Jay's arms and hugged him tightly, "You are going to love it here."

"Doesn't everybody," Rachel said, as she lifted her glass in a mock toast.

Wanting to avoid another argument, Seth said, "Oh, come on, Rachel. Let's not go there again tonight, okay?"

"Yeah guys, this is a celebration," interjected Jay, pouring his boyfriend another glass of wine.

"I think that's what they said in Germany in the nineteen thirties," Rachel mused.

Everyone groaned good-naturedly, but Seth had had his fill.

"Damnit, Rachel!" he almost shouted, as he slammed his beer down on the table splashing foam everywhere, "What do we have to do? What is it going to take?"

Miles quickly stepped between them, "Hey, come on guys, this is a party."

Rachel pushed past Miles accusingly, "I'd just like to see..."

"See what? What do you want me to see? Show me the starving children in Riverton. Show me the abused wives. Show me the homeless. You can't. You admit yourself this is the first social service program you've ever seen that actually works. So what is it you want to see?"

Rachel didn't know how to answer him and could only stammer, "It's... there's... just something, that not right."

"But it is right! It's working! Look out there." He pointed to the door.

"I don't care. It's not right."

"Uh, How about some more wine, you guys?" Jay offered. "Or a beer, Seth?"

"Good idea, I'll have one," Miles said, then realized he was actually already holding a full beer in his hand. It didn't matter. Neither Seth nor Rachel were going to give up.

"Jesus, Rache. Why can't you just for once be thankful for what we've got?"

"I am, but that's not enough." Turning to the rest of the silent group, she asked, "Doesn't anyone else see that there are no controls in Riverton?"

"That's not true," said Miles, "We're the controls. We're the good guys."

Rachel crossed to him and looked up into those dark eyes, "But what if you weren't. What if you weren't the good guys? What if all of a sudden, they change the rules. What if they decide that smokers are bad... or Baptists, or left-handed people?"

"That's stupid," Seth said, when Miles didn't respond.

She turned to look at all of them and said, "Is it? Is it stupid? Who came up with these rules in the first place?"

"We did," Jay said.

"Did you? Did you really or do you just think you did? Seth was a pacifist before he joined the Guardians. How did that change happen?"

"Nothing happened," protested Seth.

"You killed innocent children. Don't give me nothing happened!"

Seth's breath caught in his throat. "I told you I didn't know," he sighed, and then turned, and smashed his way out into the hallway. Miles ran after him. Everyone was silent for a moment.

Jay's voice was quiet as he turned to Rachel, "That's not fair, Rachel. He didn't know. Nobody knew. And it comes back to him at night. He's even been seeing someone about it."

Rachel didn't know this but it even made her angrier. Why hadn't he talked with her about it? She was his wife.

"He was just doing his job," Angie said.

"The job. The job. That's the problem. I just want him to think."

"That's fine in a classroom, Rachel," Angie responded. "But this isn't Psychology 101. Out there on the street, thinking can get him killed."

Cameron poured himself another drink and then turned to face the group. "What say, I propose a toast?"

All eyes turned to face him as he raised his glass.

"Here's to the tarnished side to gold. Cheers!"

Nobody joined him. So he drank alone.

CHAPTER XLVII

Three nights later, Glide pulled up to the curb in his father's Mercedes, and Wayne Thomas stepped out of the shadows. Rebok, Addidas, and Nike were excitedly waiting in the backseat.

"You guys ready for this?" Wayne Thomas asked, as he slid into the front seat.

The response was unanimous. This was a night they had always been waiting for, a night they would always remember, a night when they would move from pretending to be tough, to being tough. After tonight, they would be part of a real gang, the WT Panthers, and they'd all get to choose new street names, jungle animal names.

As the car pulled away from the curb and headed for the outskirts of town, "yips" of excitement rang from the open windows, sounding more like prowling wolves or rabid dogs than young boys.

Back in Junisha's temporary housing, Lyle was helping her and the two younger children pack up their belongings in boxes. Both children were bouncing up and down, getting in the way more than helping, but Junisha loved seeing their joy at the prospect of the new house. She and Lyle had been over to the house several times since social services contacted her. It seemed the lady at social services, Rachel, had told Wayne Thomas about the house a week or so earlier, but he had failed to let his mother know. Rachel had suspected as much and came bearing the good news herself.

Since that time, Junisha had been barely able to sleep, and spent every waking minute that she wasn't working or in class planning exactly how she wanted the new house to look. Lyle had taken his day off to go over and clean the yard to make it safe and repair a broken window and a couple of the closet doors. Also, he had planted roses all around the front porch. She had scoured the kitchen and bathroom until the old fixtures looked almost brand new.

"And it's got a big backyard with a tree," bounced Robert James.

"For our dog," chimed in Tamara.

"No dogs," said Junisha, not even bothering to look up.

"But Uncle Lyle says backyards were made for dogs," pleaded Tamara. "Front yards for flowers, backyards for dogs."

Junisha glanced over towards Lyle who suddenly was extra busy packing his box. "Well, I hope Uncle Lyle likes cleaning up after dogs, cause I don't touch that stuff. You hear me, Uncle Lyle?"

Lyle looked up and smiled, and then, so did Junisha. Turning to her children she said, "Robert James, be sure and leave something out to wear for tomorrow. You too, Tamara."

"Who's gonna pack for Wayne Thomas?" asked Robert James.

"Oh, you know Wayne Thomas," said Lyle, as he ran his hand over young Robert's hair. "I'm sure he'll be along directly to pack himself. Now, don't forget to brush your teeth. Tomorrow's going to be a big day."

Both children dutifully grabbed their toothbrushes and headed out the door, but Robert James turned back.

"Uncle Lyle, what's a 'nitiation?"

"Initiation? Oh, sort of a ceremony. People do it when they join things... like clubs. Why?"

"'Cause that's what Wayne Thomas is doing. Gettin' 'nitiated and then, he's gonna show 'em. That's what he said."

The child rushed off as Junisha sank to the bed.

"Oh, God, no."

"Now come on, honey. Don't jump to conclusions," Lyle hoped as he reached out a hand to Junisha.

"He's gonna do it to us," cried Junisha, as she began to rock back and forth, holding her sides. "He's finally gonna do it to us."

"Honey, they don't have any gangs in Riverton."

"Then what's he doing tonight?" she cried.

"I don't know. Maybe he's found a girl, and that's what he's talking about," Lyle said hopefully as he moved a box to sit beside her. "Yeah, that's probably it. That's a big night in a boy's life and it isn't against the law."

Junisha didn't seem convinced.

"Look," he offered. "I'll go out and see if I can't find him. It's nothing, honey. Everything's gonna be fine."

He left Junisha sitting on the bed, her body wracked with sobs. Then suddenly, she got up, searched the small desk in the corner until she found a quarter, then crossed the hall to the payphone and dialed.

Rachel picked up on the second ring. Cameron was over entertaining the baby because Angie and Jay had pulled the same rotation. She was driving, and he was riding shotgun. Seth and Miles were also on night call, Miles driving.

"So how's it feel to have Cameron back permanently?" Angie asked, as she drove along the river road.

"Great," Jay answered, "though I didn't know what was going to happen after that Seth and Rachel fiasco."

"Yeah, I know what you mean. I sure didn't see that coming," Angie agreed. "I thought she had adjusted. Maybe it just takes some people longer?"

"I thought Cameron would be packing his bags after that, but he said, no, he'd give it a year. We'd just have to take it a step at a time."

"A year's a pretty long step," encouraged Angie.

"Yeah, I know. And I also know he'll end up loving it here. He's already scouting out businesses that could use graphic artists."

The patrol car turned away from the River and headed for the outskirts of town.

As they drove, Jay went back to matchmaking. He'd been the one who introduced her to the infamous Enrique. Fortunately she had forgiven him for that. Enrique was at least endowed, and Angie was nothing if not a size queen.

"Now, if we can just get you hooked up with somebody," Jay suggested to her, "it'll be like old times."

Angie smiled and said, "Oh, don't lose any sleep on my account. I'm not spending all my nights alone."

Jay turned in the seat with a startled "What? You mean, the cowboy?"

"Don't ask," laughed Angie, "'cause I'm not telling. If it works out, maybe. But until then, I don't want any of my so-called 'friends' scaring him off."

"Ange?" Jay laughed with her. "How can you say that? You wound me. How could we scare him off? We're just two queens, a couple of Jews, and the biggest black brother God ever put on this earth. What kind of threat are we?"

"I was thinking more along the lines of us all being Californians. That'll scare just about anybody," Angie said, and then, they both laughed.

"Fair enough," Jay finally agreed, "as long as you realize if we don't like him, the guy is dust."

"It's a deal," she agreed, as they knocked knuckles.

"So, what's his name?" Jay teased again.

"I told you, forget it, until I know for sure."

Cresting a rise in the road, Angie suddenly leaned forward seeing something reflecting on the road ahead.

"What's that? Up there... at the edge of the road?"

"What?" Jay asked, straining to see what she was talking about.

Angie pulled the patrol car to the side of the road and turned on its spotlight.

Fanning the road ahead, it took only a few seconds to come to rest on the body of what appeared to be a young boy, lying in the gravel at the edge, a pool of dark blood spreading on the pavement.

Jumping out, Angie shouted back to Jay before he could fully join her, "Call for an ambulance. It looks like we're going to need it."

Jay reached back into the patrol car and called in.

"AZ-2 to GC-4, we need a medical assist... Jackson Highway, 013 marker, copy."

About three miles away, Jakes patrol car quickly pulled over when he heard the radio call. Seth turned up the volume.

The radio dispatcher was responding, "GC-4 to AZ-2... Medical unit dispatched, Jackson Highway, 013 Marker, ETA 7 minutes. Do you need further assist?"

There was no immediate response.

Angie cautiously approached the body. "It looks like a teenager, lying face down," she called back, and heard Jay relay the message.

She could see the blood, and wondered whether it was a hit and run, or something worse. Glancing around for any sign of anyone or anything else, all she heard was the wind rustling through the trees and brush crowding the rural lane.

The body groaned and Angie instantly forgot all reservations, and instantly kneeled beside the body.

"It's okay. It's okay." She whispered. "We're here."

The body groaned again.

Angie shouted back to Jay, "He's alive. Looks like a hit and run, but I can't tell."

Gently she reached under the young man to try to turn him over.

"Okay, easy does it. Let's see if we can't turn you a little and... "

Suddenly the body rolled over on its own and she found herself facing a smiling Harry Small and a very loaded pistol.

The gun exploded and Angie was hurled backwards. Instantly Harry dove off the side of the road and into the brush.

Jay was halfway between the patrol car and Angie when all this happened.

"Angie!!!!" he screamed, as he grabbed for his side arm, but at that very moment, the woods beside the patrol car erupted in gunfire and Jay, caught off guard, was struck in the shoulder and knocked to the road. Regaining his feet, he was struck again, this time in the arm, but he managed to dive for cover behind the still open car door.

Dragging himself across the seat of the patrol car, he grabbed for the car phone fumbling in his pain to press the call button.

Both Miles and Seth could hear Jay shouting, "Guardian down. Guardian down. Ambush."

Miles switched on the sirens and floored his patrol car. Seth was already on the phone.

"GC-4, AZ-5 going to assist. ERT 2 minutes."

Jay heard the response, and then, Miles' unorthodox, "Shit!"

If he hadn't been in so much pain or so worried about Angie, he would probably have laughed.

Sliding back out of the car, Jay crouched behind the door, fighting to keep conscious as he fired into the brush ahead of the car. He never noticed Wayne Thomas coming up slowly behind him.

Wayne Thomas fired straight into Jay's back. Jay wheeled around and found himself facing a kid...

What the fuck, he thought, as Wayne Thomas fired again.

Wayne Thomas wanted to keep shooting. It had been too easy.

"We did it, we did it," he heard his new gang shouting. They all came out of the woods high-fiving each other and pounding each other on the back.

"Too cool, man! Yeah."

Joey Wilkie, who wanted to change his gang name to Fire Dragon, although it wasn't officially a jungle animal, was bouncing up and down in excitement.

"Come on, let's torch the car." This was from Nike.

"All right!" The response was unanimous.

Then, they heard the siren approaching.

"Holy Shit! Come on! Get out of here."

Scattering back into the darkness of the woods like giant roaches, they dove into the brush and fought their way through to the trail, whooping like wild savages, racing for the safety of the hills.

Seconds later, Miles' patrol car raced over the rise in the road and almost slammed into the crime scene. Throwing his wheel, his car slid sideways until it completely blocked the road. Both officers were instantly out of their unit, weapons drawn and under cover of their own doors as they scanned the crime scene. The engine of Angel's car was still idling ahead of them, but from their position, neither men could see either Jay or Angie. Everything was quiet except for the receding sound of the jubilant gang.

Miles made a bolt for the other patrol car, dove in the driver's side door and slid across the seat to find Jay lying on the ground on the other side. He reached out and grabbing Jay by the shirt pulled him onto the front seat.

Jay was still alive, but barely. He looked up through dazed eyes at Seth and gasped, "Three... four... kids. Angie. Cameron?"

Seth grabbed the microphone.

"AZ-5 to GC-4, officers down. Need immediate medical assist. Gunshot wounds to chest. Copy."

The response was immediate. "GC-4 TO AZ-5. Units are already on the way."

While Miles was with Jay, Seth had worked his way over to Angie whose body lay crumpled at the side of the road. He gently rolled her over, but knew even before he did that she was dead. Still he followed procedures and checked for pulse at her neck. There was none. He wanted to cry, but couldn't. There would be time for that later. Right then the fading cheers in the woods took precedence.

Miles was putting compresses on Jay's chest, trying to stop the bleeding, when he heard Seth's voice.

"I'm going after them."

"Wait for backup," he yelled, but Seth was already gone.

CHAPTER XLVIII

Racing through the woods after the dying sounds of the boys running ahead, Seth had lost all thoughts of caution. He charged down the path, full speed, cutting between the trees, his flashlight slicing the darkness.

Ahead of him, the boys were still having the times of their lives, celebrating as they ran. The path had taken them up towards the crest of the hill leading to the train trestle that spanned the Ohio River. A series of hillocks stood between them and their planned escape route.

The first major rise was steep enough they were forced to climb, and in doing so, Billy Harker happened to look back and saw Seth's flashlight beam flickering in the darkness behind them.

"Shit! They're coming," he warned.

All four boys scrambled up the embankment, and then, ran for their lives.

Seth came out of the woods, hit the embankment and took it in three easy strides. Joey Wilkie, the youngest, was getting left further and further behind.

When his cries of, "Hey wait for me!" didn't help, he suddenly realized he still had his gun and turned back to shoot, then thought better of it. He'd never fired a gun in his life until tonight; in fact, he hated guns. Panicked, he threw the gun as far away as possible then started to run to distance himself even further from the weapon.

Seth cleared the top of the embankment and followed like a marathon killing-machine, oblivious to the brush and brambles that sliced at his legs and arms.

The other boys scrambled breathlessly up another rise.

Little Joey tried to catch up, but stumbled just as Seth came out of the woods behind him. Rolling over on his back, Joey threw up his hands and cried, "Okay, Okay, Okay, I give up."

Seth put a bullet through his head, and continued on without missing a step.

Thirteen year old Tyler, at the top of the rise, heard the shot and wheeled in the moonlight to return fire. He was blown completely off his feet by a series of shots to the chest.

Harry Small screamed as Tyler's blood splattered his face. And he continued to scream, frozen in terror, until another shot showered his body with his own blood.

The two older boys were still running. Billy Harker, aka Glide, split off from Wayne Thomas, literally throwing himself over the protection of the next rise. Wayne Thomas started to climb after Billy, but hearing Seth's crashing through the trees so close behind, decided instead to dive under the cover of the brush beside the path. And he made it just before Seth burst out of the trees and without breaking stride raced past, never noticing the completely terrified teen barely covered by the shadows of the brush. Wayne Thomas fought with every ounce of strength he had left to not move a muscle and hold his breath.

Seth was halfway up the hill when he suddenly stopped and turned back, questioning which direction the boys had gone. Listening, all he could hear were the sounds of shifting dirt and rock beneath his own feet, settling under his weight.

Billy lay just over the lip of the rise, equally quiet, like Wayne Thomas, not daring to breathe. From the sound of shifting dirt, he could tell the Guardian was only about twenty feet away, just over the ridge. Knowing he now had the advantage, he drew a deep breath and threw himself to the top of the rise, raised his gun, aimed and fired straight into Seth's back.

The audible click of an empty chamber brought the last meal he'd eaten spewing out of his mouth, and he was still vomiting as he turned in panic and continued his desperate run. He threw the useless gun away and crashed through a wall of briars, the thorns tearing at him, grabbing at him, pulling him down into a small completely isolated patch of brown earth. Lying there, his breath coming in sobs, he listened for his stalker's footsteps and the shot he knew would follow. But he heard nothing. The Guardian must have gone after Wayne Thomas, he realized. "Oh, Jesus," he whispered in relief. He still had a chance.

Glancing behind him, Billy saw that he was at the base of the railroad trestle. Quietly, cautiously, he slipped behind the wooden beams and begins to silently climb.

Sweat was streaming off his face as he made his way slowly and silently up the treacherous fifty or sixty feet to the underside of the track. Sweat was pouring down his face, burning his eyes, but he couldn't chance letting go with either hand or he'd crash to the ground below.

His hands finally grasped the metal rails through the wooden ties and he pulled himself through the gap to find himself facing the giant shape of Seth silhouetted in the moonlight waiting for him. He almost let go, but Seth brutally grabbed him and pulled him onto the bridge.

"What are you going to do to me?" Billy cried in terror.

Seth kneed the boy in the groin, then backhanded him until he was laying half-on and half-off the trestle, threatening to slip.

"No, no! Stop! Stop!" he pleaded, the pain doubling him over.

"Who was the other boy?"

"I don't know," Billy lied.

Seth grabbed him by the neck of his shirt and lifted him up off the tracks. "I don't believe you."

"I promise, I don't know. I don't..."

Seth suddenly jerked the boy up over his head and Billy realized the Guardian was going to throw him off the trestle and into the ravine hundreds of feet below.

"Wayne Thomas! Wayne Thomas!" he screamed in terror. "That black kid from the station house. Please! Don't!"

There was a long moment when the sobbing Billy didn't know whether he had done enough, or said enough. The Guardian still held him over his head, and he could feel the wind coming off the river far below and he promised Jesus he'd never do anything bad again, if someone would save him.

Slowly, Seth began to relax and lowered the sobbing boy to the wooden ties of the track.

Lying there, Billy looked up at the man towering over him. "Are you still going to kill me?"

Seth answered with exhausted resignation. "Yes."

Billy started to cry again as the man knelt down quietly beside him.
"Aw... shit, man! Do you have to?"

There was a sparking sound and Billy's body jerked once, then sagged, his limp body slipping between the ties. He hung for a moment, and then, dropped away into the darkness below. Seth had already turned and walked away, his memory erased of the boy who had once been.

Back on the road, an ambulance had arrived and was taking Jay away, its sirens blaring. Angel's body still lay where it had fallen, covered now with a sheet. Forensic photographers were taking pictures when the Channel 7 News truck pulled up. Whether they would be allowed to stay didn't concern Seth as he stepped out of the woods and made his way over to Miles, who was sitting on the front seat of their cruiser.

Miles looked up and looked older than Seth could ever remember.

Still he asked, "Seth, are you all right?"

"Yeah. How's Jay?"

Miles slowly stepped away from the car. "They're taking Jay now. I don't know. He doesn't look good. I think we ought to get to the hospital."

"Not yet," Seth said as he started back to his own patrol car. "I've got one more place to go first."

A blinding light suddenly caused Seth to wince as Foster forced a microphone into his face. The cameras were already rolling and the newsman was blocking his way.

"Officer, it's our understanding that..."

Seth's single right hook sent the reporter flying back into his cameraman, knocking both to the ground.

Seth opened the car door and got in. Miles ran to get in the car with him, but Seth screeched away without him.

"Seth? Seth!"

CHAPTER IL

Junisha and Lyle were waiting on the jail steps when Rachel arrived. They both rushed to her car before she could even pull to a stop.

"Ms. Slavin, he's still not back, and we've looked. I think something bad's gonna happen. Some sort of initiation," Junisha said as Rachel got out of the car.

Lyle looked equally worried. "I checked over by the school. Thought maybe they'd be doing something over there, you know, messing up or something. But I didn't see anybody. Could be inside, but I don't think so."

"Maybe he's... has he got a girlfriend or something like that?" Rachel offered, but Junisha was shaking her head.

"That's what Lyle kept trying to say, but I know my boy. If there was a girl he was interested in, I'd have heard."

"Okay. Maybe he just stayed over at somebody's house. Does he have any friends?"

The sound made them all turn. Wayne Thomas bolted around the corner of the building and was racing for the door when Junisha cut him off.

"Wayne Thomas, where have you been?"

"Nowhere," he tried to push past.

Blocking his path, she kept on him. "You're all sweaty and been running."

"No, I ain't. Just hot," he argued.

A siren could be heard in the distance, and Wayne Thomas cut his eyes in that direction, then again tried to push past his mother.

"I'm tired. Going to bed."

It was Lyle this time who stepped in his way. "Those sirens for you, boy?"

"It's none of your goddamned business."

"What sort of initiation we talking about here?" Lyle persisted.

Wayne Thomas took a frightened step back, "Who said anything about, anything like that?"

The sirens were getting closer.

"I said, I got to get to bed. Got school tomorrow."

"Son, what have you done?" Junisha cried.

"I ain't done nothing," Wayne Thomas shouted at her as he backed up. "Just leave me alone."

Lyle gripped Wayne Thomas' arm tighter this time. "If you haven't done anything, then what are you running from? We can't help you unless you tell us."

Wayne Thomas pulled to get lose, but Lyle held firm.

"I don't need your help. Just let me go." Then, seeing the flashing patrol car rounding the corner, the boy seemed to explode in panic, "I said, let me go!"

Seth was out of his car as soon as it stopped. Using the car as a shield, he aimed across its roof at the boy. "Freeze!"

"Seth?" It was Rachel.

"Everybody step away from him," Seth ordered ignoring her.

Wayne Thomas ducked behind Lyle crying, "He's gonna kill me, the dumb shit, he's gonna kill me."

"What did he do?" Junisha begged Seth.

"I didn't do nothing," Wayne Thomas protested, still cowering behind Lyle.

Seth had not moved a muscle. His gun never wavered. "Step away from him, before I shoot."

Rachel tried to intercede, "Seth, what's going on? What did he do?"

Lyle, who was still shielding the boy slightly, asked, "Can't we at least talk about this?"

Seth's shot hit Lyle in the arm and spun him away from Wayne Thomas. Everyone was screaming now. Junisha ran to Lyle's aid as Seth slowly swiveled his gun towards the boy he had come after. Wayne Thomas was backing up now, his hands out in front of him, pleading. "I didn't do anything. I promise."

Rachel jumped in front of Seth. "Seth! For God's sake, don't!"

Junisha was pleading as she struggled to help Lyle to his feet. "What did he do? Just tell me what my Wayne Thomas did?"

"He murdered a Guardian and possibly two."

"Oh, no," cried Junisha.

"I don't know what you're talking about, man, I didn't do nothin'," denied Wayne Thomas, trying to keep Rachel between himself and the pointing gun.

"Seth, please."

"Get out of my way, Rachel."

"No. He says he doesn't know what you're talking about. What about proof? Don't you need proof?"

"One of the other kids fingered him."

"They're lying. I've been here. I haven't been anywhere."

"Seth, you can't shoot him down in cold blood."

"Yes, I can," came his answer.

"But what if he didn't do it?"

"He did."

"No, he didn't."

"Get out of the way, Rachel."

"He was with me. I've been with him for the last hour. He's been having trouble in school, and I came by to work with him."

"No, Rachel. That's not true."

"Yes, it is. You can't shoot him. No matter how much they've brainwashed you. Think."

Seth slowly lowered his gun and walked towards his wife and the group.

Wayne Thomas ducked back trying to keep at least two people between himself and Seth.

"I was with her, man," he shouted, pointing at Rachel. "With her."

"Please, Seth. Think... Think," begged Rachel keeping herself as one of those between Seth and the boy.

Seth stopped in front of Junisha. "You, his mother?"

"Yes, sir."

"Then you have two choices. One, you can pack up tonight, take your son and leave Riverton for good."

"All right!" shouted Wayne Thomas in relief and excitement.

"Or two, you turn him over to me now and be done with it."

"What do you mean, 'Be done with it?'" Rachel asked.

"Done with it."

"Shit, Mom. Come on, let's go."

Junisha stood for a moment looking at her belligerent son, then back to the wounded man who had been shot because of him.

"I can't," she said to herself, then turned to Seth and pleaded, "Don't make me do this."

Wayne Thomas was confused and suddenly frightened again. "What are you talking about, bitch? Mom? Come on, let's go."

Junisha wasn't even looking at her son. Her focus was on Seth.

"We're doing so well here," she tried to explain. "I mean, the two young 'uns are doing so well."

"Are you crazy or something?" Wayne Thomas was shouting now and had run to his mother's side.

Rachel turned to Junisha and said, "Mrs. Butler, surely you don't..."

Junisha turned to her son, crying angrily, "I did this for you. I did this all for you and you don't care, but I do."

In her anguish and frustration, she suddenly slapped the boy, and then, pulled him instantly into her arms in a shattering embrace.

"Don't you understand. It's the first time in my life I have ever felt safe... like I had something. Like my kids had a chance to amount to something and me too. Robert James and Tamara, they love it here, even in this cell. And we have a new house. And..."

She turned once more to Seth still holding her son, "Please God, give us another chance. Don't do this to us."

Seth's voice showed absolutely no emotion. "Mrs. Butler. You have two choices."

Junisha looked at Lyle as though to asking what she should do. "Oh God."

"Hey. Hey," screamed Wayne Thomas as he held on to her tighter. "Wait a minute. I'm your son. What's to decide?"

Junisha pried his arms loose and stepped back. "Wayne Thomas, I have two other children. I can't save you, but maybe I can save them."

Seth nodded at the decision and moved forward with his taser raised. Wayne Thomas backed up in terror like a trapped animal.

"You can't do this," he screamed. "I didn't do anything. I was here all along. She said so." He was pointing at Rachel. "She said I was here. I was here."

Rachel stepped in front of Seth again.

"Seth, please. Just send him away by himself."

"He's not old enough," Seth said. "We don't throw children out onto the streets."

"No, you kill them." It was Rachel who was yelling now. "So this is what they taught you! So this is the great training you forgot to remember!"

Seth looked at his wife and said, "Get out of my way, Rachel."

"No. Don't you dare touch him," she challenged, as she backed up to put herself completely in front of the boy. "He's a boy, a child. Look at the background he came from. It's not his fault. You can't blame him for society's failures."

"That doesn't work any more, Rachel. Maybe out there, but not in here. This society has not failed him. We have not failed him. The rules here are clear. We gave him options. We gave him choices. He chose. 'He' chose."

"But he was too young to understand the consequences. Can't you understand that?"

Seth stood there a long moment as though considering and then said, "No. Now get out of my way."

"No!" she cried. "I won't let you do this. It's wrong. No matter how you explain it. It's wrong. I'll take him."

Junisha who had buried her head in Lyle's shoulder suddenly was looking at Rachel with a mixture of hope and salvation in her eyes. "Mrs. Slavin?"

Seth was just as stunned. All he could say was, "You can't."

"Yes, I can," Rachel assured him, then shouted to Wayne Thomas without taking her eyes off her husband, "Get in my car."

When he hesitated, she warned, "I said, get in my car."

Wayne Thomas ran for the car with Rachel keeping herself between Seth and running boy.

The pain and indecision in Seth's eyes was overwhelming.

"Rachel. Please. It's my job."

"It's wrong, Seth," she said, as she backed herself to the car and reached behind for its door handle. "And I won't let you kill an innocent boy."

"You can't do this. They'll never let you come back."

"Then maybe that's the way it's supposed to be. You're not the man I married. You're a robot, worse than the Gestapo! At least they could remember what they did."

She turned to get into the car when Seth cried out, "Rachel, please. He killed Angie and probably Jay."

Rachel was stunned, as if he had slapped her face and had to lean against the car to get her balance. Turning back to Seth and seeing the pain there, she knew he was telling the truth. She leaned down to look at the frightened face of Wayne Thomas, and then back at her husband, and she wanted to cry or go to sleep and never wake up. But she couldn't. Seth was still holding that lethal weapon in his hand.

Opening the car door, she slowly slid inside. "I'm going to get our son. We'll be gone before you get home."

With that, she started the engine and slowly pulled away from the parking lot, her husband and everything Riverton stood for.

It all looked so familiar now, the new trees in the park, the building where she'd worked, the street where she lived.

"Shit, that man's crazy," said the kid sitting across the front seat from her. It was only when she started to pull into the drive that she realized Cameron was watching the baby, and she really did begin to cry.

Seth arrived at the hospital about the same time Cameron did and his own pain of losing Rachel quietly took a back seat to the complete anguish he saw in Cameron's face as a doctor in green scrubs stepped out of the operating room to talk with him. Miles and several other Guardians had already shown up to hold vigil. They had risen as one upon the doctor's entrance, and surrounded Jay's lover offering silent support and concern. Except for Seth and Miles, Cameron did not know any of the other men and women standing there, but he felt their love for his man and felt their pain at his needless shooting.

As soon as the doctor left, everyone reached as one to touch him and Cameron cried.

#

Rachel was also crying as her car crossed the border leaving Riverton.

Her passenger, Wayne Thomas, was jubilant and shot a bird out the back window at the attendant Guardian.

"Yeah!" he shouted to no one in particular. The baby stirred in the back seat and then, went back to sleep.

Wayne Thomas reached for the radio dial. "Hey, how 'bout some music? Some good music?"

From that point on, hot rock music blasted the night as the rays of the morning sun crested the mountains.

Rachel was so numb; she was not even aware of the noise.

CHAPTER L

Three days later, a fifteen-gun salute rocketed through the silence of the cemetery as Angie Castillio's casket was lowered into the ground. It appeared everyone in Riverton had turned out for the funeral. Even Enrique had driven out from Los Angeles and just happened to be standing next to Jerry, Angie's cowboy. But those standing closest to the coffin were Seth, Cameron and Miles. Jay had officially been taken off the critical list, but he was a long way from being healed. As Cameron started to turn away, Seth took him in his arms and held him. Miles protectively surrounded both of these men in his arms and whispered, "Shhhhh, it'll be all right now. We'll make it all right."

Angie's parents did not attend the funeral.

The funeral was broadcast nationally and internationally, and all programming in America had been interrupted with a live feed of the funeral, the procession to the funeral and grave site.

#

Lou's diner on the outskirts of Chicago was open 24-hours a day and catered mostly to junkies looking for a connection and hookers between johns. Lou's biggest crowd didn't start at night until after ten, and lasted until three or four in the morning. It was that kind of place. This early in the evening, Lou was lucky to have two or three of his tables in use, but tonight even those sitting there weren't buying. Every eye was on the funeral in Riverton playing on the mounted T.V. over the service window.

The battered little brass bell over the door rang as a black teenager entered followed by a young white woman carrying a baby and a diaper bag. The kid seemed hyper, almost strung out. The woman just looked exhausted.

"What can I get you?" the waitress asked from behind the counter. The kid spun the counter stools until he settled on one at the end. The woman made her way into a faded booth still cradling the baby in her arms. She placed the diaper bag on the table and tried reaching in with her one free hand.

"Gimme a hamburger with all you got. Make it two," shouted the kid, spinning himself around on his new perch.

The waitress pushed a stray strand of graying hair back under her required hair net and glared at Wayne Thomas in disgust. She'd been a hooker herself at one time a long time ago, and jerks like this kid had always been a pain in the ass and lousy tippers. So she ignored him for the time being and made her way over to the booth where Rachel was holding up a baby bottle.

"Could you please warm this for me, and is there a phone somewhere?"

The waitress took the bottle and indicated the phone on the wall.

On the television, Marshall Foster was saying, "I don't think I realized how unified this community had become. As much as I've protested its founding, I can't help feeling its tragedy as though it were my own. And I'm not alone in that feeling. It seems as though the entire city of Riverton has turned out, everyone shocked by the very violence they thought they had escaped."

At the phone, Rachel balanced the baby on her hip and dialed a number. She glanced up at the screen as she waited for the call to go through.

"But Director Ryder is quick to point out that this young Guardian's life has not been lost in vain."

The image on the screen changed to a raid on a suburban household in Riverton with a man brought out in handcuffs.

"The weapons used in this senseless gangland attack on the Guardians were traced back to one of the fathers of the boys. His entire collection has been destroyed, and he has officially been terminated."

The image changed again to stacks upon stacks of weapons piled in front of the courthouse.

"This morning, city trash collectors reported finding over 8,000 other illegal weapons dumped in city receptacles during the night. As much as I hate to admit it, maybe they really have learned something this time. Maybe we've all been wrong. Maybe the rest of the country could take a lesson from Riverton."

Rachel's call went through and upon hearing the familiar voice, she cried, "Mama Slavin, It's me, Rachel...Yes, I know. Is it okay if I come home?"

At the counter, Wayne Thomas was getting more hyper. "What the fuck is taking so long with those burgers?" he shouted at the waitress as she passed.

Grabbing a red table napkin from one of the booths, he wrapped it around his arm and started towards the front of the diner. Seeing a tip someone left on a table, he scooped it up and turned back to the waitress whose tip he had just stolen, "You got smokes?"

The waitress indicated outside.

Rachel watched as Wayne Thomas shoved through the front door and crossed to the cigarette machine.

Foster's voice continued in the background, "Maybe Riverton has proven that guns will continue to kill until there are no more guns."

All eyes in the cafe were back on the television. Surprisingly no one laughed or jeered. This was an area where guns were a fact of life.

Wayne Thomas dropped his coins into the machine, but found it wasn't enough. Pounding the return coin button did nothing. Traffic on the street had dwindled, but Wayne Thomas was so busy taking out his frustration on the cigarette machine, he didn't notice the lowrider that passed, and then, did a U-turn to pass by again.

Inside, Rachel was still on the phone when a blast rang out. Wayne Thomas' bloodied body was hurled through the shattered door. Everyone in the diner dove for cover.

Rachel dropped to the floor, covering her screaming baby as glass showered down on them both.

Wayne Thomas' body lay half-in and half-out of the diner door, a pool of blood already racing across the floor.

"Maybe it's time to wake up America." Foster's voice intoned on the still playing T.V. "Maybe Riverton is right."

Rachel remained huddled on the filthy floor, surrounded by the graffiti marred walls. A trickle of blood made its way slowly down her face as she clutched her terrified, screaming baby to her. She was still in that same position twenty minutes later when the police finally showed up.

"Reality can be a real bitch," Angie used to say. "The trick is to never let it bite you in the ass."

Rachel could already feel the teeth marks.

THE END